NINJAK

THE
SHADOW
WARS

MATT KINDT | RAÚL ALLÉN | JUAN JOSÉ RYP | STEPHEN SEGOVIA | CLAY MANN

CONTENTS

Collection Cover Art: Mico Suayan
with Ulises Arreola

THE LOST FILES
NINJAK #6-9

Writer: Matt Kindt
Artists: Stephen Segovia (#6-7),
Juan José Ryp (#8-9)
Color Art: Ulises Arreola
Letterer: Dave Sharpe

SPECIFICATIONS & INSIGHTS
NINJAK #6-9

Text and art: Matt Kindt

Associate Editor: Tom Brennan
Editor: Warren Simons

VALIANT

Peter Cuneo
Chairman

Dinesh Shamdasani
CEO & Chief Creative Officer

Gavin Cuneo
Chief Operating Officer & CFO

Fred Pierce
Publisher

Warren Simons
VP Editor-in-Chief

Walter Black
VP Operations

Hunter Gorinson
Director of Marketing,
Communications & Digital Media

Atom! Freeman
Director of Sales

Matthew Klein
Andy Liegl
John Petrie
Sales Managers

Josh Johns
Digital Sales & Special Projects Manager

Travis Escarfullery
Jeff Walker
Production & Design Managers

Alejandro Arbona
Tom Brennan
Editors

Kyle Andrukiewicz
Associate Editor

Peter Stern
Publishing & Operations Manager

Andrew Steinbeiser
Marketing & Communications Manager

Danny Khazem
Editorial Operations Manager

Ivan Cohen
Collection Editor

Steve Blackwell
Collection Designer

Lauren Hitzhusen
Editorial Assistant

Rian Hughes/Device
Trade Dress & Book Design

Russell Brown
President, Consumer Products,
Promotions and Ad Sales

Geeta Singh
Licensing Manager

Ninjak®: The Shadow Wars. Published by Valiant Entertainment LLC. Office of Publication: 350 Seventh Avenue, New York, NY 10001. Printed in the U.S.A. First Printing. ISBN: 9781939346940.

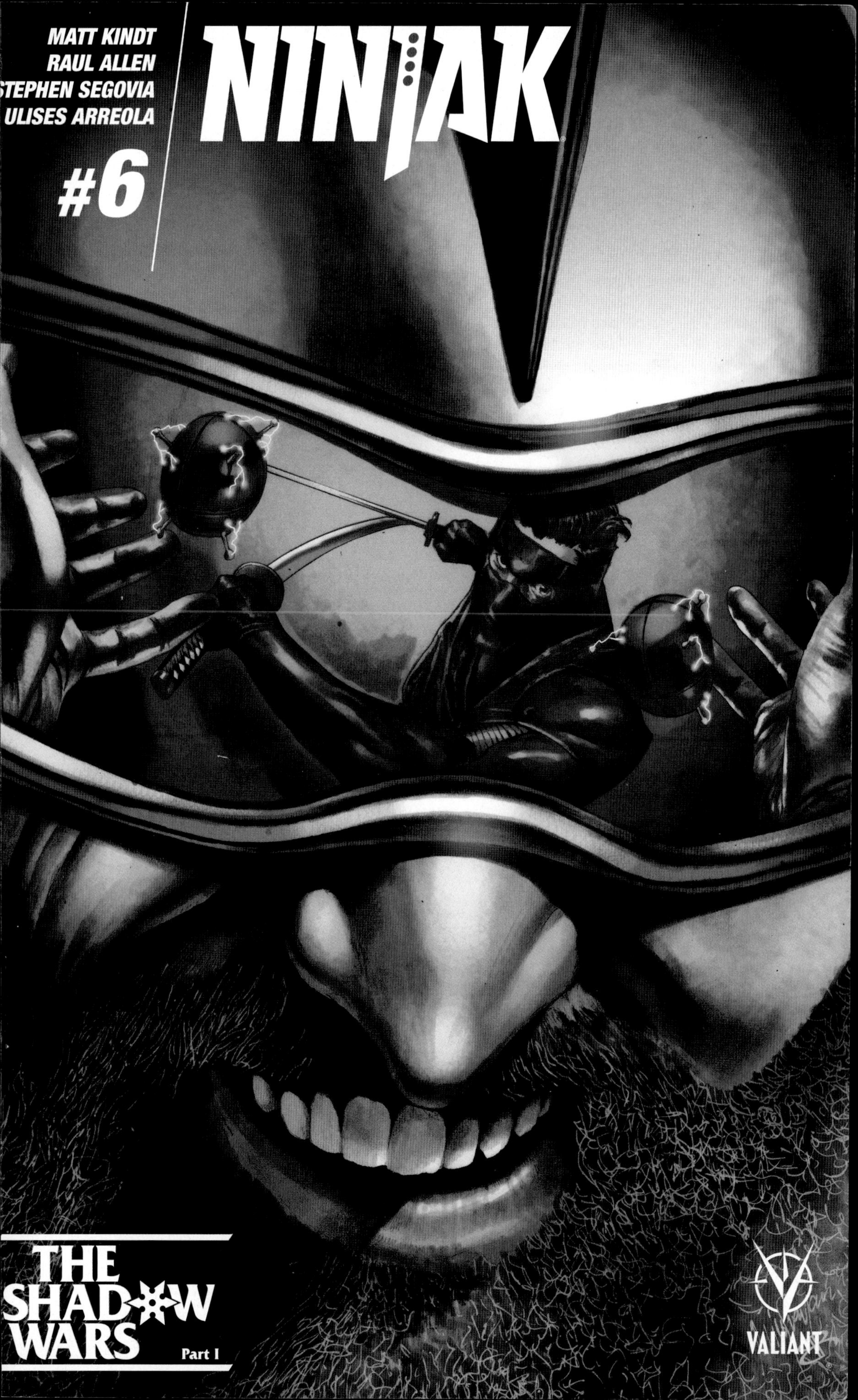

MATT KINDT
RAUL ALLEN
STEPHEN SEGOVIA
ULISES ARREOLA
NINJAK
#6
THE SHADOW WARS
Part I
VALIANT

NINJAK SPECIFICATIONS & INSIGHTS

CLASSIFIED

Fountain Pen

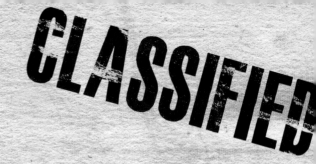

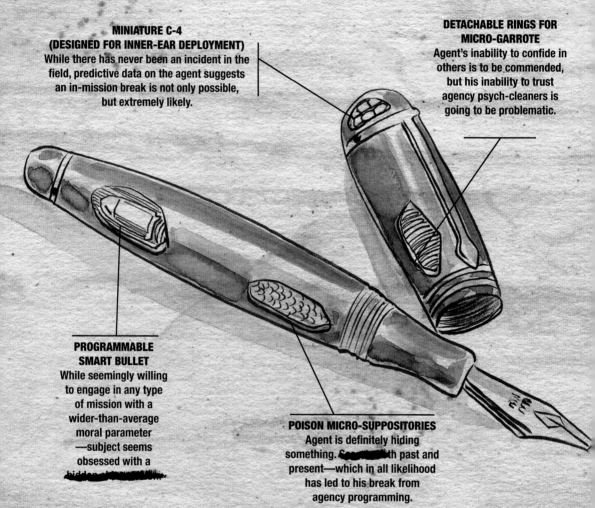

MINIATURE C-4 (DESIGNED FOR INNER-EAR DEPLOYMENT)
While there has never been an incident in the field, predictive data on the agent suggests an in-mission break is not only possible, but extremely likely.

DETACHABLE RINGS FOR MICRO-GARROTE
Agent's inability to confide in others is to be commended, but his inability to trust agency psych-cleaners is going to be problematic.

PROGRAMMABLE SMART BULLET
While seemingly willing to engage in any type of mission with a wider-than-average moral parameter—subject seems obsessed with a [redacted]

POISON MICRO-SUPPOSITORIES
Agent is definitely hiding something. [redacted] past and present—which in all likelihood has led to his break from agency programming.

THE SHADOW WARS

PREVIOUSLY IN NINJAK...

His name is Ninjak—spy and mercenary for hire. He is also Colin King, wealthy son of privilege.

The British espionage organization MI-6 tasked Colin with infiltrating and destroying Weaponeer, a criminal empire that designs arms for the highest, most illicit bidder. Disguised as businessman Henry Collins, Ninjak ingratiated himself to the group's imposing leader, Kannon. He also met Kannon's right-hand woman, Roku, an assassin so feared that skilled warriors have taken their own lives rather than face her razor-sharp locks of hair and her deadly skills.

Ninjak eventually engaged Kannon in open combat, dismembering him and leaving him in the custody of MI-6 director Neville Alcott. Colin then took over as CEO of Weaponeer. He aims to take down Weaponeer from the inside...

Ninjak is hunting the Shadow Seven. First up: La Barbe...

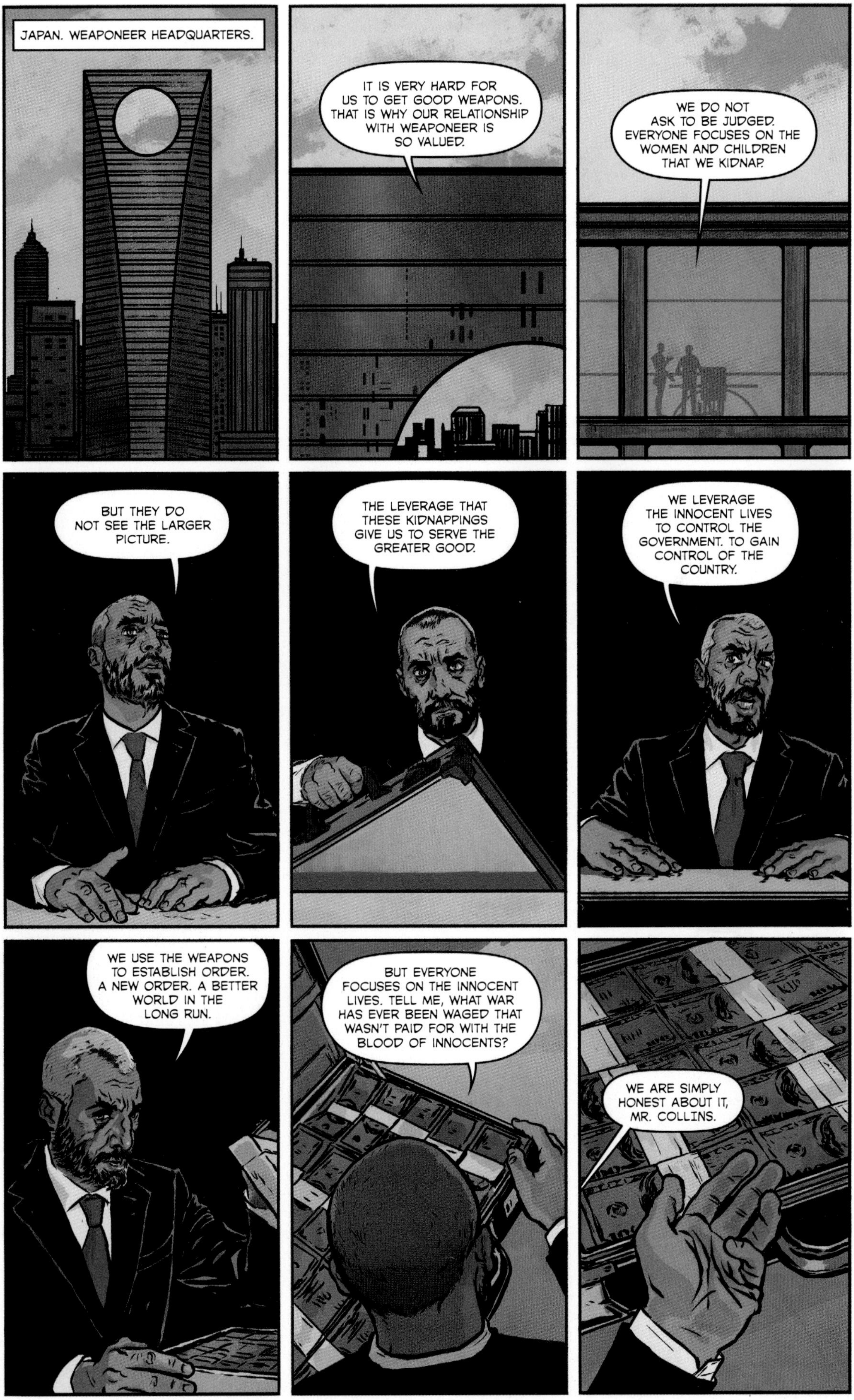
JAPAN. WEAPONEER HEADQUARTERS.
IT IS VERY HARD FOR US TO GET GOOD WEAPONS. THAT IS WHY OUR RELATIONSHIP WITH WEAPONEER IS SO VALUED.
WE DO NOT ASK TO BE JUDGED. EVERYONE FOCUSES ON THE WOMEN AND CHILDREN THAT WE KIDNAP.
BUT THEY DO NOT SEE THE LARGER PICTURE.
THE LEVERAGE THAT THESE KIDNAPPINGS GIVE US TO SERVE THE GREATER GOOD.
WE LEVERAGE THE INNOCENT LIVES TO CONTROL THE GOVERNMENT. TO GAIN CONTROL OF THE COUNTRY.
WE USE THE WEAPONS TO ESTABLISH ORDER. A NEW ORDER. A BETTER WORLD IN THE LONG RUN.
BUT EVERYONE FOCUSES ON THE INNOCENT LIVES. TELL ME, WHAT WAR HAS EVER BEEN WAGED THAT WASN'T PAID FOR WITH THE BLOOD OF INNOCENTS?
WE ARE SIMPLY HONEST ABOUT IT, MR. COLLINS.

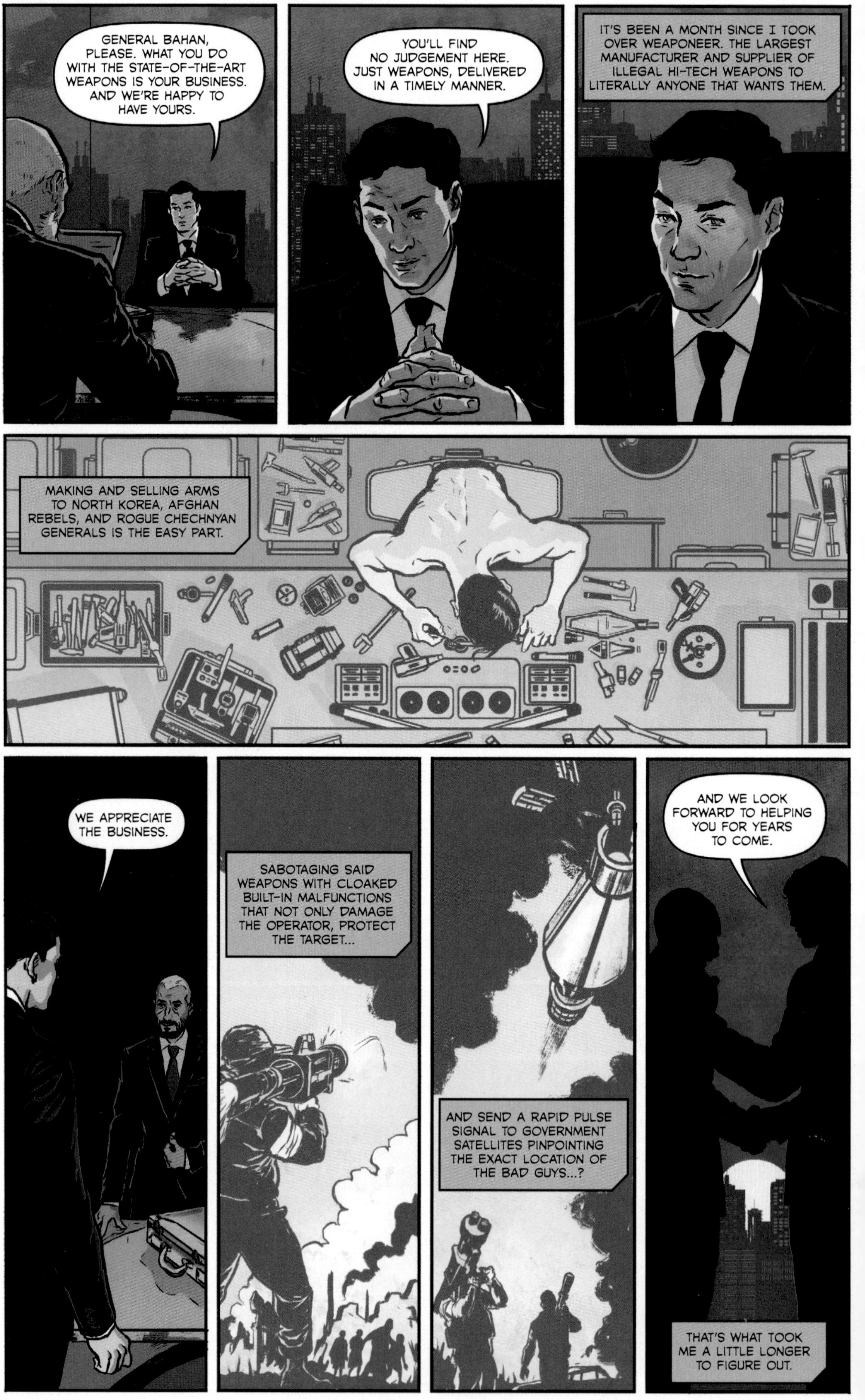
GENERAL BAHAN, PLEASE. WHAT YOU DO WITH THE STATE-OF-THE-ART WEAPONS IS YOUR BUSINESS. AND WE'RE HAPPY TO HAVE YOURS.
YOU'LL FIND NO JUDGEMENT HERE. JUST WEAPONS, DELIVERED IN A TIMELY MANNER.
IT'S BEEN A MONTH SINCE I TOOK OVER WEAPONEER. THE LARGEST MANUFACTURER AND SUPPLIER OF ILLEGAL HI-TECH WEAPONS TO LITERALLY ANYONE THAT WANTS THEM.
MAKING AND SELLING ARMS TO NORTH KOREA, AFGHAN REBELS, AND ROGUE CHECHNYAN GENERALS IS THE EASY PART.
WE APPRECIATE THE BUSINESS.
SABOTAGING SAID WEAPONS WITH CLOAKED BUILT-IN MALFUNCTIONS THAT NOT ONLY DAMAGE THE OPERATOR, PROTECT THE TARGET...
AND SEND A RAPID PULSE SIGNAL TO GOVERNMENT SATELLITES PINPOINTING THE EXACT LOCATION OF THE BAD GUYS...?
AND WE LOOK FORWARD TO HELPING YOU FOR YEARS TO COME.
THAT'S WHAT TOOK ME A LITTLE LONGER TO FIGURE OUT.

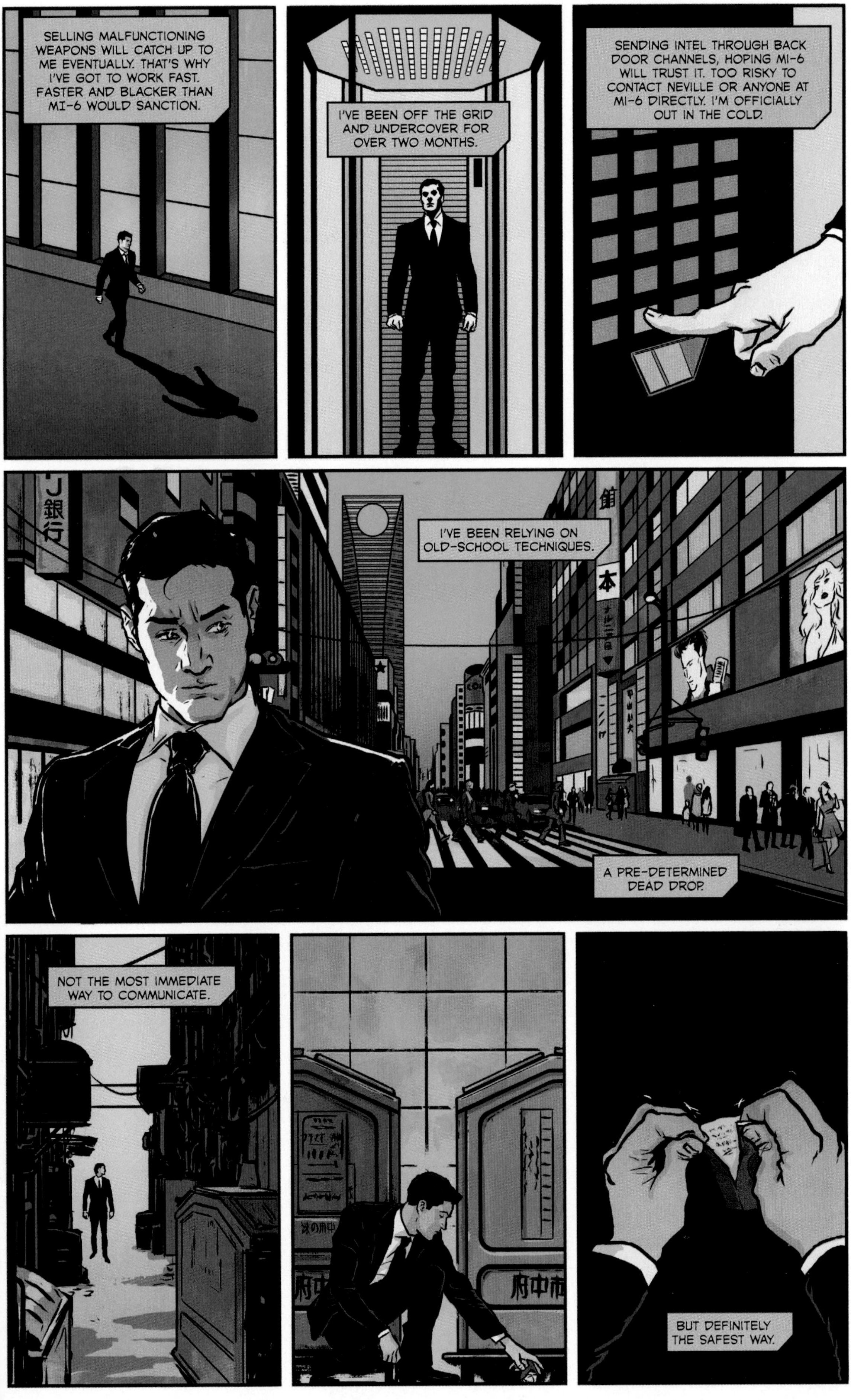
SELLING MALFUNCTIONING WEAPONS WILL CATCH UP TO ME EVENTUALLY. THAT'S WHY I'VE GOT TO WORK FAST. FASTER AND BLACKER THAN MI-6 WOULD SANCTION.
I'VE BEEN OFF THE GRID AND UNDERCOVER FOR OVER TWO MONTHS.
SENDING INTEL THROUGH BACK DOOR CHANNELS, HOPING MI-6 WILL TRUST IT. TOO RISKY TO CONTACT NEVILLE OR ANYONE AT MI-6 DIRECTLY. I'M OFFICIALLY OUT IN THE COLD.
I'VE BEEN RELYING ON OLD-SCHOOL TECHNIQUES.
A PRE-DETERMINED DEAD DROP.
NOT THE MOST IMMEDIATE WAY TO COMMUNICATE.
BUT DEFINITELY THE SAFEST WAY.

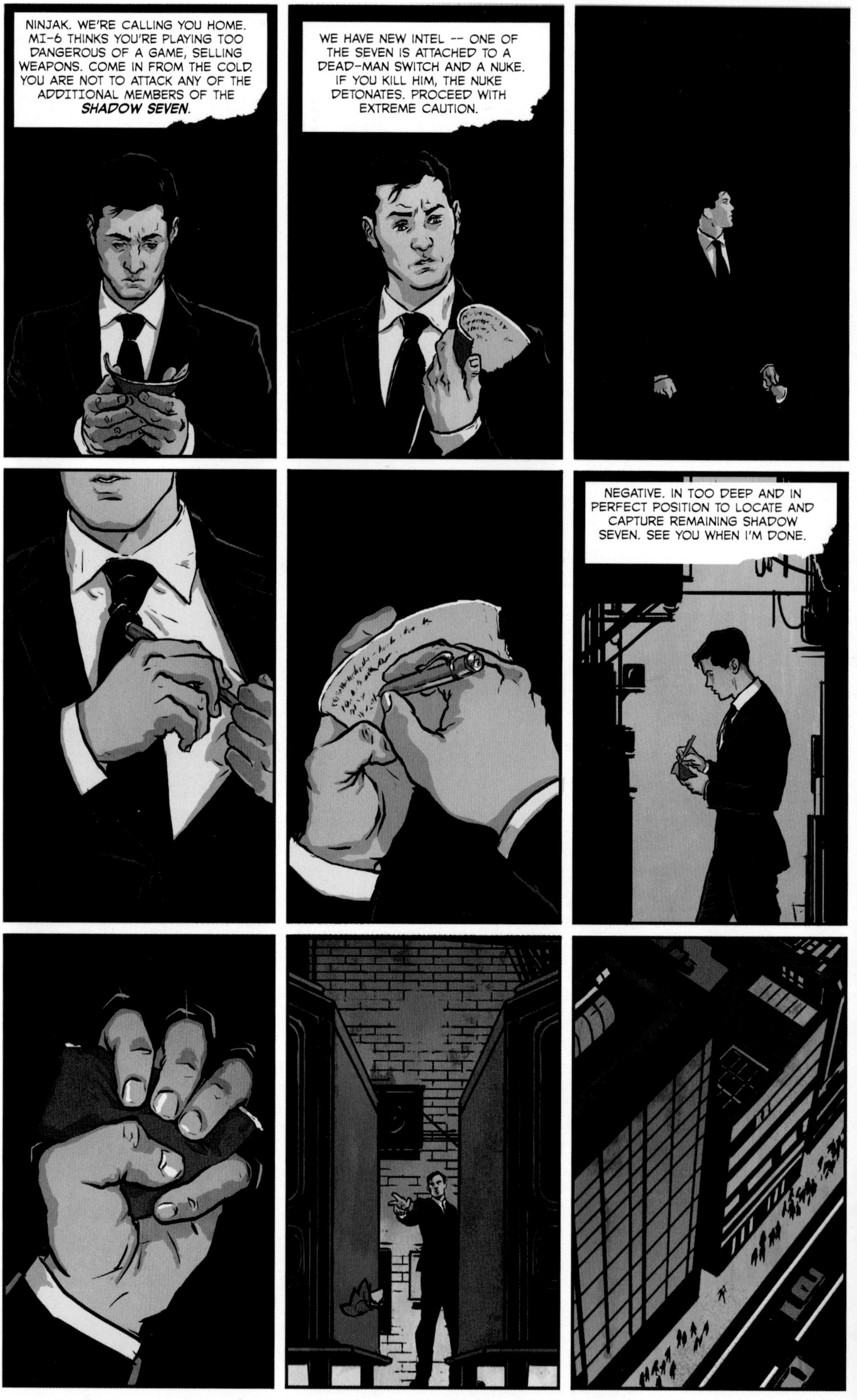
NINJAK. WE'RE CALLING YOU HOME. MI-6 THINKS YOU'RE PLAYING TOO DANGEROUS OF A GAME, SELLING WEAPONS. COME IN FROM THE COLD. YOU ARE NOT TO ATTACK ANY OF THE ADDITIONAL MEMBERS OF THE ***SHADOW SEVEN***.
WE HAVE NEW INTEL -- ONE OF THE SEVEN IS ATTACHED TO A DEAD-MAN SWITCH AND A NUKE. IF YOU KILL HIM, THE NUKE DETONATES. PROCEED WITH EXTREME CAUTION.
NEGATIVE. IN TOO DEEP AND IN PERFECT POSITION TO LOCATE AND CAPTURE REMAINING SHADOW SEVEN. SEE YOU WHEN I'M DONE.

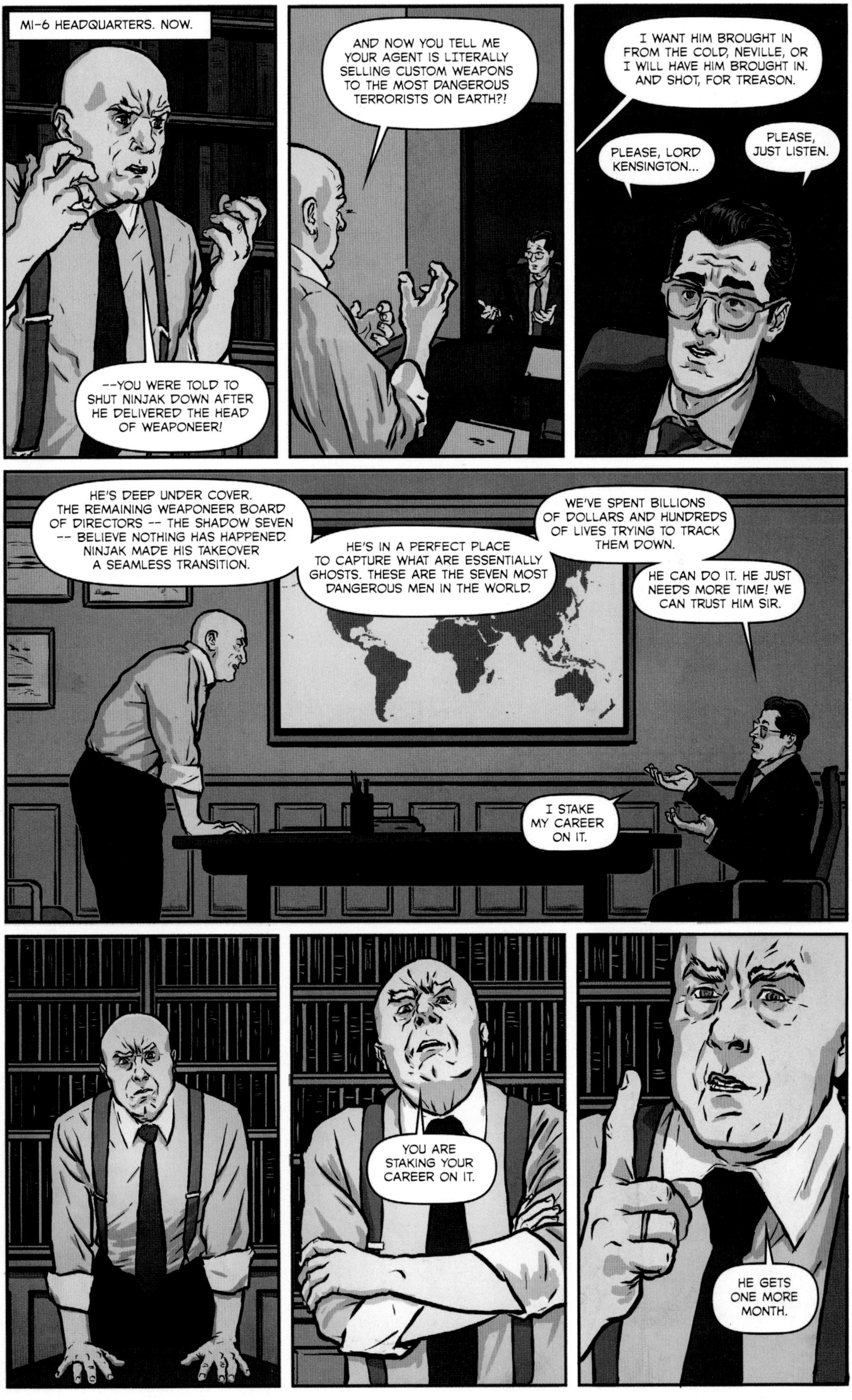
MI-6 HEADQUARTERS. NOW.
--YOU WERE TOLD TO SHUT NINJAK DOWN AFTER HE DELIVERED THE HEAD OF WEAPONEER!
AND NOW YOU TELL ME YOUR AGENT IS LITERALLY SELLING CUSTOM WEAPONS TO THE MOST DANGEROUS TERRORISTS ON EARTH?!
I WANT HIM BROUGHT IN FROM THE COLD, NEVILLE, OR I WILL HAVE HIM BROUGHT IN. AND SHOT, FOR TREASON.
PLEASE, LORD KENSINGTON...
PLEASE, JUST LISTEN.
HE'S DEEP UNDER COVER. THE REMAINING WEAPONEER BOARD OF DIRECTORS -- THE SHADOW SEVEN -- BELIEVE NOTHING HAS HAPPENED. NINJAK MADE HIS TAKEOVER A SEAMLESS TRANSITION.
HE'S IN A PERFECT PLACE TO CAPTURE WHAT ARE ESSENTIALLY GHOSTS. THESE ARE THE SEVEN MOST DANGEROUS MEN IN THE WORLD.
WE'VE SPENT BILLIONS OF DOLLARS AND HUNDREDS OF LIVES TRYING TO TRACK THEM DOWN.
HE CAN DO IT. HE JUST NEEDS MORE TIME! WE CAN TRUST HIM SIR.
I STAKE MY CAREER ON IT.
YOU ARE STAKING YOUR CAREER ON IT.
HE GETS ONE MORE MONTH.

TOKYO. WEAPONEER HEADQUARTERS.

EVEN WITH UNFETTERED ACCESS TO WEAPONEER'S FILES, FINDING THE REMAINING SHADOW SEVEN IS GOING TO BE TOUGH.

THESE AREN'T YOUR EVERY DAY EXECUTIVES PUSHING MONEY AROUND ALL DAY.

FIRST ON MY LIST. LA BARBE. QUIETLY, HE'S BECOME THE RICHEST MAN ON EARTH THAT NO ONE HAS EVER HEARD OF. A RECLUSE.

WHAT DOES ALL HIS MONEY BUY? ANONYMITY. SECLUSION. I'VE SEEN HIS TYPE BEFORE. WHEN YOU'VE AMASSED AS MUCH WEALTH AS HE HAS, IT'S NOT ABOUT THE MONEY ANYMORE. THE MONEY IS JUST A WAY OF KEEPING SCORE.

AND SINCE HE'S RUN OUT OF WORTHY COMPETITION, HE'S JUST MELTED AWAY.

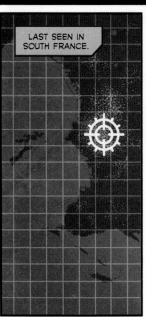

LAST SEEN IN SOUTH FRANCE.

PROVENCE TO BE EXACT.

SOUTH FRANCE...BRINGS BACK A LOT OF MEMORIES.

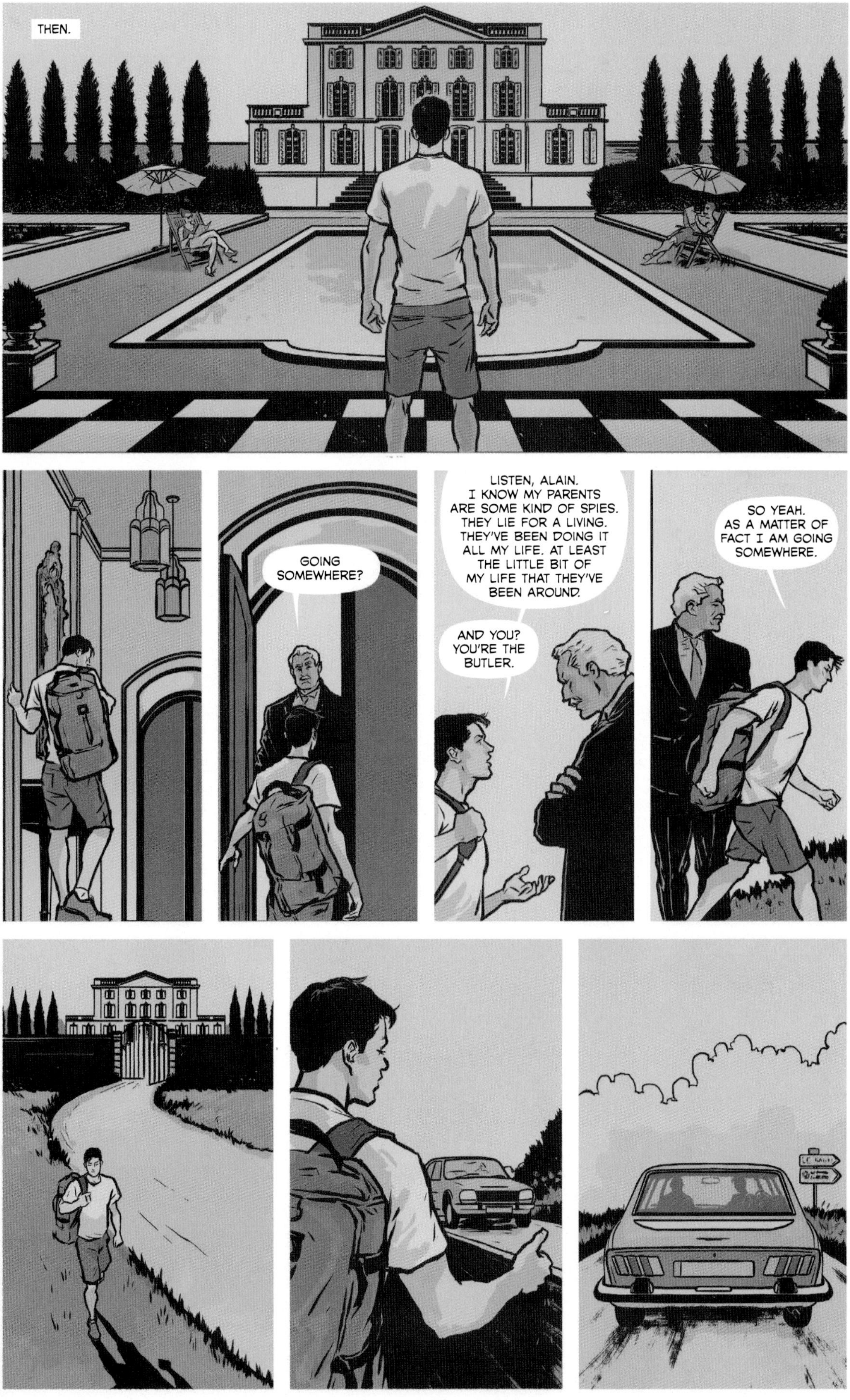
THEN.
GOING SOMEWHERE?
LISTEN, ALAIN. I KNOW MY PARENTS ARE SOME KIND OF SPIES. THEY LIE FOR A LIVING. THEY'VE BEEN DOING IT ALL MY LIFE. AT LEAST THE LITTLE BIT OF MY LIFE THAT THEY'VE BEEN AROUND.
AND YOU? YOU'RE THE BUTLER.
SO YEAH. AS A MATTER OF FACT I AM GOING SOMEWHERE.

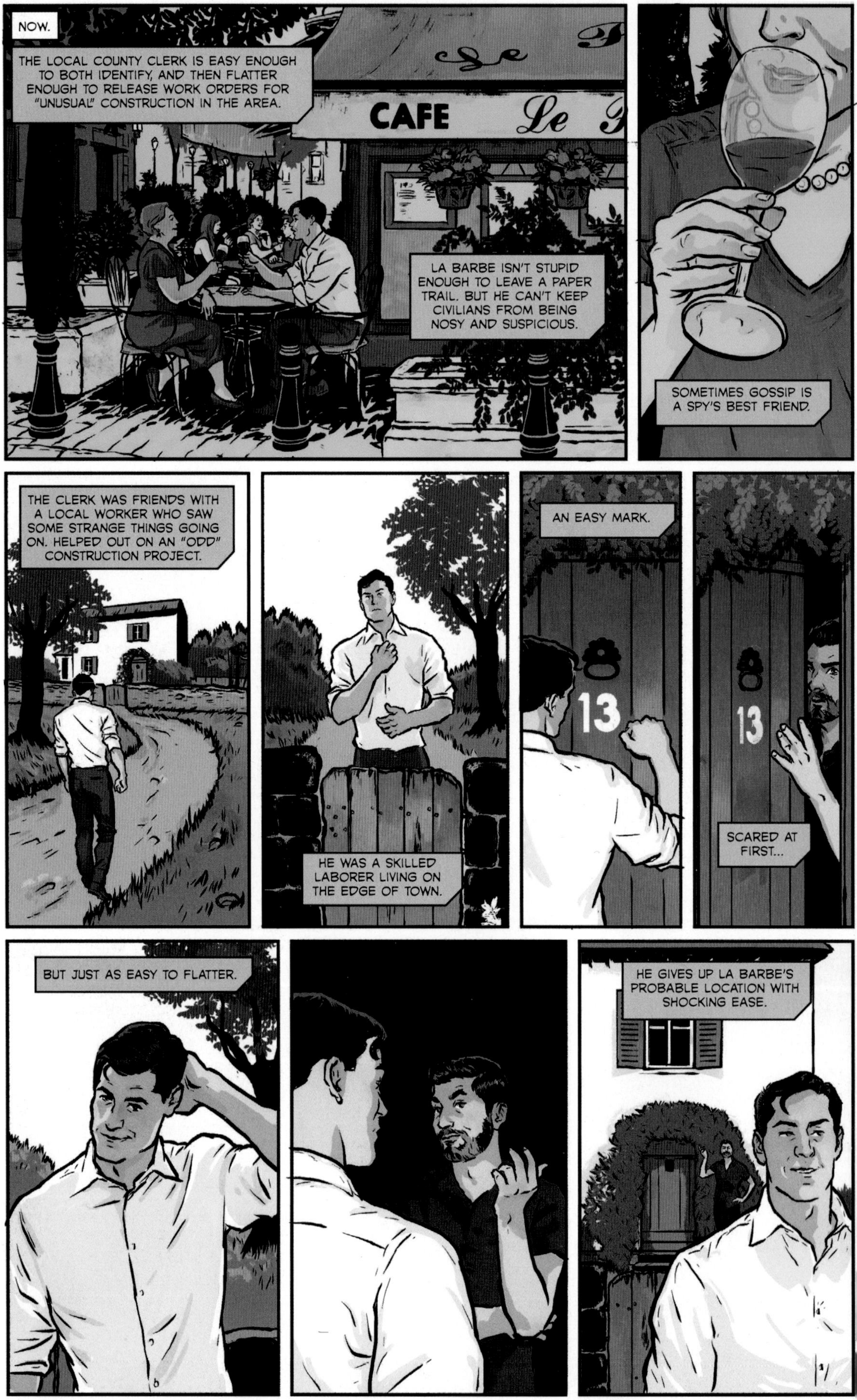
NOW.
THE LOCAL COUNTY CLERK IS EASY ENOUGH TO BOTH IDENTIFY, AND THEN FLATTER ENOUGH TO RELEASE WORK ORDERS FOR "UNUSUAL" CONSTRUCTION IN THE AREA.
CAFE Le
LA BARBE ISN'T STUPID ENOUGH TO LEAVE A PAPER TRAIL. BUT HE CAN'T KEEP CIVILIANS FROM BEING NOSY AND SUSPICIOUS.
SOMETIMES GOSSIP IS A SPY'S BEST FRIEND.
THE CLERK WAS FRIENDS WITH A LOCAL WORKER WHO SAW SOME STRANGE THINGS GOING ON. HELPED OUT ON AN "ODD" CONSTRUCTION PROJECT.
HE WAS A SKILLED LABORER LIVING ON THE EDGE OF TOWN.
AN EASY MARK.
13
13
SCARED AT FIRST...
BUT JUST AS EASY TO FLATTER.
HE GIVES UP LA BARBE'S PROBABLE LOCATION WITH SHOCKING EASE.

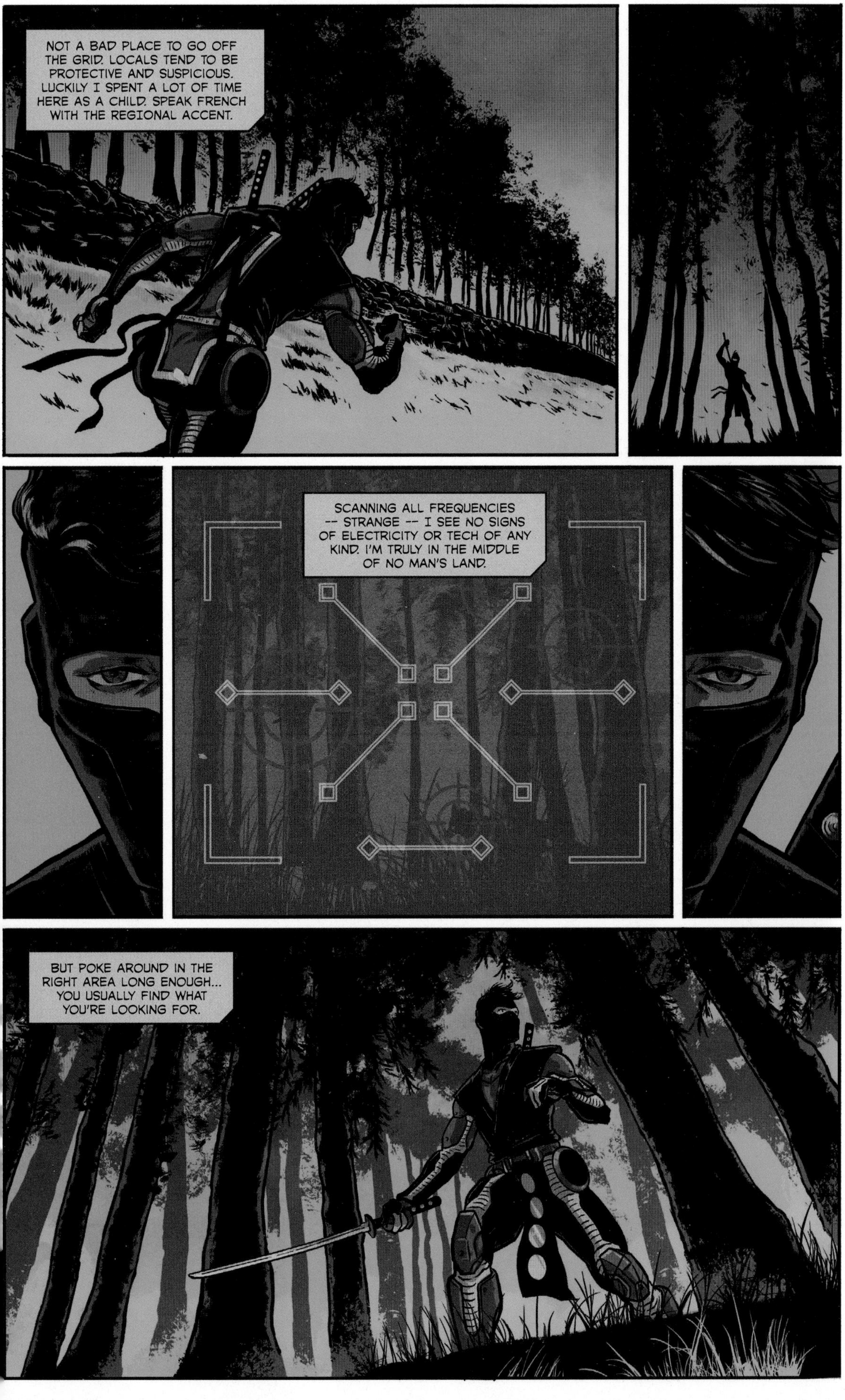
NOT A BAD PLACE TO GO OFF THE GRID. LOCALS TEND TO BE PROTECTIVE AND SUSPICIOUS. LUCKILY I SPENT A LOT OF TIME HERE AS A CHILD. SPEAK FRENCH WITH THE REGIONAL ACCENT.
SCANNING ALL FREQUENCIES -- STRANGE -- I SEE NO SIGNS OF ELECTRICITY OR TECH OF ANY KIND. I'M TRULY IN THE MIDDLE OF NO MAN'S LAND.
BUT POKE AROUND IN THE RIGHT AREA LONG ENOUGH... YOU USUALLY FIND WHAT YOU'RE LOOKING FOR.

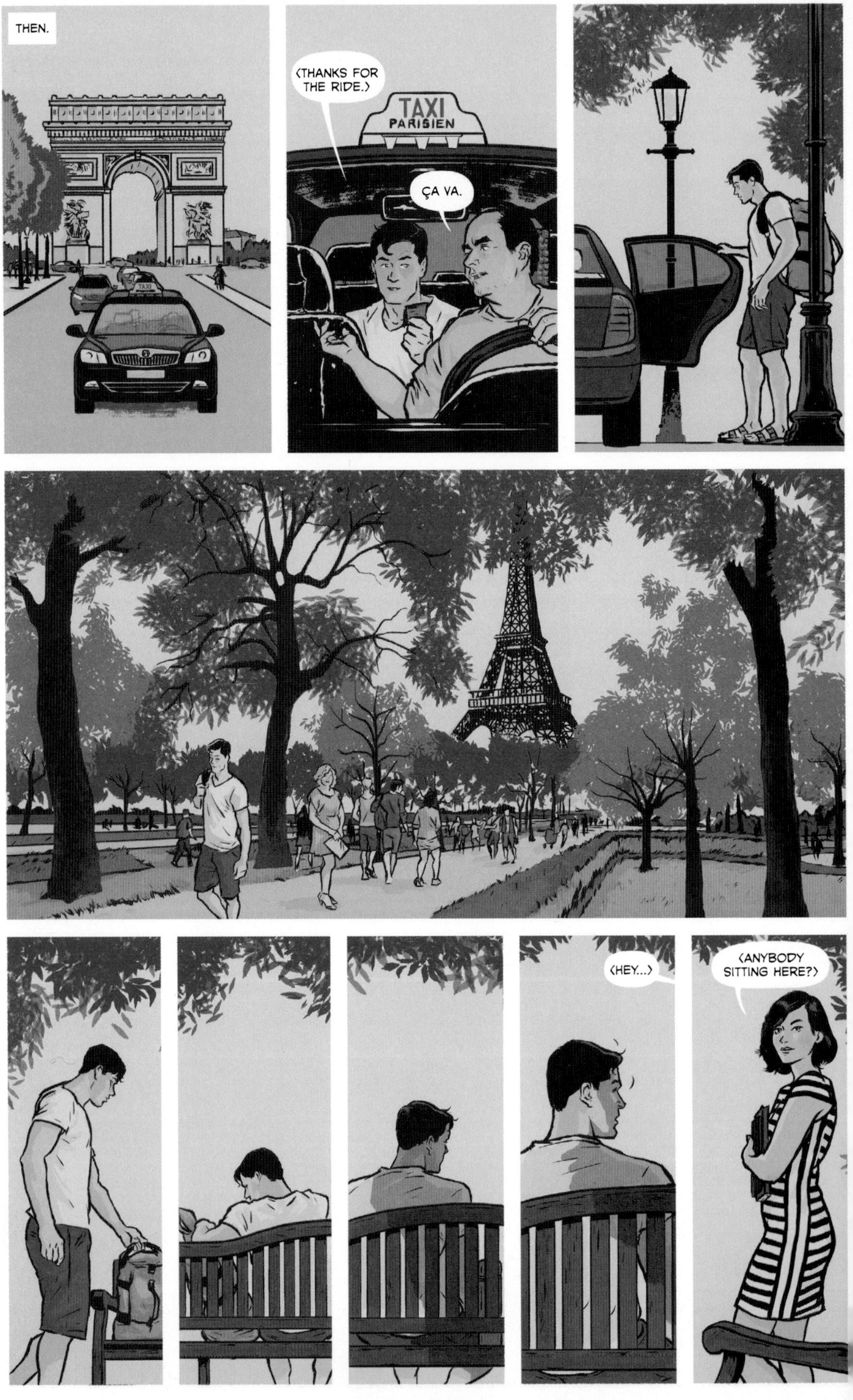
THEN.
‹THANKS FOR THE RIDE.›
TAXI PARISIEN
ÇA VA.
‹HEY...›
‹ANYBODY SITTING HERE?›

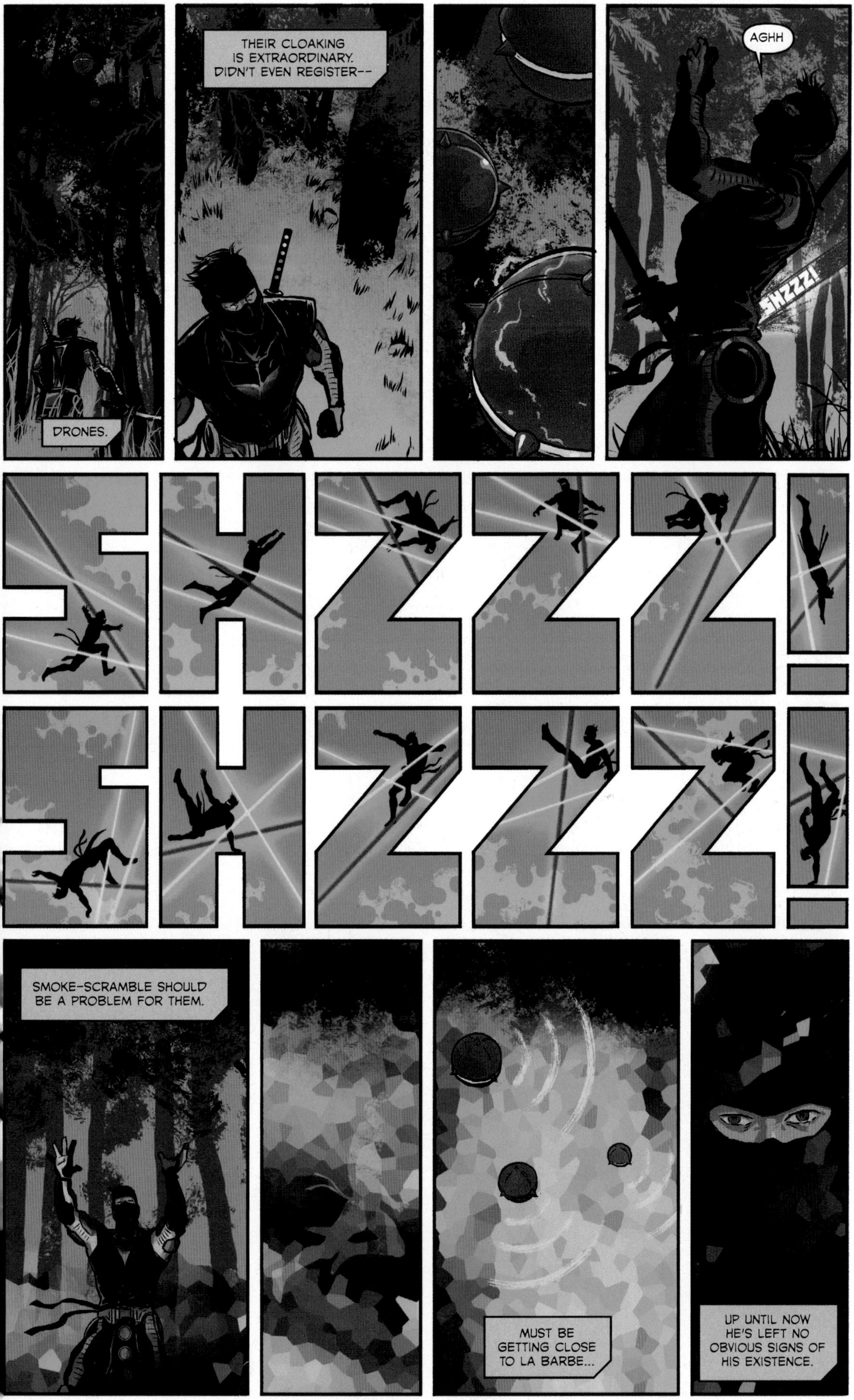
DRONES.
THEIR CLOAKING IS EXTRAORDINARY. DIDN'T EVEN REGISTER--
AGHH
SHZZZ!
SHZZZ!
SHZZZ!
SMOKE-SCRAMBLE SHOULD BE A PROBLEM FOR THEM.
MUST BE GETTING CLOSE TO LA BARBE...
UP UNTIL NOW HE'S LEFT NO OBVIOUS SIGNS OF HIS EXISTENCE.

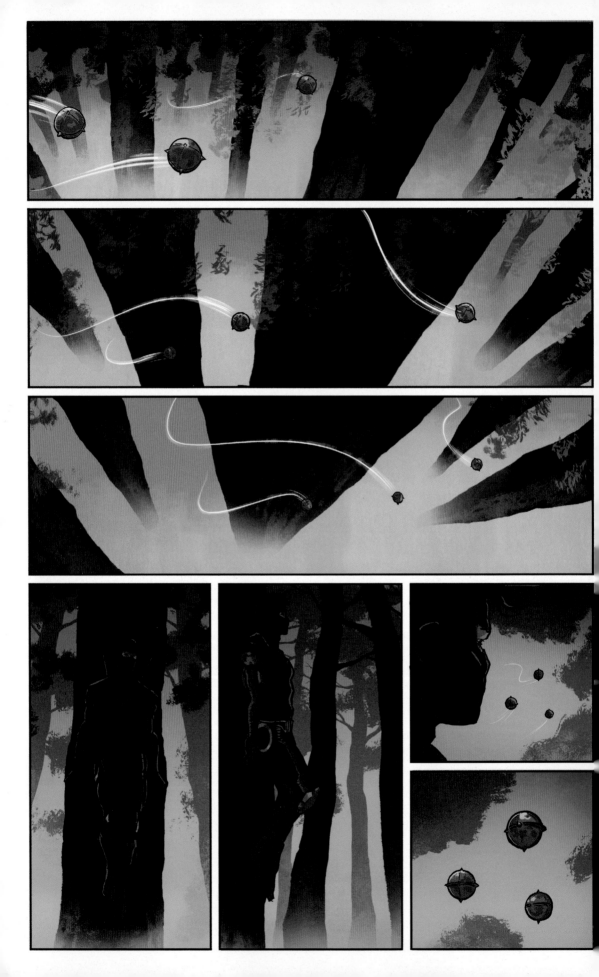

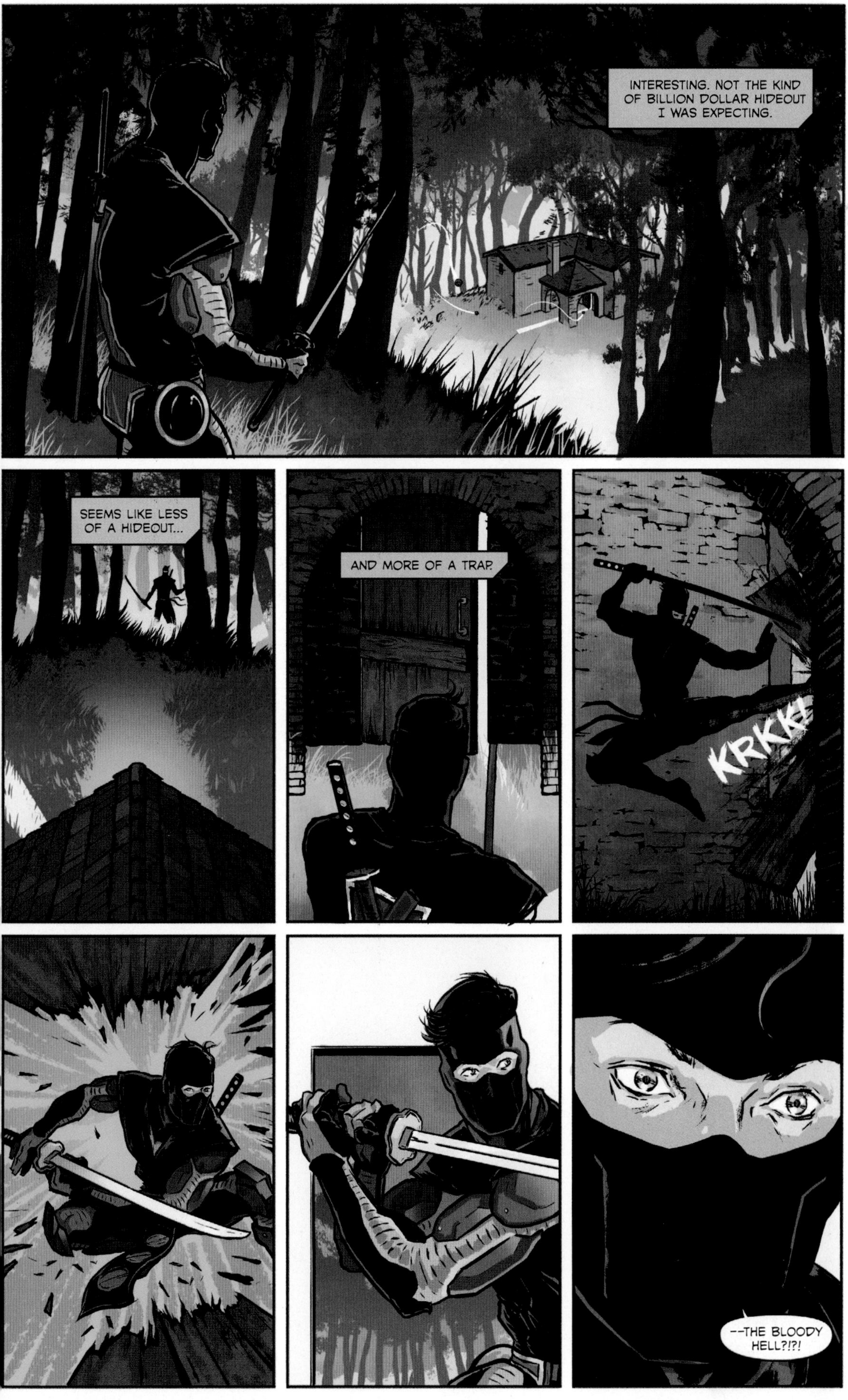
INTERESTING. NOT THE KIND OF BILLION DOLLAR HIDEOUT I WAS EXPECTING.
SEEMS LIKE LESS OF A HIDEOUT...
AND MORE OF A TRAP.
KRKK!
--THE BLOODY HELL?!?!

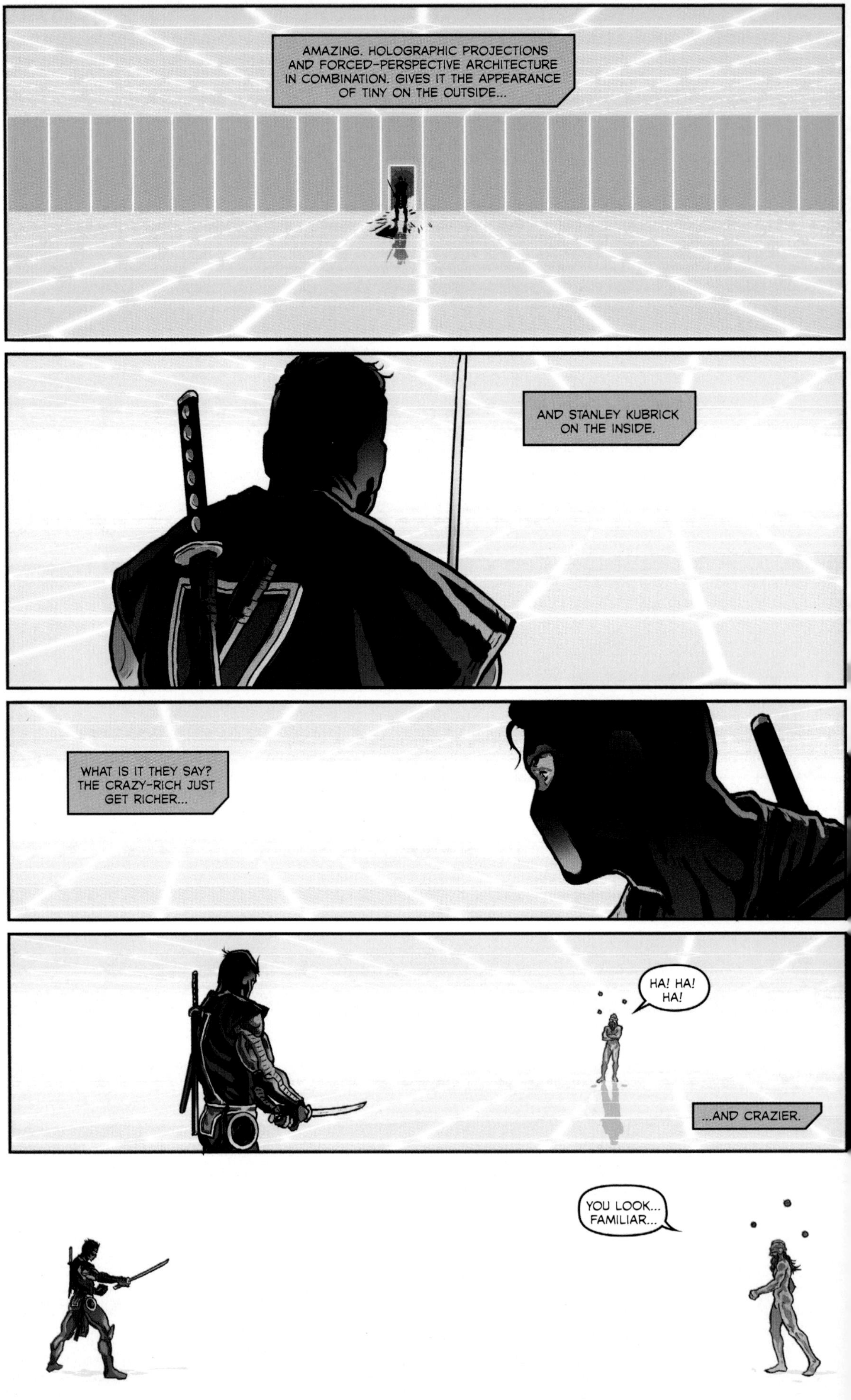
AMAZING. HOLOGRAPHIC PROJECTIONS AND FORCED-PERSPECTIVE ARCHITECTURE IN COMBINATION. GIVES IT THE APPEARANCE OF TINY ON THE OUTSIDE...
AND STANLEY KUBRICK ON THE INSIDE.
WHAT IS IT THEY SAY? THE CRAZY-RICH JUST GET RICHER...
HA! HA! HA!
...AND CRAZIER.
YOU LOOK... FAMILIAR...

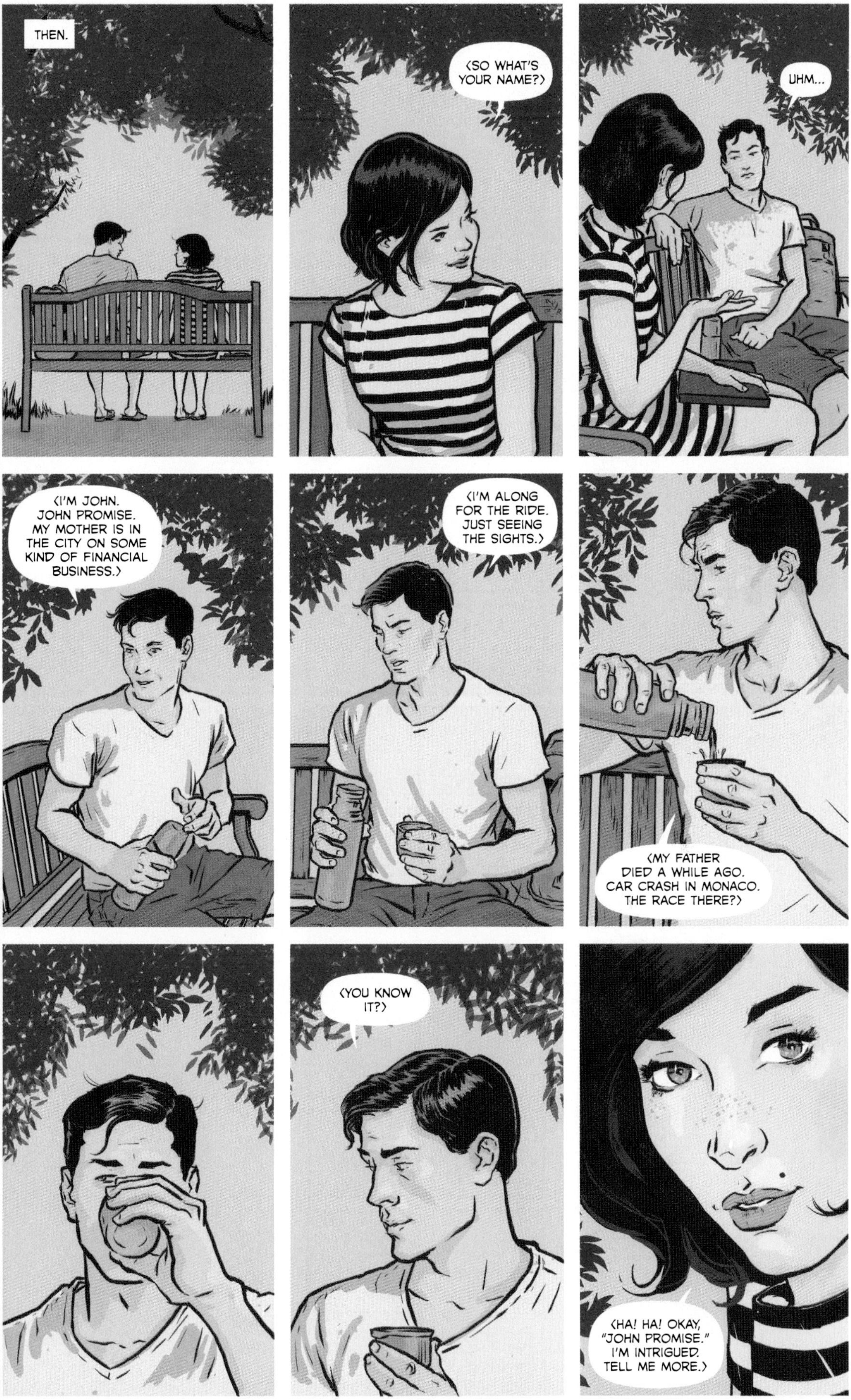
THEN.
<SO WHAT'S YOUR NAME?>
UHM...
<I'M JOHN. JOHN PROMISE. MY MOTHER IS IN THE CITY ON SOME KIND OF FINANCIAL BUSINESS.>
<I'M ALONG FOR THE RIDE. JUST SEEING THE SIGHTS.>
<MY FATHER DIED A WHILE AGO. CAR CRASH IN MONACO. THE RACE THERE?>
<YOU KNOW IT?>
<HA! HA! OKAY, "JOHN PROMISE." I'M INTRIGUED. TELL ME MORE.>

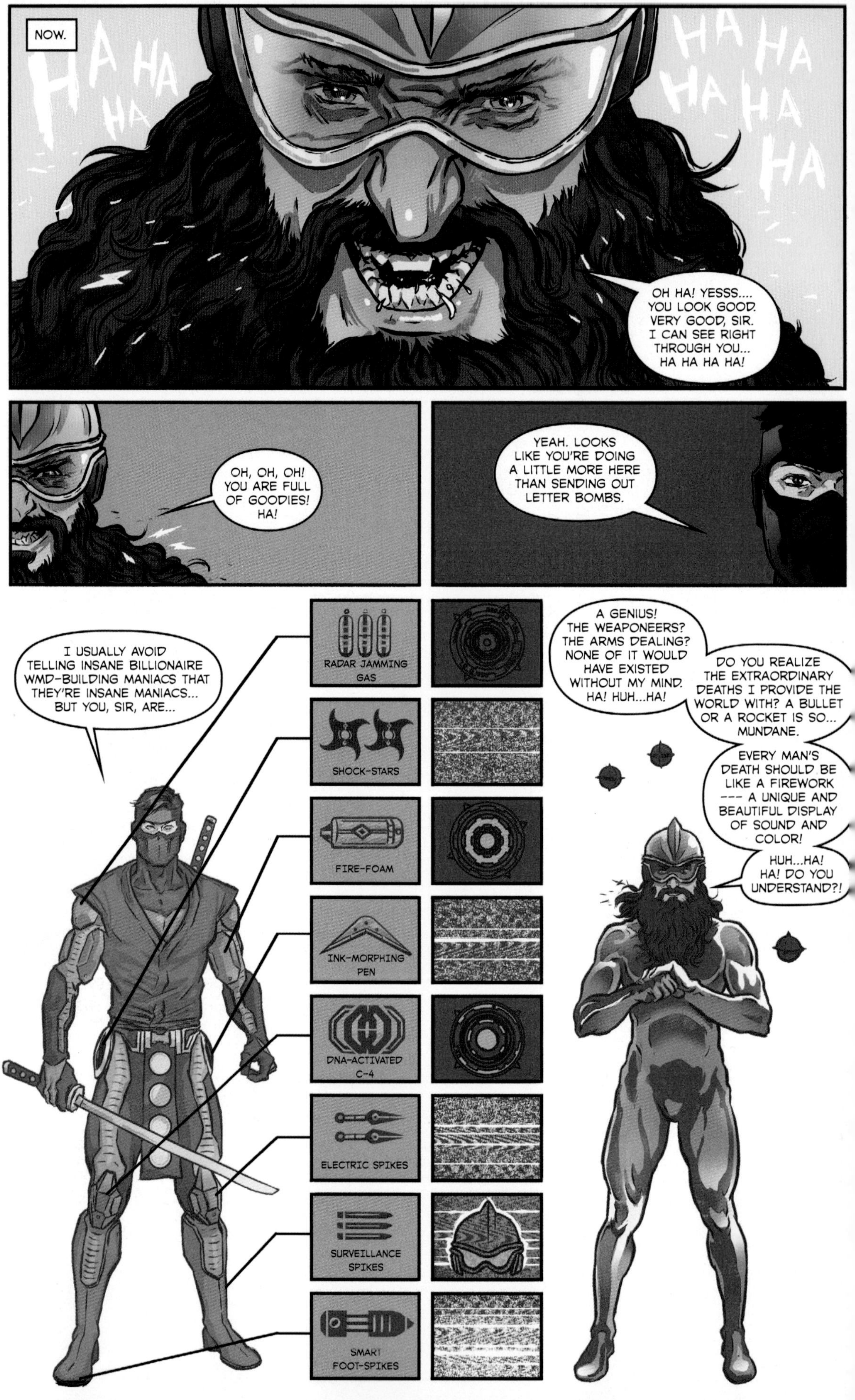
NOW.
HA HA HA HA
HA HA HA HA HA HA
OH HA! YESSS.... YOU LOOK GOOD. VERY GOOD, SIR. I CAN SEE RIGHT THROUGH YOU... HA HA HA HA!
OH, OH, OH! YOU ARE FULL OF GOODIES! HA!
YEAH. LOOKS LIKE YOU'RE DOING A LITTLE MORE HERE THAN SENDING OUT LETTER BOMBS.
I USUALLY AVOID TELLING INSANE BILLIONAIRE WMD-BUILDING MANIACS THAT THEY'RE INSANE MANIACS... BUT YOU, SIR, ARE...
RADAR JAMMING GAS
SHOCK-STARS
FIRE-FOAM
INK-MORPHING PEN
DNA-ACTIVATED C-4
ELECTRIC SPIKES
SURVEILLANCE SPIKES
SMART FOOT-SPIKES
A GENIUS! THE WEAPONEERS? THE ARMS DEALING? NONE OF IT WOULD HAVE EXISTED WITHOUT MY MIND. HA! HUH...HA!
DO YOU REALIZE THE EXTRAORDINARY DEATHS I PROVIDE THE WORLD WITH? A BULLET OR A ROCKET IS SO... MUNDANE.
EVERY MAN'S DEATH SHOULD BE LIKE A FIREWORK --- A UNIQUE AND BEAUTIFUL DISPLAY OF SOUND AND COLOR!
HUH...HA! HA! DO YOU UNDERSTAND?!

WOW. YOU'VE TAKEN FOIL HATS TO A WHOLE NEW LEVEL.
HA! HA-HA!
BOO!
DAMN. THAT HELMET PACKS A PUNCH...HE'S LITERALLY HACKING INTO EVERYTHING I'VE GOT SIMULTANEOUSLY...
AGHHH!!!
GOT TO GET IT ALL OFF...
NEVER SEEN TECH LIKE THIS...
ANYTHING WITH A CIRCUIT...
HE'S GOT AHOLD OF IT...
KILLING ME WITH MY OWN TECH.
SHZZZ!
SHZZZ!
SHZZZ!
SHZZZ!
SHZZZ!

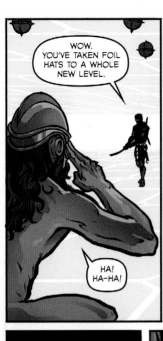

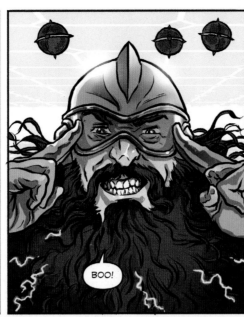

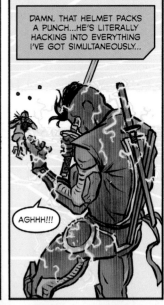

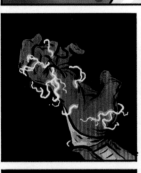

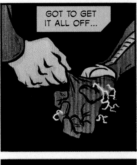

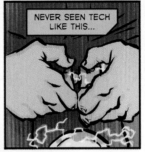

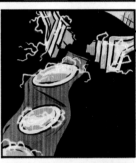

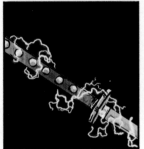

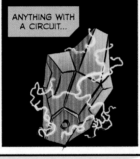

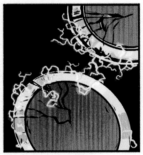

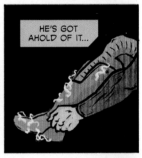

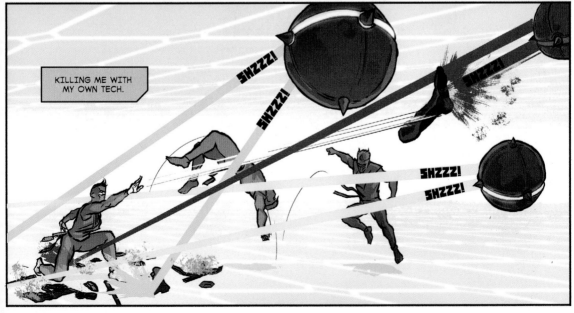

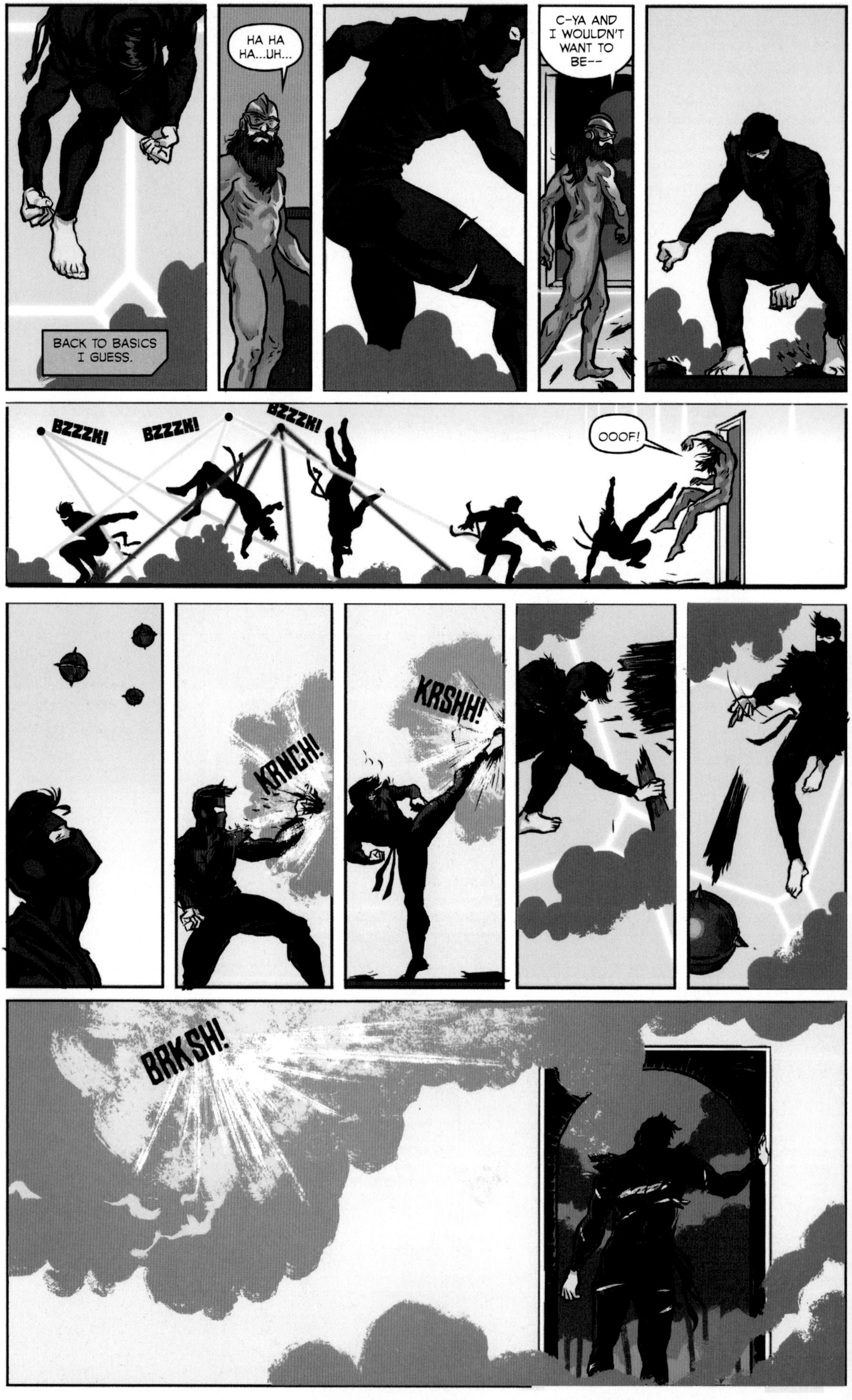
BACK TO BASICS I GUESS.
HA HA HA...UH...
C-YA AND I WOULDN'T WANT TO BE--
BZZZK!
BZZZK!
BZZZK!
OOOF!
KRNCH!
KRSHH!
BRKSH!

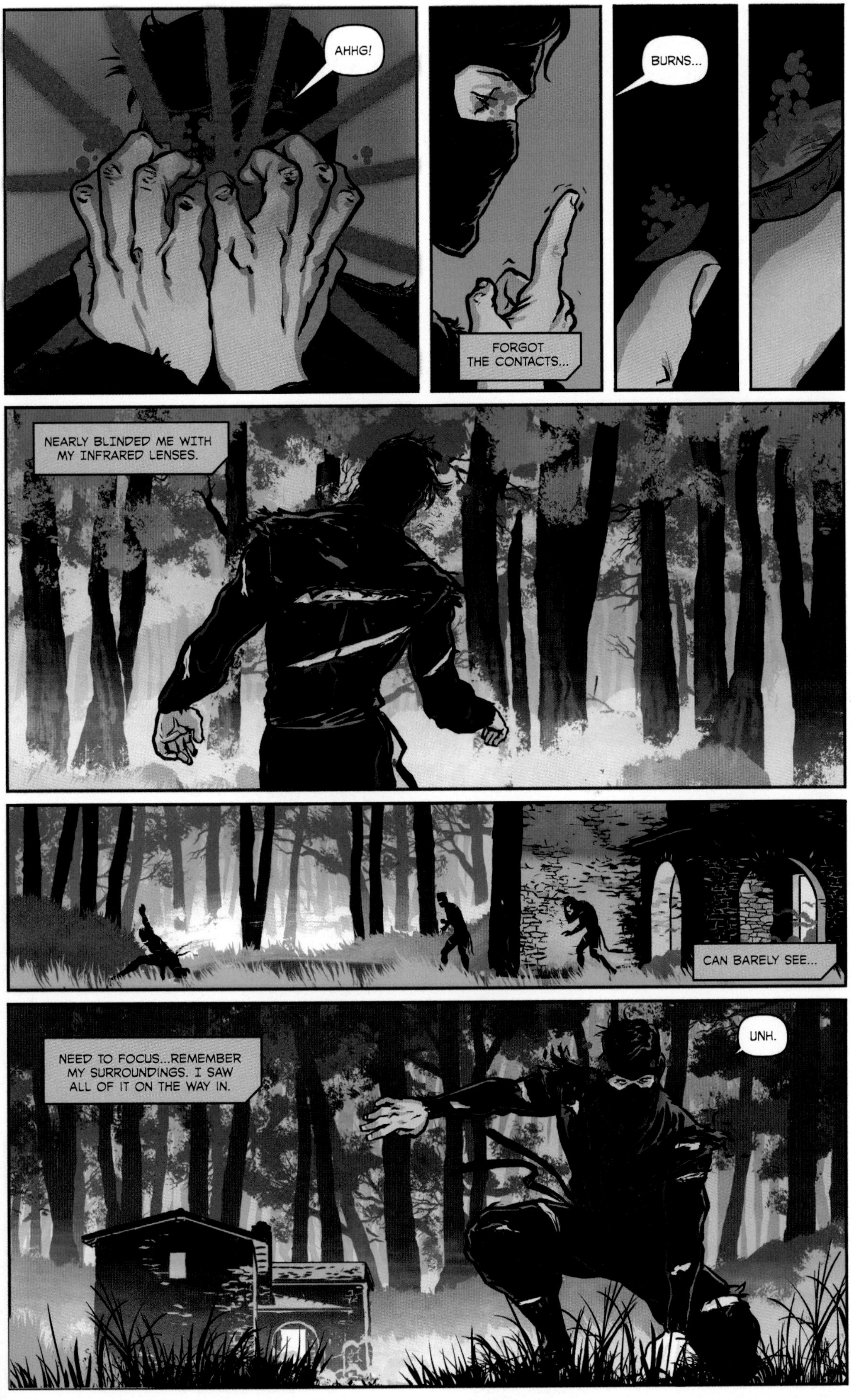
AHHG!
BURNS...
FORGOT THE CONTACTS...
NEARLY BLINDED ME WITH MY INFRARED LENSES.
CAN BARELY SEE...
NEED TO FOCUS...REMEMBER MY SURROUNDINGS. I SAW ALL OF IT ON THE WAY IN.
UNH.

GOT TO USE HEARING.

SMELL.

TOUCH.

MEMORY.

"A NINJA'S TRUE SKILL IS DEMONSTRATED...

"WITH NOTHING BUT HIS EMPTY HANDS."

MINIMIZE MY SENSORY FOOTPRINT...

AND OPEN MY SENSES TO HIS...

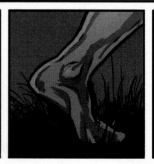

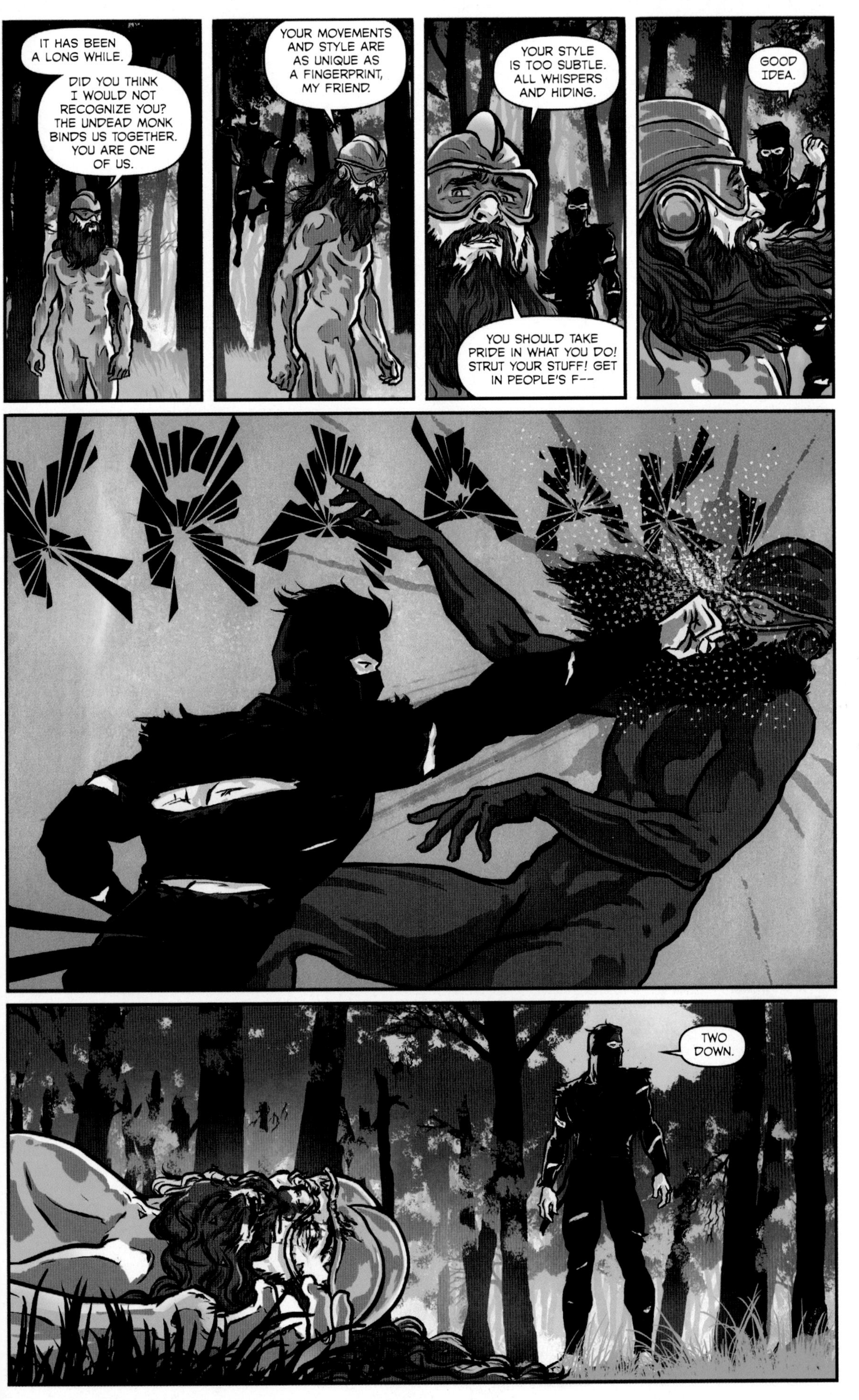
IT HAS BEEN A LONG WHILE.
DID YOU THINK I WOULD NOT RECOGNIZE YOU? THE UNDEAD MONK BINDS US TOGETHER. YOU ARE ONE OF US.
YOUR MOVEMENTS AND STYLE ARE AS UNIQUE AS A FINGERPRINT, MY FRIEND.
YOUR STYLE IS TOO SUBTLE. ALL WHISPERS AND HIDING.
YOU SHOULD TAKE PRIDE IN WHAT YOU DO! STRUT YOUR STUFF! GET IN PEOPLE'S F--
GOOD IDEA.
TWO DOWN.

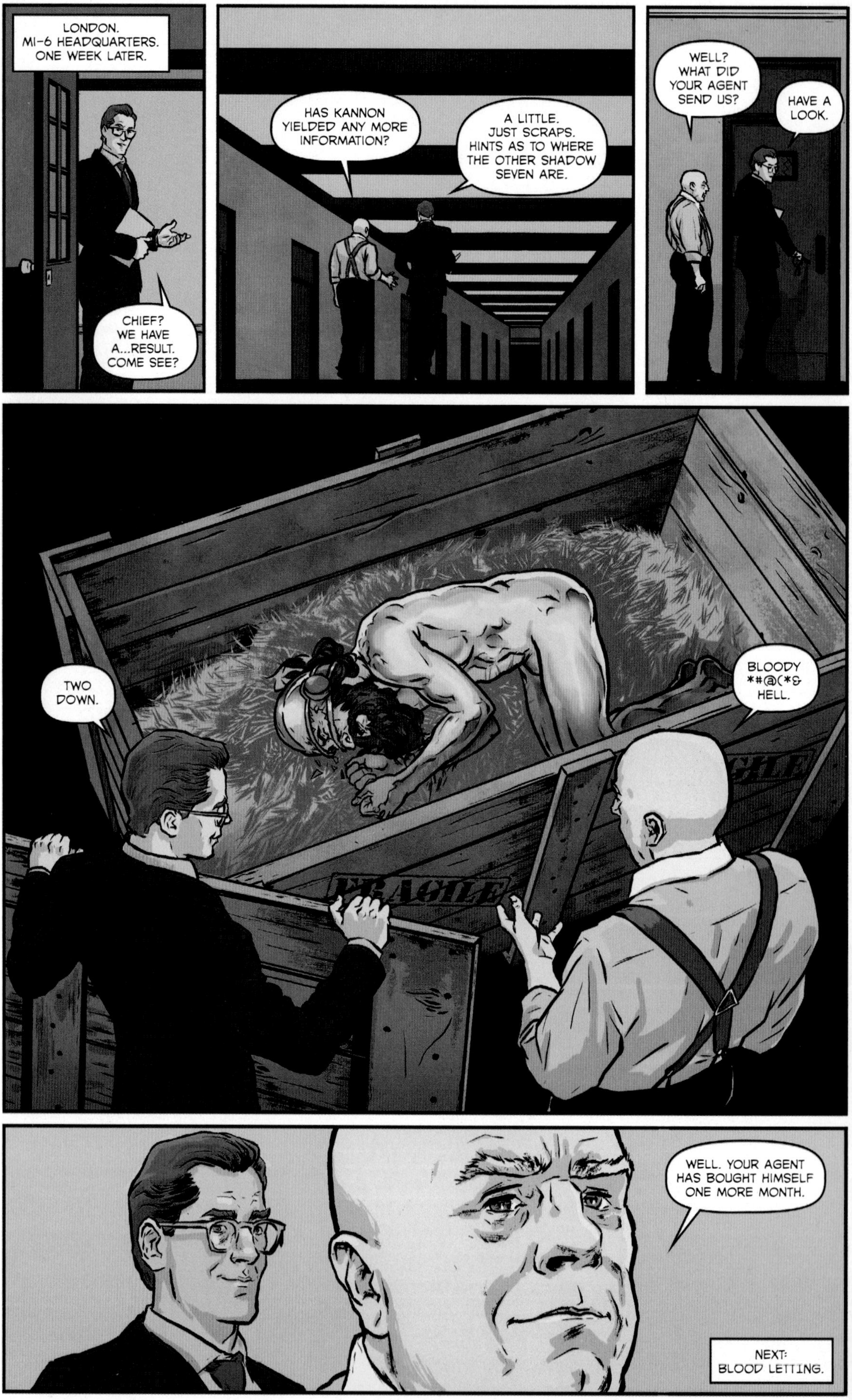
LONDON.
MI-6 HEADQUARTERS.
ONE WEEK LATER.
CHIEF? WE HAVE A...RESULT. COME SEE?
HAS KANNON YIELDED ANY MORE INFORMATION?
A LITTLE. JUST SCRAPS. HINTS AS TO WHERE THE OTHER SHADOW SEVEN ARE.
WELL? WHAT DID YOUR AGENT SEND US?
HAVE A LOOK.
FRAGILE
TWO DOWN.
BLOODY *#@(*& HELL.
WELL. YOUR AGENT HAS BOUGHT HIMSELF ONE MORE MONTH.
NEXT: BLOOD LETTING.

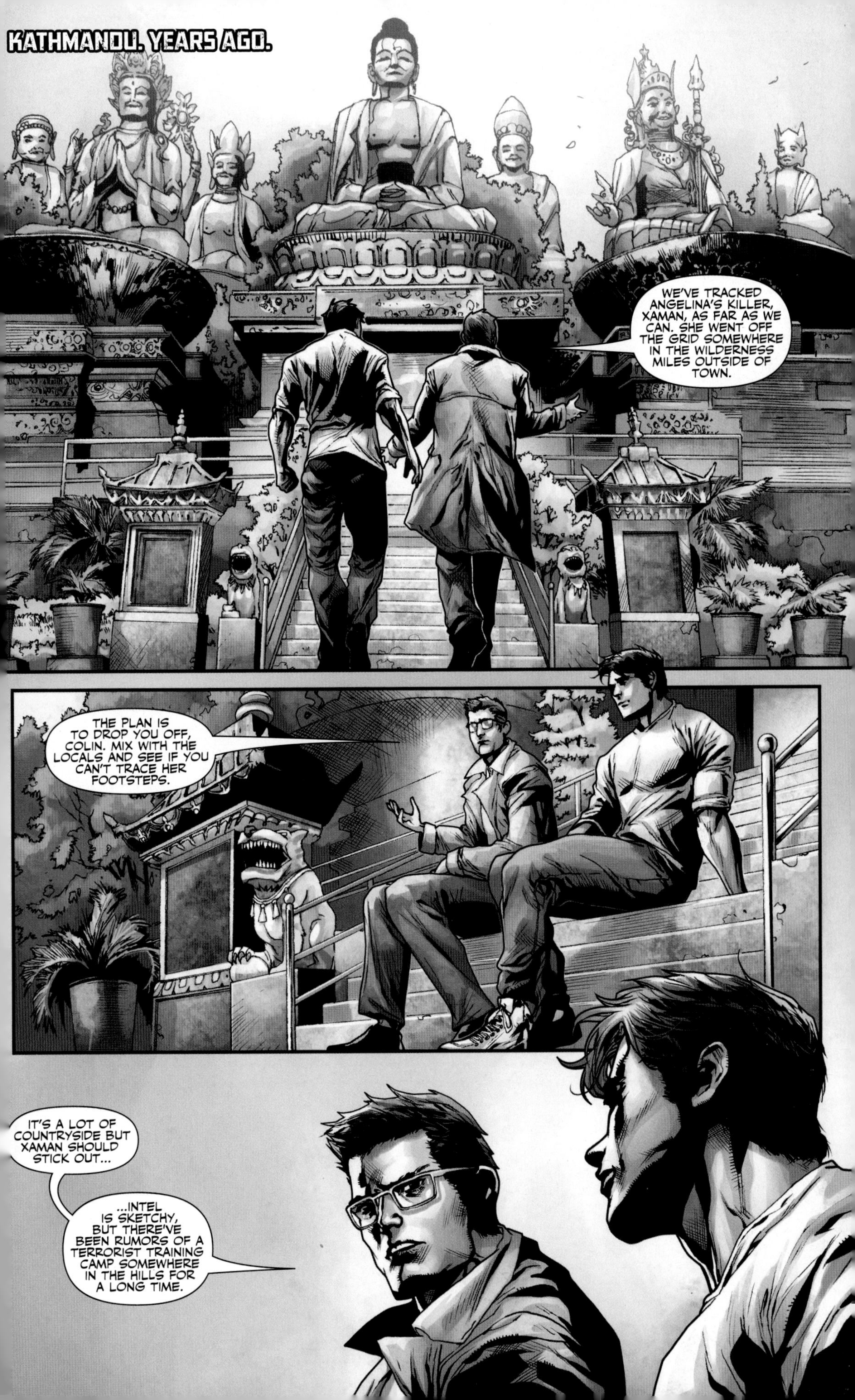
KATHMANDU. YEARS AGO.
WE'VE TRACKED ANGELINA'S KILLER, XAMAN, AS FAR AS WE CAN. SHE WENT OFF THE GRID SOMEWHERE IN THE WILDERNESS MILES OUTSIDE OF TOWN.
THE PLAN IS TO DROP YOU OFF, COLIN. MIX WITH THE LOCALS AND SEE IF YOU CAN'T TRACE HER FOOTSTEPS.
IT'S A LOT OF COUNTRYSIDE BUT XAMAN SHOULD STICK OUT...
...INTEL IS SKETCHY, BUT THERE'VE BEEN RUMORS OF A TERRORIST TRAINING CAMP SOMEWHERE IN THE HILLS FOR A LONG TIME.

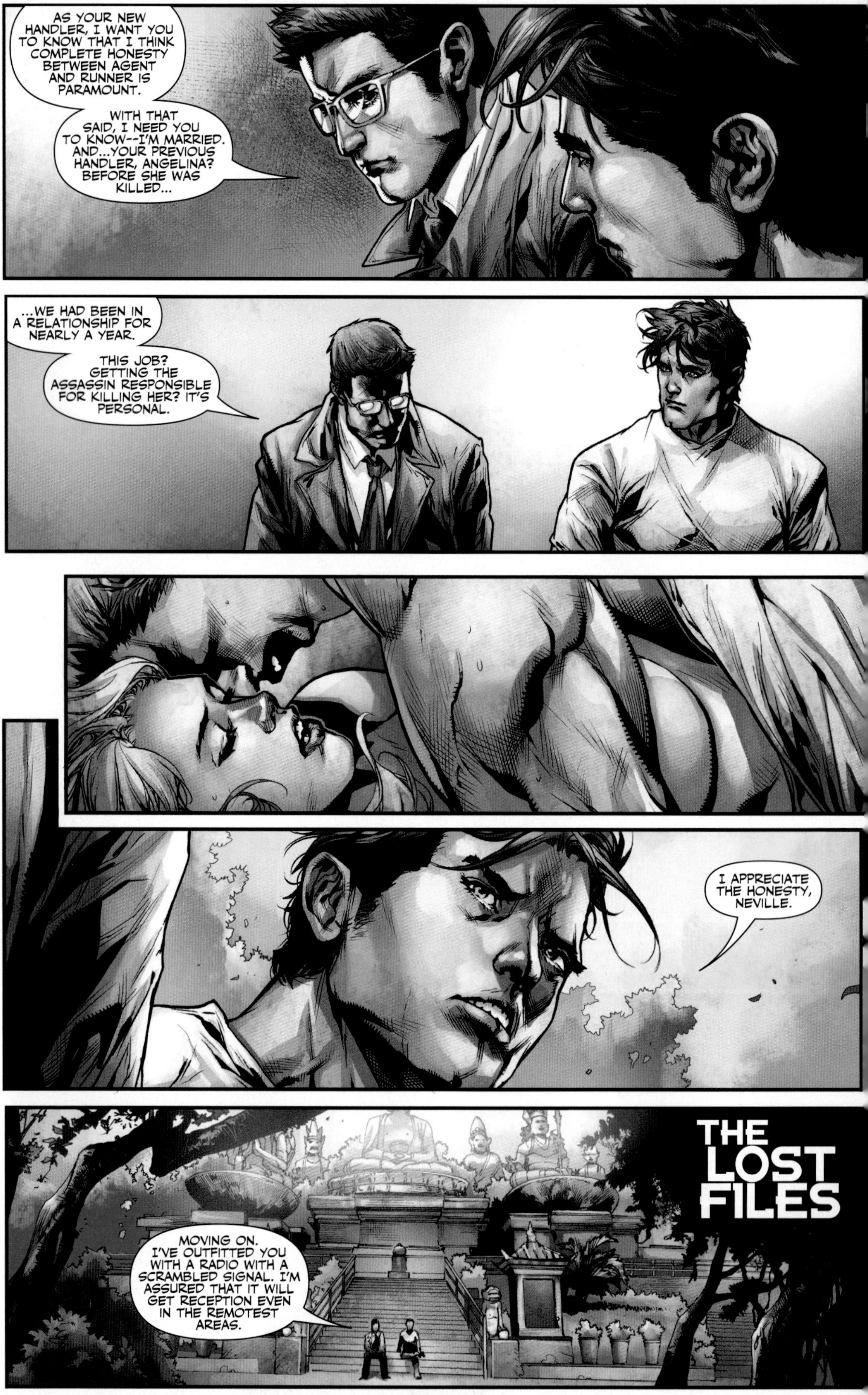
AS YOUR NEW HANDLER, I WANT YOU TO KNOW THAT I THINK COMPLETE HONESTY BETWEEN AGENT AND RUNNER IS PARAMOUNT.
WITH THAT SAID, I NEED YOU TO KNOW--I'M MARRIED. AND...YOUR PREVIOUS HANDLER, ANGELINA? BEFORE SHE WAS KILLED...
...WE HAD BEEN IN A RELATIONSHIP FOR NEARLY A YEAR.
THIS JOB? GETTING THE ASSASSIN RESPONSIBLE FOR KILLING HER? IT'S PERSONAL.
I APPRECIATE THE HONESTY, NEVILLE.
THE LOST FILES
MOVING ON. I'VE OUTFITTED YOU WITH A RADIO WITH A SCRAMBLED SIGNAL. I'M ASSURED THAT IT WILL GET RECEPTION EVEN IN THE REMOTEST AREAS.

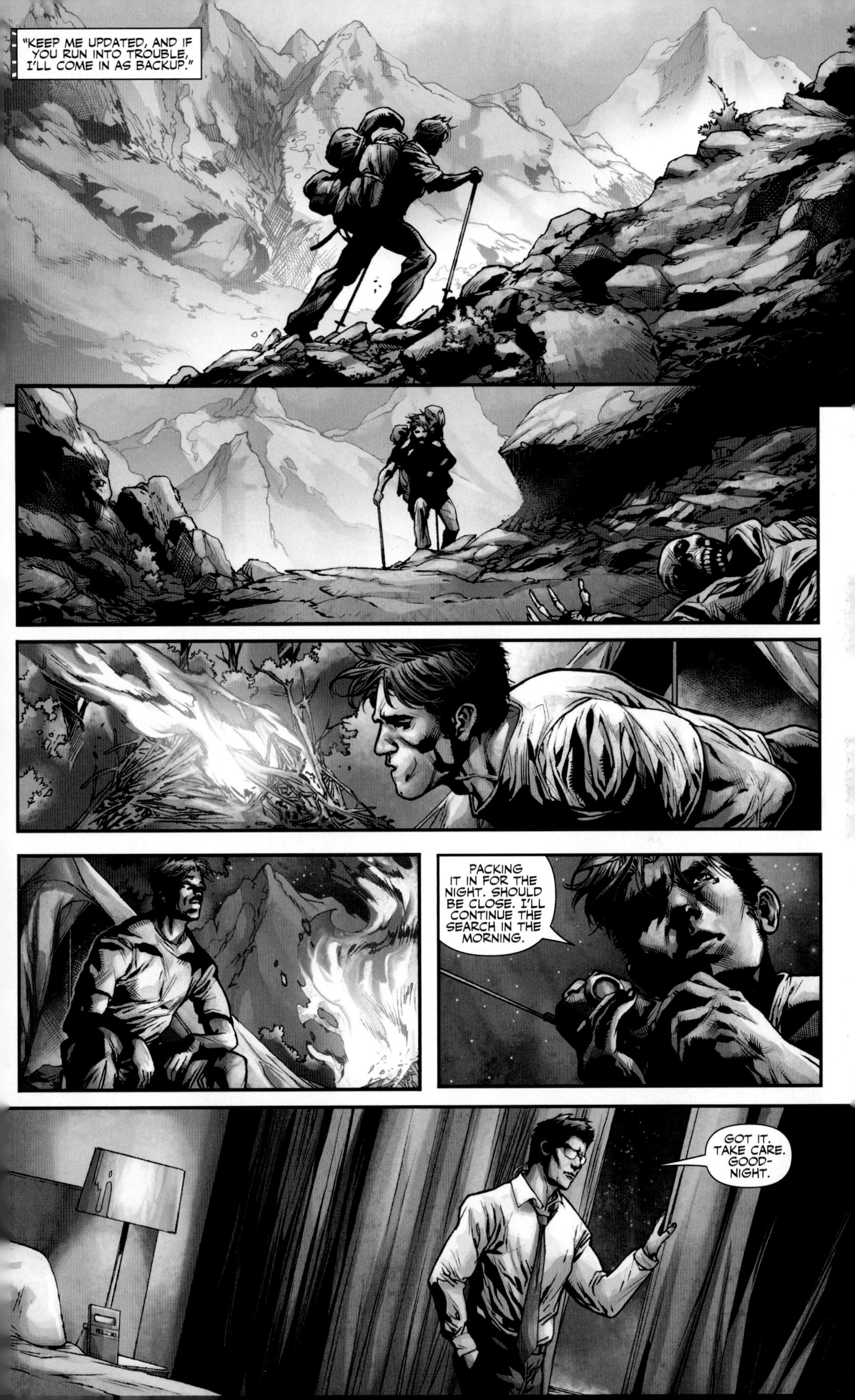
"KEEP ME UPDATED, AND IF YOU RUN INTO TROUBLE, I'LL COME IN AS BACKUP."
PACKING IT IN FOR THE NIGHT. SHOULD BE CLOSE. I'LL CONTINUE THE SEARCH IN THE MORNING.
GOT IT. TAKE CARE. GOOD-NIGHT.

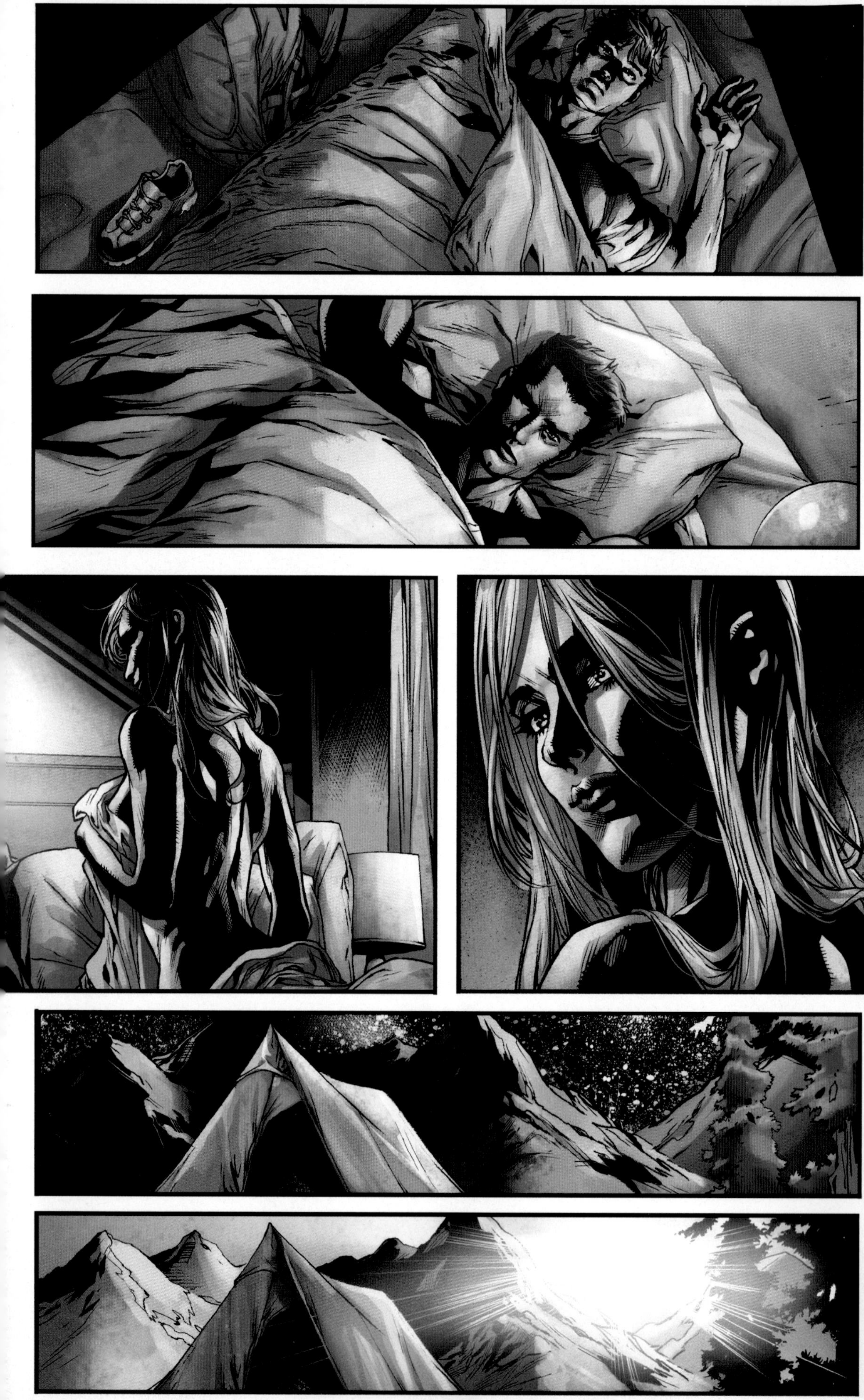

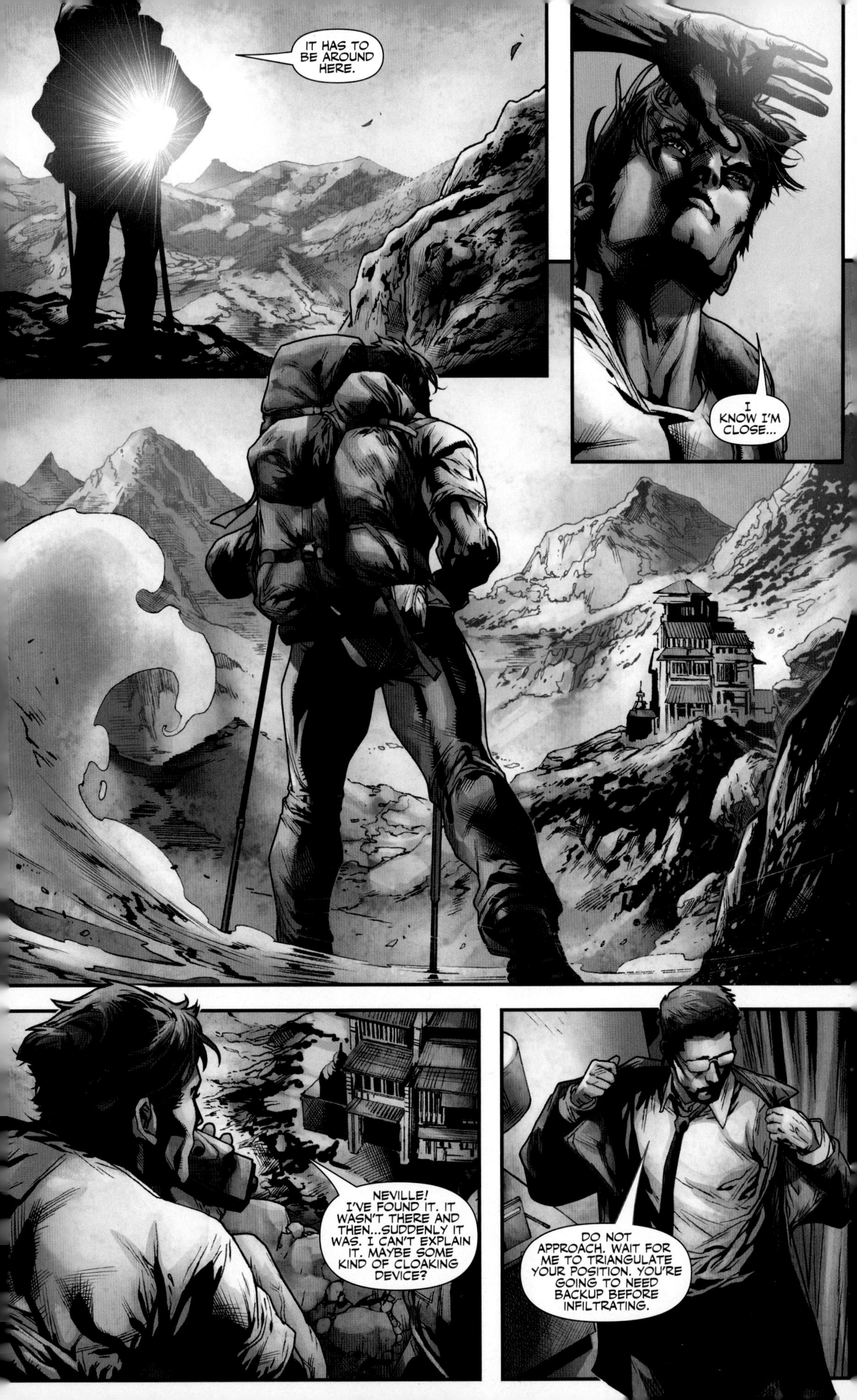
IT HAS TO BE AROUND HERE.
I KNOW I'M CLOSE...
NEVILLE! I'VE FOUND IT. IT WASN'T THERE AND THEN...SUDDENLY IT WAS. I CAN'T EXPLAIN IT. MAYBE SOME KIND OF CLOAKING DEVICE?
DO NOT APPROACH. WAIT FOR ME TO TRIANGULATE YOUR POSITION. YOU'RE GOING TO NEED BACKUP BEFORE INFILTRATING.

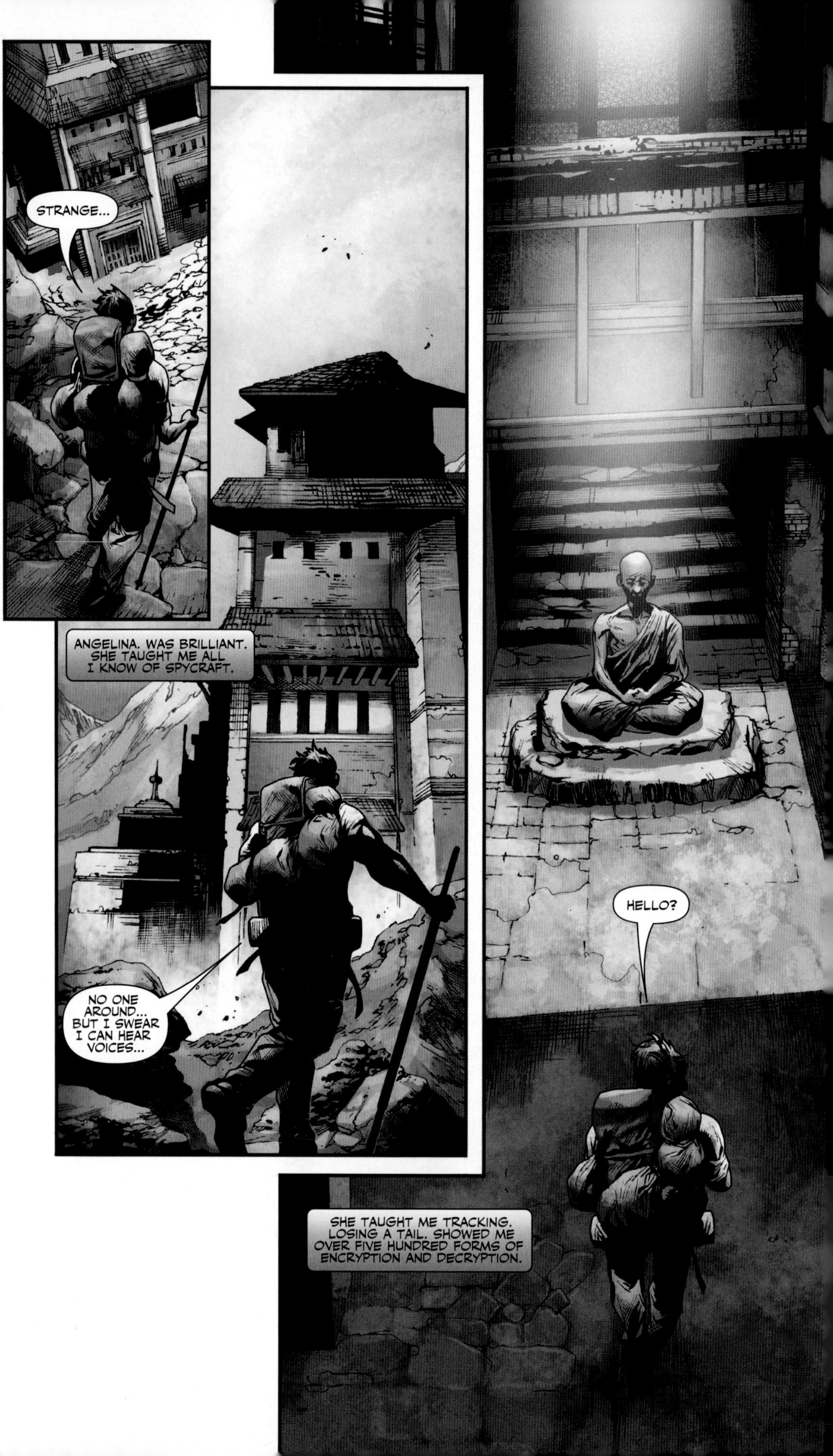
STRANGE...
ANGELINA. WAS BRILLIANT. SHE TAUGHT ME ALL I KNOW OF SPYCRAFT.
NO ONE AROUND... BUT I SWEAR I CAN HEAR VOICES...
HELLO?
SHE TAUGHT ME TRACKING. LOSING A TAIL. SHOWED ME OVER FIVE HUNDRED FORMS OF ENCRYPTION AND DECRYPTION.

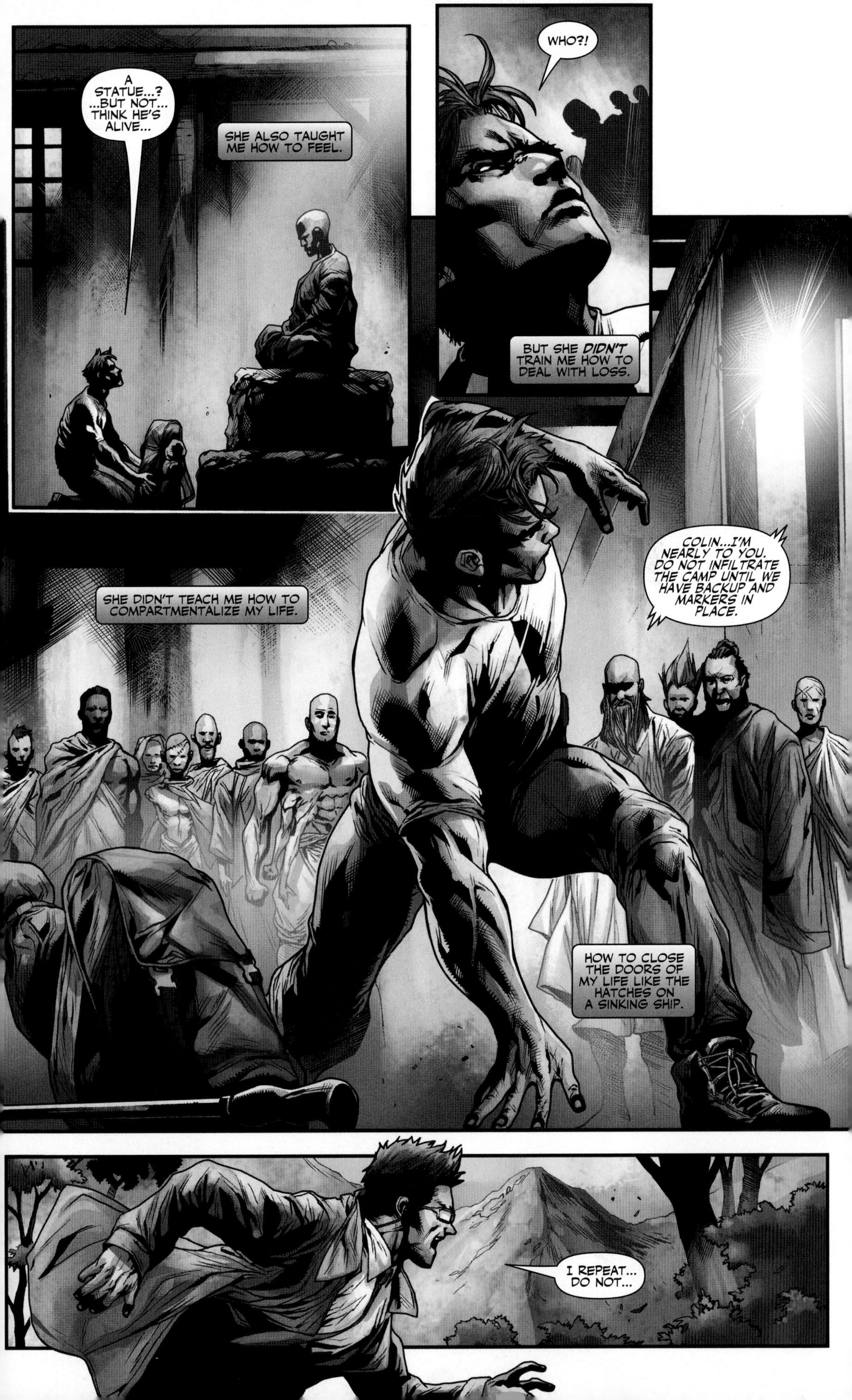

A STATUE...? ...BUT NOT... THINK HE'S ALIVE...
SHE ALSO TAUGHT ME HOW TO FEEL.
WHO?!
BUT SHE *DIDN'T* TRAIN ME HOW TO DEAL WITH LOSS.
SHE DIDN'T TEACH ME HOW TO COMPARTMENTALIZE MY LIFE.
COLIN...I'M NEARLY TO YOU. DO NOT INFILTRATE THE CAMP UNTIL WE HAVE BACKUP AND MARKERS IN PLACE.
HOW TO CLOSE THE DOORS OF MY LIFE LIKE THE HATCHES ON A SINKING SHIP.
I REPEAT... DO NOT...

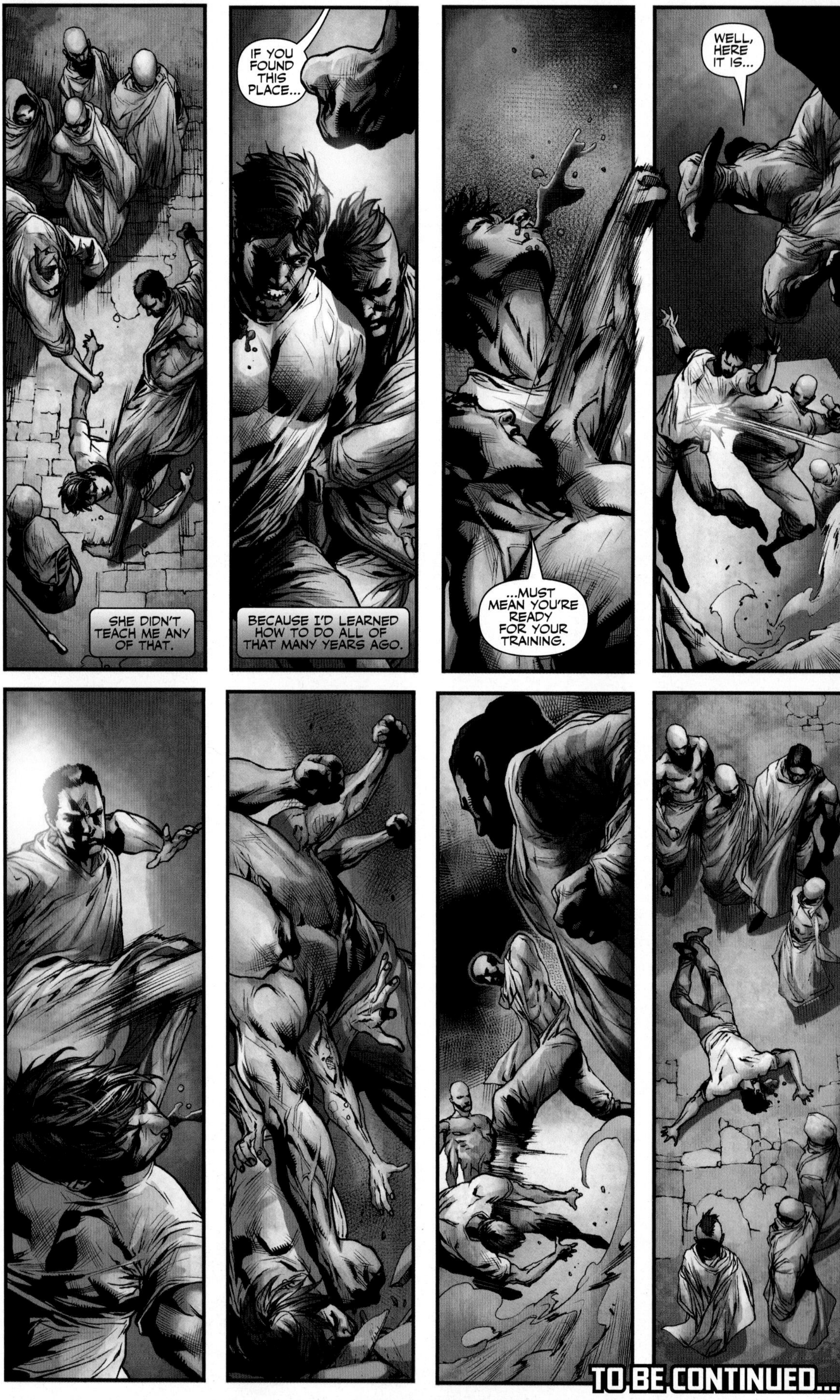
SHE DIDN'T TEACH ME ANY OF THAT.
IF YOU FOUND THIS PLACE...
BECAUSE I'D LEARNED HOW TO DO ALL OF THAT MANY YEARS AGO.
...MUST MEAN YOU'RE READY FOR YOUR TRAINING.
WELL, HERE IT IS...
TO BE CONTINUED...

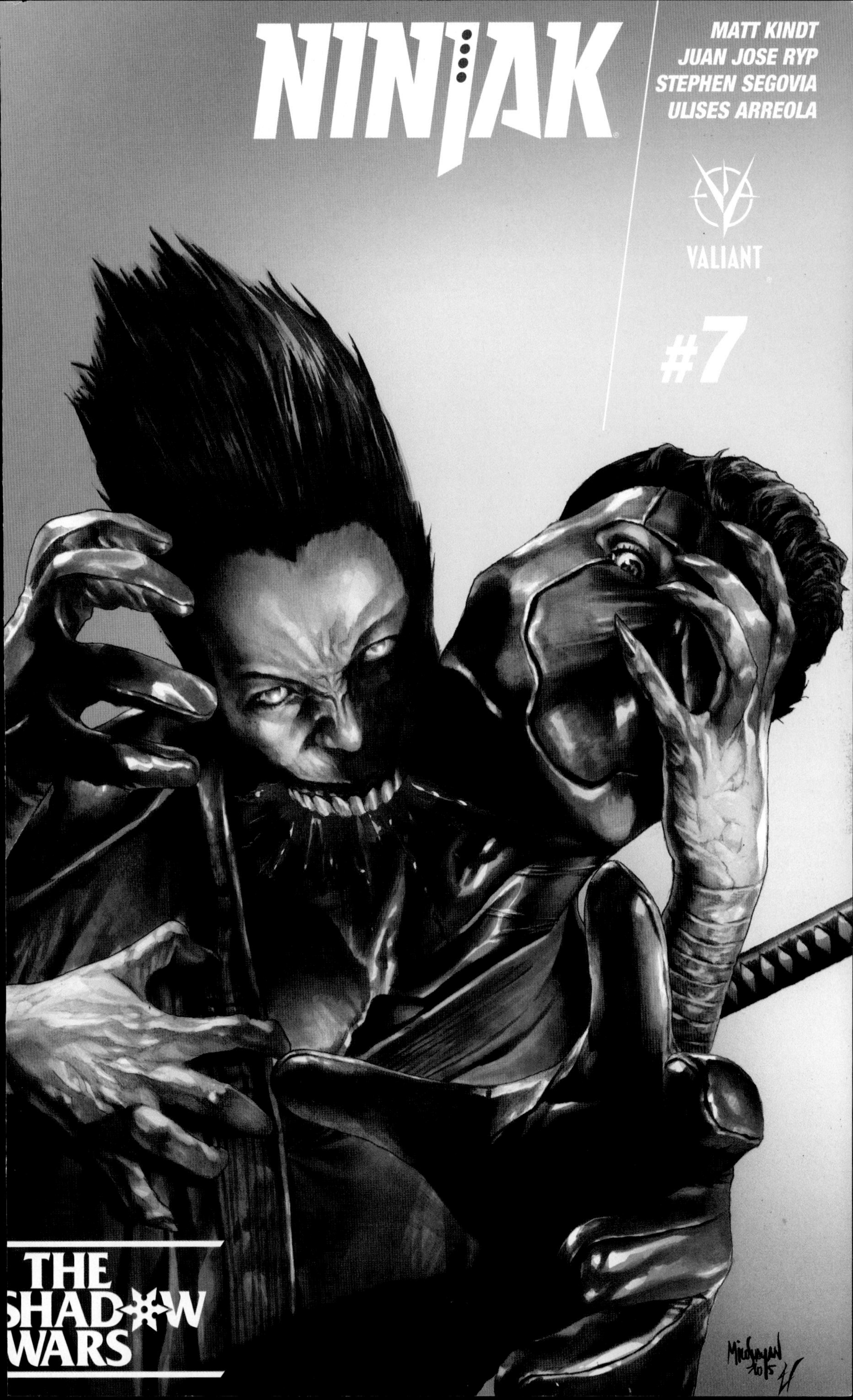
NINJAK
MATT KINDT
JUAN JOSE RYP
STEPHEN SEGOVIA
ULISES ARREOLA
VALIANT
#7
THE SHADOW WARS

NINJAK SPECIFICATIONS
& INSIGHTS

Battle Mask

CLASSIFIED

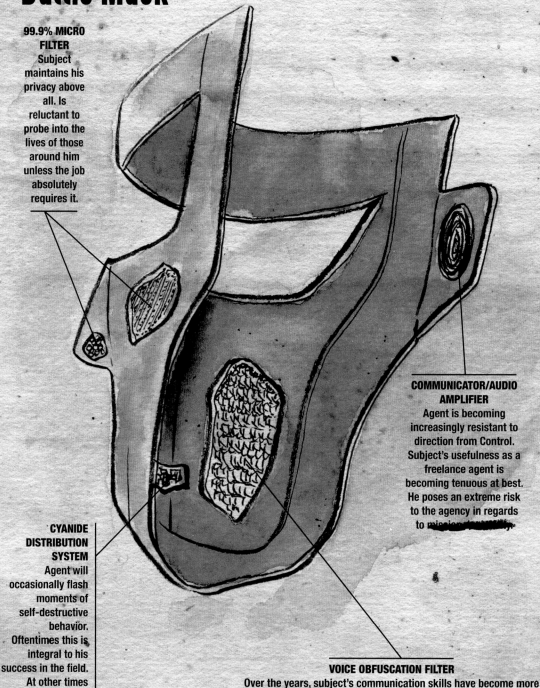

99.9% MICRO FILTER
Subject maintains his privacy above all. Is reluctant to probe into the lives of those around him unless the job absolutely requires it.

COMMUNICATOR/AUDIO AMPLIFIER
Agent is becoming increasingly resistant to direction from Control. Subject's usefulness as a freelance agent is becoming tenuous at best. He poses an extreme risk to the agency in regards to ~~mission~~.

CYANIDE DISTRIBUTION SYSTEM
Agent will occasionally flash moments of self-destructive behavior. Oftentimes this is integral to his success in the field. At other times it results in unnecessary risk taking.

VOICE OBFUSCATION FILTER
Over the years, subject's communication skills have become more and more stilted. Agent only seems comfortable in social situations while incognito. Personal life is in ~~danger of~~.

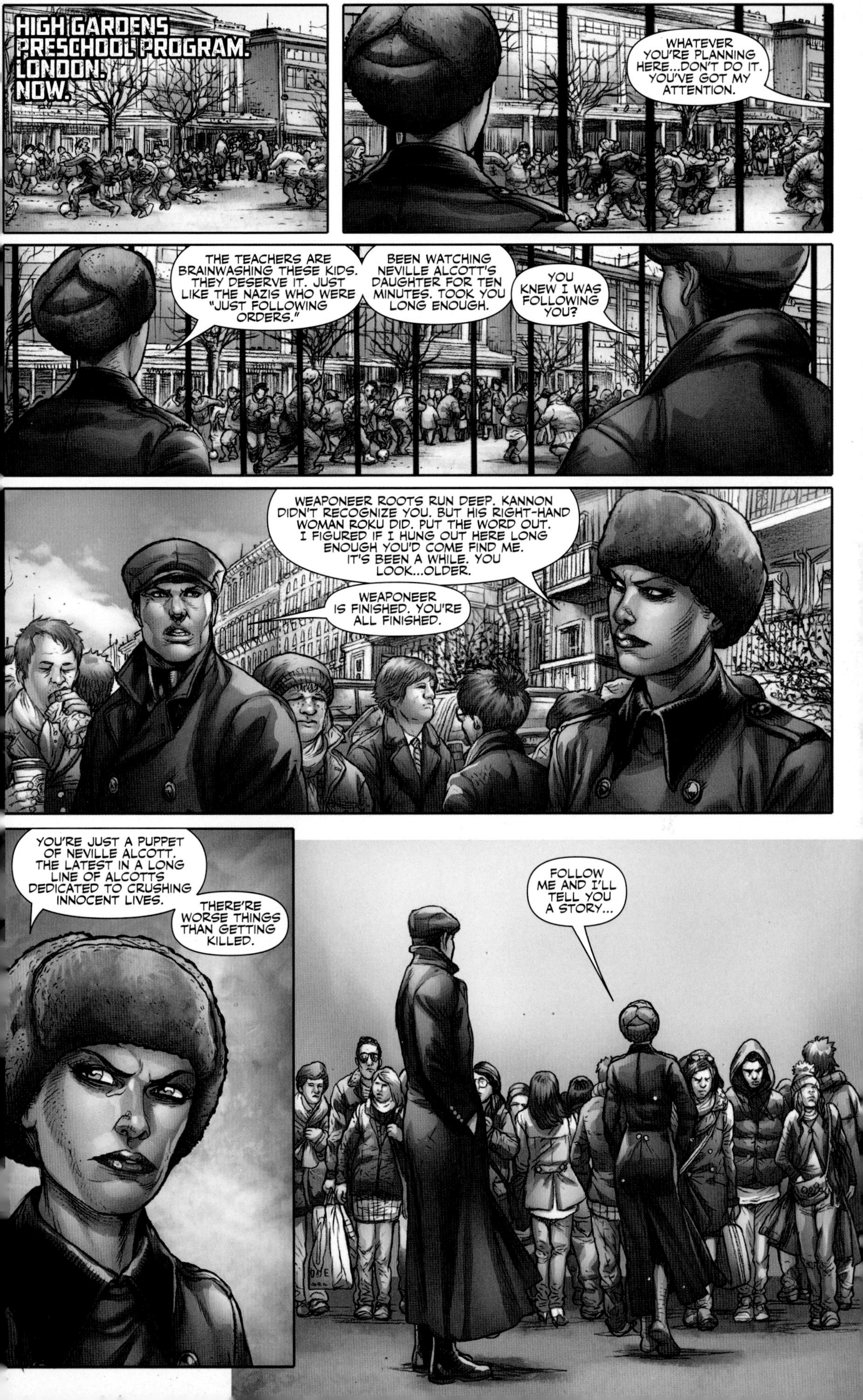

HIGH GARDENS PRESCHOOL PROGRAM. LONDON. NOW.
WHATEVER YOU'RE PLANNING HERE...DON'T DO IT. YOU'VE GOT MY ATTENTION.
THE TEACHERS ARE BRAINWASHING THESE KIDS. THEY DESERVE IT. JUST LIKE THE NAZIS WHO WERE "JUST FOLLOWING ORDERS."
BEEN WATCHING NEVILLE ALCOTT'S DAUGHTER FOR TEN MINUTES. TOOK YOU LONG ENOUGH.
YOU KNEW I WAS FOLLOWING YOU?
WEAPONEER ROOTS RUN DEEP. KANNON DIDN'T RECOGNIZE YOU. BUT HIS RIGHT-HAND WOMAN ROKU DID. PUT THE WORD OUT. I FIGURED IF I HUNG OUT HERE LONG ENOUGH YOU'D COME FIND ME. IT'S BEEN A WHILE. YOU LOOK...OLDER.
WEAPONEER IS FINISHED. YOU'RE ALL FINISHED.
YOU'RE JUST A PUPPET OF NEVILLE ALCOTT. THE LATEST IN A LONG LINE OF ALCOTTS DEDICATED TO CRUSHING INNOCENT LIVES.
THERE'RE WORSE THINGS THAN GETTING KILLED.
FOLLOW ME AND I'LL TELL YOU A STORY...

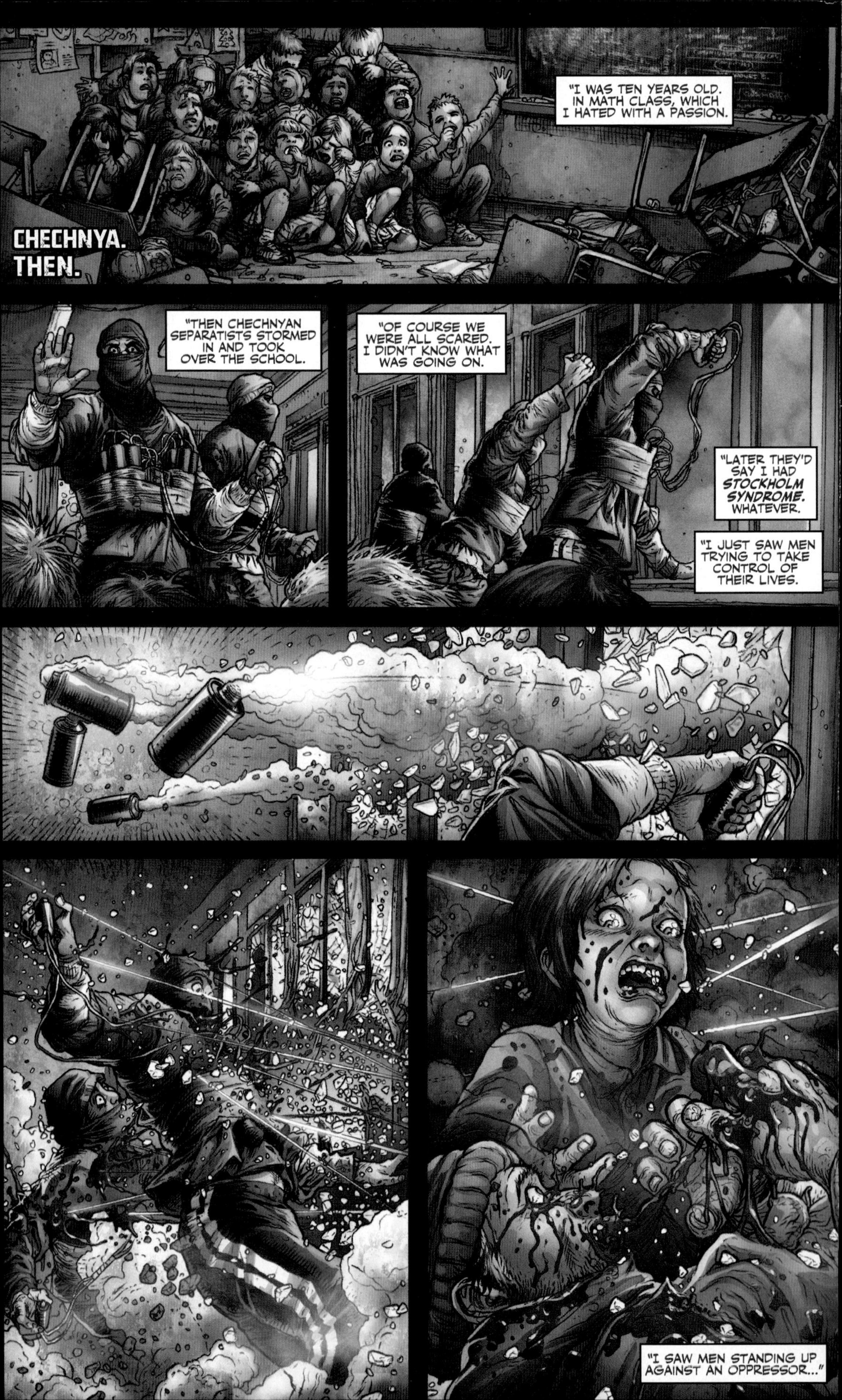

CHECHNYA. THEN.
"I WAS TEN YEARS OLD. IN MATH CLASS, WHICH I HATED WITH A PASSION.
"THEN CHECHNYAN SEPARATISTS STORMED IN AND TOOK OVER THE SCHOOL.
"OF COURSE WE WERE ALL SCARED. I DIDN'T KNOW WHAT WAS GOING ON.
"LATER THEY'D SAY I HAD *STOCKHOLM SYNDROME.* WHATEVER.
"I JUST SAW MEN TRYING TO TAKE CONTROL OF THEIR LIVES.
"I SAW MEN STANDING UP AGAINST AN OPPRESSOR..."

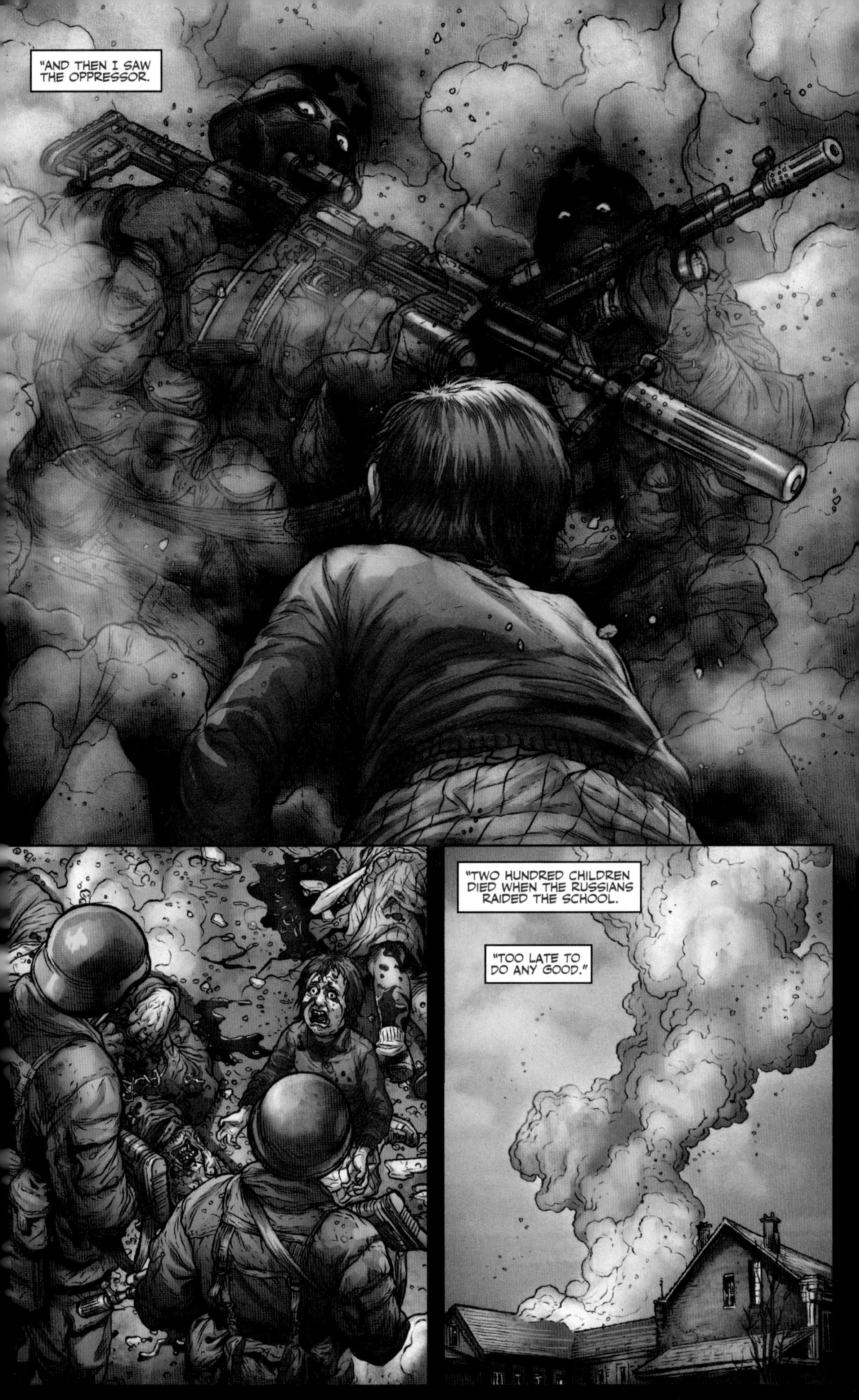
"AND THEN I SAW THE OPPRESSOR.
"TWO HUNDRED CHILDREN DIED WHEN THE RUSSIANS RAIDED THE SCHOOL.
"TOO LATE TO DO ANY GOOD."

"SOME OF US ESCAPED.

"BUT MY LESSON WAS LEARNED.

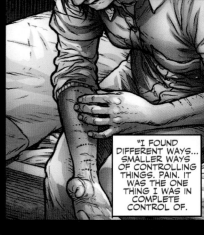

"I FOUND DIFFERENT WAYS... SMALLER WAYS OF CONTROLLING THINGS. PAIN. IT WAS THE ONE THING I WAS IN COMPLETE CONTROL OF.

"AS I GREW OLDER I KEPT SEARCHING FOR NEW WAYS OF CONTROLLING MY FATE. SINGING ON THE STREETS OF MOSCOW WAS THE ONLY WAY I COULD THINK TO FIGHT THE KREMLIN.

"EVERYTHING I DID SEEMED TO PUT ME BACK IN THE SAME RUSSIAN PRISON. WITH NO CONTROL.

"I WAS IN A JAIL IN MOSCOW WHEN KANNON SHOWED UP.

"HE WAS COLLECTING LOST SOULS. AND REVIVING THEM."

WHEN YOU GET OUT IN SIX MONTHS COME SEE ME. I'LL SHOW YOU A NEW WAY TO LIVE.

"STILL, PAIN WAS THE ONLY THING I COULD CONTROL.

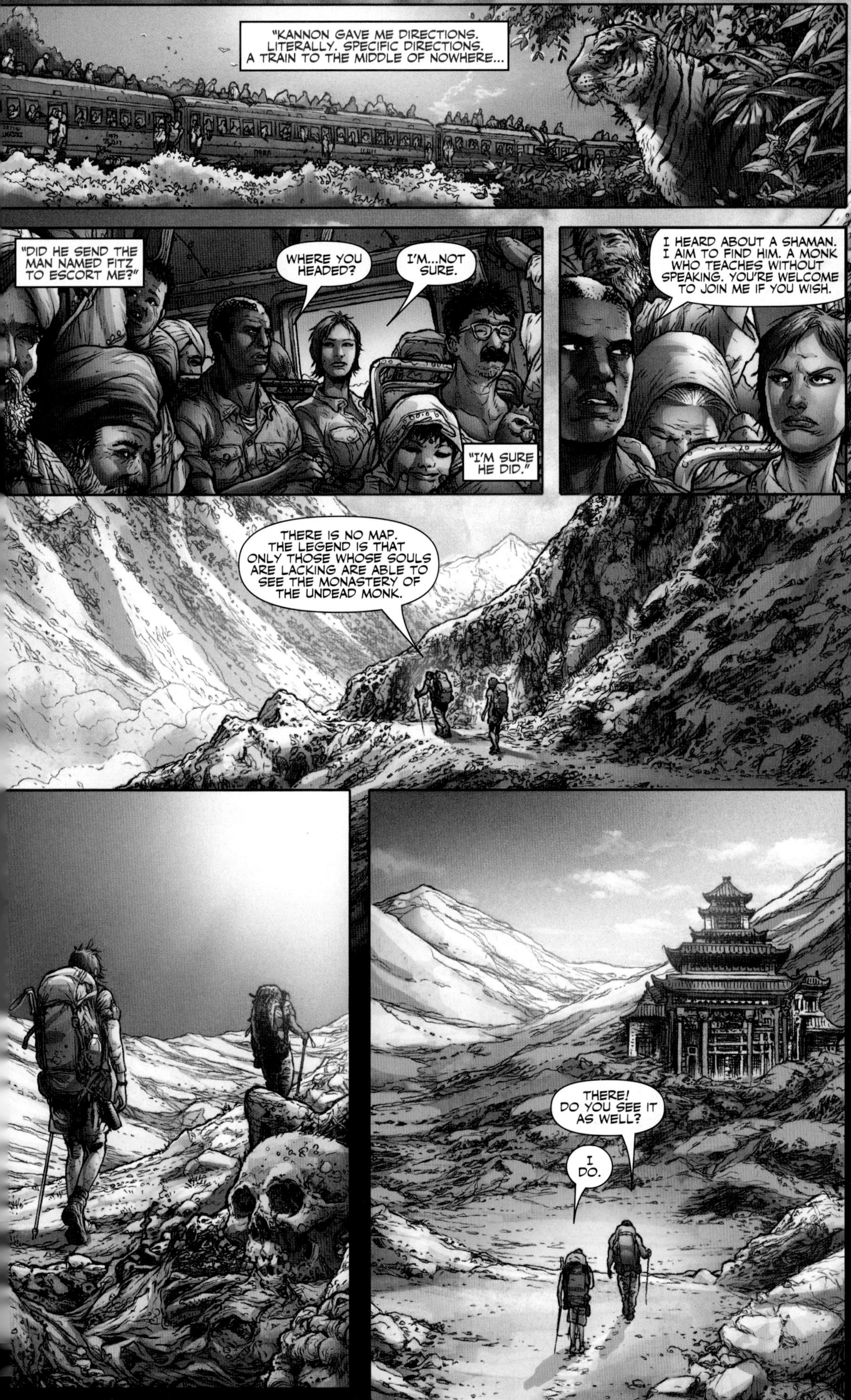
"KANNON GAVE ME DIRECTIONS. LITERALLY. SPECIFIC DIRECTIONS. A TRAIN TO THE MIDDLE OF NOWHERE...
"DID HE SEND THE MAN NAMED FITZ TO ESCORT ME?"
WHERE YOU HEADED?
I'M...NOT SURE.
"I'M SURE HE DID."
I HEARD ABOUT A SHAMAN. I AIM TO FIND HIM. A MONK WHO TEACHES WITHOUT SPEAKING. YOU'RE WELCOME TO JOIN ME IF YOU WISH.
THERE IS NO MAP. THE LEGEND IS THAT ONLY THOSE WHOSE SOULS ARE LACKING ARE ABLE TO SEE THE MONASTERY OF THE UNDEAD MONK.
THERE! DO YOU SEE IT AS WELL?
I DO.

"I COULD HEAR HIS VOICE. BUT *NOT* HIS VOICE. I COULD JUST HEAR...HIM.

"HIS MIND. HIS IDEAS. HE WAS THE WISEST CREATURE I'D EVER SEEN.

"I CALL HIM CREATURE BECAUSE I'M NOT SURE HE REALLY WAS A MAN.

"HE NEVER TALKED.

"BUT HE SPOKE *VOLUMES.*

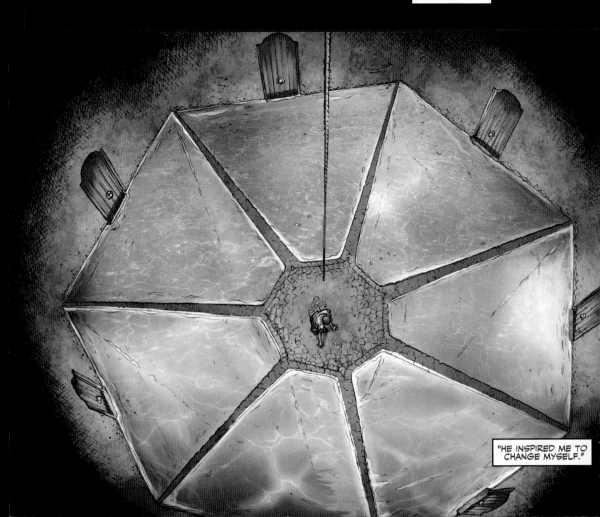

"HE INSPIRED ME TO CHANGE MYSELF."

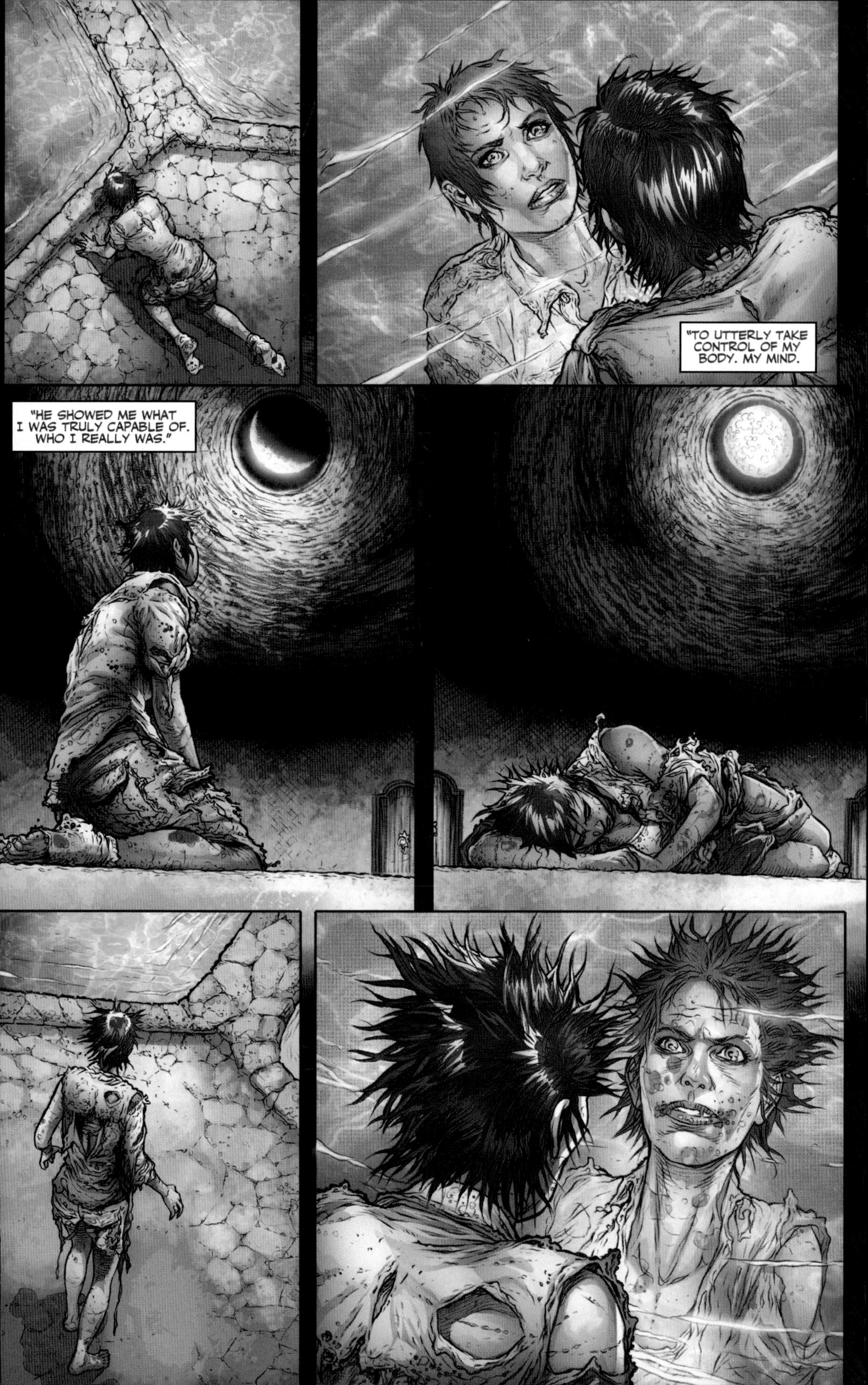
"TO UTTERLY TAKE CONTROL OF MY BODY. MY MIND.
"HE SHOWED ME WHAT I WAS TRULY CAPABLE OF. WHO I REALLY WAS."

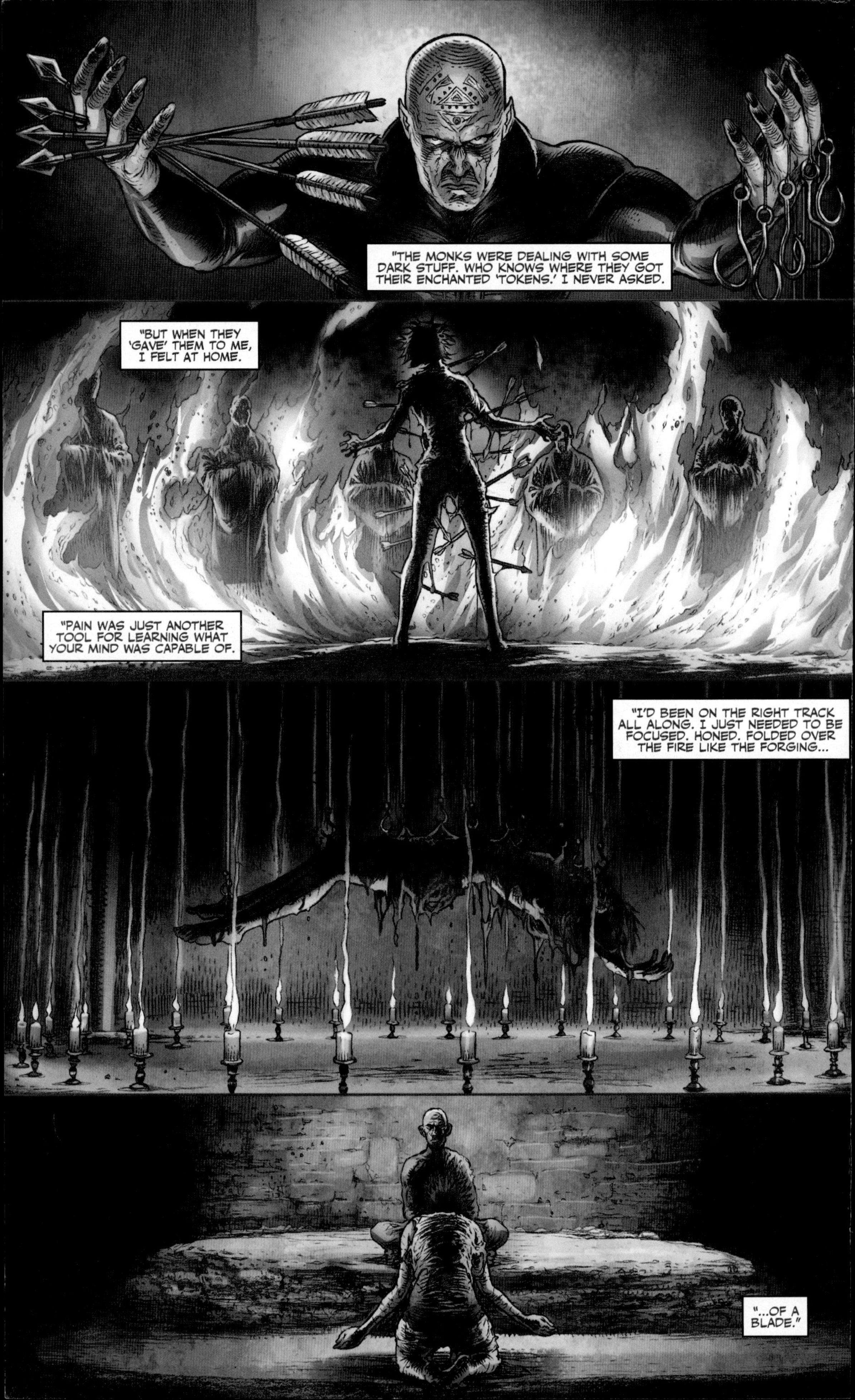
"THE MONKS WERE DEALING WITH SOME DARK STUFF. WHO KNOWS WHERE THEY GOT THEIR ENCHANTED 'TOKENS.' I NEVER ASKED.
"BUT WHEN THEY 'GAVE' THEM TO ME, I FELT AT HOME.
"PAIN WAS JUST ANOTHER TOOL FOR LEARNING WHAT YOUR MIND WAS CAPABLE OF.
"I'D BEEN ON THE RIGHT TRACK ALL ALONG. I JUST NEEDED TO BE FOCUSED. HONED. FOLDED OVER THE FIRE LIKE THE FORGING...
"...OF A BLADE."

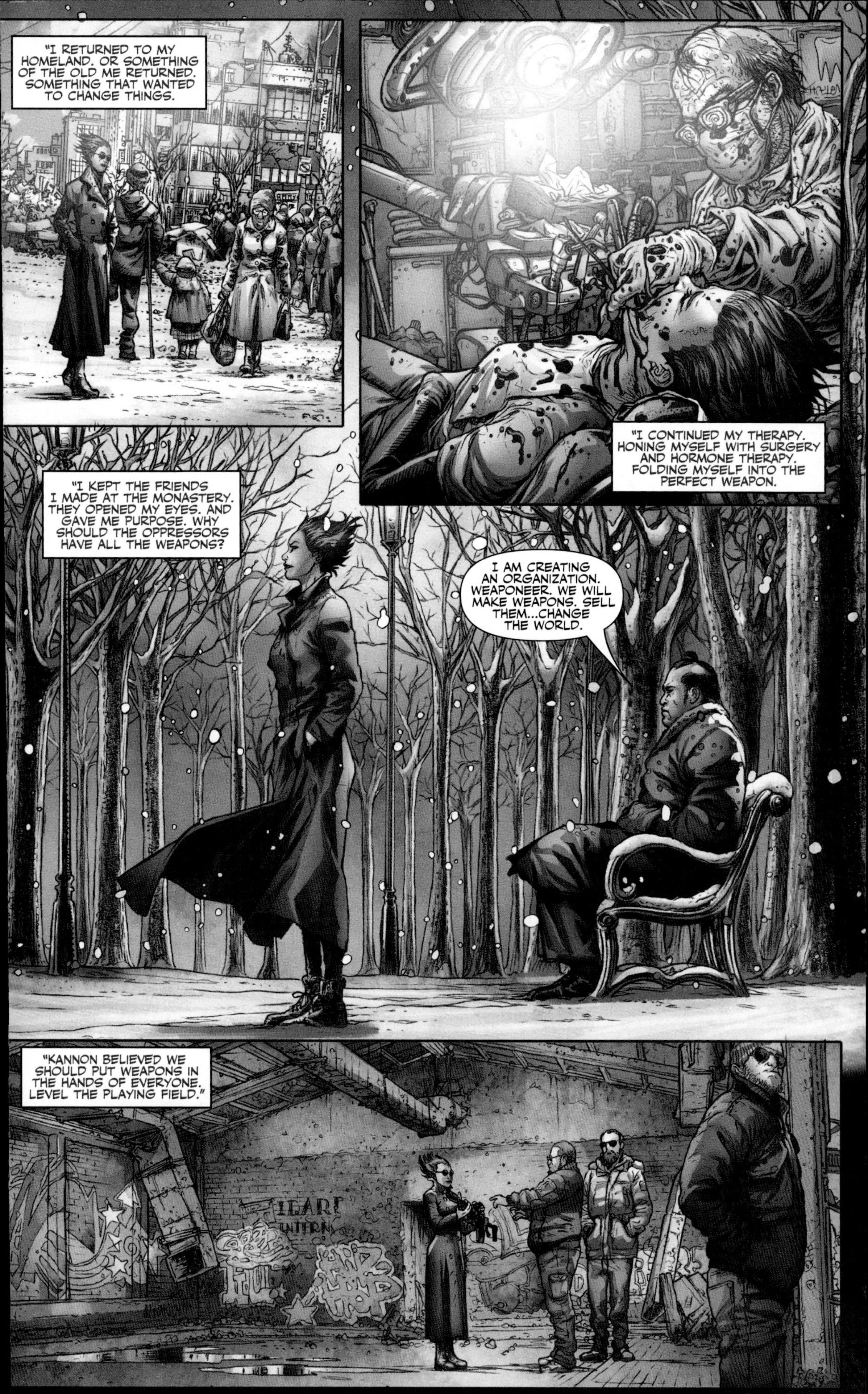
"I RETURNED TO MY HOMELAND. OR SOMETHING OF THE OLD ME RETURNED. SOMETHING THAT WANTED TO CHANGE THINGS.
"I CONTINUED MY THERAPY. HONING MYSELF WITH SURGERY AND HORMONE THERAPY. FOLDING MYSELF INTO THE PERFECT WEAPON.
"I KEPT THE FRIENDS I MADE AT THE MONASTERY. THEY OPENED MY EYES. AND GAVE ME PURPOSE. WHY SHOULD THE OPPRESSORS HAVE ALL THE WEAPONS?
I AM CREATING AN ORGANIZATION. WEAPONEER. WE WILL MAKE WEAPONS. SELL THEM...CHANGE THE WORLD.
"KANNON BELIEVED WE SHOULD PUT WEAPONS IN THE HANDS OF EVERYONE. LEVEL THE PLAYING FIELD."

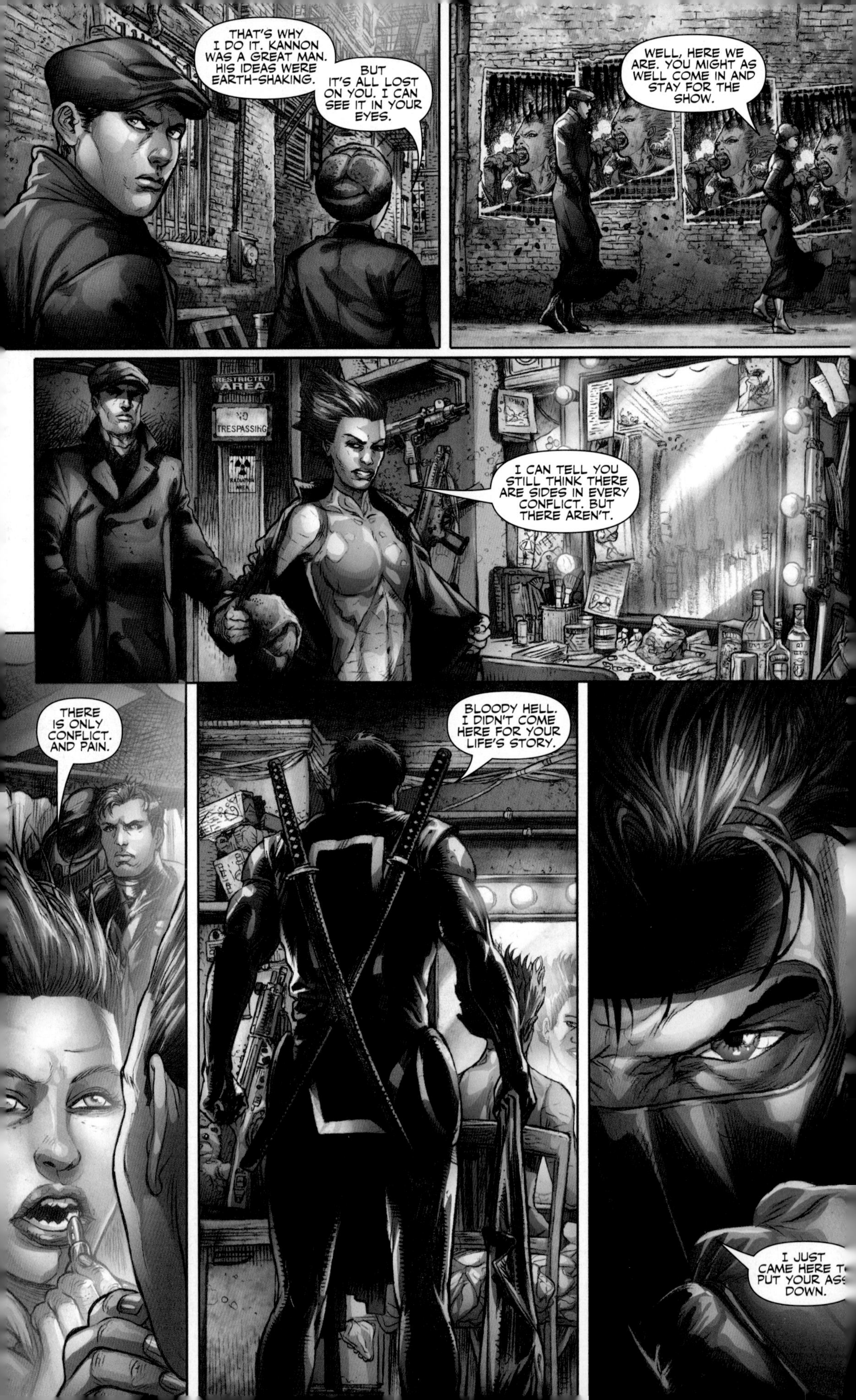
THAT'S WHY I DO IT. KANNON WAS A GREAT MAN. HIS IDEAS WERE EARTH-SHAKING.
BUT IT'S ALL LOST ON YOU. I CAN SEE IT IN YOUR EYES.
WELL, HERE WE ARE. YOU MIGHT AS WELL COME IN AND STAY FOR THE SHOW.
RESTRICTED AREA
NO TRESPASSING
RADIATION AREA
I CAN TELL YOU STILL THINK THERE ARE SIDES IN EVERY CONFLICT. BUT THERE AREN'T.
THERE IS ONLY CONFLICT. AND PAIN.
BLOODY HELL. I DIDN'T COME HERE FOR YOUR LIFE'S STORY.
I JUST CAME HERE T PUT YOUR AS DOWN.

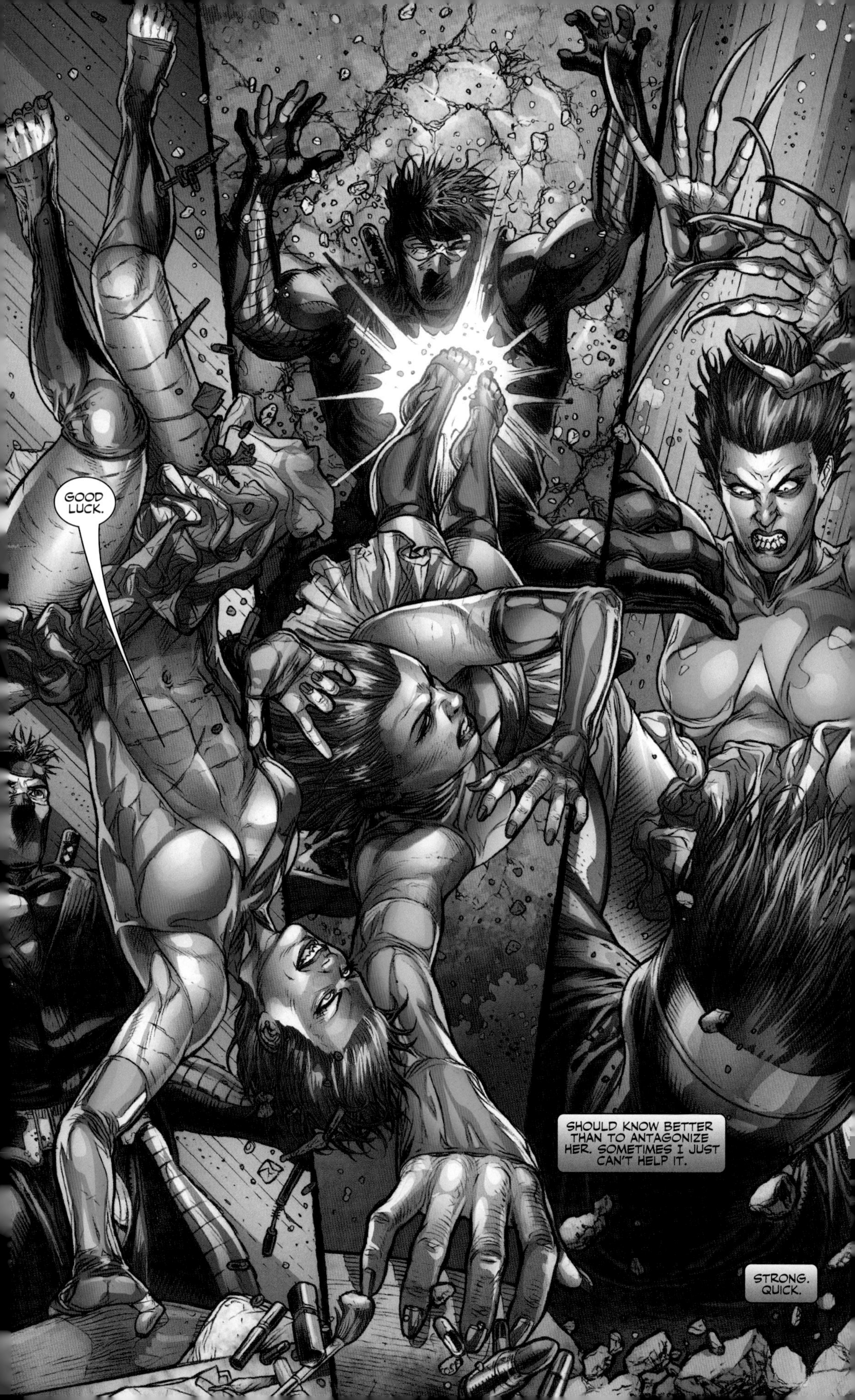
GOOD LUCK.
SHOULD KNOW BETTER THAN TO ANTAGONIZE HER. SOMETIMES I JUST CAN'T HELP IT.
STRONG. QUICK.

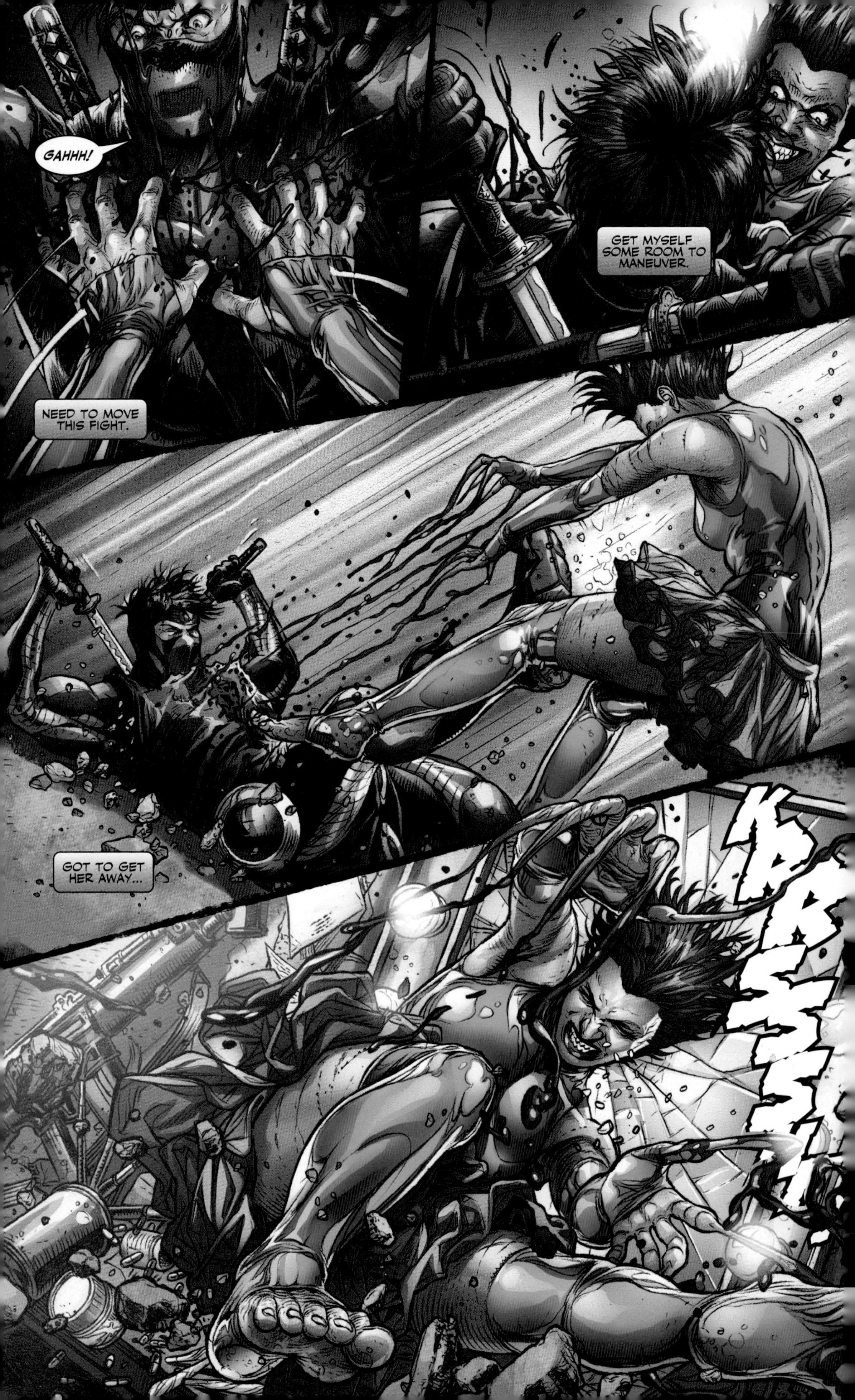
GAHHH!
GET MYSELF SOME ROOM TO MANEUVER.
NEED TO MOVE THIS FIGHT.
GOT TO GET HER AWAY...

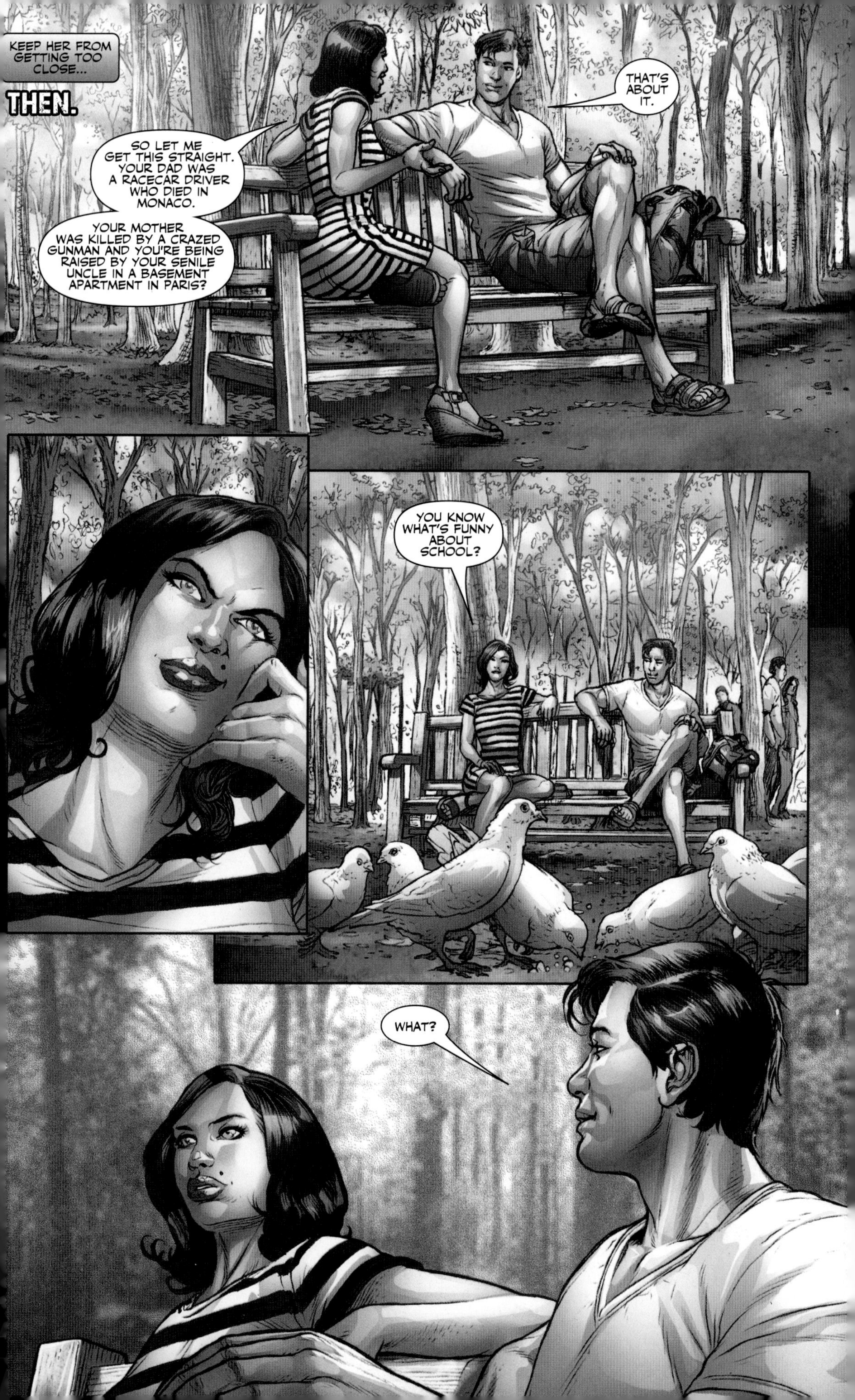
KEEP HER FROM GETTING TOO CLOSE...
THEN.
SO LET ME GET THIS STRAIGHT. YOUR DAD WAS A RACECAR DRIVER WHO DIED IN MONACO.
YOUR MOTHER WAS KILLED BY A CRAZED GUNMAN AND YOU'RE BEING RAISED BY YOUR SENILE UNCLE IN A BASEMENT APARTMENT IN PARIS?
THAT'S ABOUT IT.
YOU KNOW WHAT'S FUNNY ABOUT SCHOOL?
WHAT?

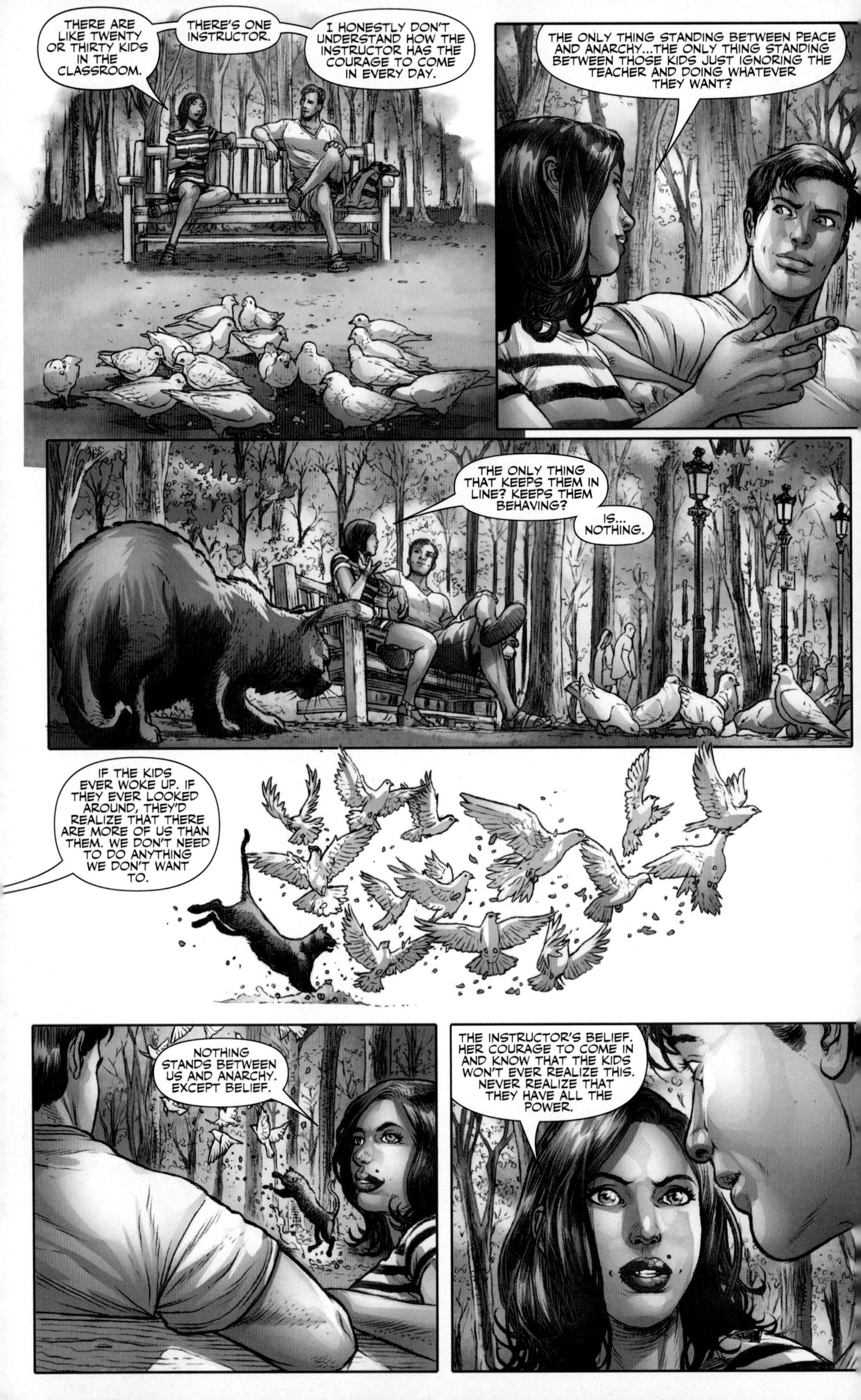
THERE ARE LIKE TWENTY OR THIRTY KIDS IN THE CLASSROOM.
THERE'S ONE INSTRUCTOR.
I HONESTLY DON'T UNDERSTAND HOW THE INSTRUCTOR HAS THE COURAGE TO COME IN EVERY DAY.
THE ONLY THING STANDING BETWEEN PEACE AND ANARCHY...THE ONLY THING STANDING BETWEEN THOSE KIDS JUST IGNORING THE TEACHER AND DOING WHATEVER THEY WANT?
THE ONLY THING THAT KEEPS THEM IN LINE? KEEPS THEM BEHAVING?
IS... NOTHING.
IF THE KIDS EVER WOKE UP. IF THEY EVER LOOKED AROUND, THEY'D REALIZE THAT THERE ARE MORE OF US THAN THEM. WE DON'T NEED TO DO ANYTHING WE DON'T WANT TO.
NOTHING STANDS BETWEEN US AND ANARCHY. EXCEPT BELIEF.
THE INSTRUCTOR'S BELIEF. HER COURAGE TO COME IN AND KNOW THAT THE KIDS WON'T EVER REALIZE THIS. NEVER REALIZE THAT THEY HAVE ALL THE POWER.

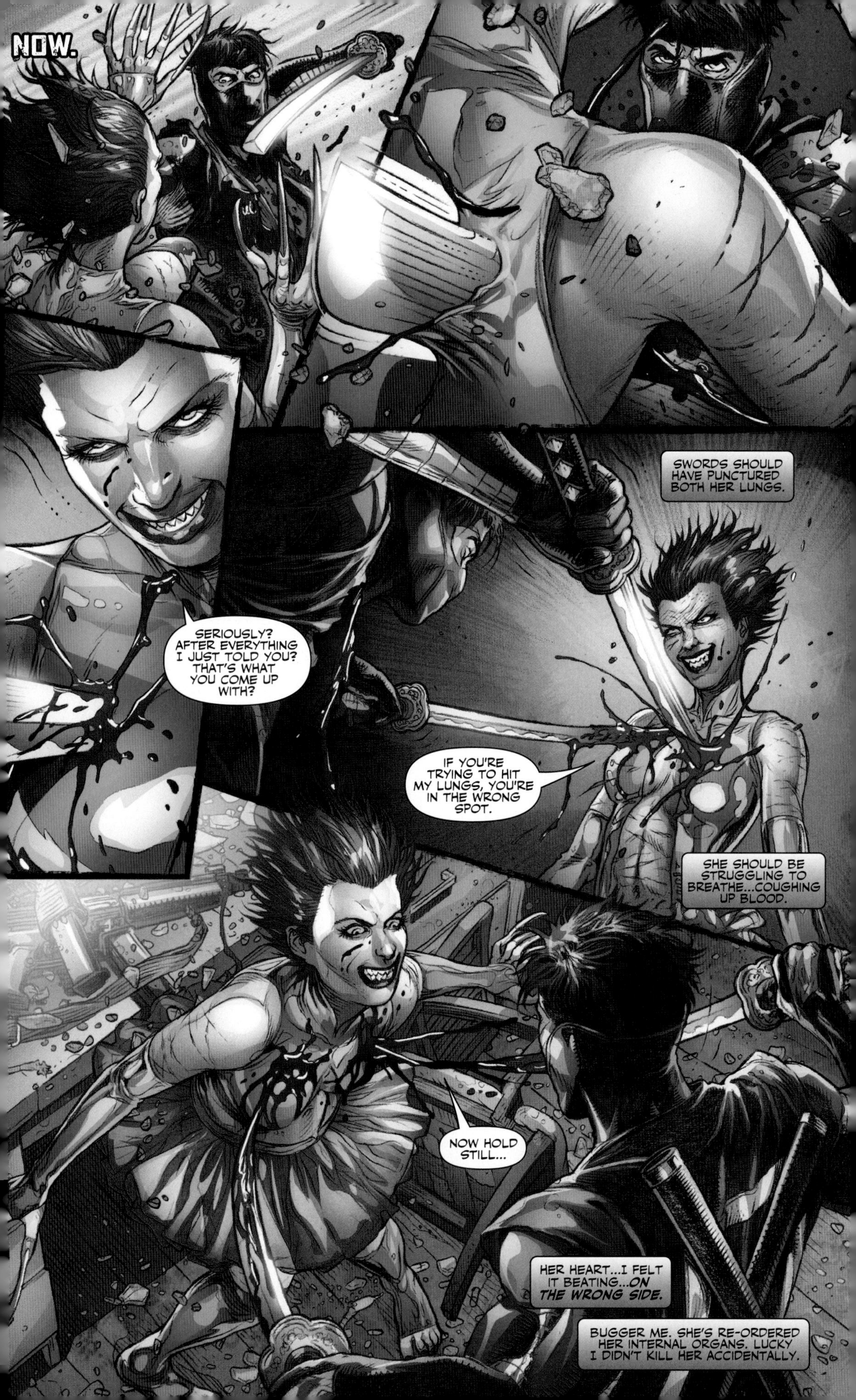
NOW.
SWORDS SHOULD HAVE PUNCTURED BOTH HER LUNGS.
SERIOUSLY? AFTER EVERYTHING I JUST TOLD YOU? THAT'S WHAT YOU COME UP WITH?
IF YOU'RE TRYING TO HIT MY LUNGS, YOU'RE IN THE WRONG SPOT.
SHE SHOULD BE STRUGGLING TO BREATHE...COUGHING UP BLOOD.
NOW HOLD STILL...
HER HEART...I FELT IT BEATING...ON THE WRONG SIDE.
BUGGER ME. SHE'S RE-ORDERED HER INTERNAL ORGANS. LUCKY I DIDN'T KILL HER ACCIDENTALLY.

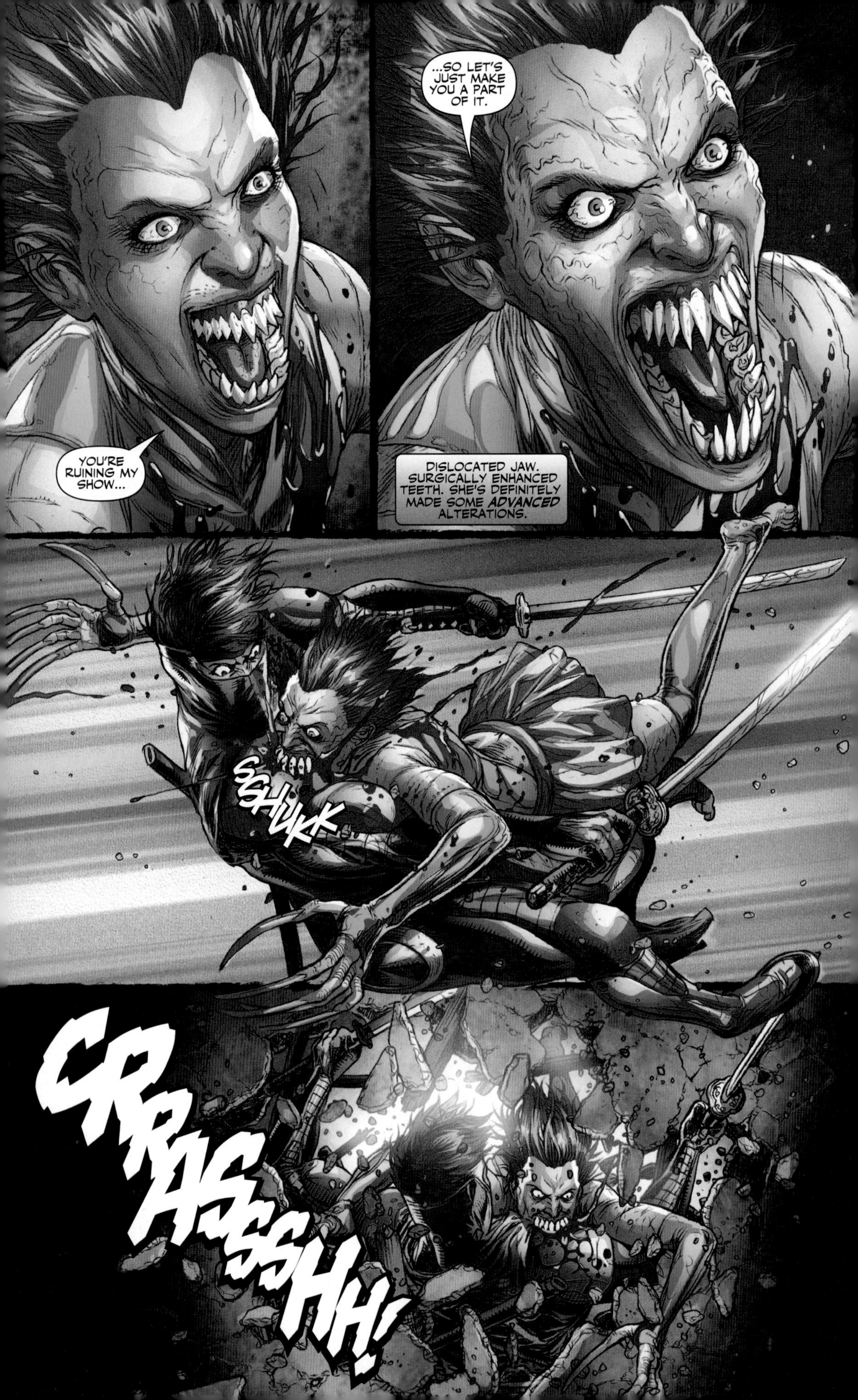
YOU'RE RUINING MY SHOW...
...SO LET'S JUST MAKE YOU A PART OF IT.
DISLOCATED JAW. SURGICALLY ENHANCED TEETH. SHE'S DEFINITELY MADE SOME *ADVANCED* ALTERATIONS.
SCHLUKK
CRASSSHH!

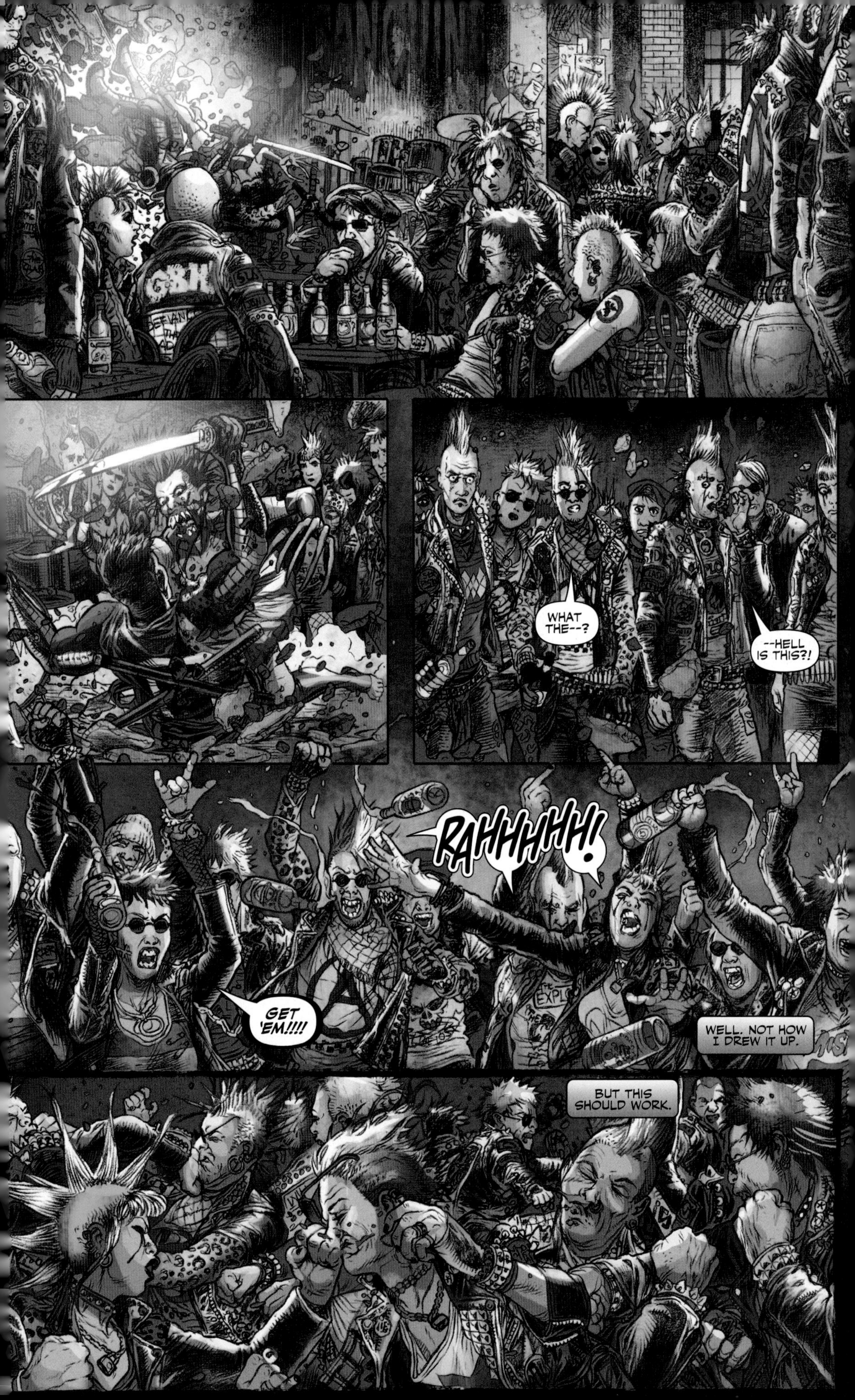
WHAT THE--?
--HELL IS THIS?!
RAHHHHH!
GET 'EM!!!!
WELL. NOT HOW I DREW IT UP.
BUT THIS SHOULD WORK.

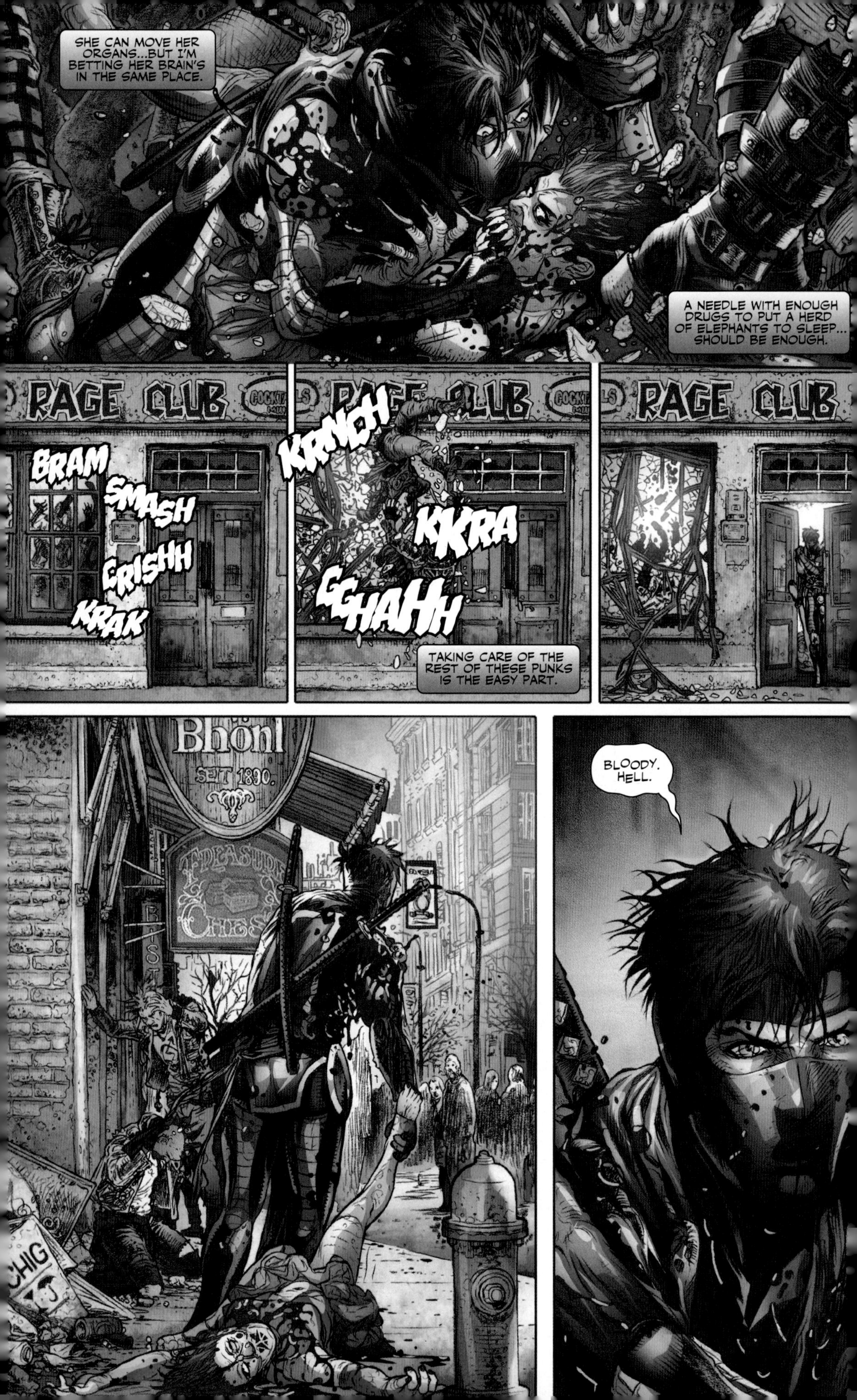
SHE CAN MOVE HER ORGANS...BUT I'M BETTING HER BRAIN'S IN THE SAME PLACE.
A NEEDLE WITH ENOUGH DRUGS TO PUT A HERD OF ELEPHANTS TO SLEEP... SHOULD BE ENOUGH.
RAGE CLUB
BRAM
SMASH
CRISHH
KRAK
RAGE CLUB
KRNCH
KKRA
GGHAHH
TAKING CARE OF THE REST OF THESE PUNKS IS THE EASY PART.
RAGE CLUB
Bhönl
SEIT 1890.
BLOODY. HELL.

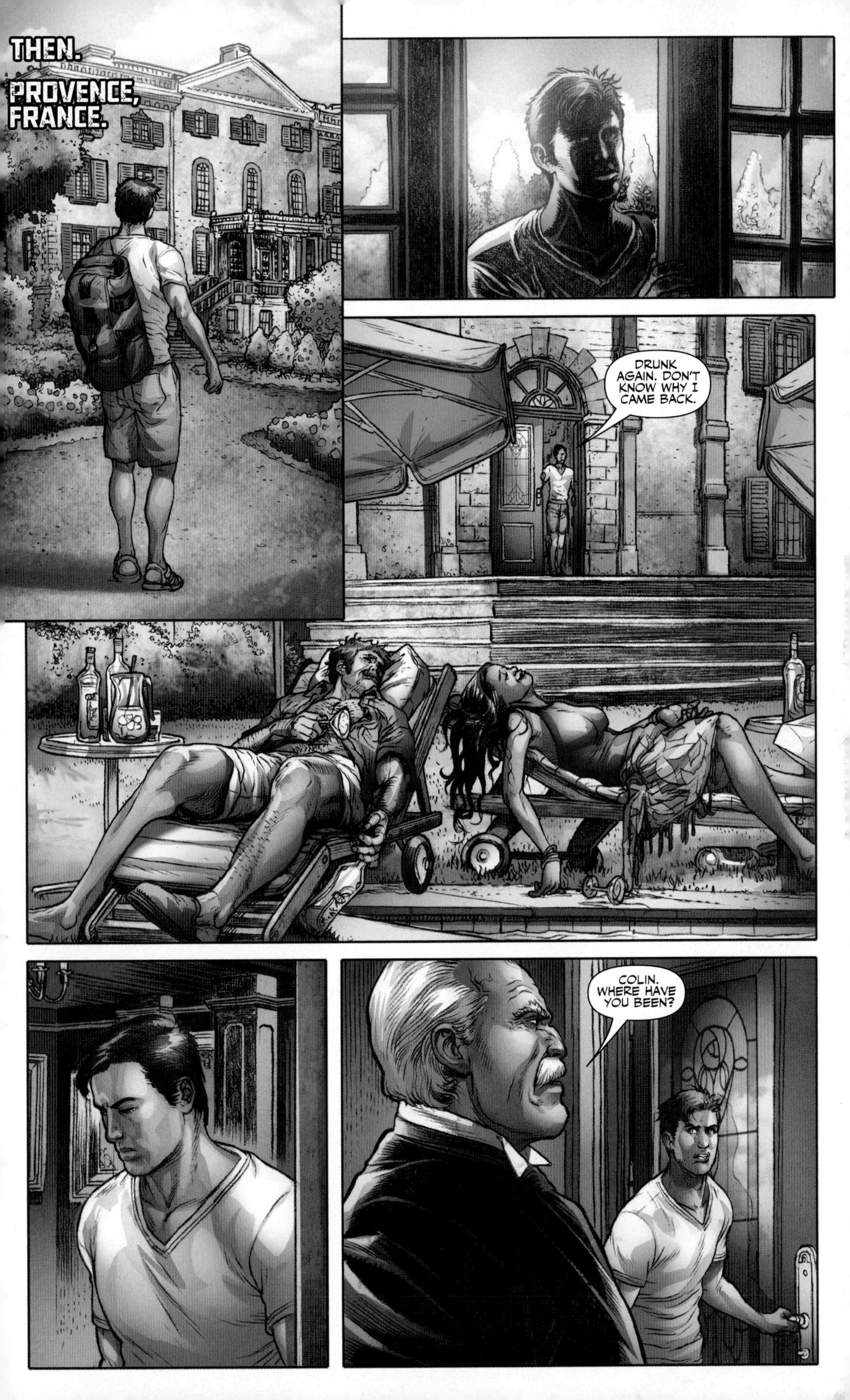
THEN.
PROVENCE, FRANCE.
DRUNK AGAIN. DON'T KNOW WHY I CAME BACK.
COLIN. WHERE HAVE YOU BEEN?

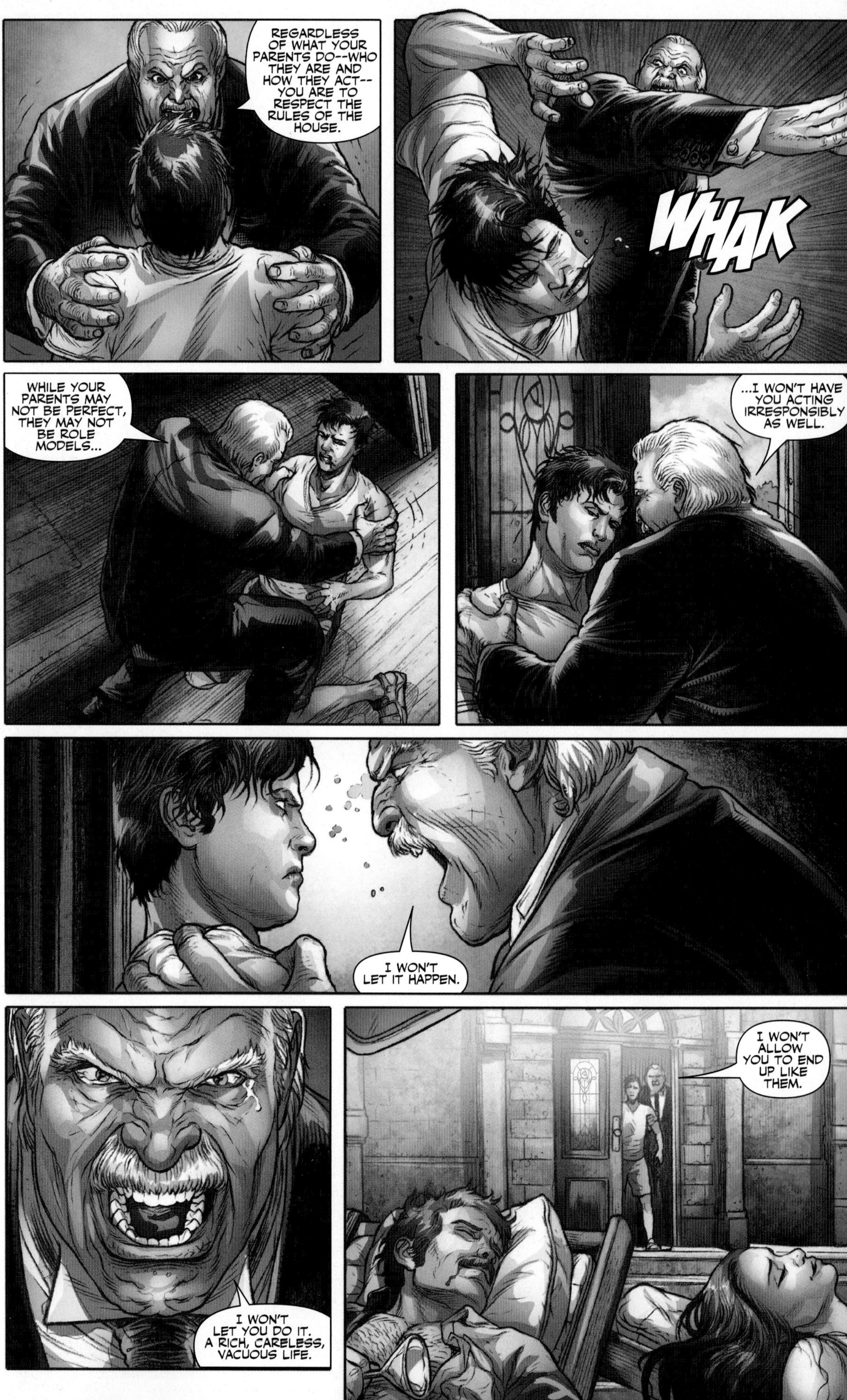
REGARDLESS OF WHAT YOUR PARENTS DO--WHO THEY ARE AND HOW THEY ACT--YOU ARE TO RESPECT THE RULES OF THE HOUSE.
WHAK
WHILE YOUR PARENTS MAY NOT BE PERFECT, THEY MAY NOT BE ROLE MODELS...
...I WON'T HAVE YOU ACTING IRRESPONSIBLY AS WELL.
I WON'T LET IT HAPPEN.
I WON'T LET YOU DO IT. A RICH, CARELESS, VACUOUS LIFE.
I WON'T ALLOW YOU TO END UP LIKE THEM.

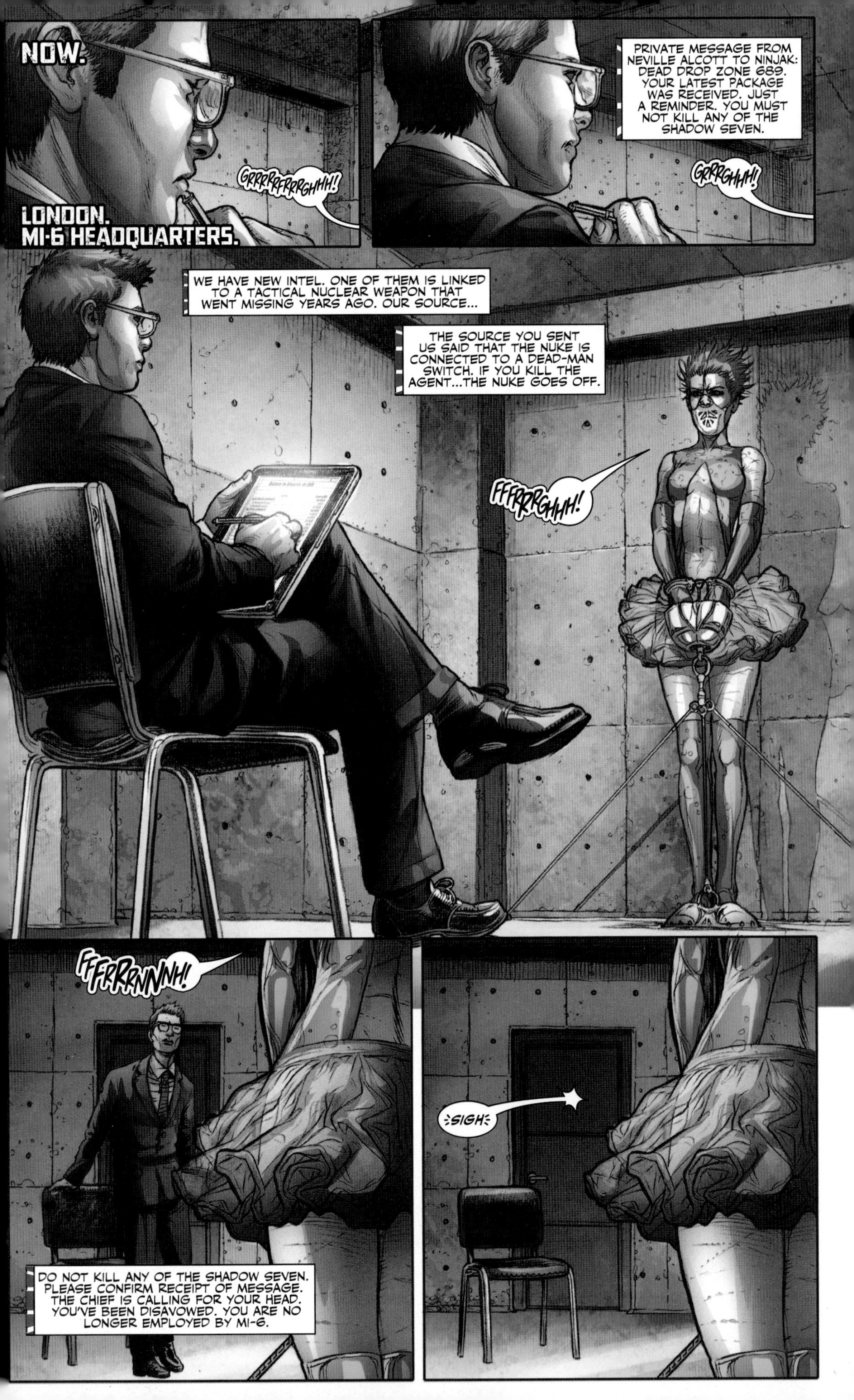
NOW.
LONDON.
MI-6 HEADQUARTERS.
GRRRRFRRRGHHH!
PRIVATE MESSAGE FROM NEVILLE ALCOTT TO NINJAK: DEAD DROP ZONE 689. YOUR LATEST PACKAGE WAS RECEIVED. JUST A REMINDER. YOU MUST NOT KILL ANY OF THE SHADOW SEVEN.
GRRRGHHH!
WE HAVE NEW INTEL. ONE OF THEM IS LINKED TO A TACTICAL NUCLEAR WEAPON THAT WENT MISSING YEARS AGO. OUR SOURCE...
THE SOURCE YOU SENT US SAID THAT THE NUKE IS CONNECTED TO A DEAD-MAN SWITCH. IF YOU KILL THE AGENT...THE NUKE GOES OFF.
FFFRRRGHHH!
FFFRRRNNNH!
DO NOT KILL ANY OF THE SHADOW SEVEN. PLEASE CONFIRM RECEIPT OF MESSAGE. THE CHIEF IS CALLING FOR YOUR HEAD. YOU'VE BEEN DISAVOWED. YOU ARE NO LONGER EMPLOYED BY MI-6.
SIGH

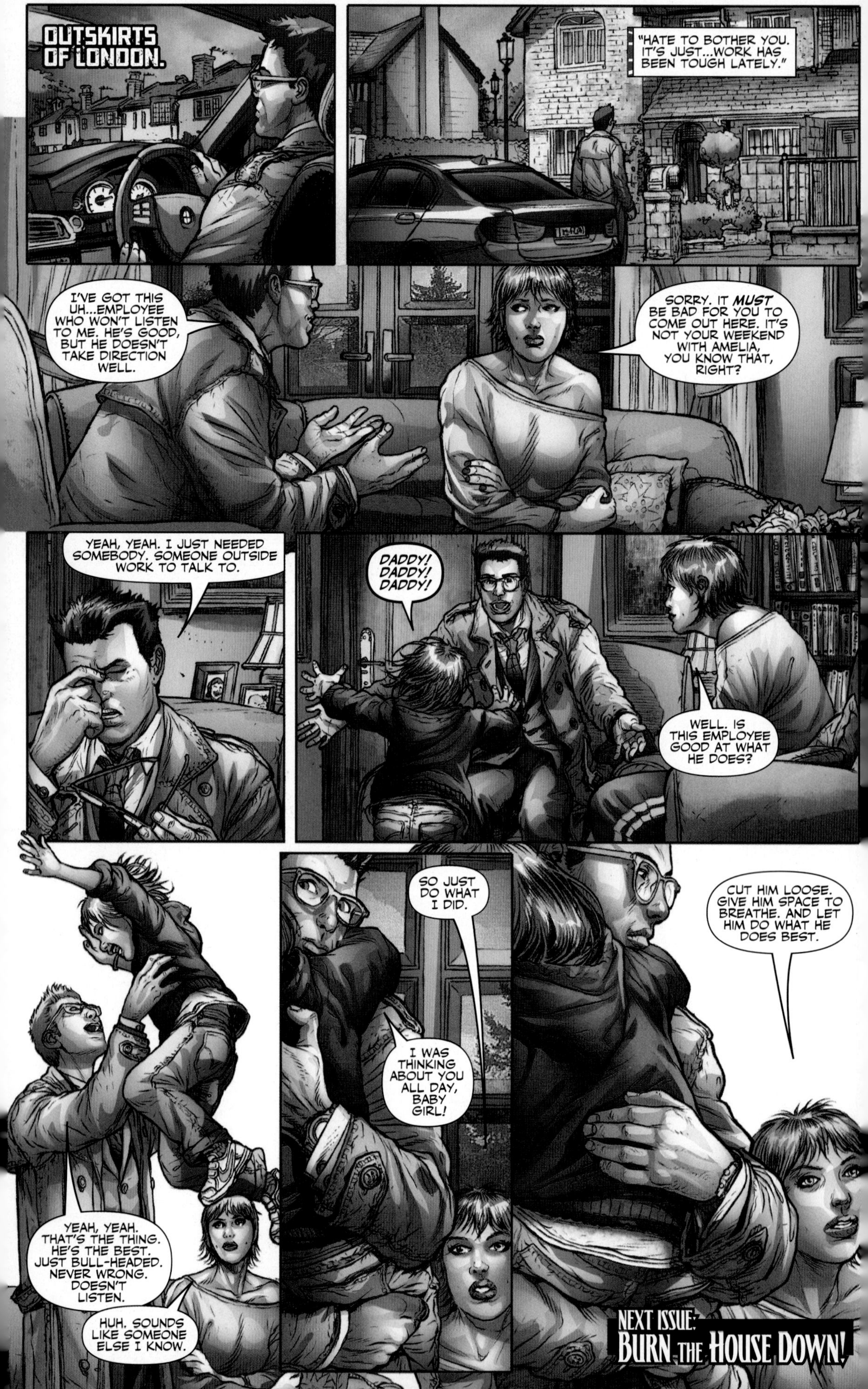
OUTSKIRTS OF LONDON.
"HATE TO BOTHER YOU. IT'S JUST...WORK HAS BEEN TOUGH LATELY."
I'VE GOT THIS UH...EMPLOYEE WHO WON'T LISTEN TO ME. HE'S GOOD, BUT HE DOESN'T TAKE DIRECTION WELL.
SORRY. IT MUST BE BAD FOR YOU TO COME OUT HERE. IT'S NOT YOUR WEEKEND WITH AMELIA, YOU KNOW THAT, RIGHT?
YEAH, YEAH. I JUST NEEDED SOMEBODY. SOMEONE OUTSIDE WORK TO TALK TO.
DADDY! DADDY! DADDY!
WELL. IS THIS EMPLOYEE GOOD AT WHAT HE DOES?
YEAH, YEAH. THAT'S THE THING. HE'S THE BEST. JUST BULL-HEADED. NEVER WRONG. DOESN'T LISTEN.
HUH. SOUNDS LIKE SOMEONE ELSE I KNOW.
SO JUST DO WHAT I DID.
I WAS THINKING ABOUT YOU ALL DAY, BABY GIRL!
CUT HIM LOOSE. GIVE HIM SPACE TO BREATHE. AND LET HIM DO WHAT HE DOES BEST.
NEXT ISSUE: BURN THE HOUSE DOWN!

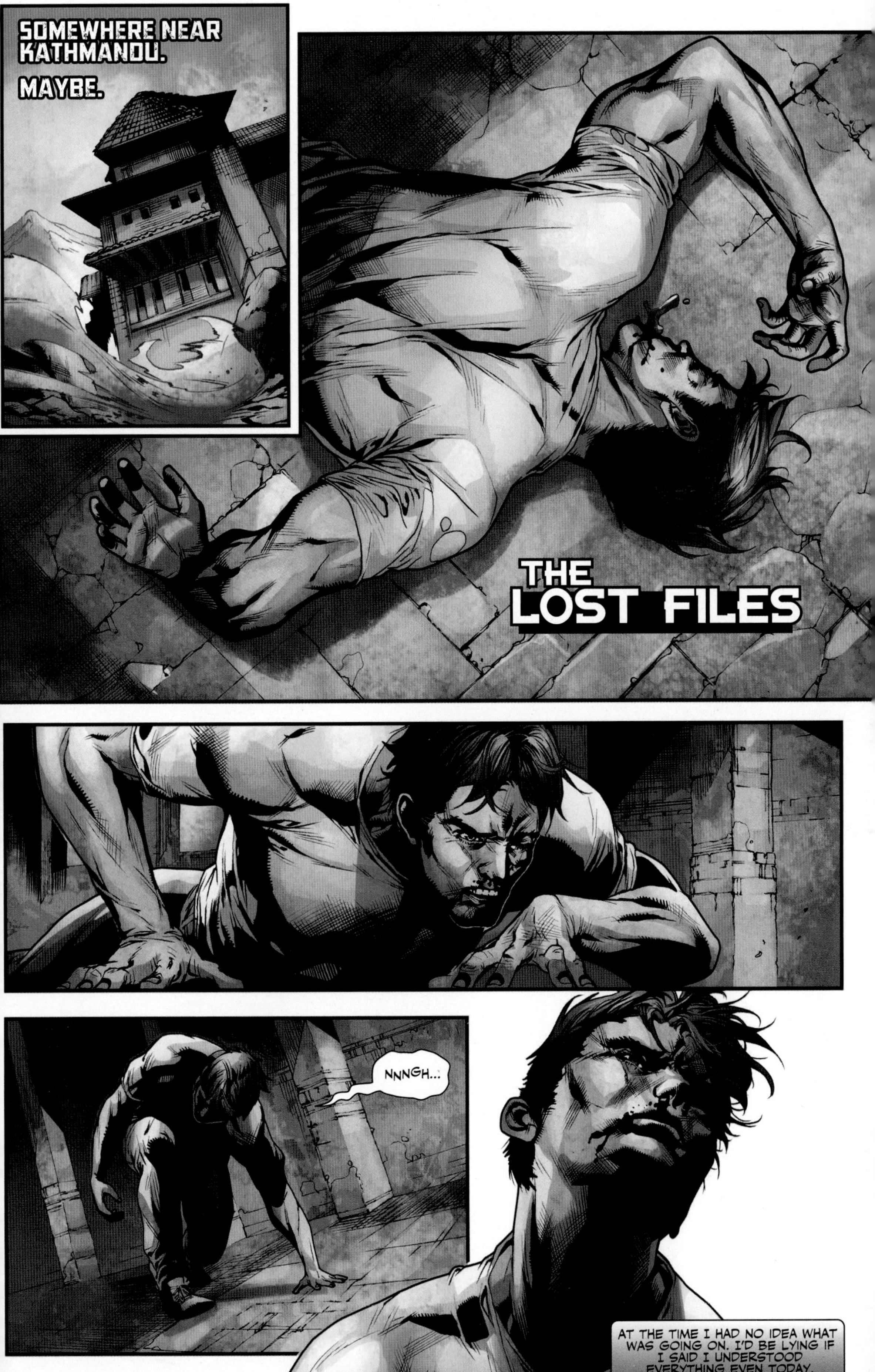
SOMEWHERE NEAR KATHMANDU.
MAYBE.
THE LOST FILES
NNNGH...
AT THE TIME I HAD NO IDEA WHAT WAS GOING ON. I'D BE LYING IF I SAID I UNDERSTOOD EVERYTHING EVEN TODAY.

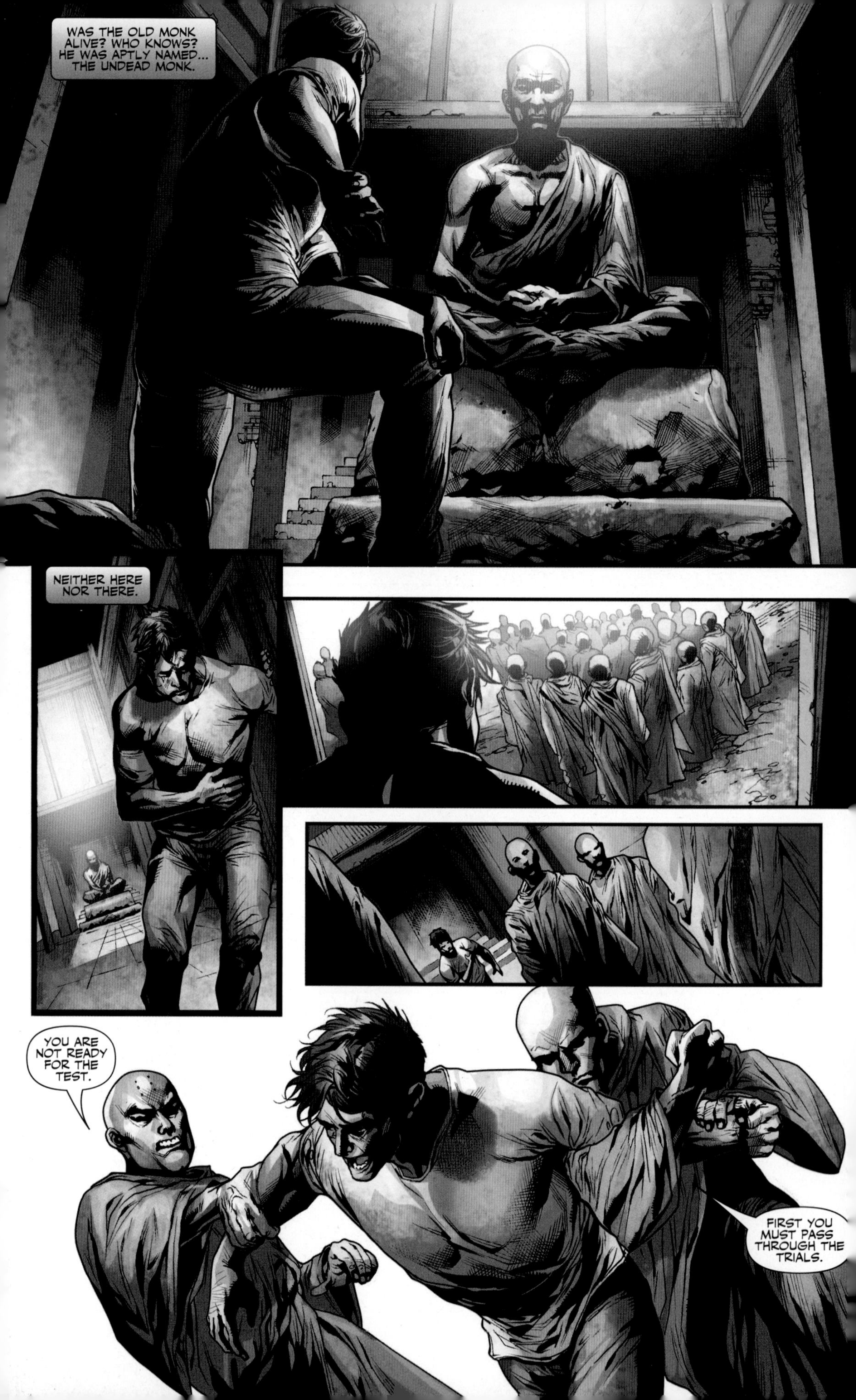
WAS THE OLD MONK ALIVE? WHO KNOWS? HE WAS APTLY NAMED... THE UNDEAD MONK.
NEITHER HERE NOR THERE.
YOU ARE NOT READY FOR THE TEST.
FIRST YOU MUST PASS THROUGH THE TRIALS.

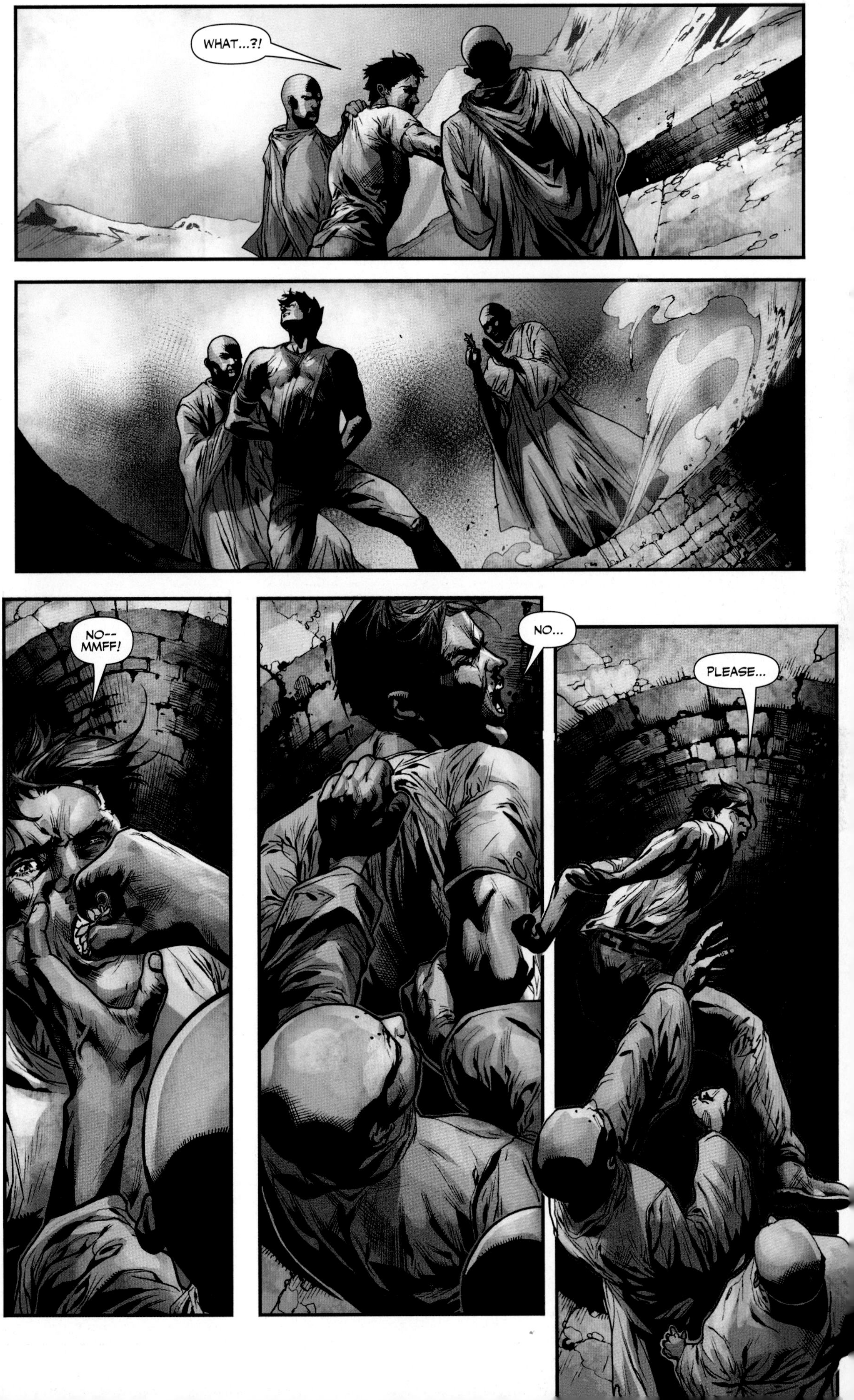
WHAT...?!
NO--
MMFF!
NO...
PLEASE...

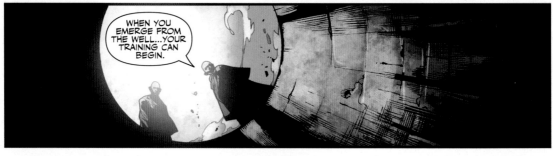

WHEN YOU EMERGE FROM THE WELL...YOUR TRAINING CAN BEGIN.

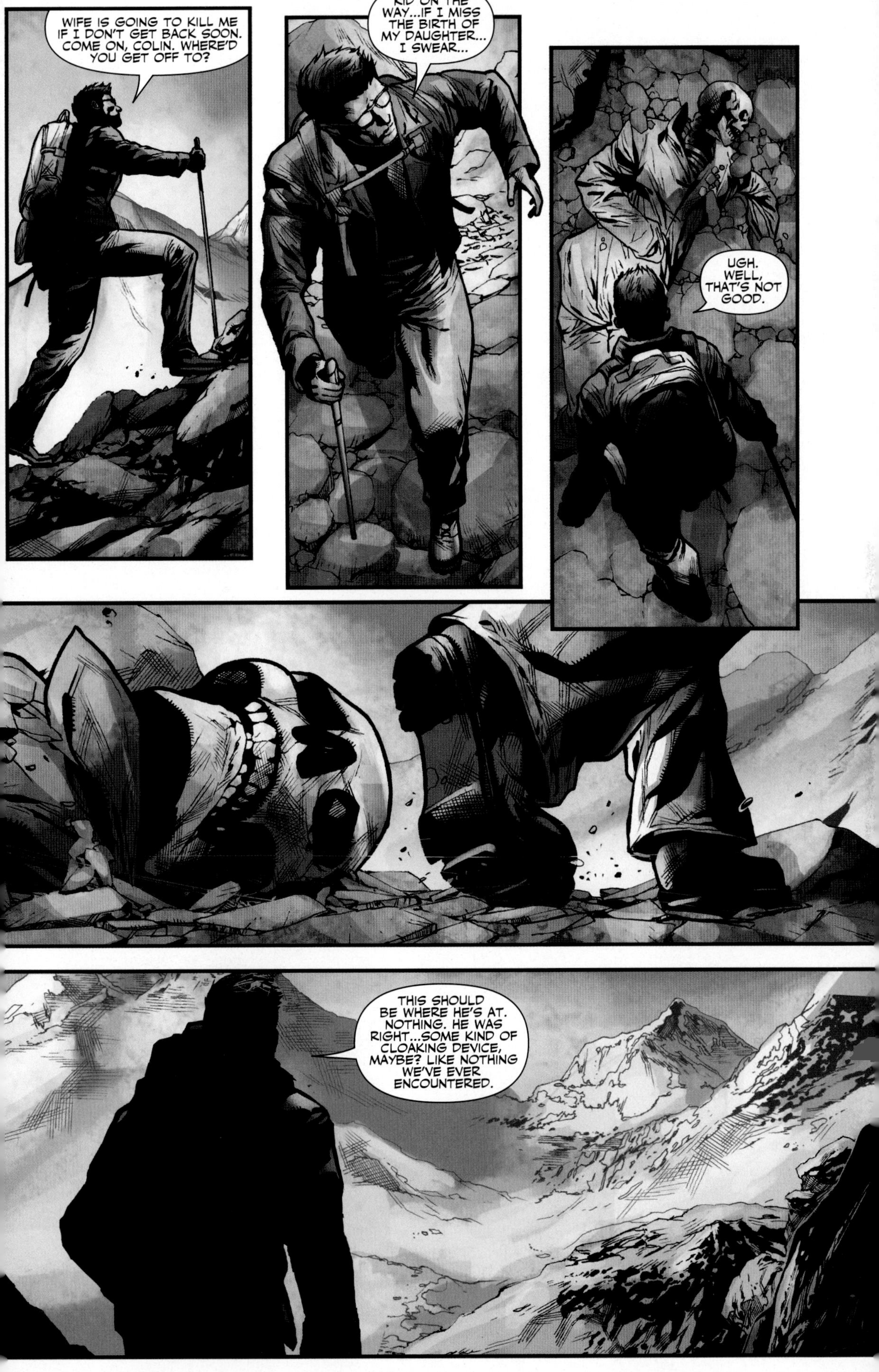
WIFE IS GOING TO KILL ME IF I DON'T GET BACK SOON. COME ON, COLIN. WHERE'D YOU GET OFF TO?
KID ON THE WAY...IF I MISS THE BIRTH OF MY DAUGHTER... I SWEAR...
UGH. WELL, THAT'S NOT GOOD.
THIS SHOULD BE WHERE HE'S AT. NOTHING. HE WAS RIGHT...SOME KIND OF CLOAKING DEVICE, MAYBE? LIKE NOTHING WE'VE EVER ENCOUNTERED.

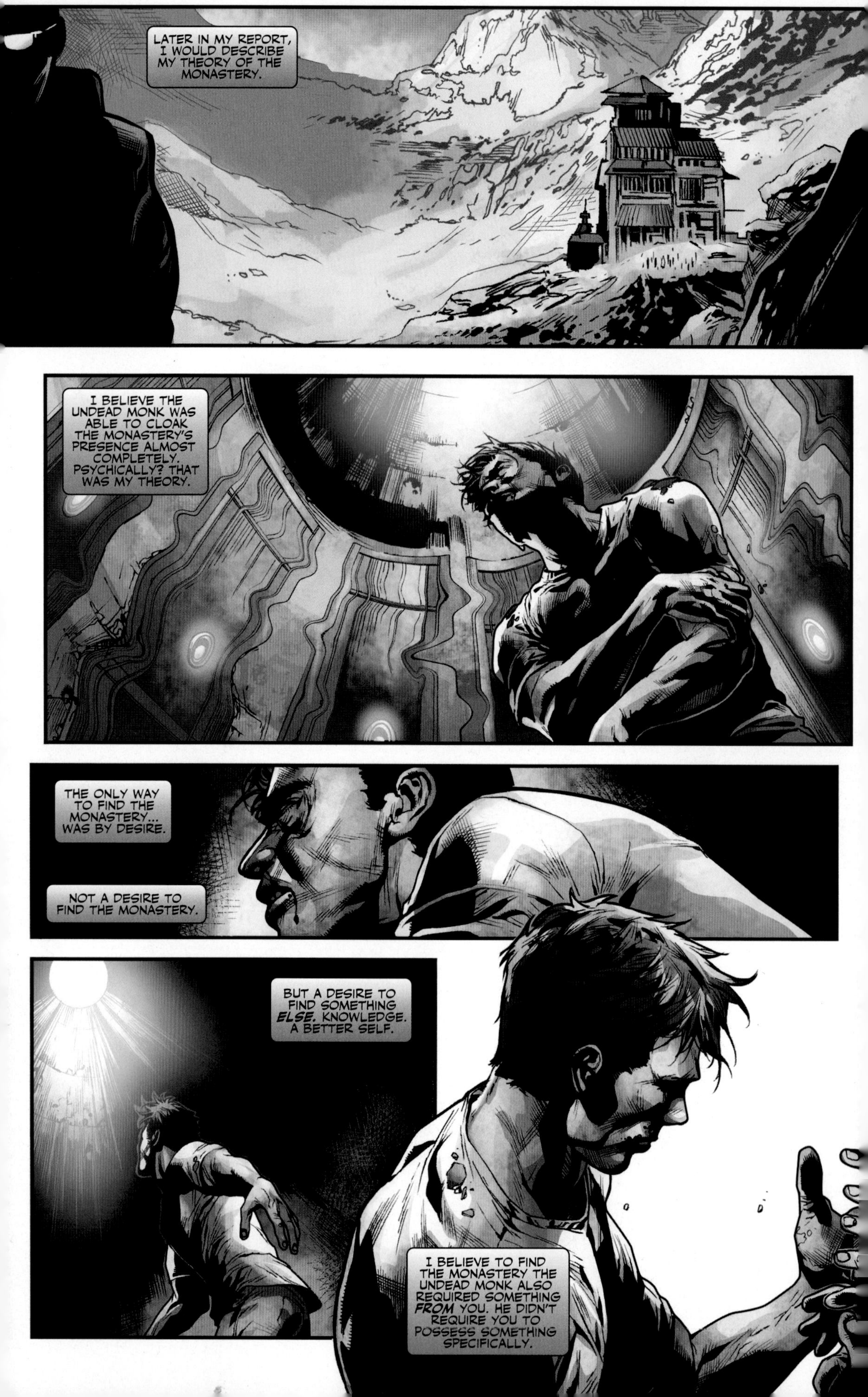

LATER IN MY REPORT, I WOULD DESCRIBE MY THEORY OF THE MONASTERY.
I BELIEVE THE UNDEAD MONK WAS ABLE TO CLOAK THE MONASTERY'S PRESENCE ALMOST COMPLETELY. PSYCHICALLY? THAT WAS MY THEORY.
THE ONLY WAY TO FIND THE MONASTERY... WAS BY DESIRE.
NOT A DESIRE TO FIND THE MONASTERY.
BUT A DESIRE TO FIND SOMETHING *ELSE*. KNOWLEDGE. A BETTER SELF.
I BELIEVE TO FIND THE MONASTERY THE UNDEAD MONK ALSO REQUIRED SOMETHING *FROM* YOU. HE DIDN'T REQUIRE YOU TO POSSESS SOMETHING SPECIFICALLY.

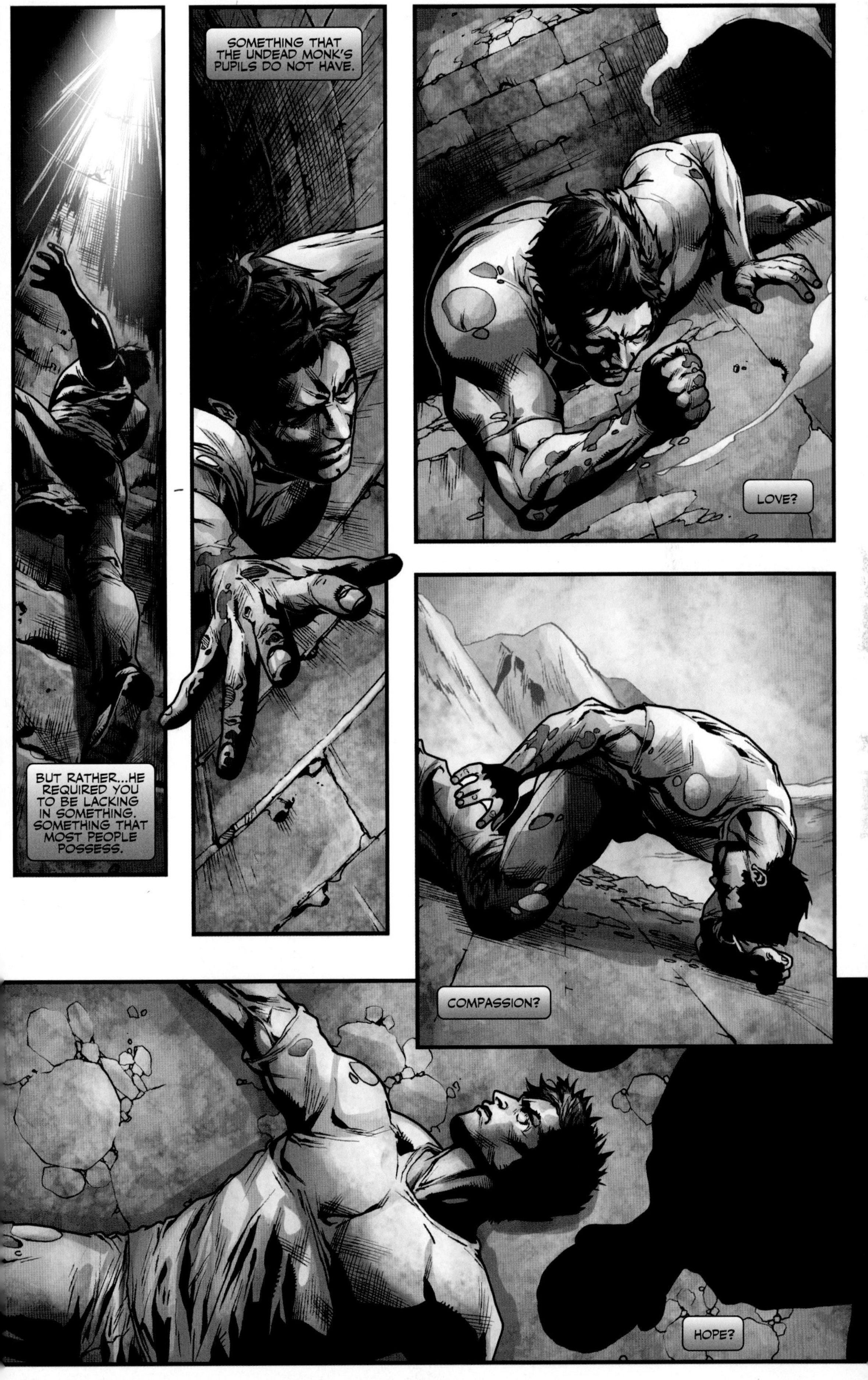
BUT RATHER...HE REQUIRED YOU TO BE LACKING IN SOMETHING. SOMETHING THAT MOST PEOPLE POSSESS.
SOMETHING THAT THE UNDEAD MONK'S PUPILS DO NOT HAVE.
LOVE?
COMPASSION?
HOPE?

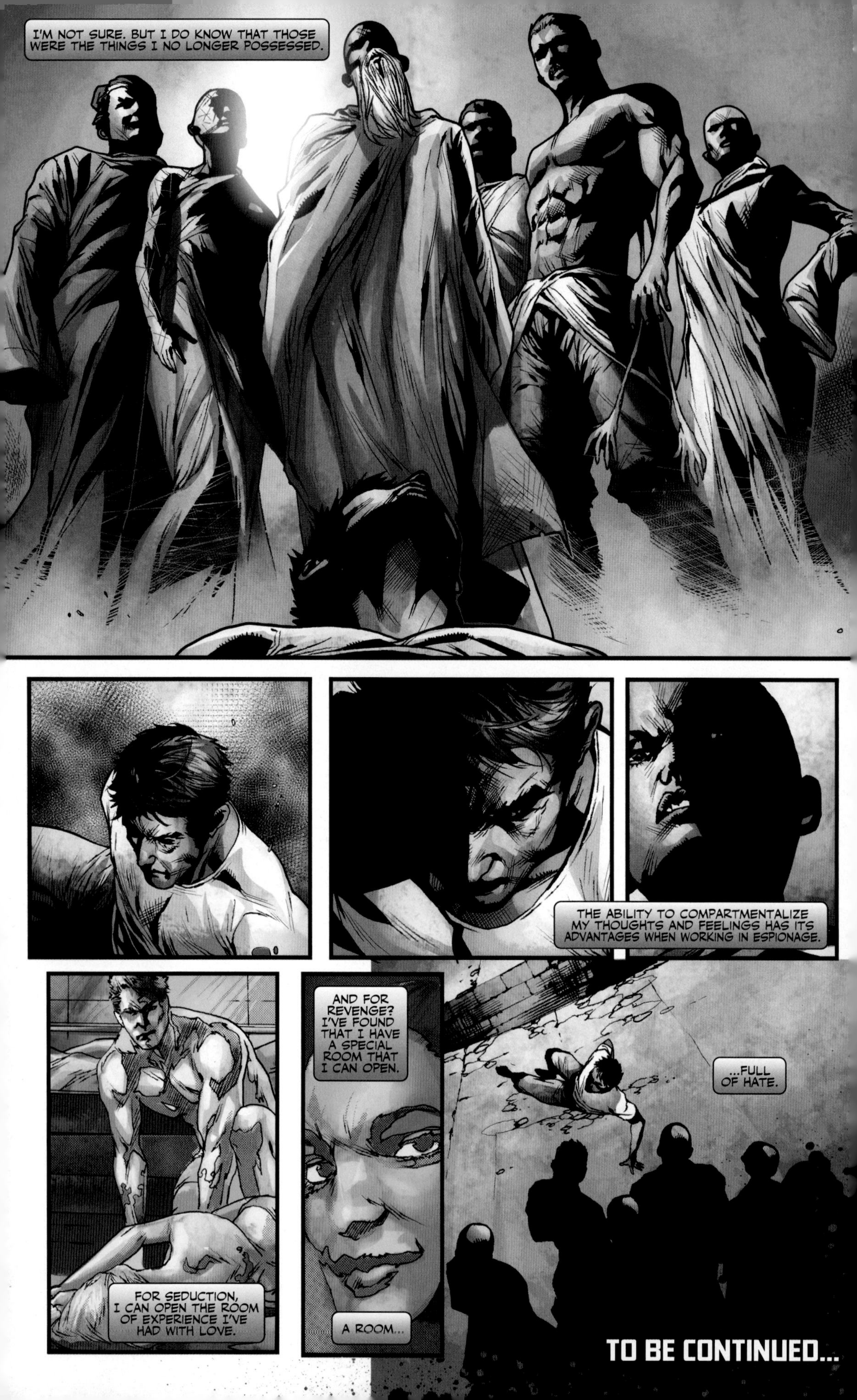

I'M NOT SURE. BUT I DO KNOW THAT THOSE WERE THE THINGS I NO LONGER POSSESSED.
THE ABILITY TO COMPARTMENTALIZE MY THOUGHTS AND FEELINGS HAS ITS ADVANTAGES WHEN WORKING IN ESPIONAGE.
FOR SEDUCTION, I CAN OPEN THE ROOM OF EXPERIENCE I'VE HAD WITH LOVE.
AND FOR REVENGE? I'VE FOUND THAT I HAVE A SPECIAL ROOM THAT I CAN OPEN.
A ROOM...
...FULL OF HATE.
TO BE CONTINUED...

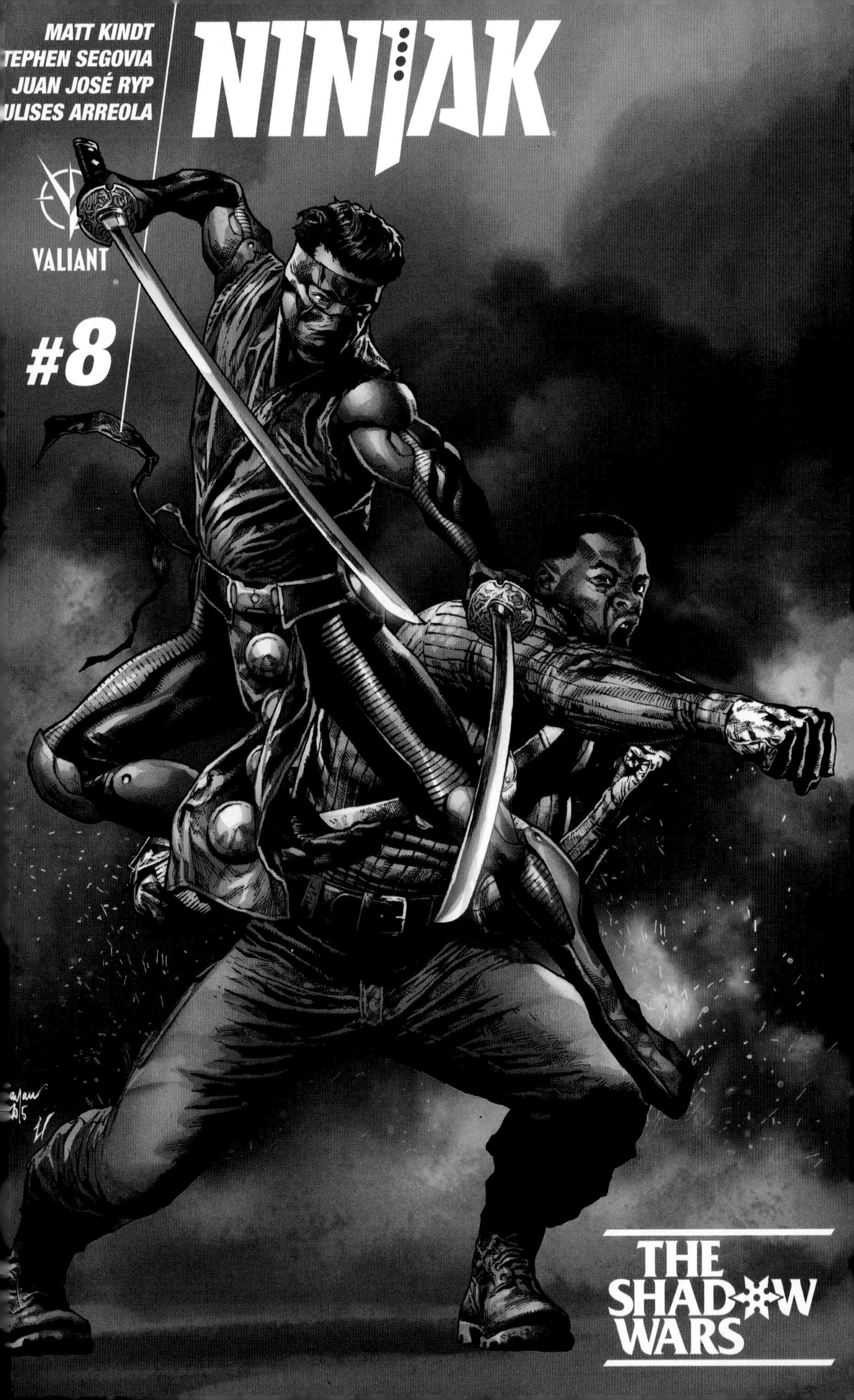
MATT KINDT
TEPHEN SEGOVIA
JUAN JOSÉ RYP
ULISES ARREOLA
NINJAK
VALIANT
#8
THE SHADOW WARS

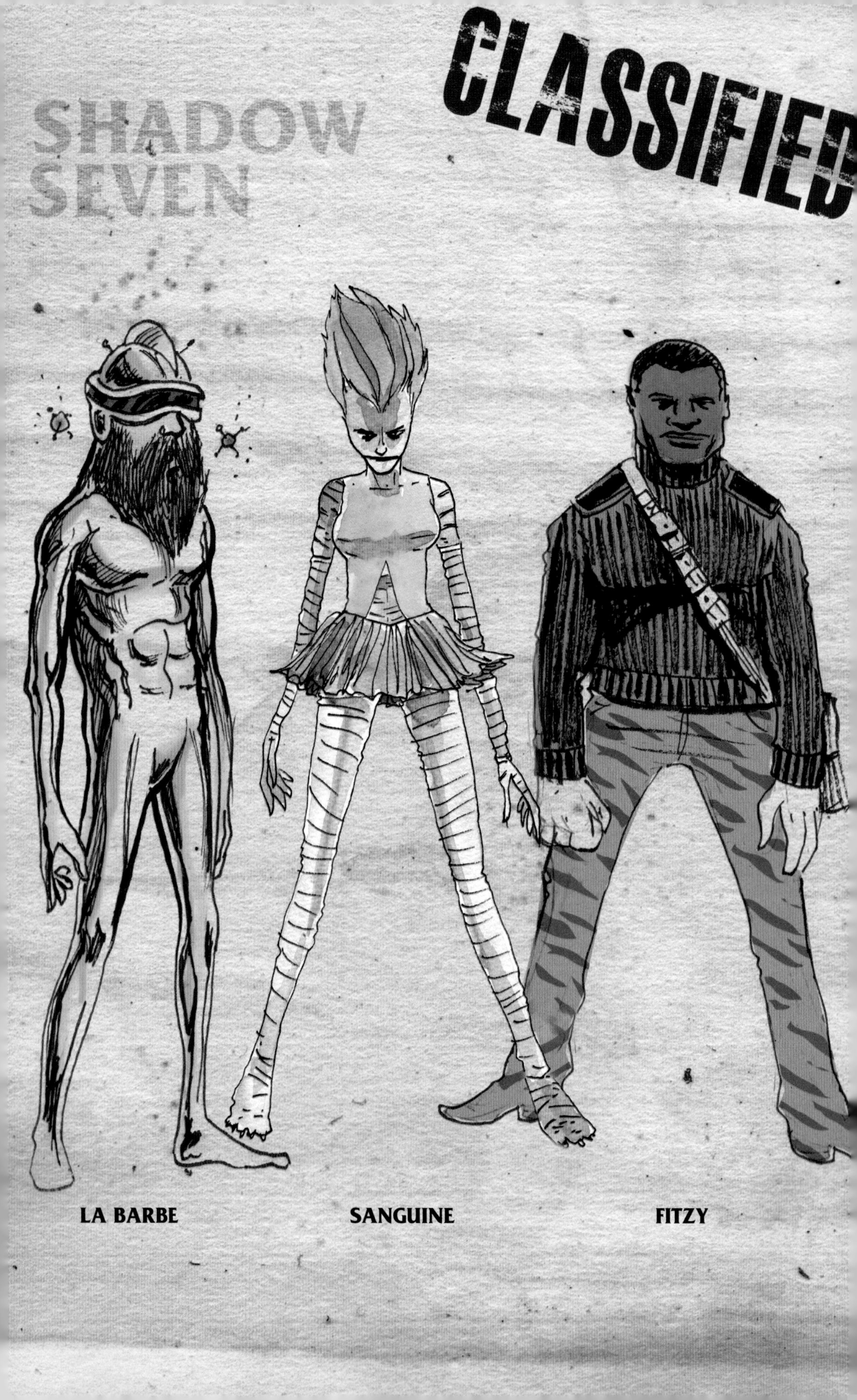
CLASSIFIED
SHADOW SEVEN
LA BARBE
SANGUINE
FITZY

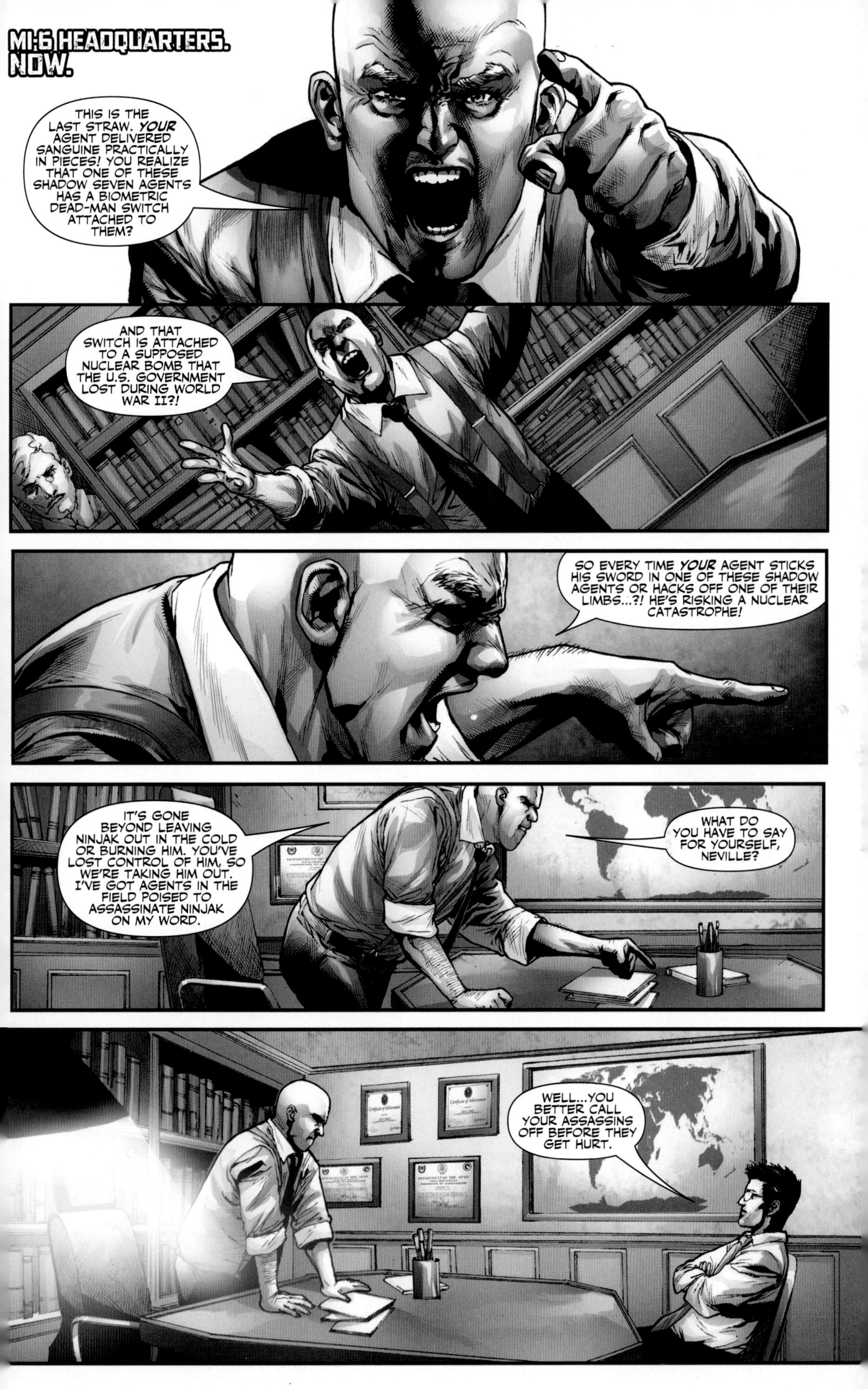
MI-6 HEADQUARTERS. NOW.
THIS IS THE LAST STRAW. YOUR AGENT DELIVERED SANGUINE PRACTICALLY IN PIECES! YOU REALIZE THAT ONE OF THESE SHADOW SEVEN AGENTS HAS A BIOMETRIC DEAD-MAN SWITCH ATTACHED TO THEM?
AND THAT SWITCH IS ATTACHED TO A SUPPOSED NUCLEAR BOMB THAT THE U.S. GOVERNMENT LOST DURING WORLD WAR II?!
SO EVERY TIME YOUR AGENT STICKS HIS SWORD IN ONE OF THESE SHADOW AGENTS OR HACKS OFF ONE OF THEIR LIMBS...?! HE'S RISKING A NUCLEAR CATASTROPHE!
IT'S GONE BEYOND LEAVING NINJAK OUT IN THE COLD OR BURNING HIM. YOU'VE LOST CONTROL OF HIM, SO WE'RE TAKING HIM OUT. I'VE GOT AGENTS IN THE FIELD POISED TO ASSASSINATE NINJAK ON MY WORD.
WHAT DO YOU HAVE TO SAY FOR YOURSELF, NEVILLE?
WELL...YOU BETTER CALL YOUR ASSASSINS OFF BEFORE THEY GET HURT.

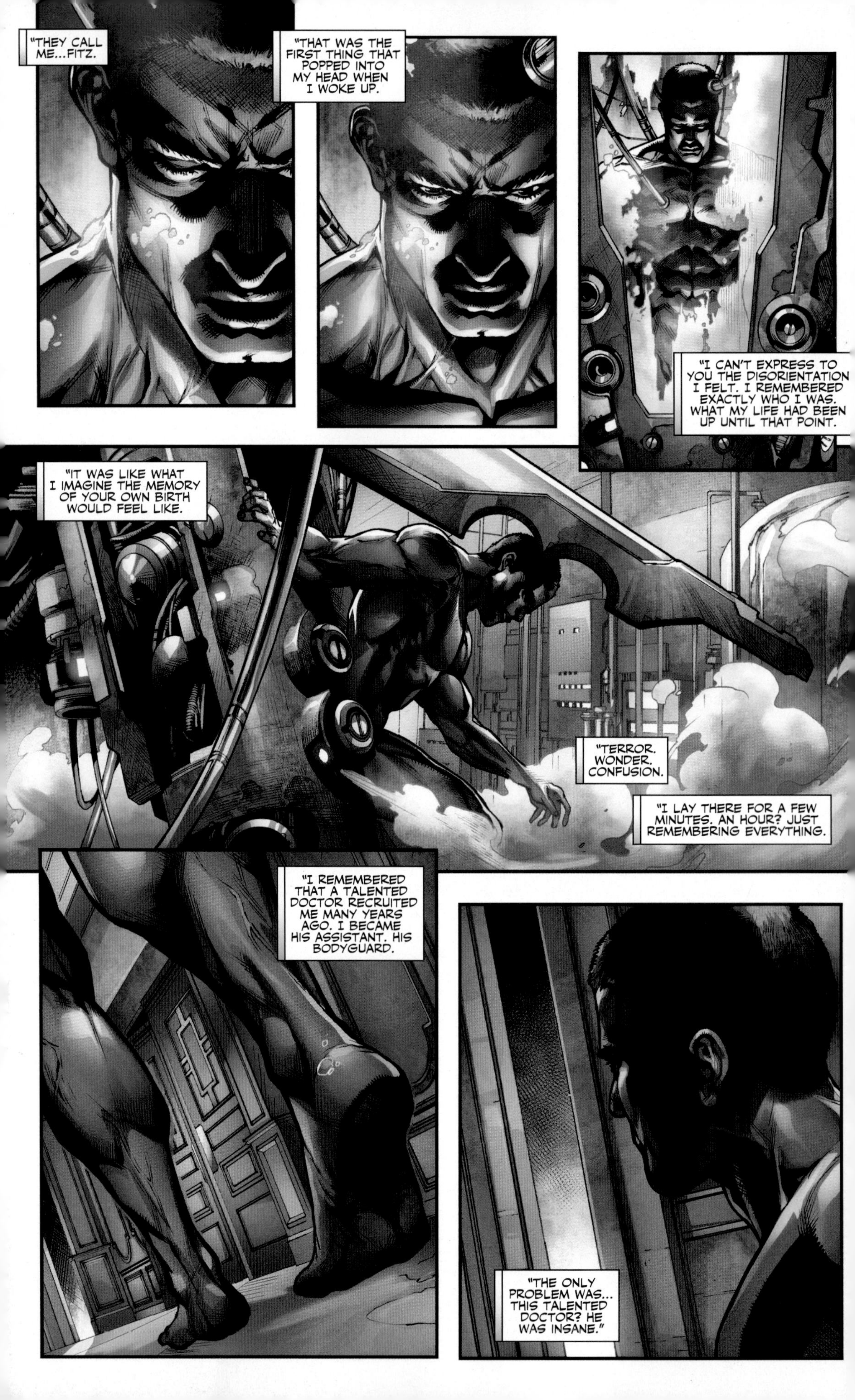
"THEY CALL ME...FITZ.
"THAT WAS THE FIRST THING THAT POPPED INTO MY HEAD WHEN I WOKE UP.
"I CAN'T EXPRESS TO YOU THE DISORIENTATION I FELT. I REMEMBERED EXACTLY WHO I WAS. WHAT MY LIFE HAD BEEN UP UNTIL THAT POINT.
"IT WAS LIKE WHAT I IMAGINE THE MEMORY OF YOUR OWN BIRTH WOULD FEEL LIKE.
"TERROR. WONDER. CONFUSION.
"I LAY THERE FOR A FEW MINUTES. AN HOUR? JUST REMEMBERING EVERYTHING.
"I REMEMBERED THAT A TALENTED DOCTOR RECRUITED ME MANY YEARS AGO. I BECAME HIS ASSISTANT. HIS BODYGUARD.
"THE ONLY PROBLEM WAS... THIS TALENTED DOCTOR? HE WAS INSANE."

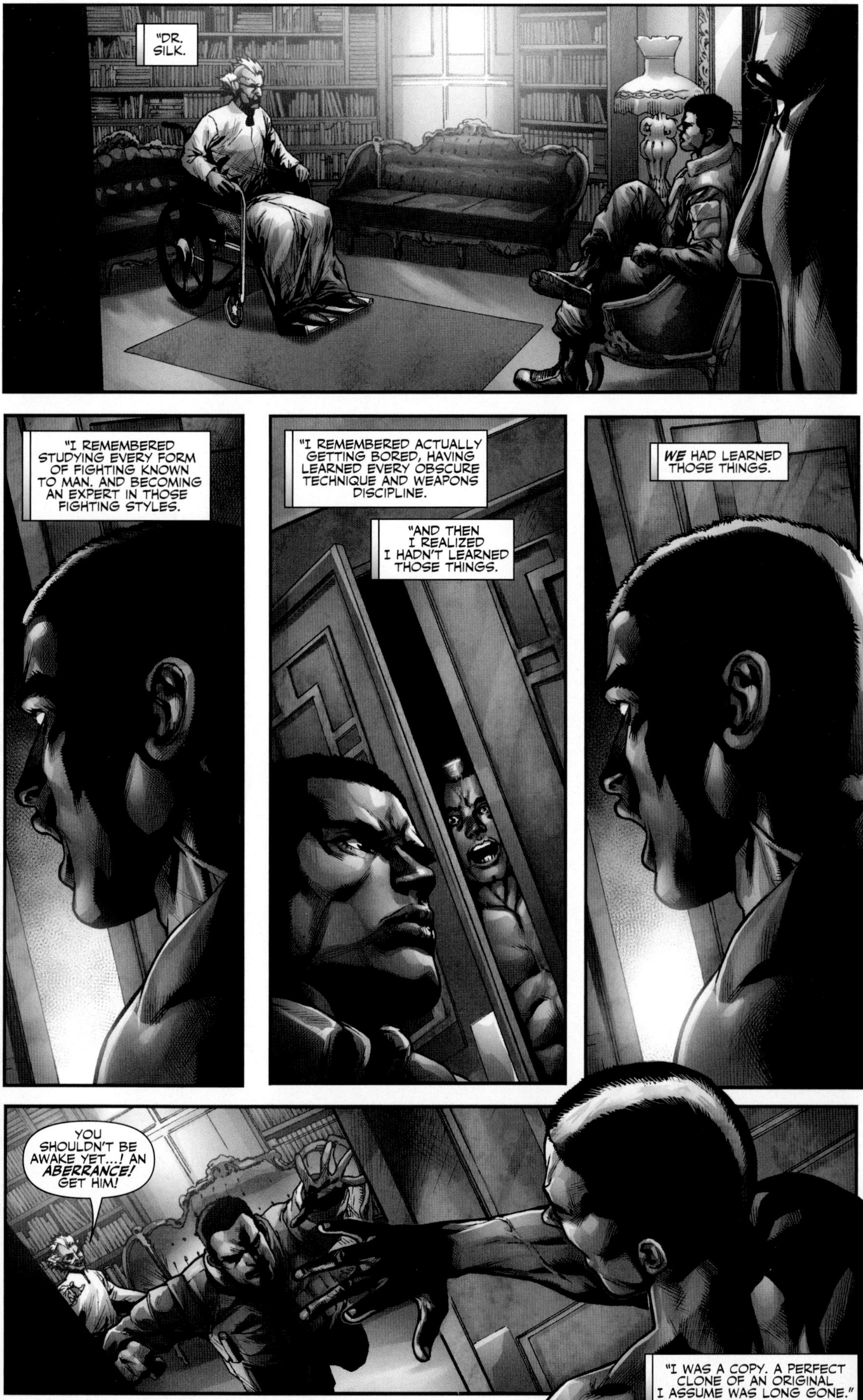
"DR. SILK.
"I REMEMBERED STUDYING EVERY FORM OF FIGHTING KNOWN TO MAN. AND BECOMING AN EXPERT IN THOSE FIGHTING STYLES.
"I REMEMBERED ACTUALLY GETTING BORED, HAVING LEARNED EVERY OBSCURE TECHNIQUE AND WEAPONS DISCIPLINE.
"AND THEN I REALIZED I HADN'T LEARNED THOSE THINGS.
WE HAD LEARNED THOSE THINGS.
YOU SHOULDN'T BE AWAKE YET...! AN *ABERRANCE!* GET HIM!
"I WAS A COPY. A PERFECT CLONE OF AN ORIGINAL I ASSUME WAS LONG GONE."

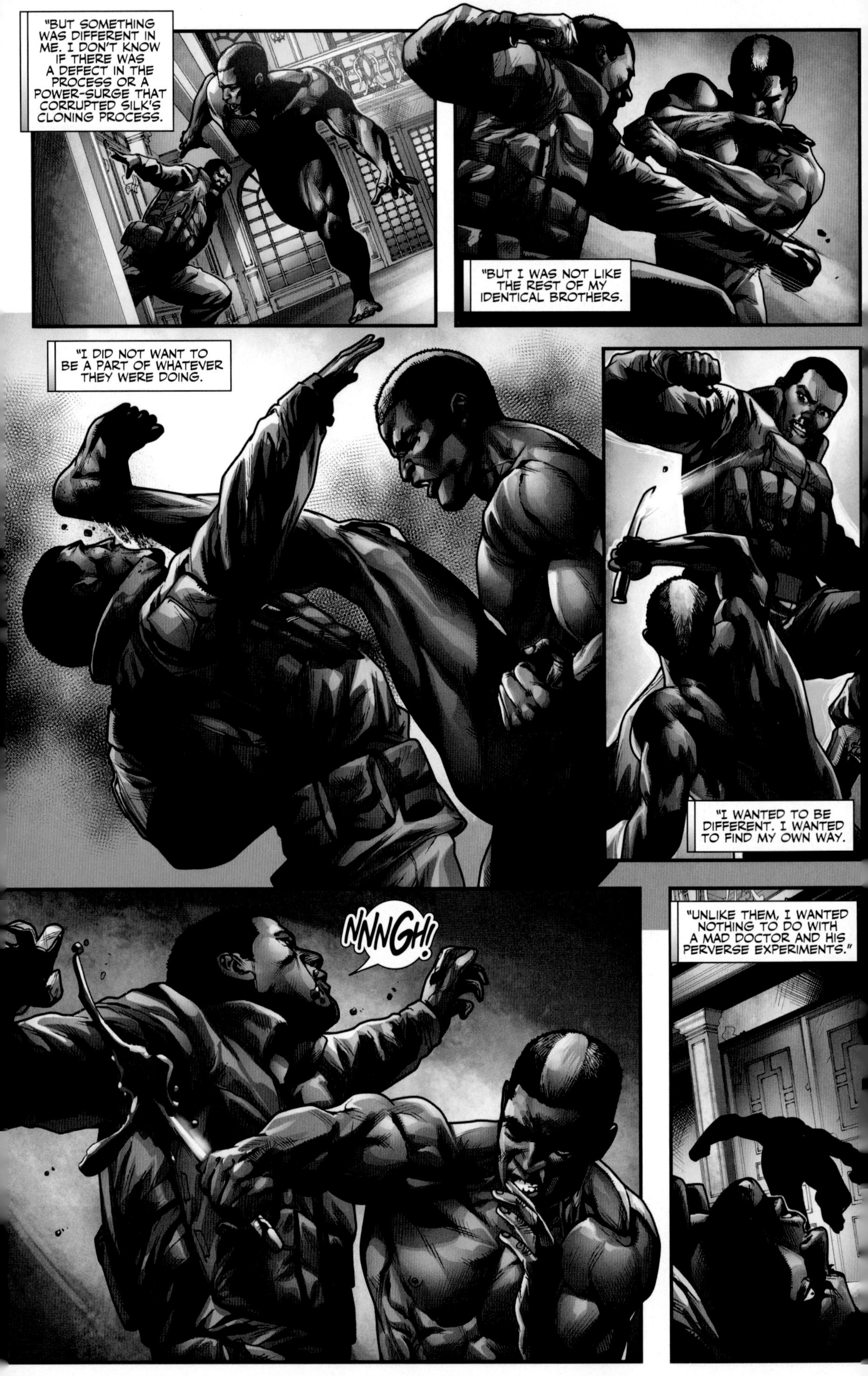
"BUT SOMETHING WAS DIFFERENT IN ME. I DON'T KNOW IF THERE WAS A DEFECT IN THE PROCESS OR A POWER-SURGE THAT CORRUPTED SILK'S CLONING PROCESS.
"BUT I WAS NOT LIKE THE REST OF MY IDENTICAL BROTHERS.
"I DID NOT WANT TO BE A PART OF WHATEVER THEY WERE DOING.
"I WANTED TO BE DIFFERENT. I WANTED TO FIND MY OWN WAY.
NNNGH!
"UNLIKE THEM, I WANTED NOTHING TO DO WITH A MAD DOCTOR AND HIS PERVERSE EXPERIMENTS."

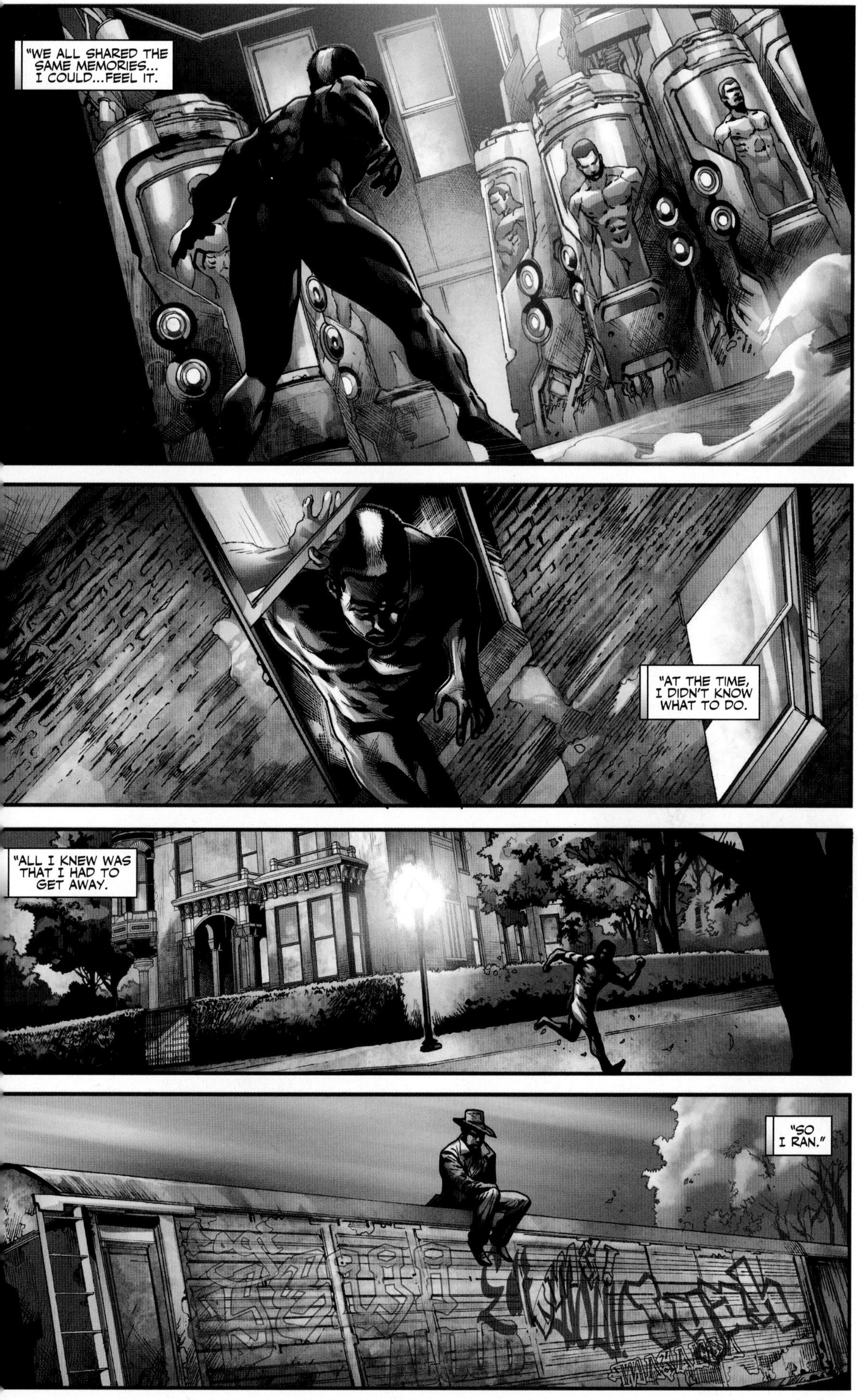
"WE ALL SHARED THE SAME MEMORIES... I COULD...FEEL IT.
"AT THE TIME, I DIDN'T KNOW WHAT TO DO.
"ALL I KNEW WAS THAT I HAD TO GET AWAY.
"SO I RAN."

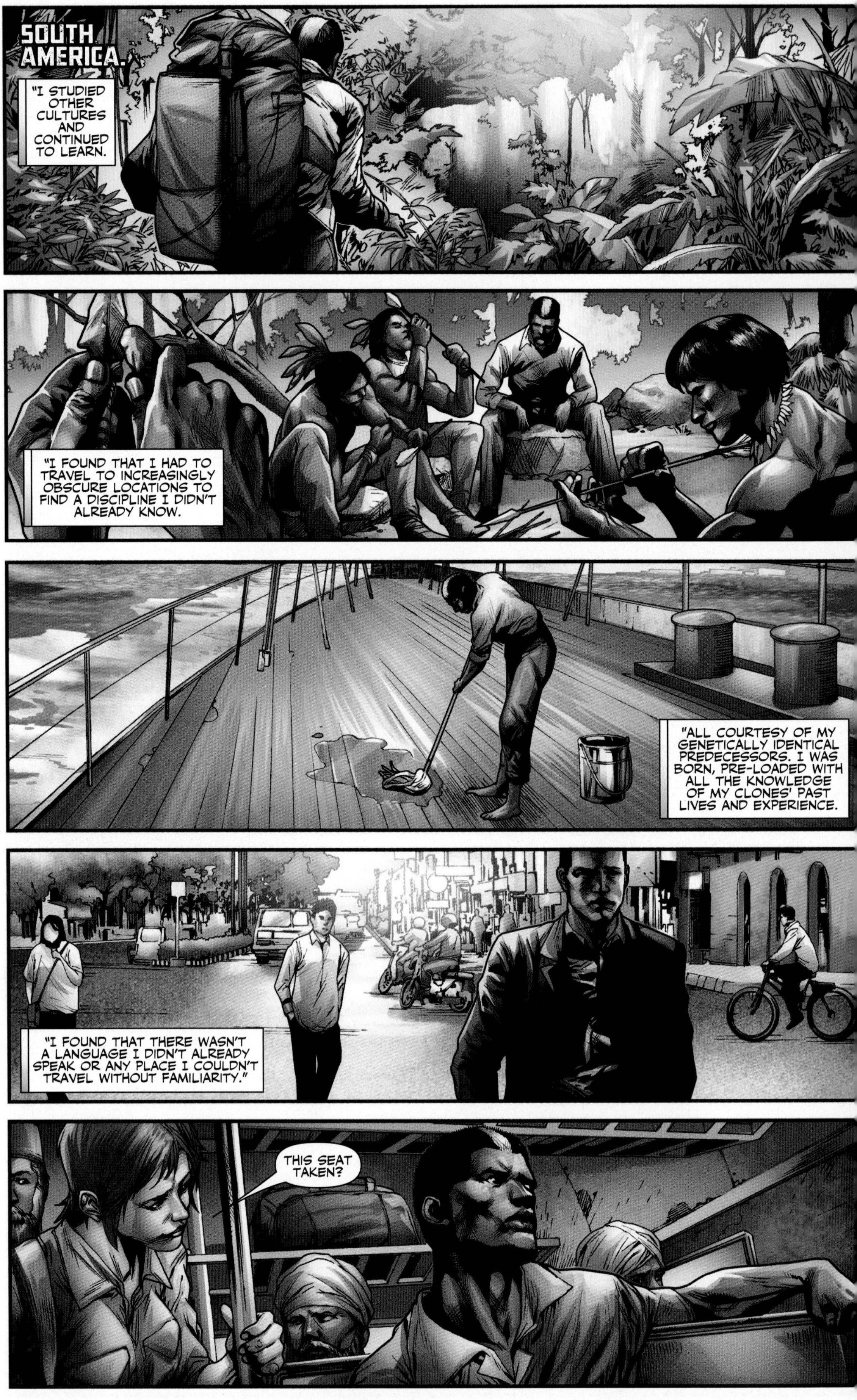
SOUTH AMERICA.
"I STUDIED OTHER CULTURES AND CONTINUED TO LEARN.
"I FOUND THAT I HAD TO TRAVEL TO INCREASINGLY OBSCURE LOCATIONS TO FIND A DISCIPLINE I DIDN'T ALREADY KNOW.
"ALL COURTESY OF MY GENETICALLY IDENTICAL PREDECESSORS. I WAS BORN, PRE-LOADED WITH ALL THE KNOWLEDGE OF MY CLONES' PAST LIVES AND EXPERIENCE.
"I FOUND THAT THERE WASN'T A LANGUAGE I DIDN'T ALREADY SPEAK OR ANY PLACE I COULDN'T TRAVEL WITHOUT FAMILIARITY."
THIS SEAT TAKEN?

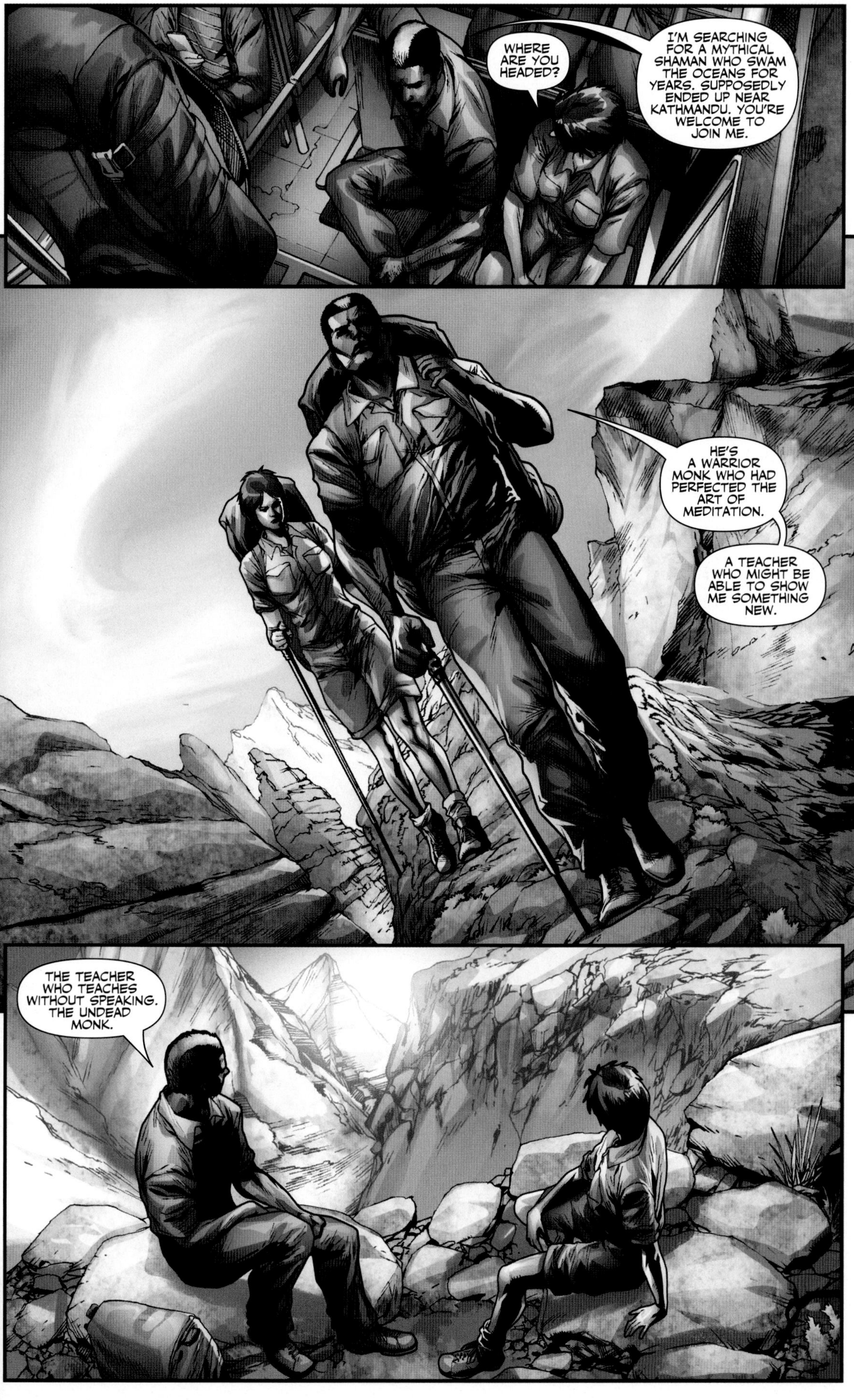
WHERE ARE YOU HEADED?
I'M SEARCHING FOR A MYTHICAL SHAMAN WHO SWAM THE OCEANS FOR YEARS. SUPPOSEDLY ENDED UP NEAR KATHMANDU. YOU'RE WELCOME TO JOIN ME.
HE'S A WARRIOR MONK WHO HAD PERFECTED THE ART OF MEDITATION.
A TEACHER WHO MIGHT BE ABLE TO SHOW ME SOMETHING NEW.
THE TEACHER WHO TEACHES WITHOUT SPEAKING. THE UNDEAD MONK.

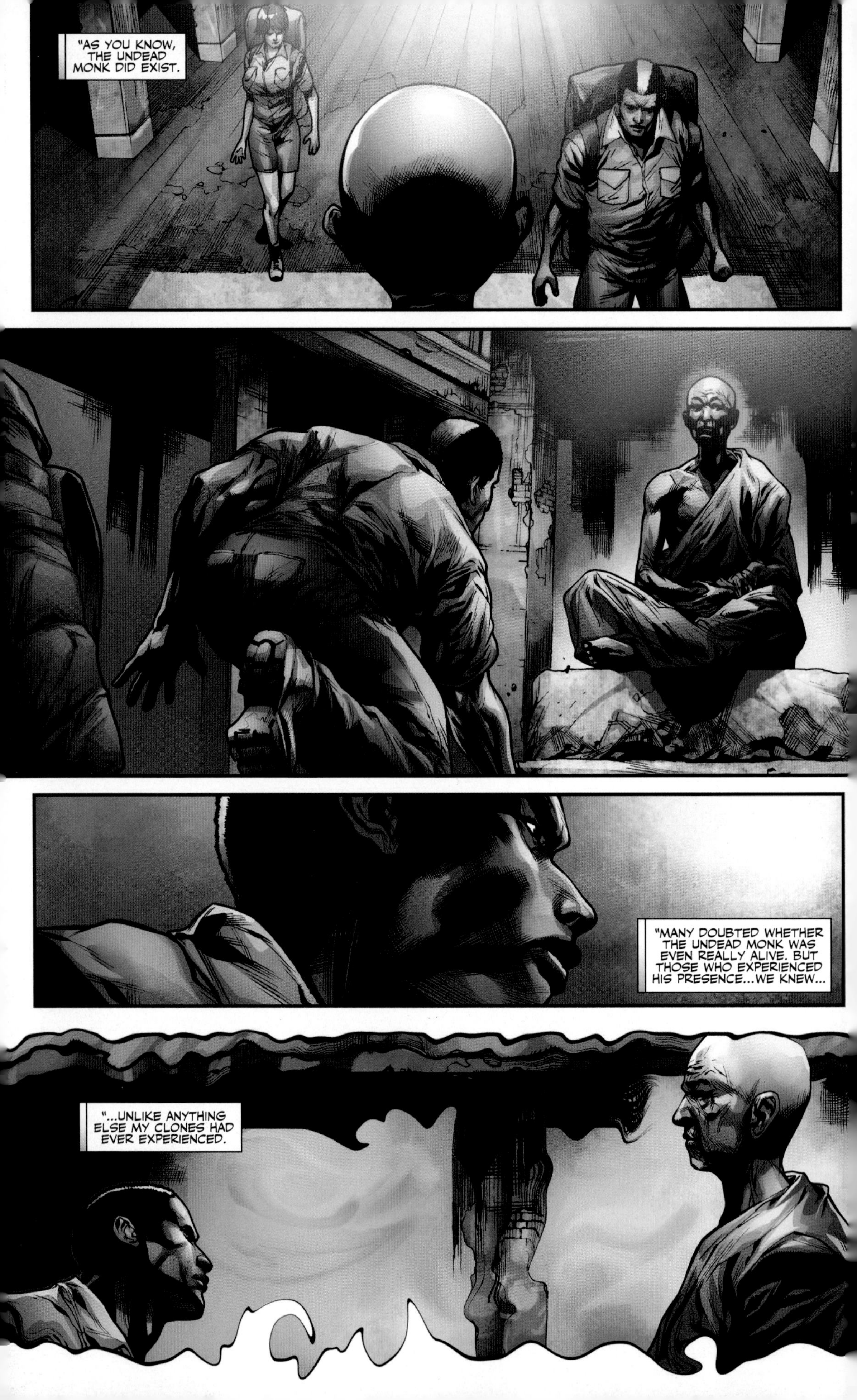
"AS YOU KNOW, THE UNDEAD MONK DID EXIST.
"MANY DOUBTED WHETHER THE UNDEAD MONK WAS EVEN REALLY ALIVE. BUT THOSE WHO EXPERIENCED HIS PRESENCE...WE KNEW...
"...UNLIKE ANYTHING ELSE MY CLONES HAD EVER EXPERIENCED.

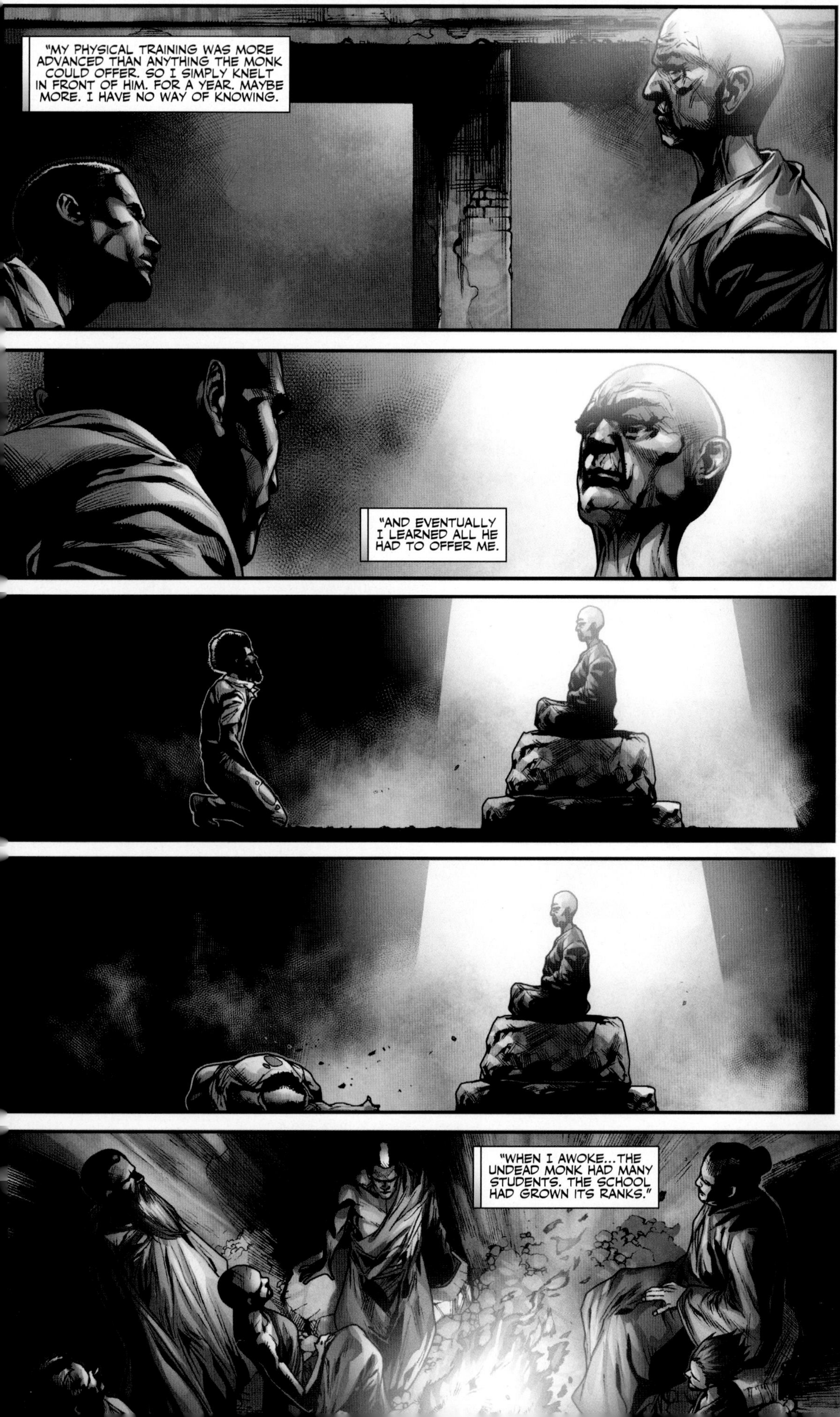
"MY PHYSICAL TRAINING WAS MORE ADVANCED THAN ANYTHING THE MONK COULD OFFER. SO I SIMPLY KNELT IN FRONT OF HIM. FOR A YEAR. MAYBE MORE. I HAVE NO WAY OF KNOWING.
"AND EVENTUALLY I LEARNED ALL HE HAD TO OFFER ME.
"WHEN I AWOKE...THE UNDEAD MONK HAD MANY STUDENTS. THE SCHOOL HAD GROWN ITS RANKS."

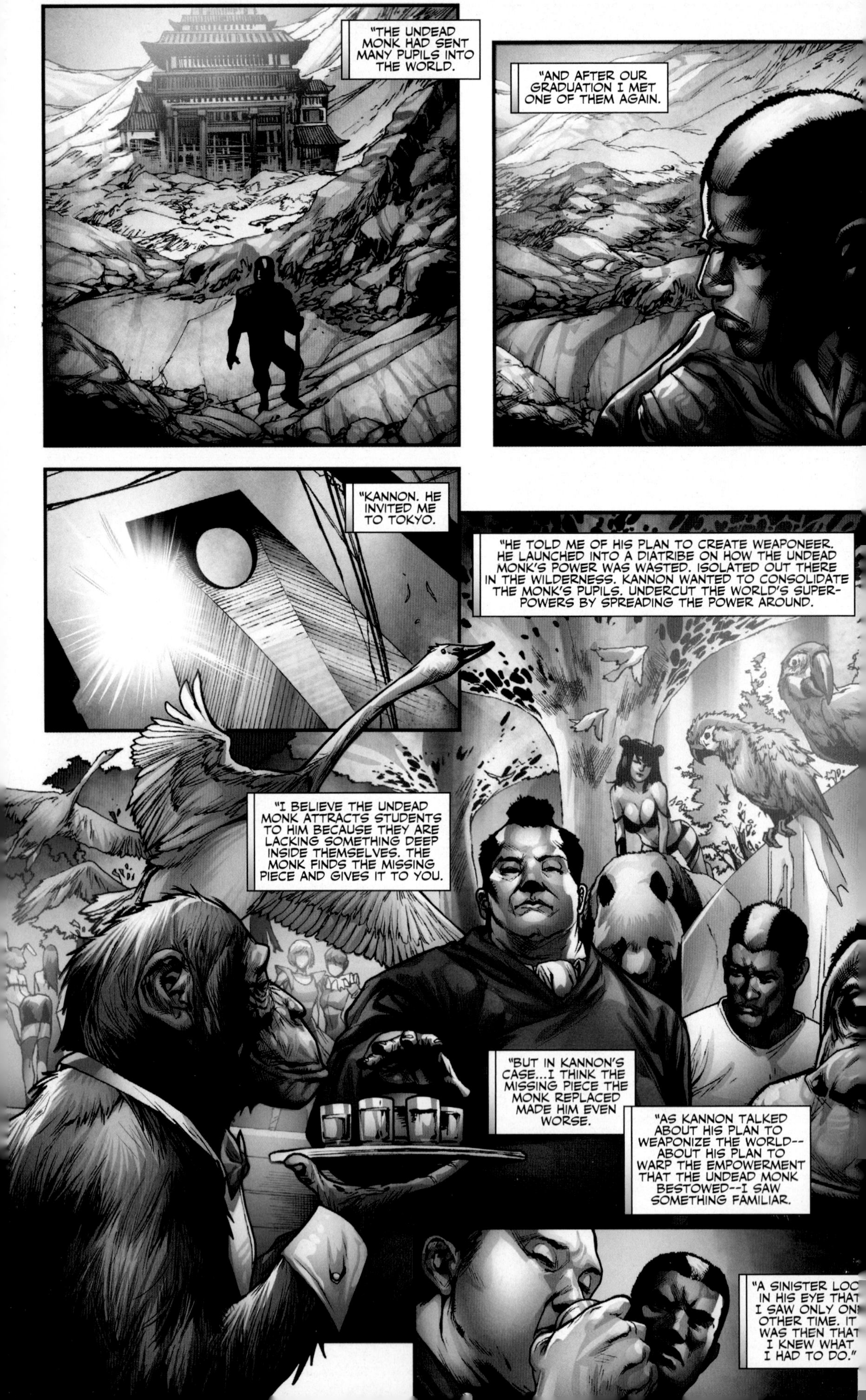
"THE UNDEAD MONK HAD SENT MANY PUPILS INTO THE WORLD.
"AND AFTER OUR GRADUATION I MET ONE OF THEM AGAIN.
"KANNON. HE INVITED ME TO TOKYO.
"HE TOLD ME OF HIS PLAN TO CREATE WEAPONEER. HE LAUNCHED INTO A DIATRIBE ON HOW THE UNDEAD MONK'S POWER WAS WASTED. ISOLATED OUT THERE IN THE WILDERNESS. KANNON WANTED TO CONSOLIDATE THE MONK'S PUPILS. UNDERCUT THE WORLD'S SUPER-POWERS BY SPREADING THE POWER AROUND.
"I BELIEVE THE UNDEAD MONK ATTRACTS STUDENTS TO HIM BECAUSE THEY ARE LACKING SOMETHING DEEP INSIDE THEMSELVES. THE MONK FINDS THE MISSING PIECE AND GIVES IT TO YOU.
"BUT IN KANNON'S CASE...I THINK THE MISSING PIECE THE MONK REPLACED MADE HIM EVEN WORSE.
"AS KANNON TALKED ABOUT HIS PLAN TO WEAPONIZE THE WORLD--ABOUT HIS PLAN TO WARP THE EMPOWERMENT THAT THE UNDEAD MONK BESTOWED--I SAW SOMETHING FAMILIAR.
"A SINISTER LOO IN HIS EYE THAT I SAW ONLY ON OTHER TIME. IT WAS THEN THAT I KNEW WHAT I HAD TO DO."

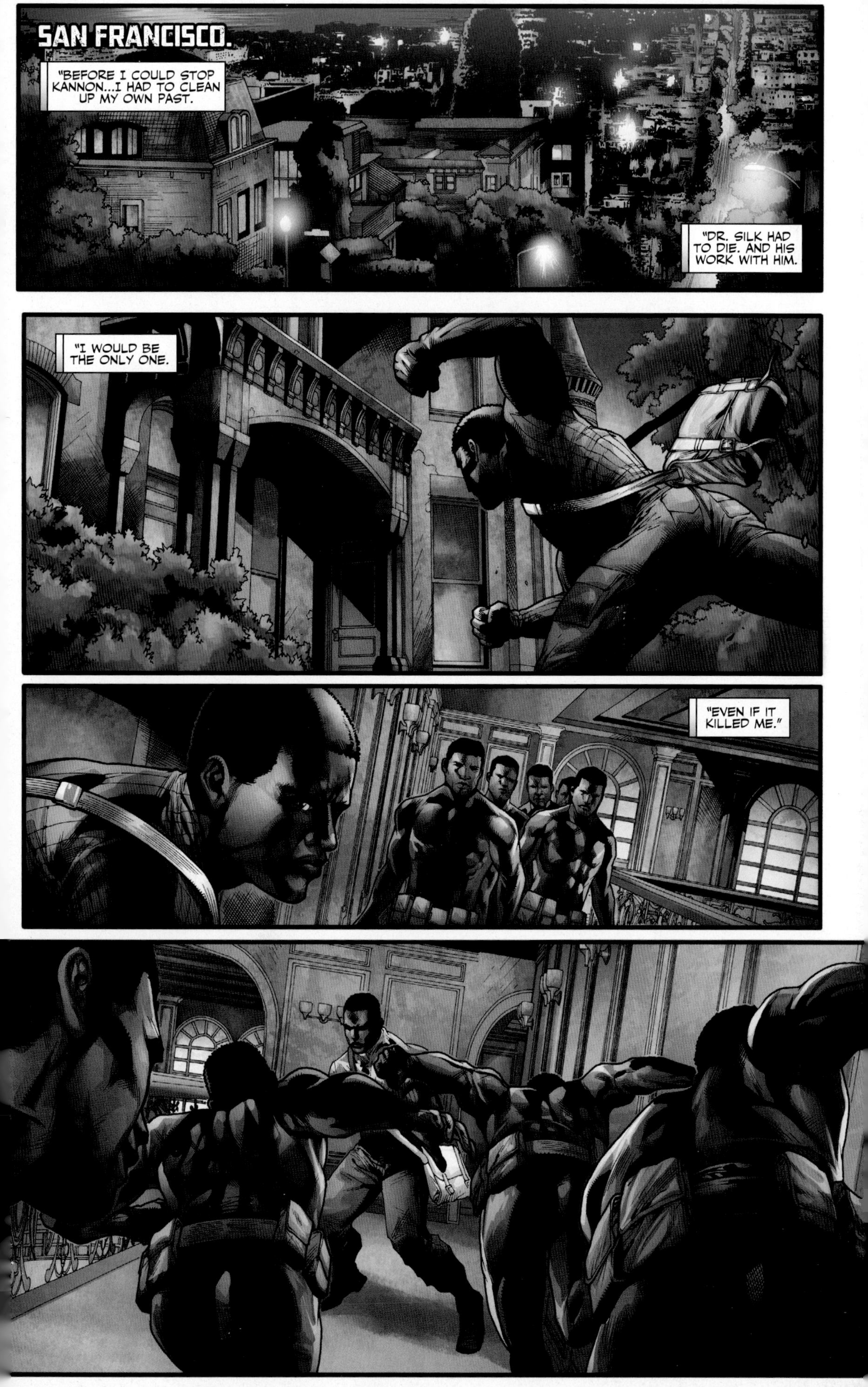
SAN FRANCISCO.
"BEFORE I COULD STOP KANNON...I HAD TO CLEAN UP MY OWN PAST.
"DR. SILK HAD TO DIE. AND HIS WORK WITH HIM.
"I WOULD BE THE ONLY ONE.
"EVEN IF IT KILLED ME."

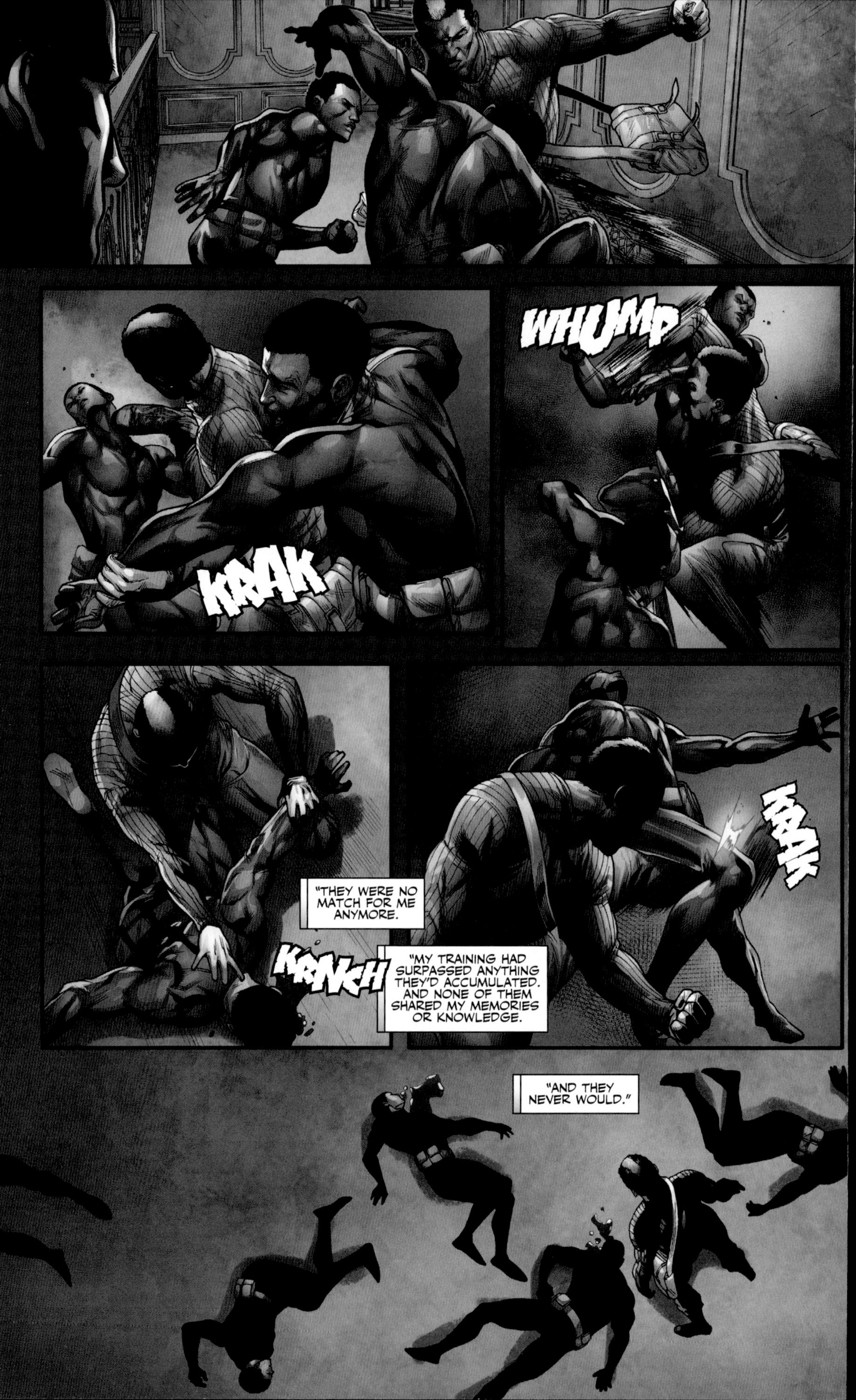
KRAK
WHUMP
"THEY WERE NO MATCH FOR ME ANYMORE.
KRNCH
KRAK
"MY TRAINING HAD SURPASSED ANYTHING THEY'D ACCUMULATED. AND NONE OF THEM SHARED MY MEMORIES OR KNOWLEDGE.
"AND THEY NEVER WOULD."

"DR. SILK WAS NOWHERE TO BE FOUND.

"SO I DID WHAT I COULD."

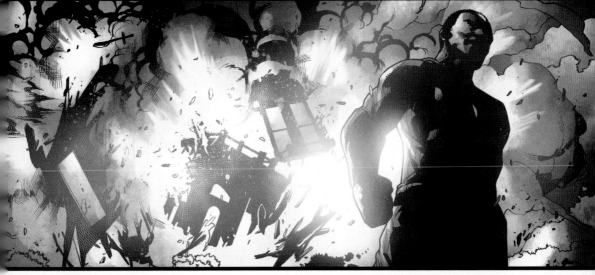

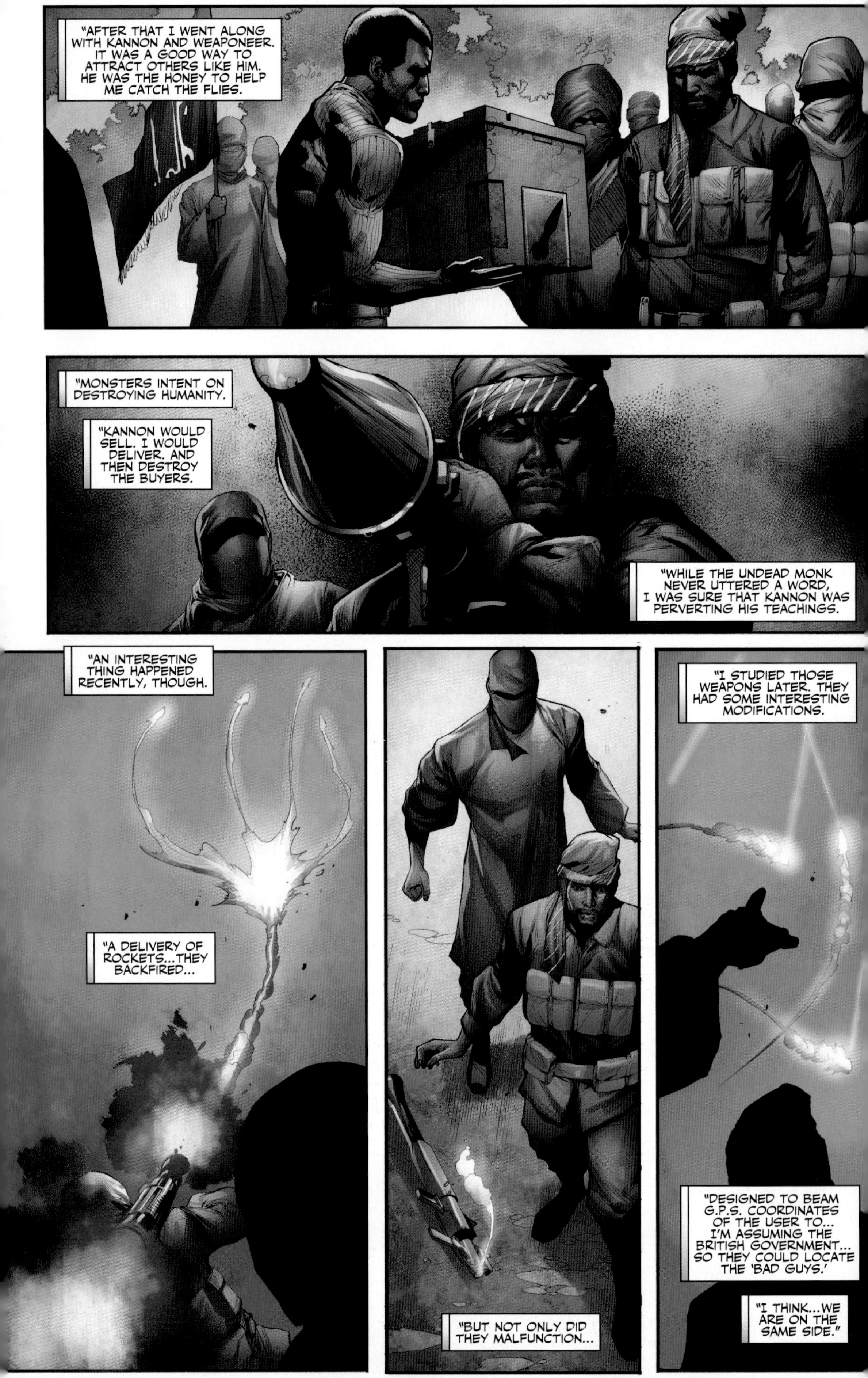
"AFTER THAT I WENT ALONG WITH KANNON AND WEAPONEER. IT WAS A GOOD WAY TO ATTRACT OTHERS LIKE HIM. HE WAS THE HONEY TO HELP ME CATCH THE FLIES.
"MONSTERS INTENT ON DESTROYING HUMANITY.
"KANNON WOULD SELL. I WOULD DELIVER. AND THEN DESTROY THE BUYERS.
"WHILE THE UNDEAD MONK NEVER UTTERED A WORD, I WAS SURE THAT KANNON WAS PERVERTING HIS TEACHINGS.
"AN INTERESTING THING HAPPENED RECENTLY, THOUGH.
"A DELIVERY OF ROCKETS...THEY BACKFIRED...
"BUT NOT ONLY DID THEY MALFUNCTION...
"I STUDIED THOSE WEAPONS LATER. THEY HAD SOME INTERESTING MODIFICATIONS.
"DESIGNED TO BEAM G.P.S. COORDINATES OF THE USER TO... I'M ASSUMING THE BRITISH GOVERNMENT... SO THEY COULD LOCATE THE 'BAD GUYS.'
"I THINK...WE ARE ON THE SAME SIDE."

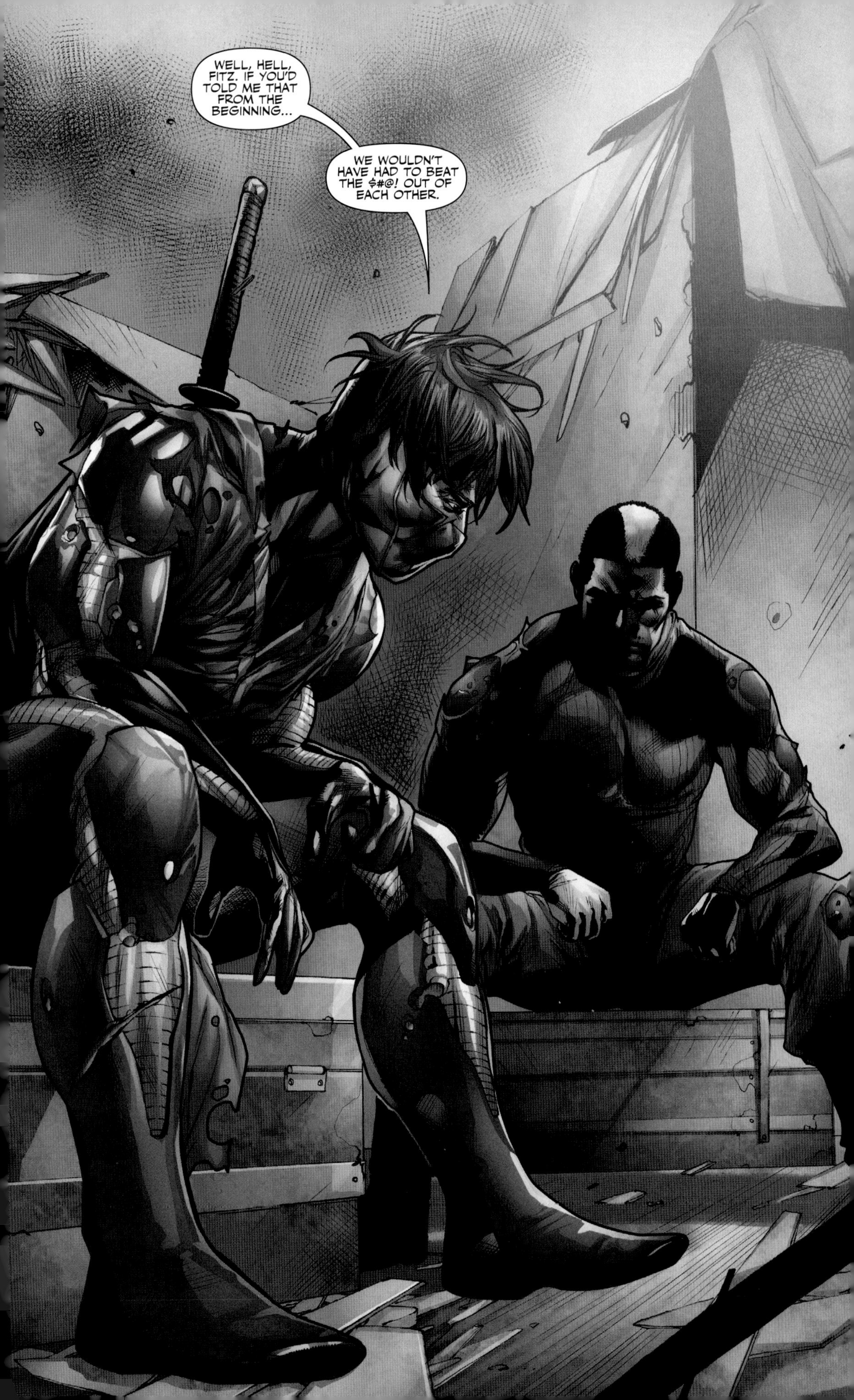

WELL, HELL, FITZ. IF YOU'D TOLD ME THAT FROM THE BEGINNING...
WE WOULDN'T HAVE HAD TO BEAT THE $#@! OUT OF EACH OTHER.

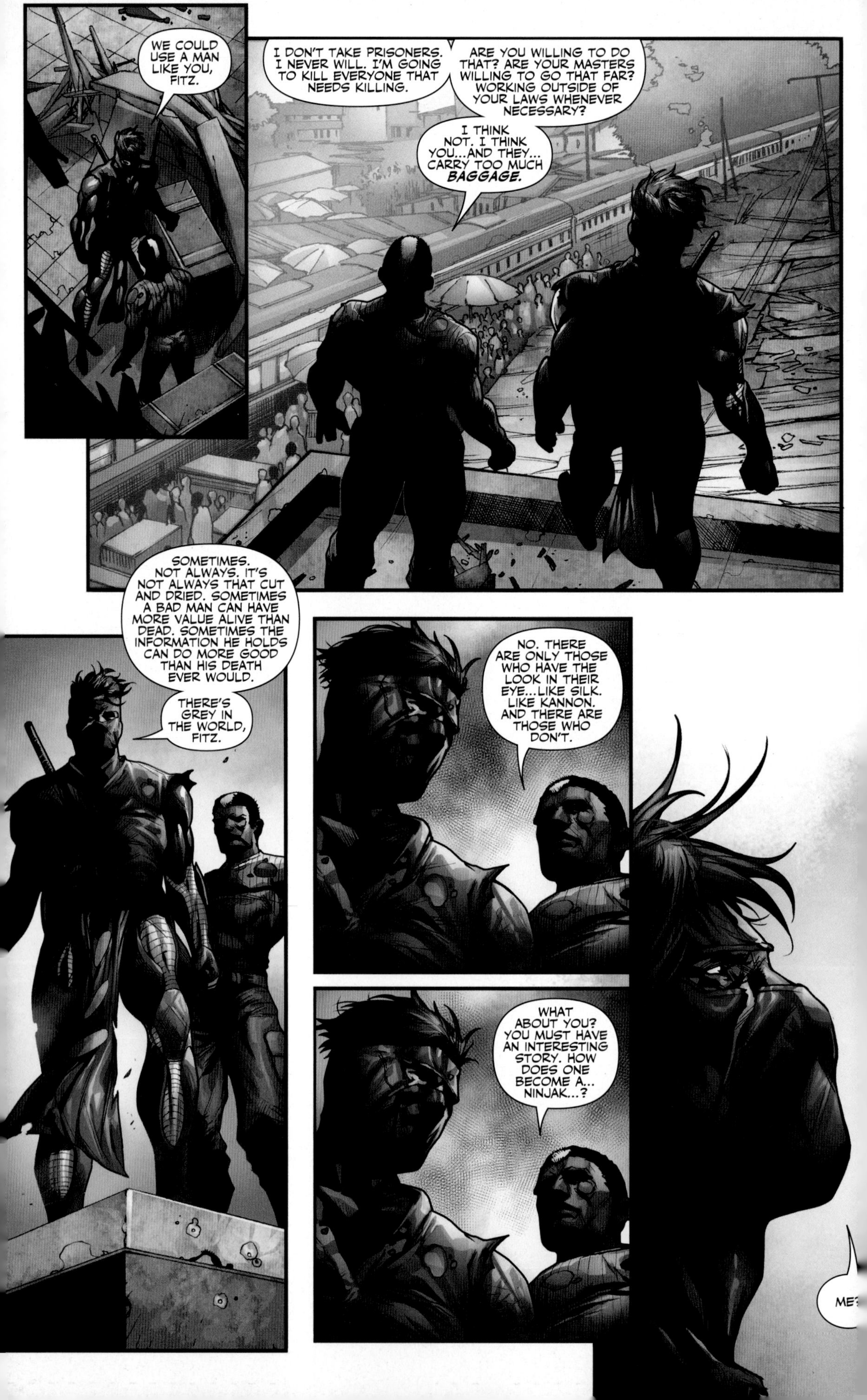
WE COULD USE A MAN LIKE YOU, FITZ.
I DON'T TAKE PRISONERS. I NEVER WILL. I'M GOING TO KILL EVERYONE THAT NEEDS KILLING.
ARE YOU WILLING TO DO THAT? ARE YOUR MASTERS WILLING TO GO THAT FAR? WORKING OUTSIDE OF YOUR LAWS WHENEVER NECESSARY?
I THINK NOT. I THINK YOU...AND THEY... CARRY TOO MUCH ***BAGGAGE.***
SOMETIMES. NOT ALWAYS. IT'S NOT ALWAYS THAT CUT AND DRIED. SOMETIMES A BAD MAN CAN HAVE MORE VALUE ALIVE THAN DEAD. SOMETIMES THE INFORMATION HE HOLDS CAN DO MORE GOOD THAN HIS DEATH EVER WOULD.
THERE'S GREY IN THE WORLD, FITZ.
NO. THERE ARE ONLY THOSE WHO HAVE THE LOOK IN THEIR EYE...LIKE SILK. LIKE KANNON. AND THERE ARE THOSE WHO DON'T.
WHAT ABOUT YOU? YOU MUST HAVE AN INTERESTING STORY. HOW DOES ONE BECOME A... NINJAK...?
ME?

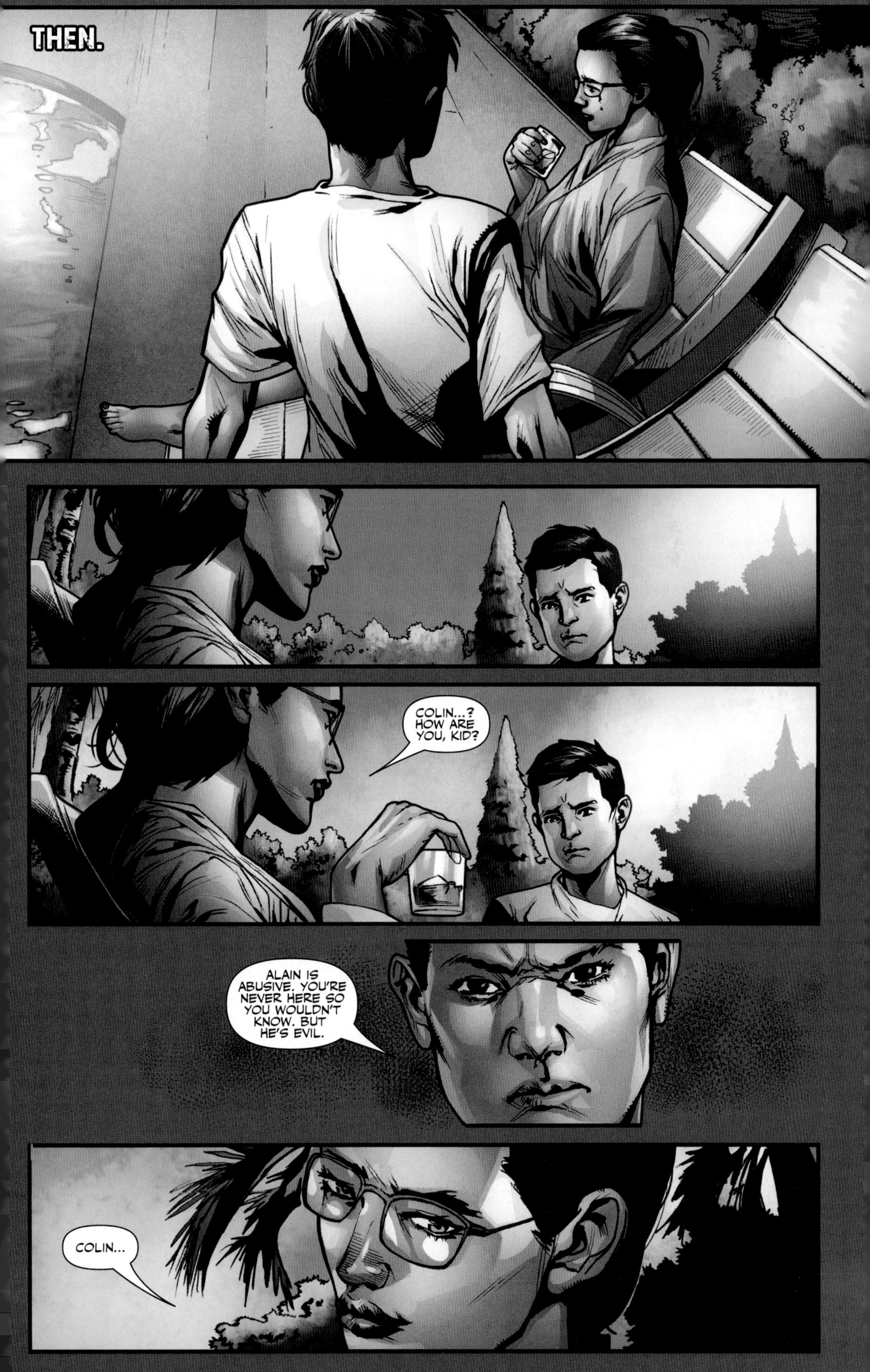
THEN.
COLIN...? HOW ARE YOU, KID?
ALAIN IS ABUSIVE. YOU'RE NEVER HERE SO YOU WOULDN'T KNOW. BUT HE'S EVIL.
COLIN...

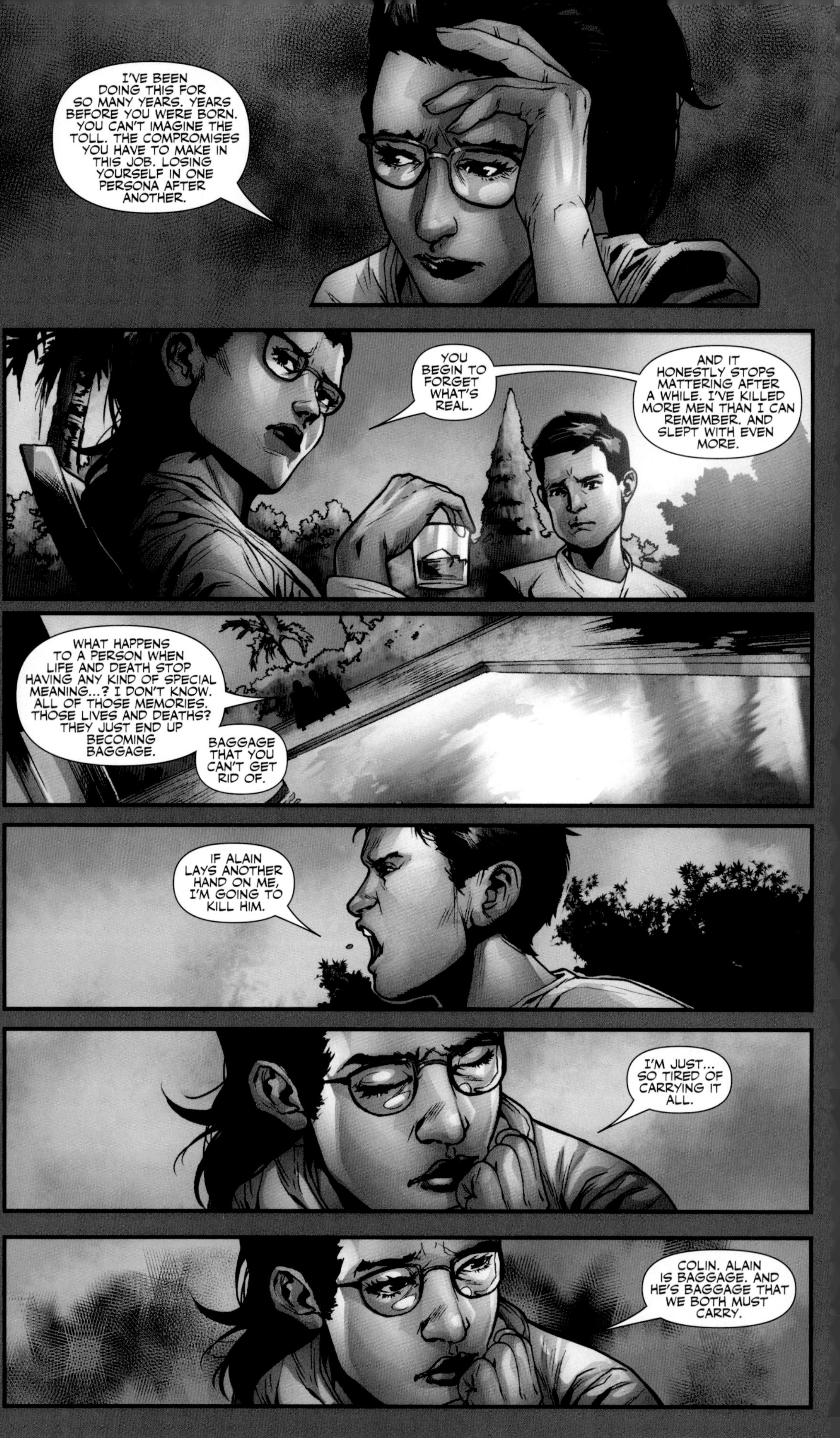
I'VE BEEN DOING THIS FOR SO MANY YEARS. YEARS BEFORE YOU WERE BORN. YOU CAN'T IMAGINE THE TOLL. THE COMPROMISES YOU HAVE TO MAKE IN THIS JOB. LOSING YOURSELF IN ONE PERSONA AFTER ANOTHER.
YOU BEGIN TO FORGET WHAT'S REAL.
AND IT HONESTLY STOPS MATTERING AFTER A WHILE. I'VE KILLED MORE MEN THAN I CAN REMEMBER. AND SLEPT WITH EVEN MORE.
WHAT HAPPENS TO A PERSON WHEN LIFE AND DEATH STOP HAVING ANY KIND OF SPECIAL MEANING...? I DON'T KNOW. ALL OF THOSE MEMORIES. THOSE LIVES AND DEATHS? THEY JUST END UP BECOMING BAGGAGE.
BAGGAGE THAT YOU CAN'T GET RID OF.
IF ALAIN LAYS ANOTHER HAND ON ME, I'M GOING TO KILL HIM.
I'M JUST... SO TIRED OF CARRYING IT ALL.
COLIN. ALAIN IS BAGGAGE. AND HE'S BAGGAGE THAT WE BOTH MUST CARRY.

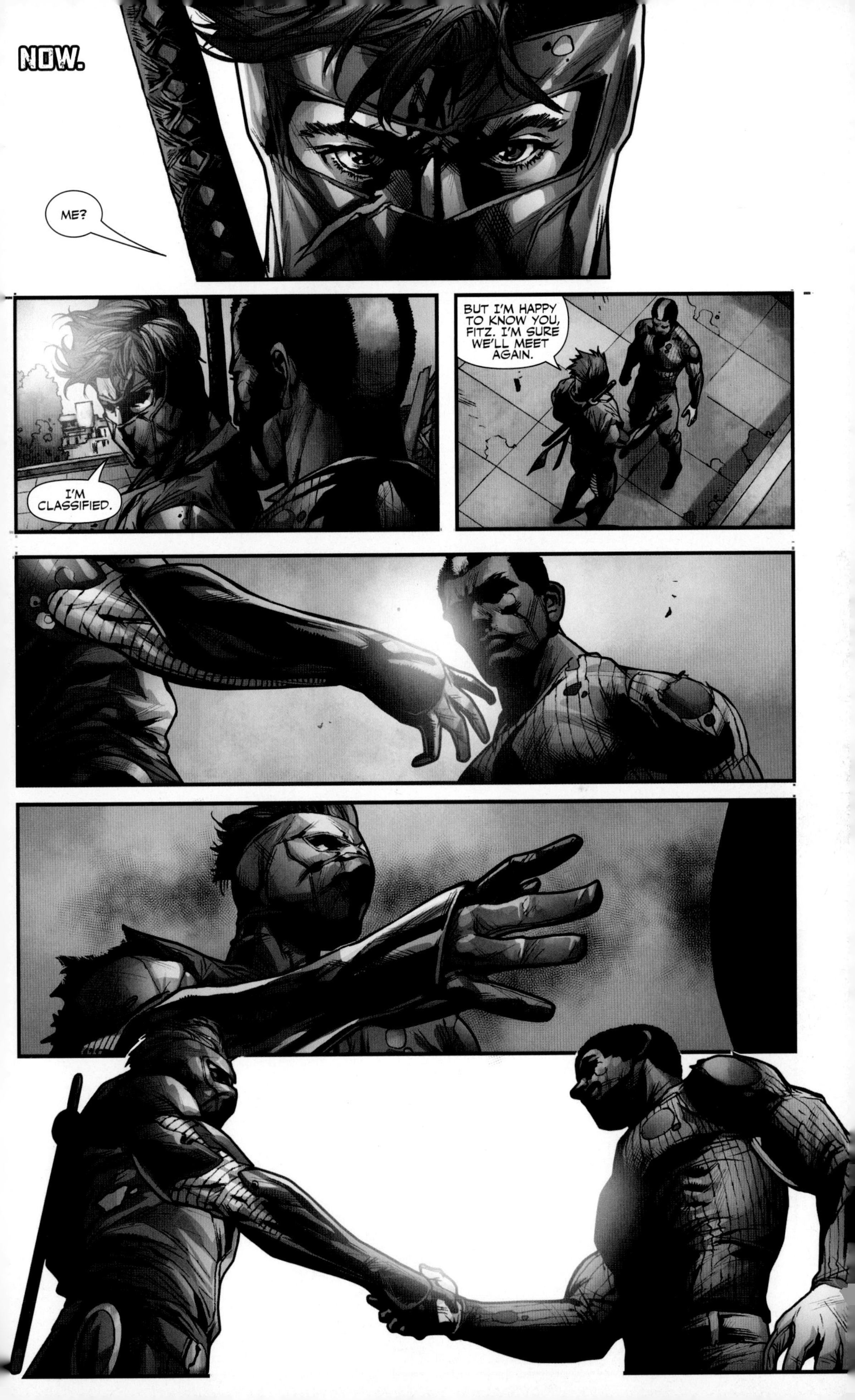
NOW.
ME?
I'M CLASSIFIED.
BUT I'M HAPPY TO KNOW YOU, FITZ. I'M SURE WE'LL MEET AGAIN.

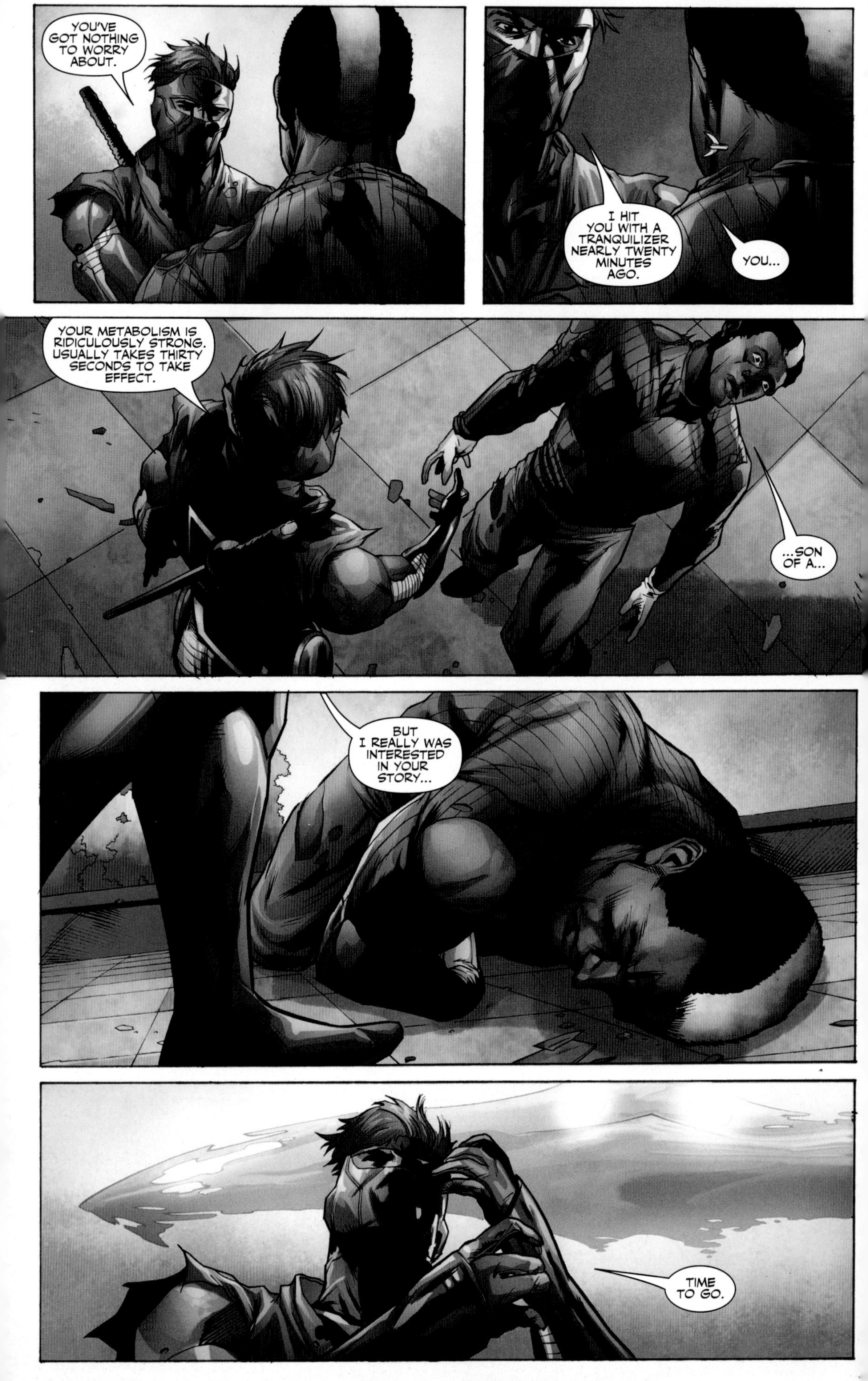
YOU'VE GOT NOTHING TO WORRY ABOUT.
I HIT YOU WITH A TRANQUILIZER NEARLY TWENTY MINUTES AGO.
YOU...
YOUR METABOLISM IS RIDICULOUSLY STRONG. USUALLY TAKES THIRTY SECONDS TO TAKE EFFECT.
...SON OF A...
BUT I REALLY WAS INTERESTED IN YOUR STORY...
TIME TO GO.

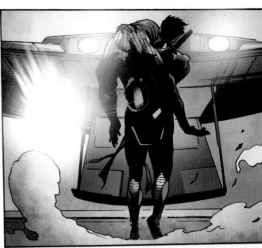

I APPRECIATE
YOU NOT KILLING
HIM, NINJAK.

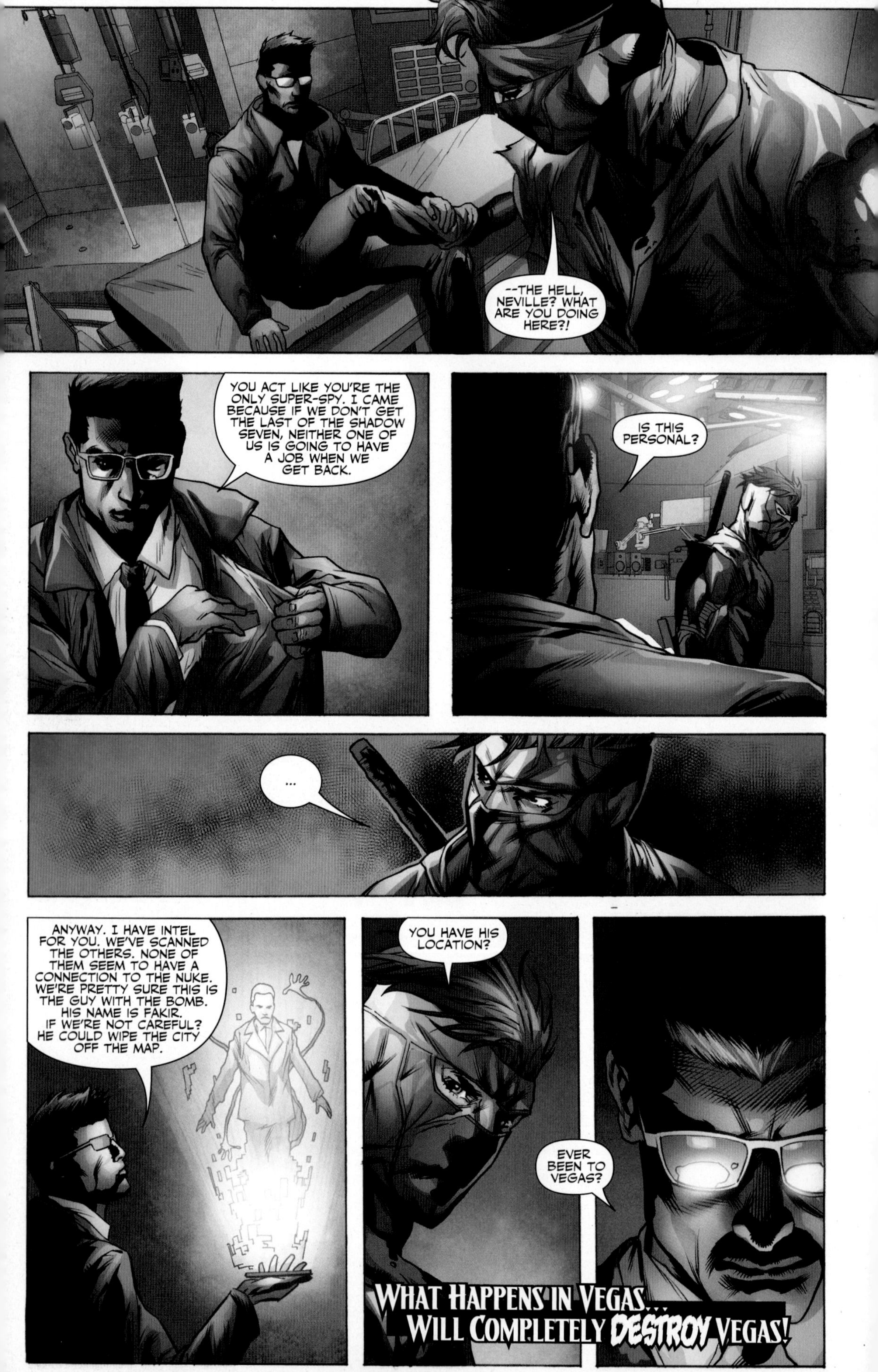
--THE HELL, NEVILLE? WHAT ARE YOU DOING HERE?!
YOU ACT LIKE YOU'RE THE ONLY SUPER-SPY. I CAME BECAUSE IF WE DON'T GET THE LAST OF THE SHADOW SEVEN, NEITHER ONE OF US IS GOING TO HAVE A JOB WHEN WE GET BACK.
IS THIS PERSONAL?
...
ANYWAY. I HAVE INTEL FOR YOU. WE'VE SCANNED THE OTHERS. NONE OF THEM SEEM TO HAVE A CONNECTION TO THE NUKE. WE'RE PRETTY SURE THIS IS THE GUY WITH THE BOMB. HIS NAME IS FAKIR. IF WE'RE NOT CAREFUL? HE COULD WIPE THE CITY OFF THE MAP.
YOU HAVE HIS LOCATION?
EVER BEEN TO VEGAS?
WHAT HAPPENS IN VEGAS... WILL COMPLETELY DESTROY VEGAS!

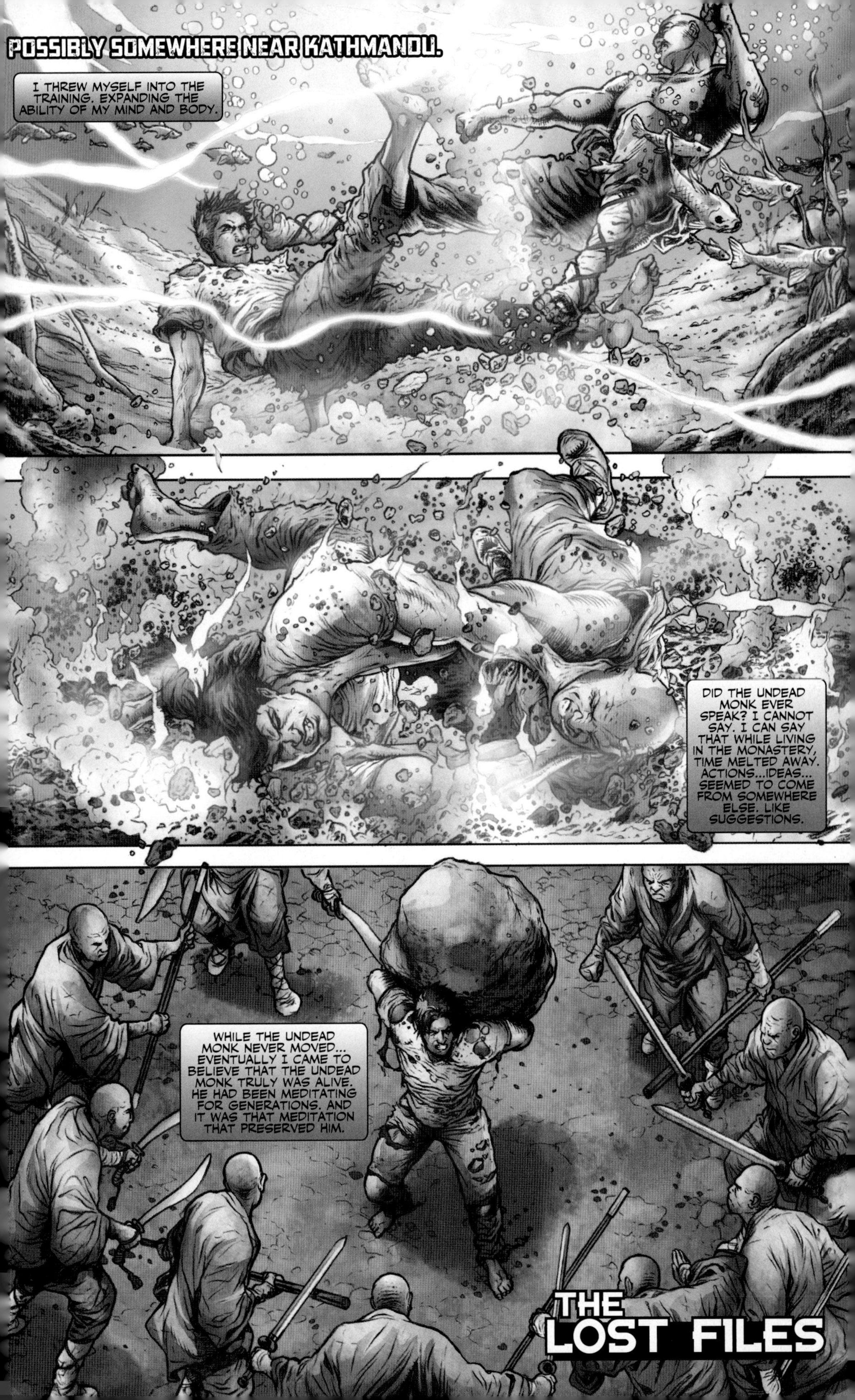
POSSIBLY SOMEWHERE NEAR KATHMANDU.
I THREW MYSELF INTO THE TRAINING. EXPANDING THE ABILITY OF MY MIND AND BODY.
DID THE UNDEAD MONK EVER SPEAK? I CANNOT SAY. I CAN SAY THAT WHILE LIVING IN THE MONASTERY, TIME MELTED AWAY. ACTIONS...IDEAS... SEEMED TO COME FROM SOMEWHERE ELSE. LIKE SUGGESTIONS.
WHILE THE UNDEAD MONK NEVER MOVED... EVENTUALLY I CAME TO BELIEVE THAT THE UNDEAD MONK TRULY WAS ALIVE. HE HAD BEEN MEDITATING FOR GENERATIONS. AND IT WAS THAT MEDITATION THAT PRESERVED HIM.
THE LOST FILES

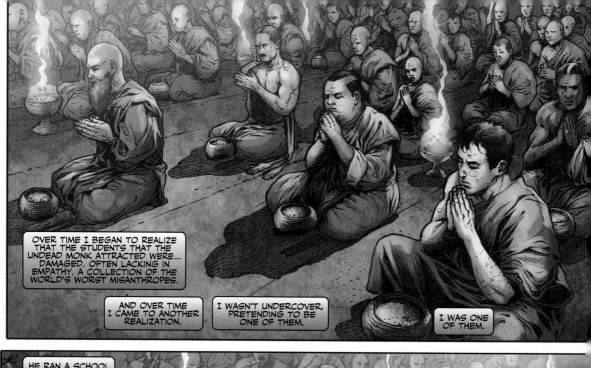

OVER TIME I BEGAN TO REALIZE THAT THE STUDENTS THAT THE UNDEAD MONK ATTRACTED WERE... DAMAGED. OFTEN LACKING IN EMPATHY. A COLLECTION OF THE WORLD'S WORST MISANTHROPES.

AND OVER TIME I CAME TO ANOTHER REALIZATION.

I WASN'T UNDERCOVER, PRETENDING TO BE ONE OF THEM.

I WAS ONE OF THEM.

HE RAN A SCHOOL BUT NEVER SPOKE A WORD.

HE TAUGHT US THE LIMITS OF OUR MINDS AND BODIES WITHOUT LIFTING EVEN A FINGER.

OUR FOOD WAS POISONED REGULARLY. WE HAD TO LEARN HOW TO ABSORB THE POISON. PROCESS THE POISON...

...OR NOT.

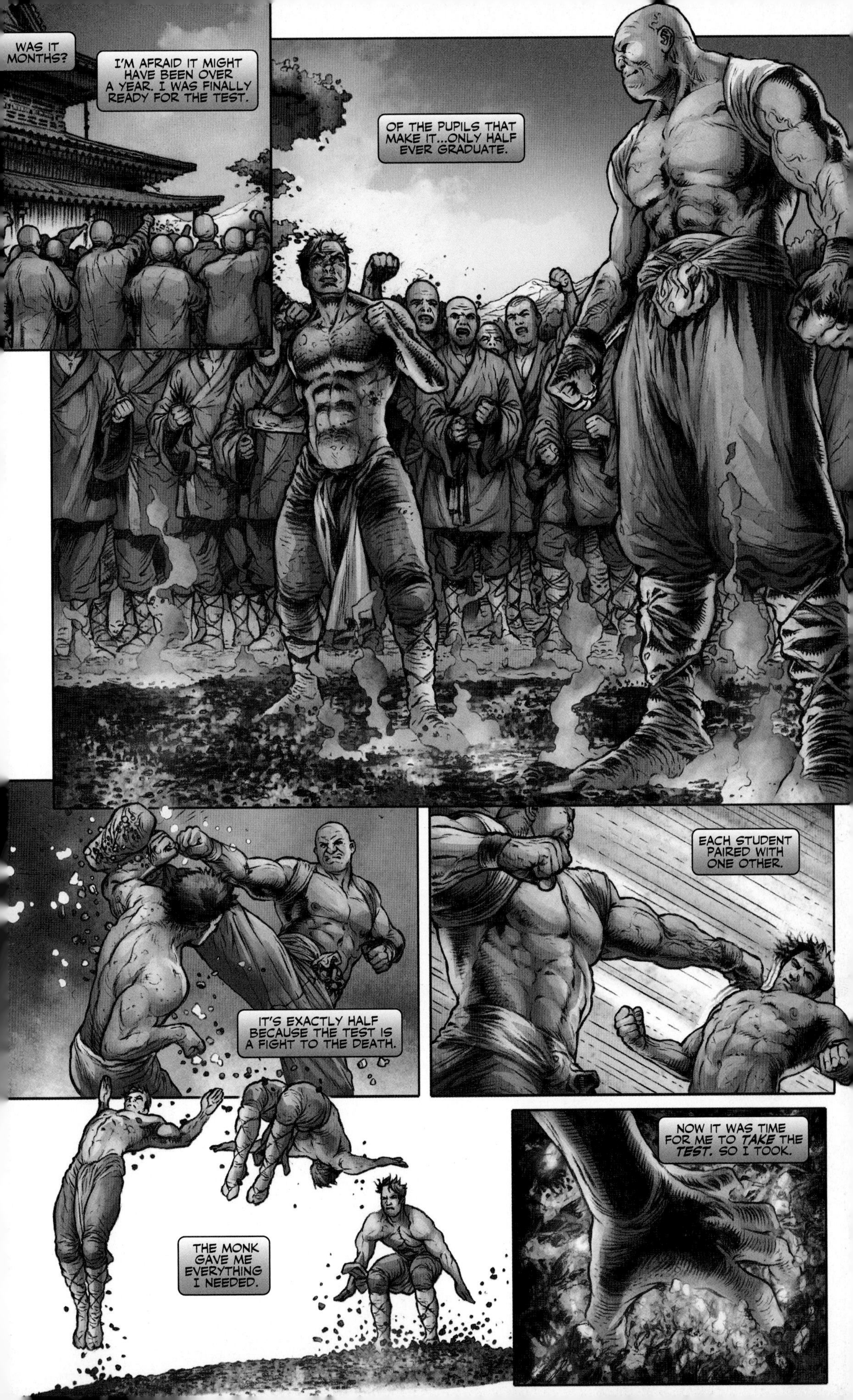
WAS IT MONTHS?
I'M AFRAID IT MIGHT HAVE BEEN OVER A YEAR. I WAS FINALLY READY FOR THE TEST.
OF THE PUPILS THAT MAKE IT...ONLY HALF EVER GRADUATE.
IT'S EXACTLY HALF BECAUSE THE TEST IS A FIGHT TO THE DEATH.
EACH STUDENT PAIRED WITH ONE OTHER.
THE MONK GAVE ME EVERYTHING I NEEDED.
NOW IT WAS TIME FOR ME TO *TAKE* THE *TEST.* SO I TOOK.

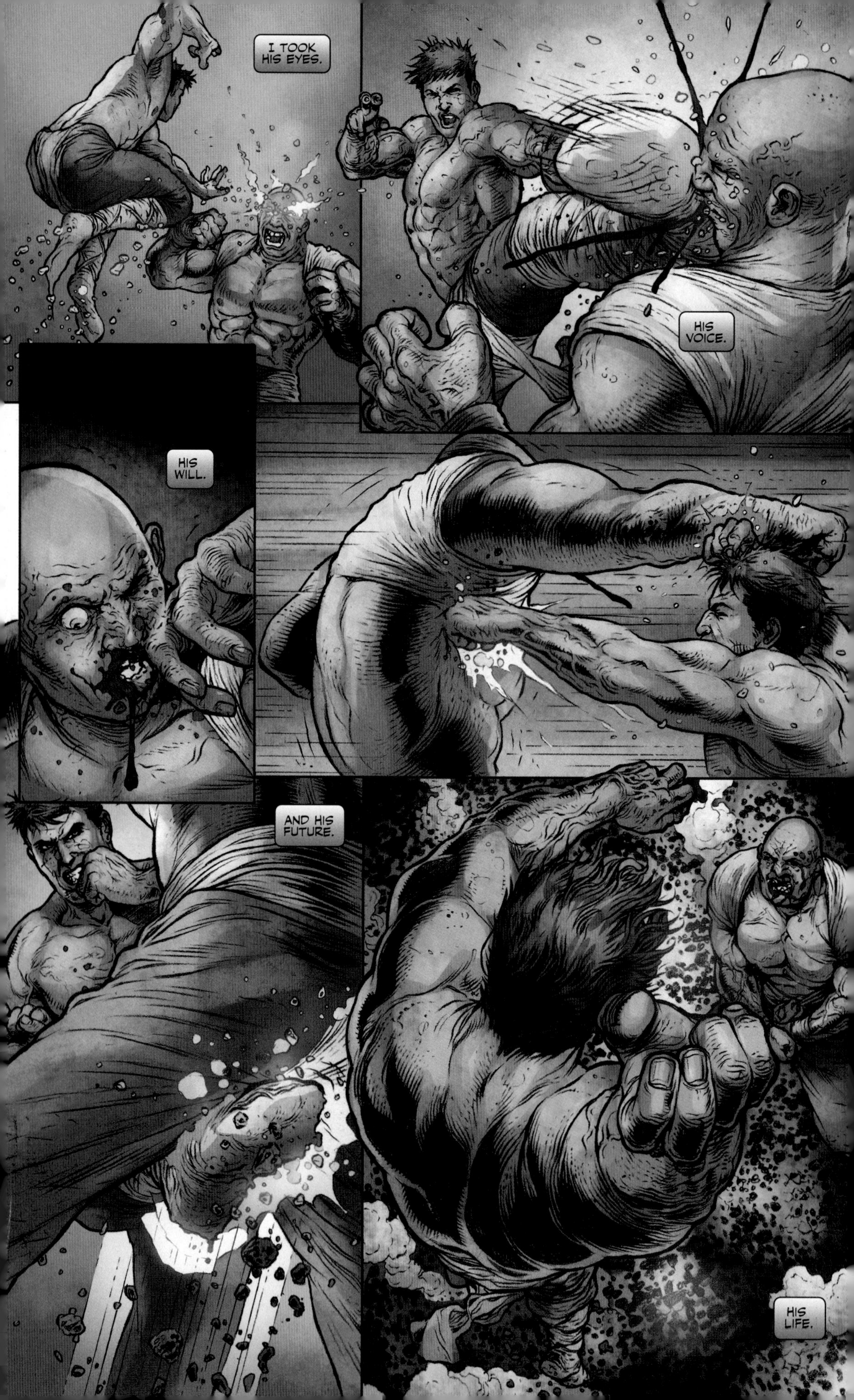
I TOOK HIS EYES.
HIS VOICE.
HIS WILL.
AND HIS FUTURE.
HIS LIFE.

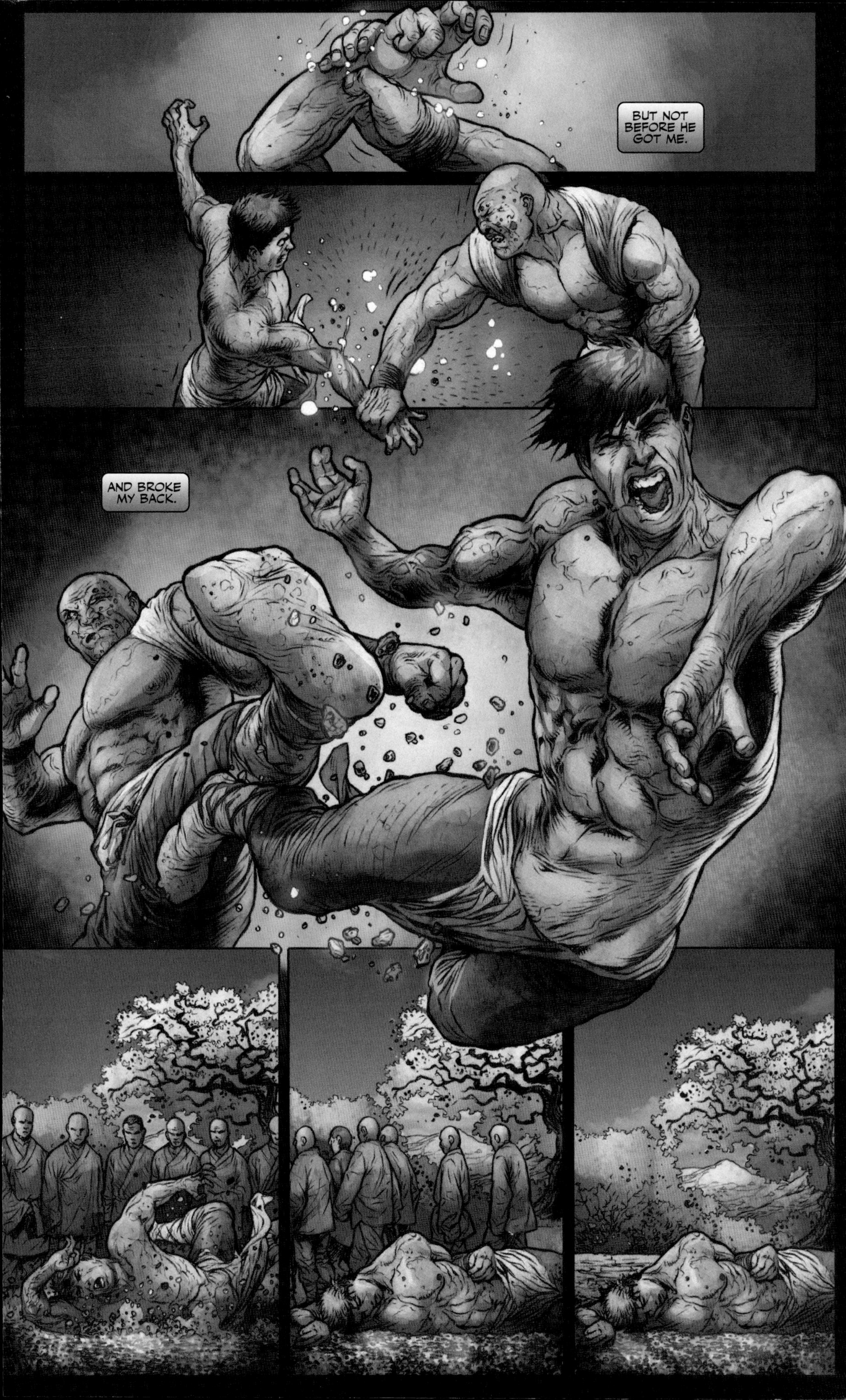
BUT NOT BEFORE HE GOT ME.
AND BROKE MY BACK.

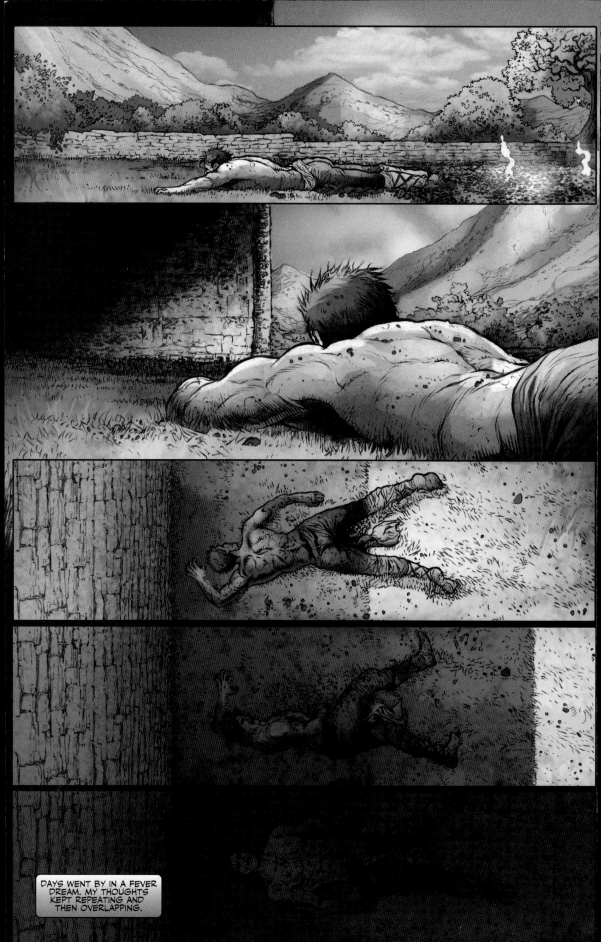

DAYS WENT BY IN A FEVER
DREAM. MY THOUGHTS
KEPT REPEATING AND
THEN OVERLAPPING.

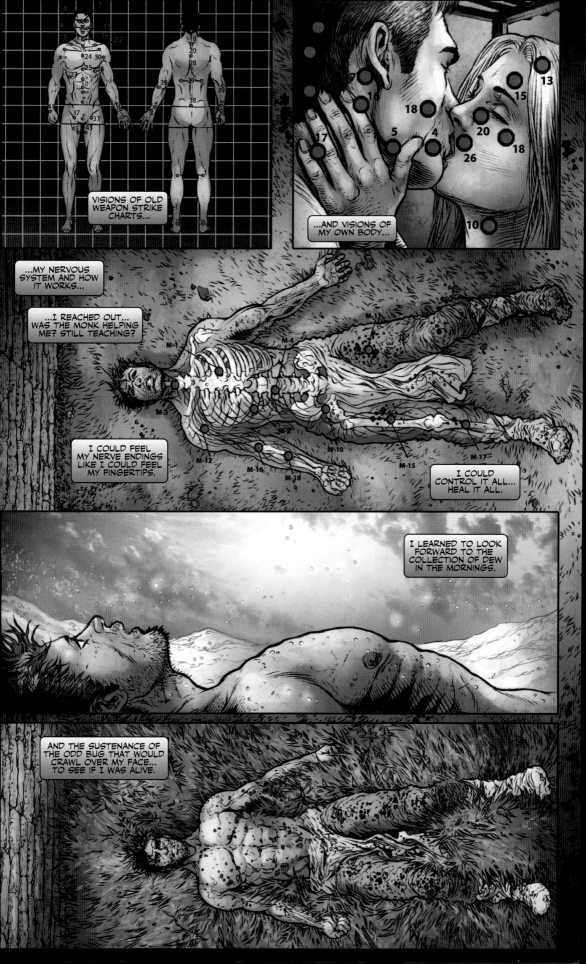

VISIONS OF OLD
WEAPON STRIKE
CHARTS...

...AND VISIONS OF
MY OWN BODY...

...MY NERVOUS
SYSTEM AND HOW
IT WORKS...

...I REACHED OUT...
WAS THE MONK HELPING
ME? STILL TEACHING?

I COULD FEEL
MY NERVE ENDINGS
LIKE I COULD FEEL
MY FINGERTIPS.

I COULD
CONTROL IT ALL...
HEAL IT ALL.

I LEARNED TO LOOK
FORWARD TO THE
COLLECTION OF DEW
IN THE MORNINGS.

AND THE SUSTENANCE OF
THE ODD BUG THAT WOULD
CRAWL OVER MY FACE...
TO SEE IF I WAS ALIVE.

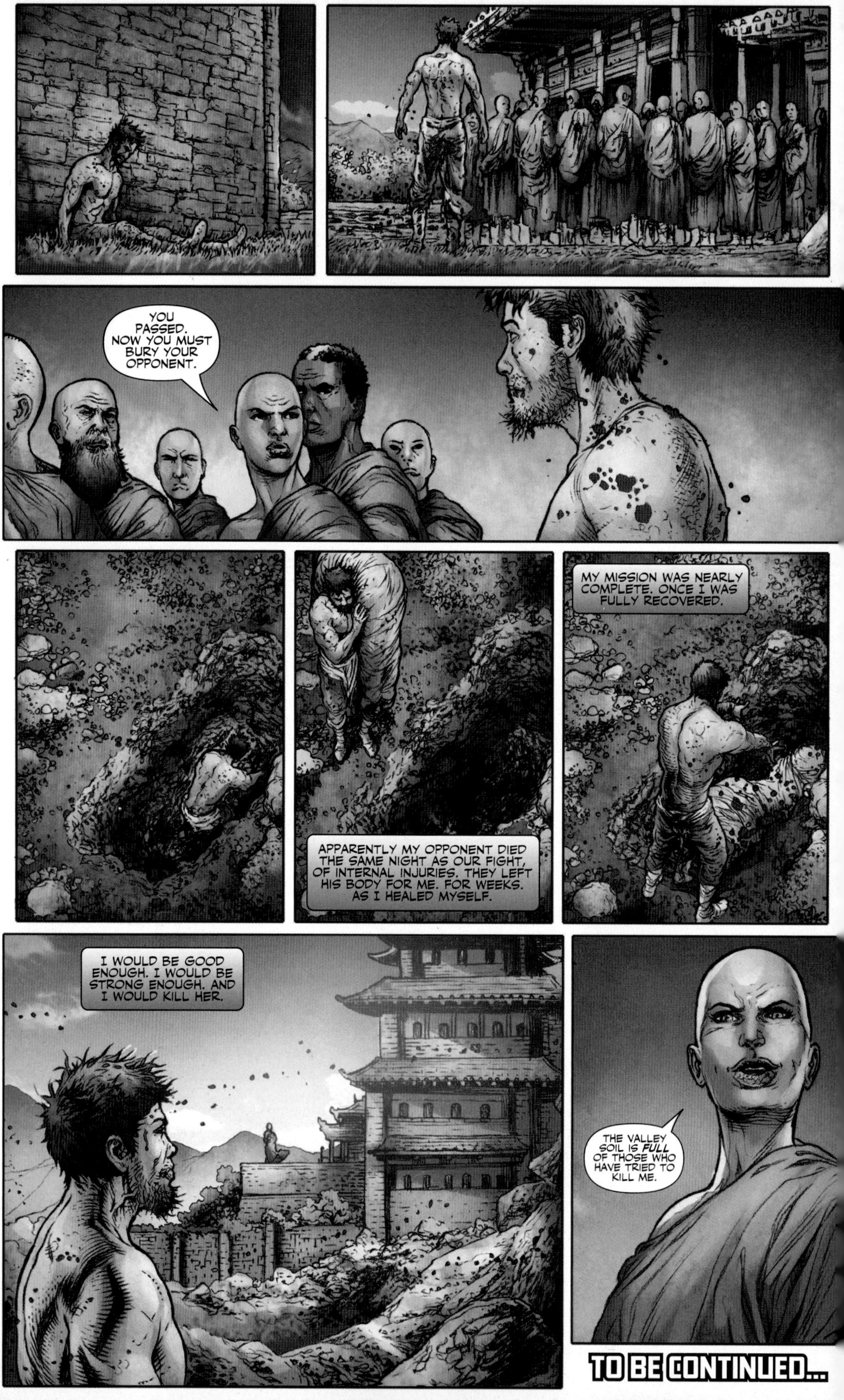
YOU PASSED. NOW YOU MUST BURY YOUR OPPONENT.
APPARENTLY MY OPPONENT DIED THE SAME NIGHT AS OUR FIGHT, OF INTERNAL INJURIES. THEY LEFT HIS BODY FOR ME. FOR WEEKS. AS I HEALED MYSELF.
MY MISSION WAS NEARLY COMPLETE. ONCE I WAS FULLY RECOVERED.
I WOULD BE GOOD ENOUGH. I WOULD BE STRONG ENOUGH. AND I WOULD KILL HER.
THE VALLEY SOIL IS FULL OF THOSE WHO HAVE TRIED TO KILL ME.
TO BE CONTINUED...

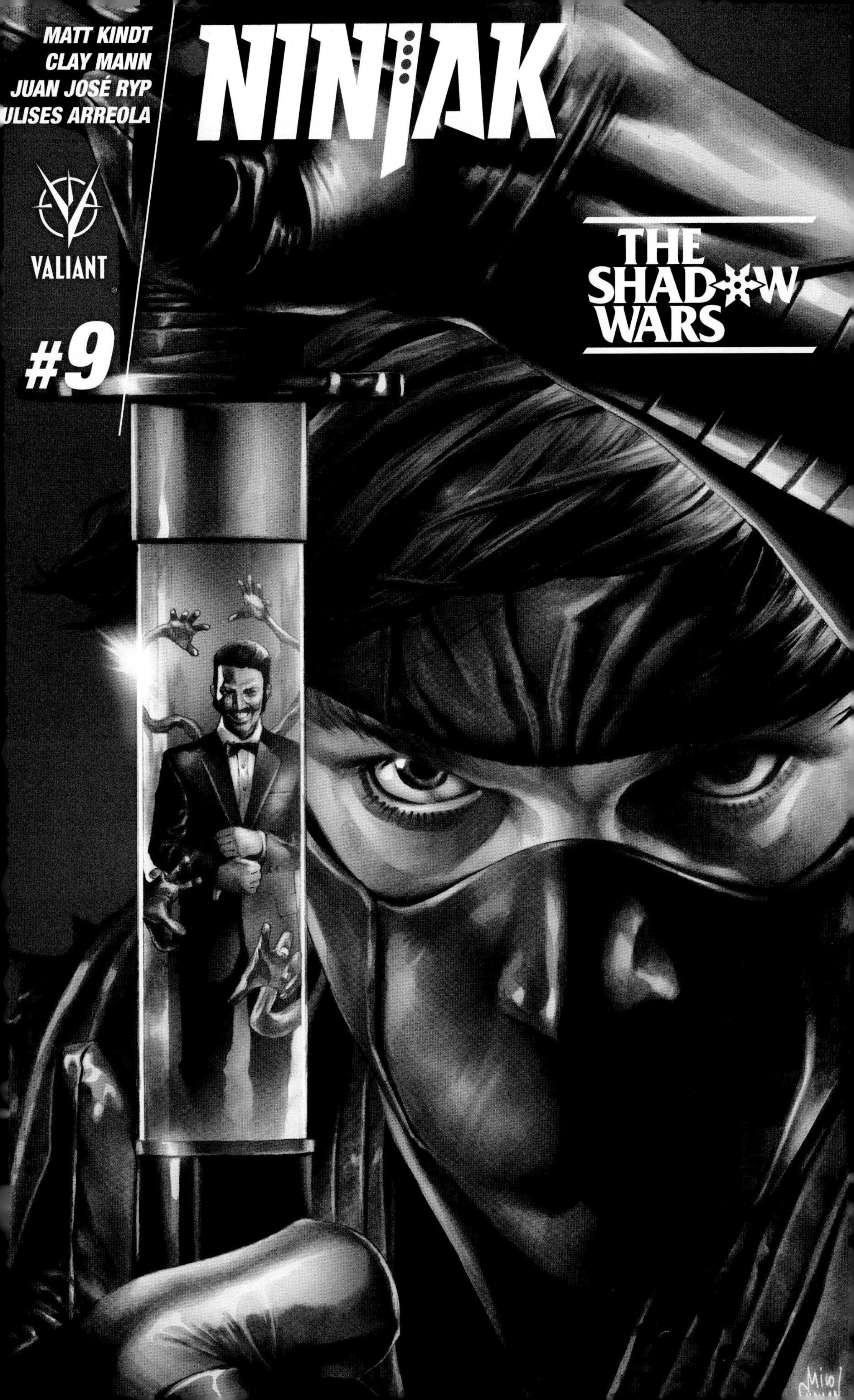
MATT KINDT
CLAY MANN
JUAN JOSÉ RYP
ULISES ARREOLA
NINJAK
VALIANT
#9
THE SHADOW WARS

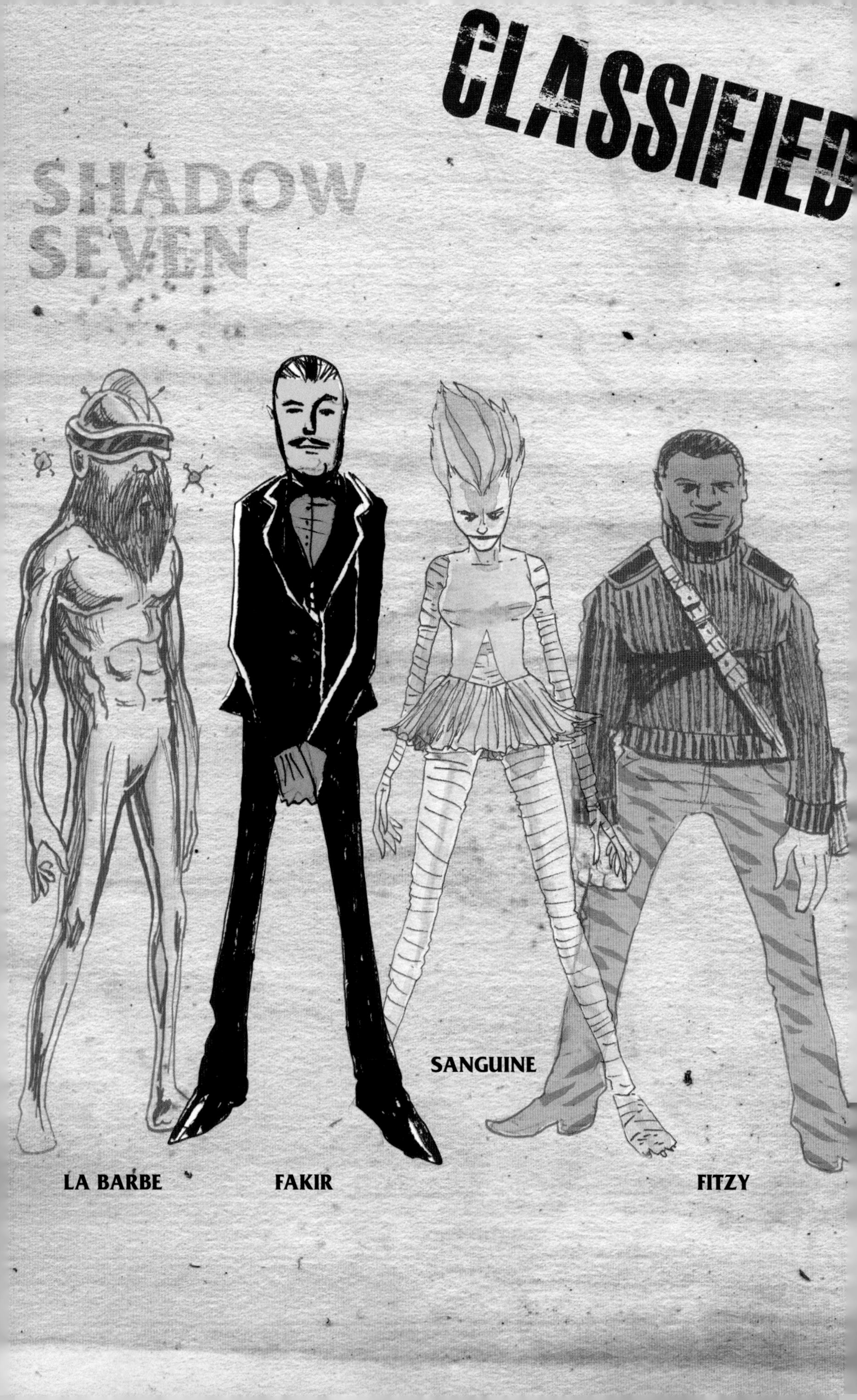
CLASSIFIED
SHADOW SEVEN
LA BARBE
FAKIR
SANGUINE
FITZY

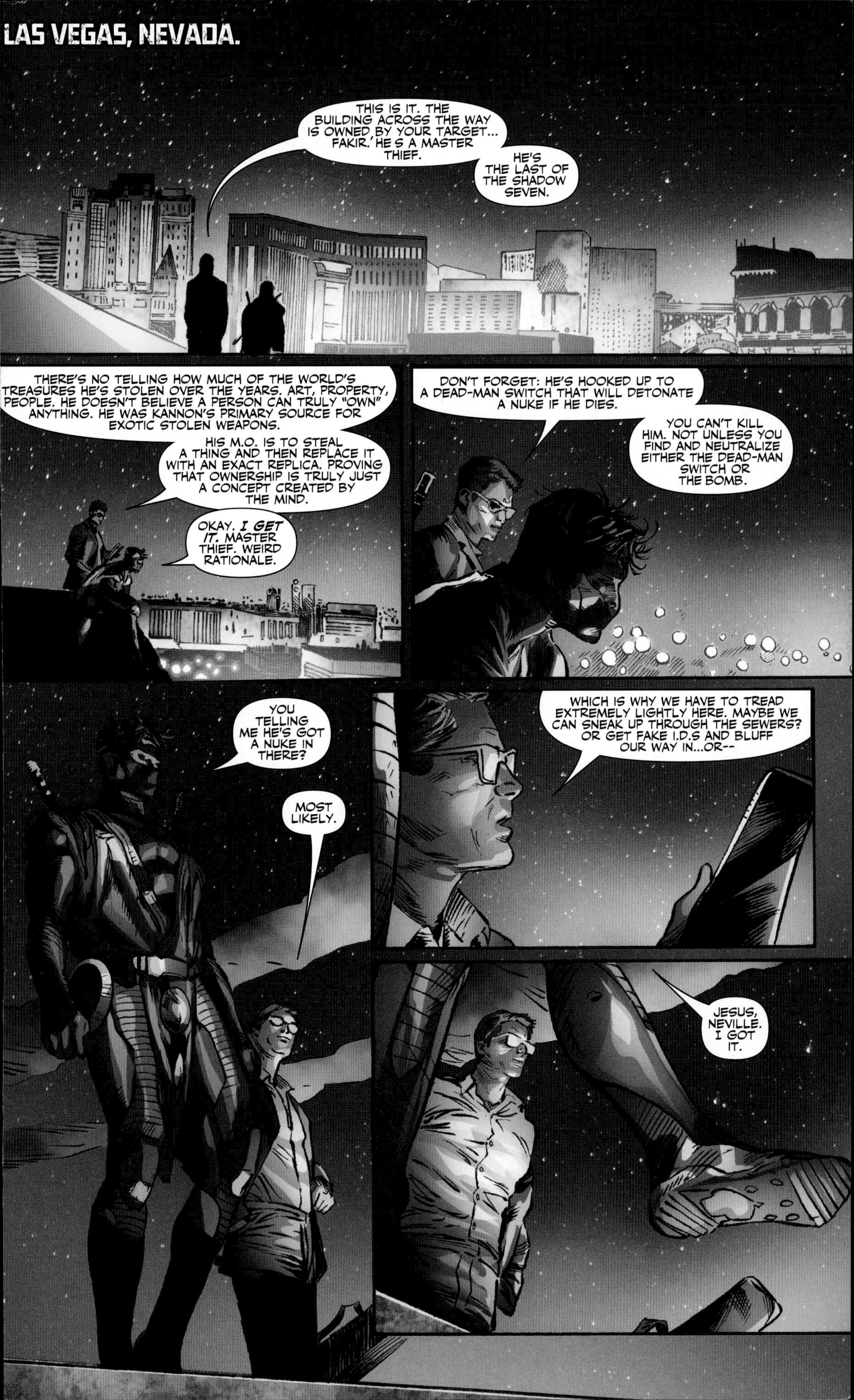
LAS VEGAS, NEVADA.
THIS IS IT. THE BUILDING ACROSS THE WAY IS OWNED BY YOUR TARGET... FAKIR. HE'S A MASTER THIEF.
HE'S THE LAST OF THE SHADOW SEVEN.
THERE'S NO TELLING HOW MUCH OF THE WORLD'S TREASURES HE'S STOLEN OVER THE YEARS. ART, PROPERTY, PEOPLE. HE DOESN'T BELIEVE A PERSON CAN TRULY "OWN" ANYTHING. HE WAS KANNON'S PRIMARY SOURCE FOR EXOTIC STOLEN WEAPONS.
HIS M.O. IS TO STEAL A THING AND THEN REPLACE IT WITH AN EXACT REPLICA. PROVING THAT OWNERSHIP IS TRULY JUST A CONCEPT CREATED BY THE MIND.
OKAY. *I GET IT.* MASTER THIEF. WEIRD RATIONALE.
DON'T FORGET: HE'S HOOKED UP TO A DEAD-MAN SWITCH THAT WILL DETONATE A NUKE IF HE DIES.
YOU CAN'T KILL HIM. NOT UNLESS YOU FIND AND NEUTRALIZE EITHER THE DEAD-MAN SWITCH OR THE BOMB.
YOU TELLING ME HE'S GOT A NUKE IN THERE?
MOST LIKELY.
WHICH IS WHY WE HAVE TO TREAD EXTREMELY LIGHTLY HERE. MAYBE WE CAN SNEAK UP THROUGH THE SEWERS? OR GET FAKE I.D.S AND BLUFF OUR WAY IN...OR--
JESUS, NEVILLE. I GOT IT.

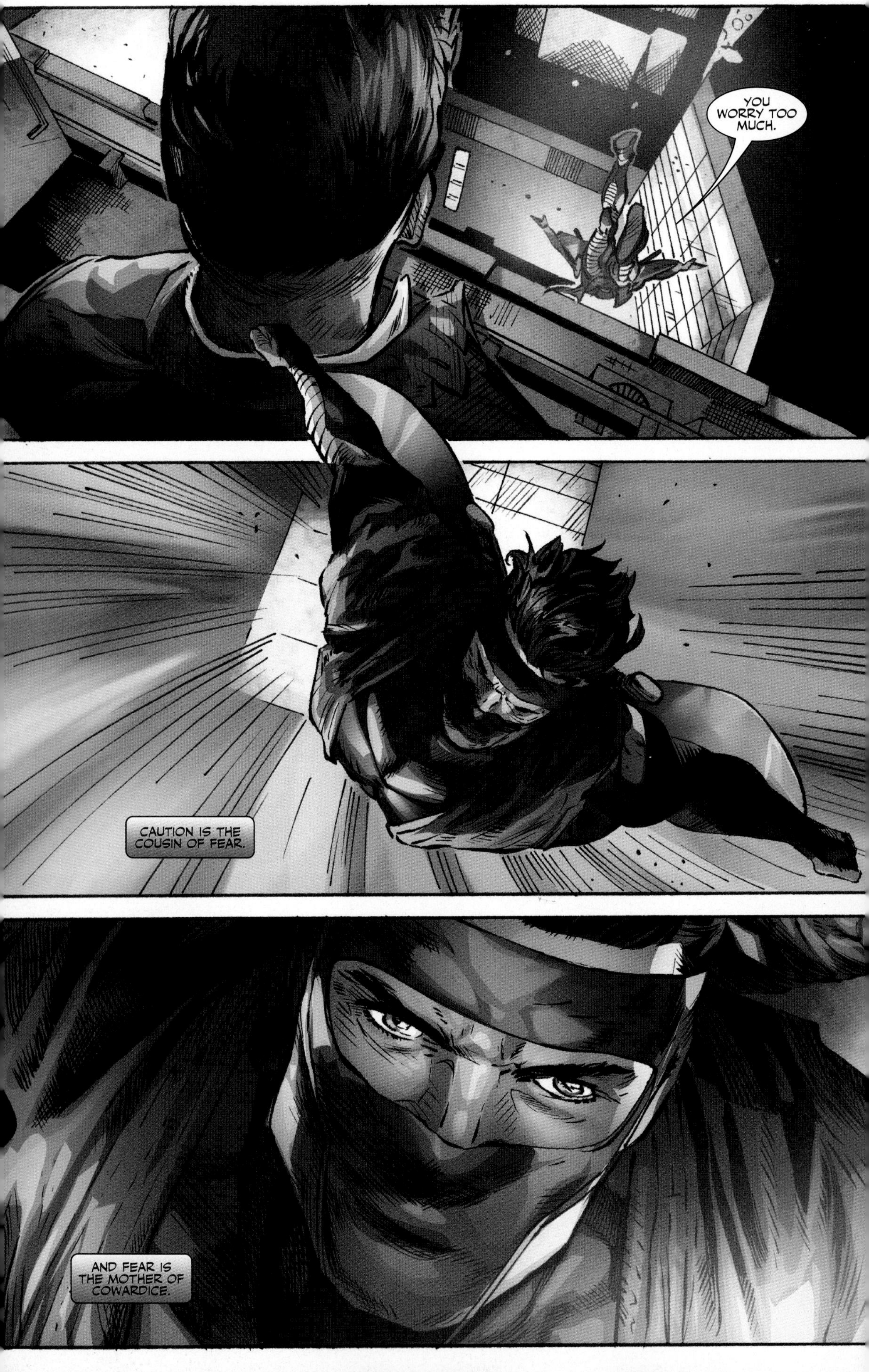
YOU WORRY TOO MUCH.
CAUTION IS THE COUSIN OF FEAR.
AND FEAR IS THE MOTHER OF COWARDICE.

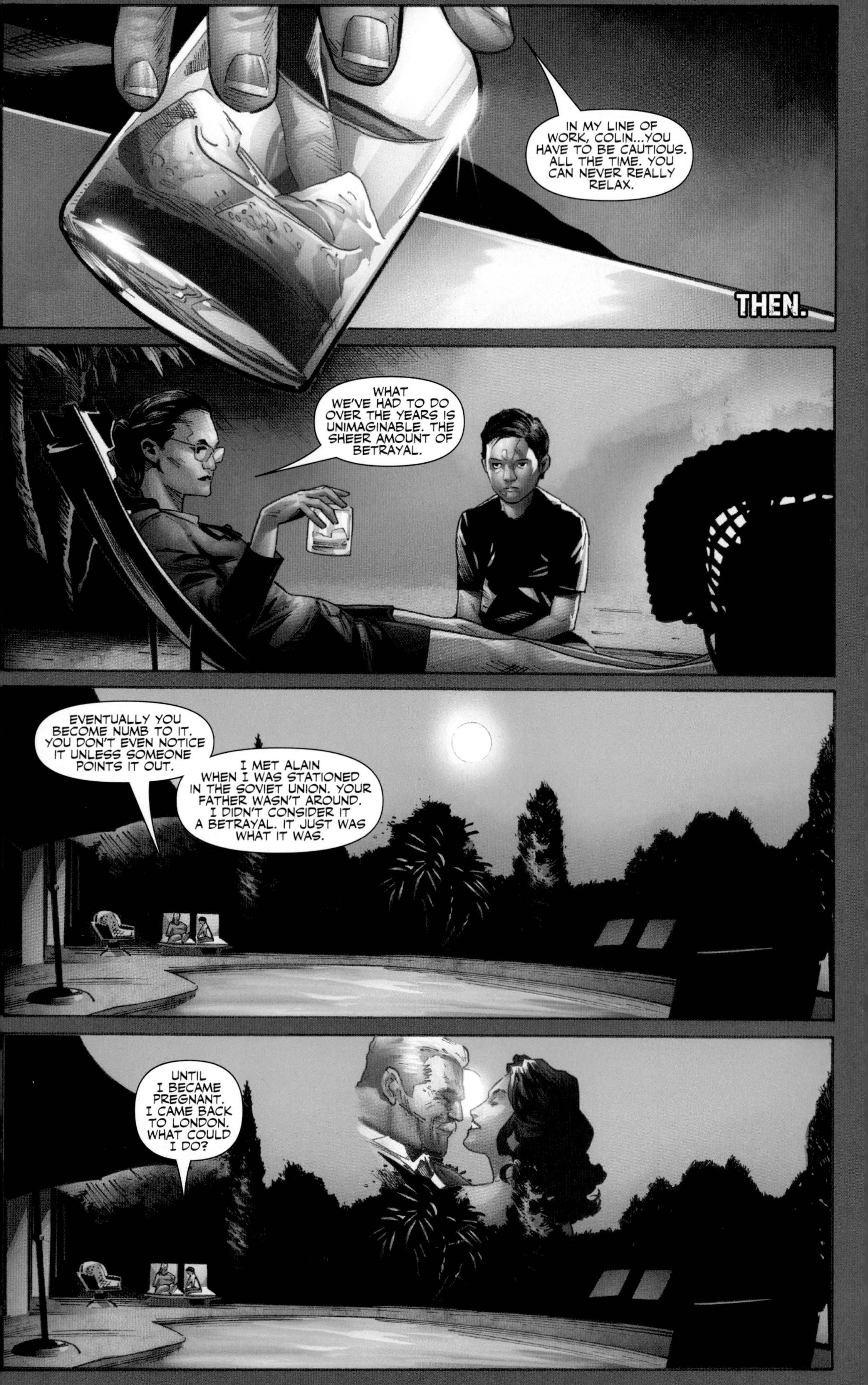
IN MY LINE OF WORK, COLIN...YOU HAVE TO BE CAUTIOUS. ALL THE TIME. YOU CAN NEVER REALLY RELAX.
THEN.
WHAT WE'VE HAD TO DO OVER THE YEARS IS UNIMAGINABLE. THE SHEER AMOUNT OF BETRAYAL.
EVENTUALLY YOU BECOME NUMB TO IT. YOU DON'T EVEN NOTICE IT UNLESS SOMEONE POINTS IT OUT.
I MET ALAIN WHEN I WAS STATIONED IN THE SOVIET UNION. YOUR FATHER WASN'T AROUND. I DIDN'T CONSIDER IT A BETRAYAL. IT JUST WAS WHAT IT WAS.
UNTIL I BECAME PREGNANT. I CAME BACK TO LONDON. WHAT COULD I DO?

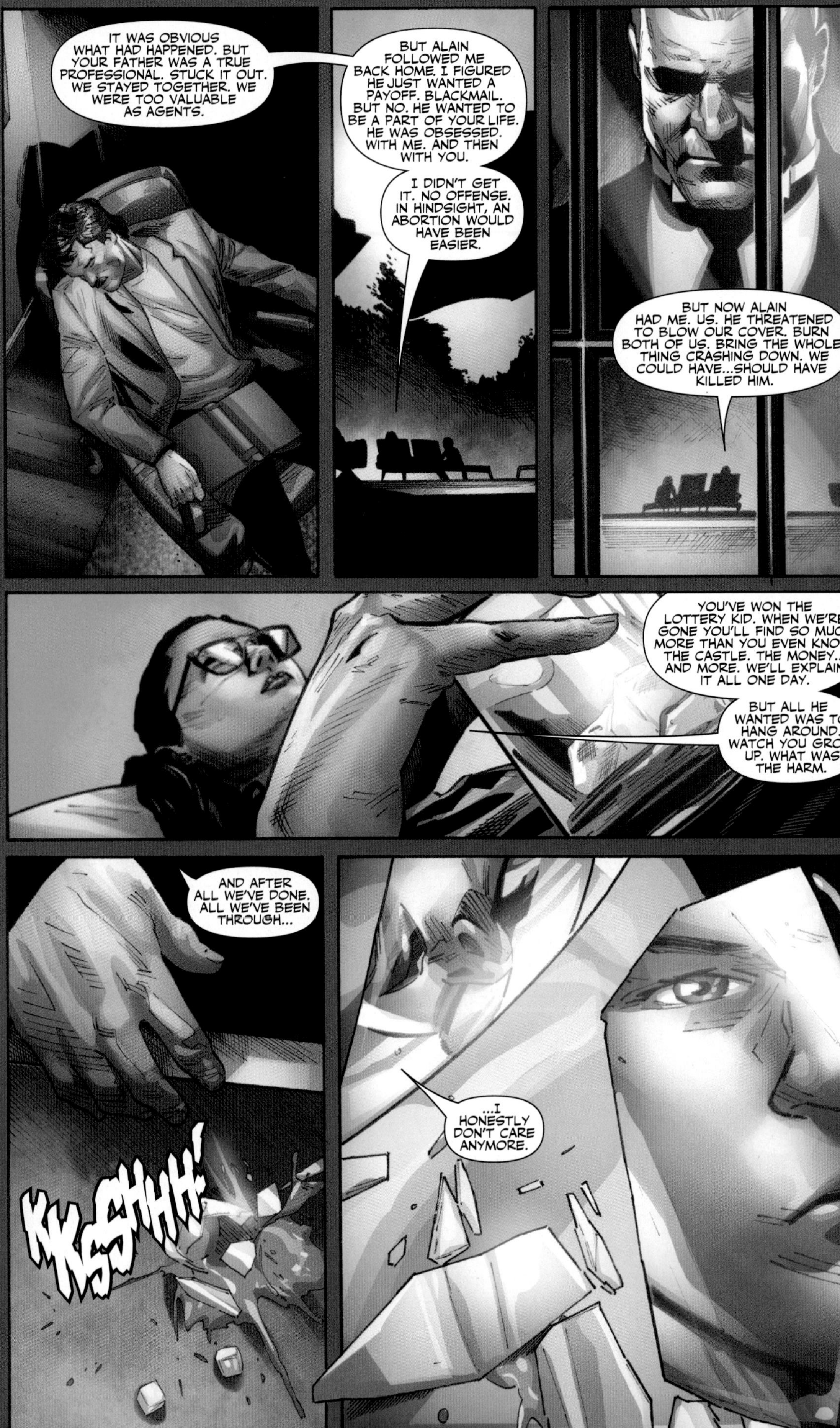
IT WAS OBVIOUS WHAT HAD HAPPENED. BUT YOUR FATHER WAS A TRUE PROFESSIONAL. STUCK IT OUT. WE STAYED TOGETHER. WE WERE TOO VALUABLE AS AGENTS.
BUT ALAIN FOLLOWED ME BACK HOME. I FIGURED HE JUST WANTED A PAYOFF. BLACKMAIL. BUT NO. HE WANTED TO BE A PART OF YOUR LIFE. HE WAS OBSESSED. WITH ME. AND THEN WITH YOU.
I DIDN'T GET IT. NO OFFENSE. IN HINDSIGHT, AN ABORTION WOULD HAVE BEEN EASIER.
BUT NOW ALAIN HAD ME. US. HE THREATENED TO BLOW OUR COVER. BURN BOTH OF US. BRING THE WHOLE THING CRASHING DOWN. WE COULD HAVE...SHOULD HAVE KILLED HIM.
YOU'VE WON THE LOTTERY KID. WHEN WE'RE GONE YOU'LL FIND SO MUCH MORE THAN YOU EVEN KNOW. THE CASTLE. THE MONEY... AND MORE. WE'LL EXPLAIN IT ALL ONE DAY.
BUT ALL HE WANTED WAS TO HANG AROUND. WATCH YOU GROW UP. WHAT WAS THE HARM.
AND AFTER ALL WE'VE DONE. ALL WE'VE BEEN THROUGH...
KKSHHH!
...I HONESTLY DON'T CARE ANYMORE.

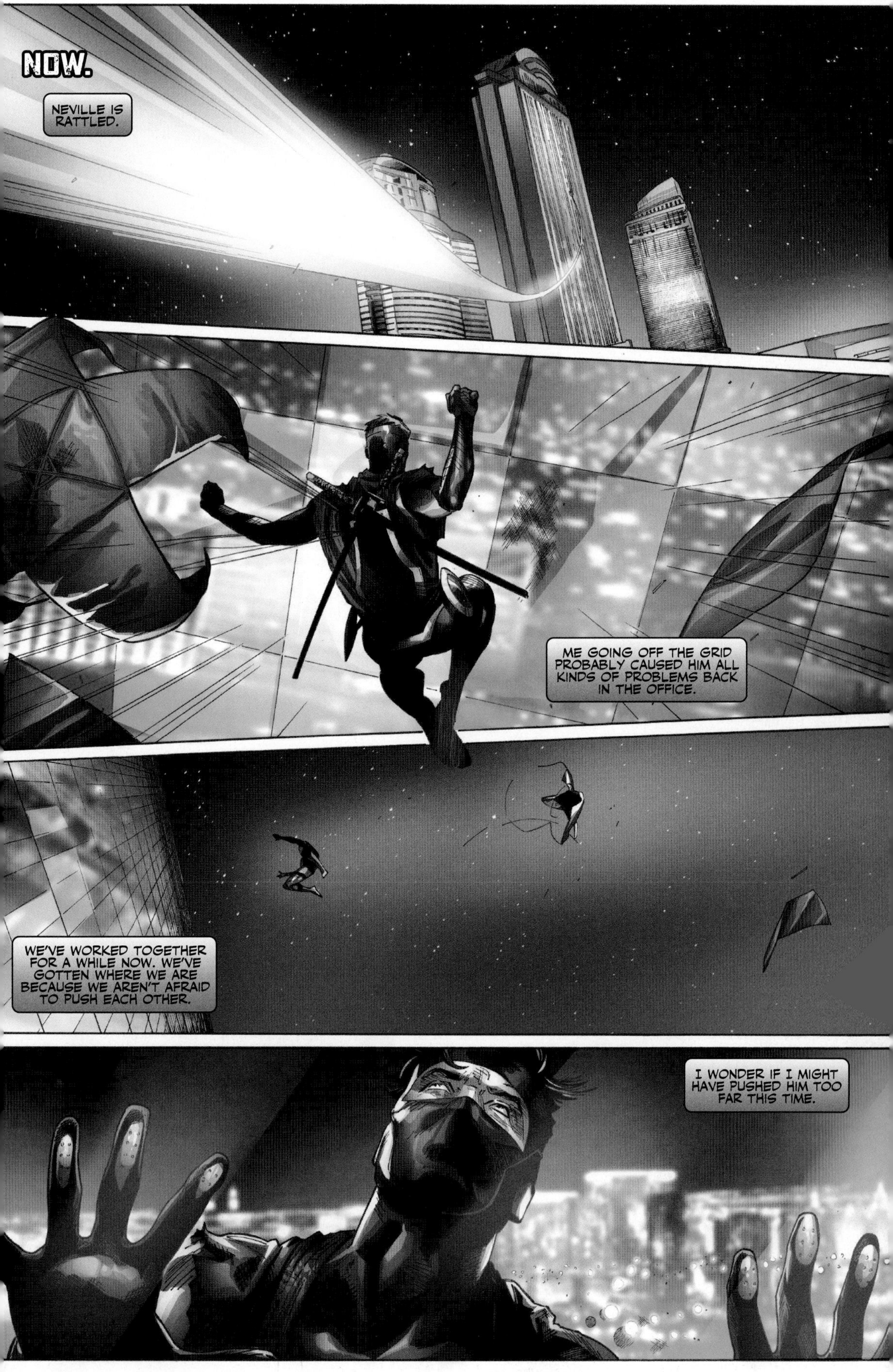
NOW.
NEVILLE IS RATTLED.
ME GOING OFF THE GRID PROBABLY CAUSED HIM ALL KINDS OF PROBLEMS BACK IN THE OFFICE.
WE'VE WORKED TOGETHER FOR A WHILE NOW. WE'VE GOTTEN WHERE WE ARE BECAUSE WE AREN'T AFRAID TO PUSH EACH OTHER.
I WONDER IF I MIGHT HAVE PUSHED HIM TOO FAR THIS TIME.

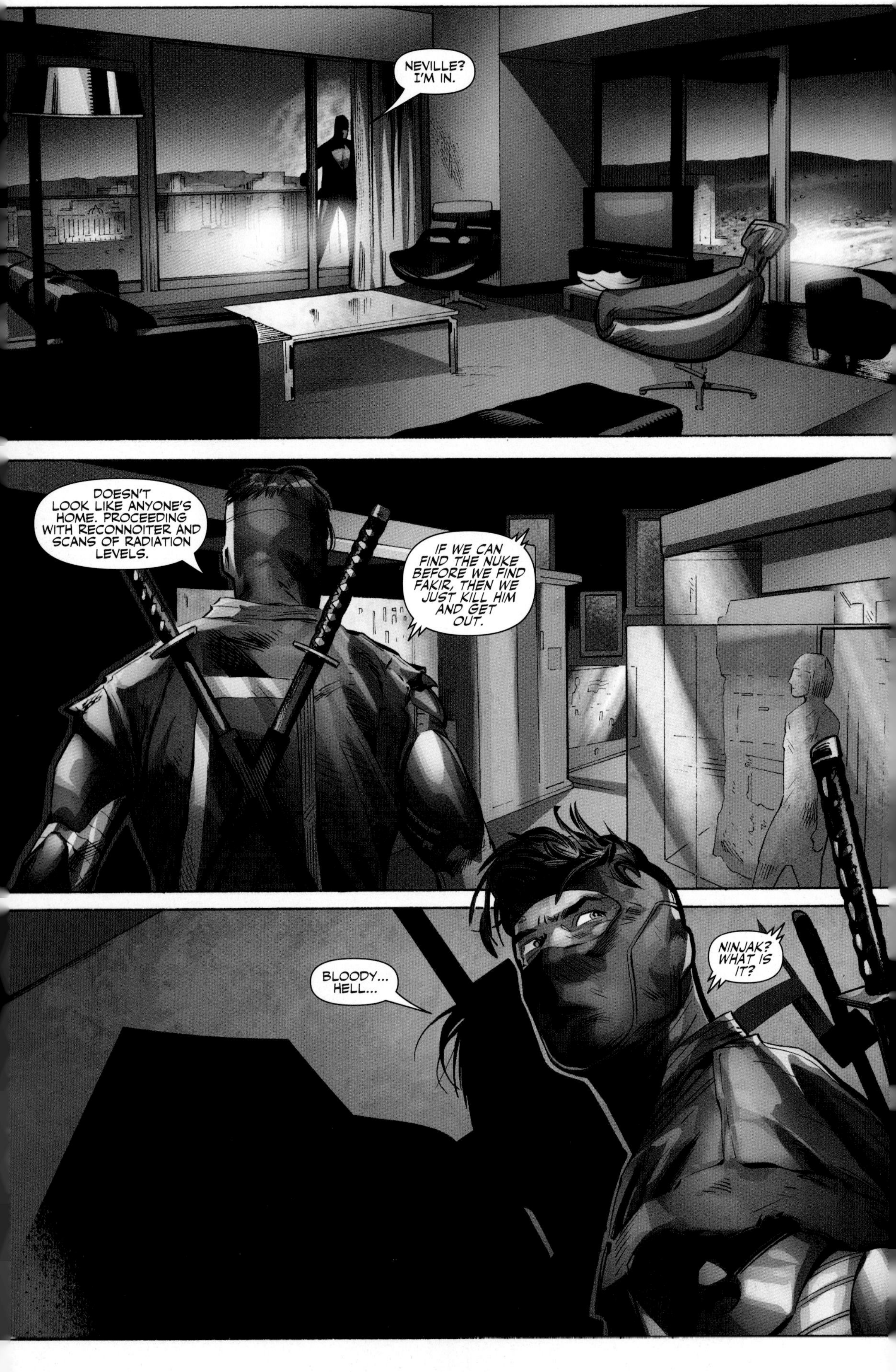
NEVILLE? I'M IN.
DOESN'T LOOK LIKE ANYONE'S HOME. PROCEEDING WITH RECONNOITER AND SCANS OF RADIATION LEVELS.
IF WE CAN FIND THE NUKE BEFORE WE FIND FAKIR, THEN WE JUST KILL HIM AND GET OUT.
BLOODY... HELL...
NINJAK? WHAT IS IT?

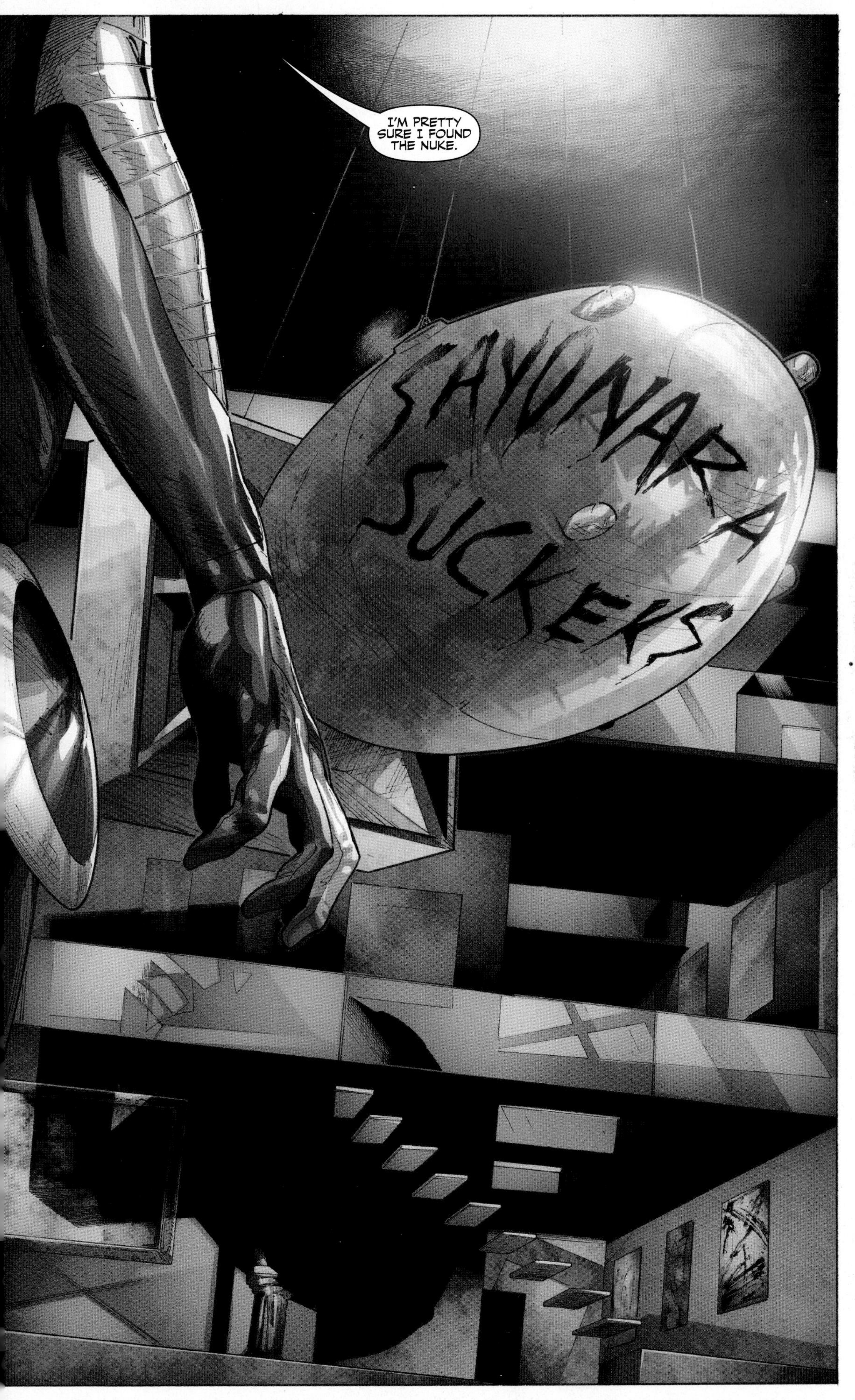
I'M PRETTY SURE I FOUND THE NUKE.
SAYONARA SUCKERS

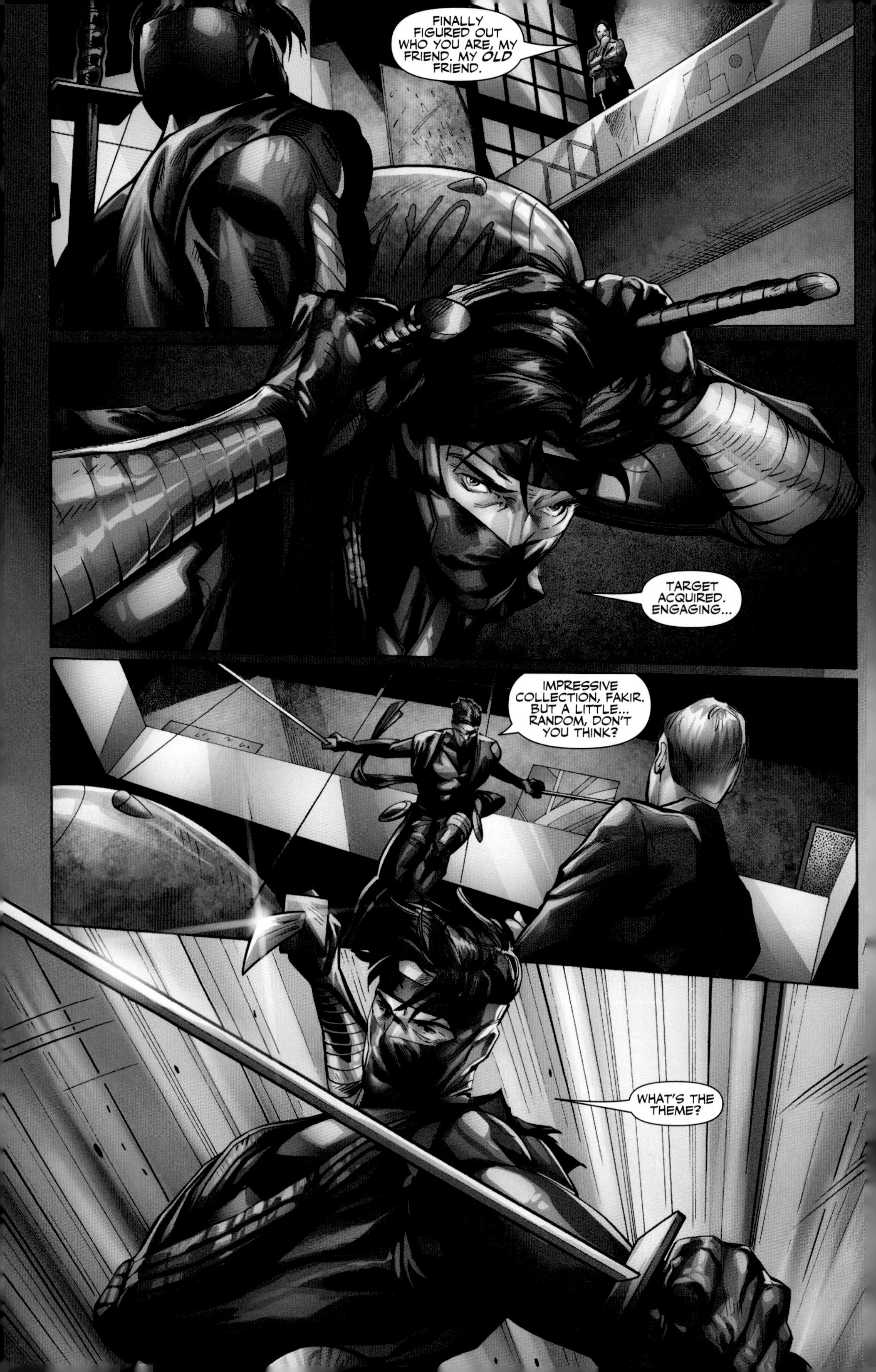
FINALLY FIGURED OUT WHO YOU ARE, MY FRIEND. MY *OLD* FRIEND.
TARGET ACQUIRED. ENGAGING...
IMPRESSIVE COLLECTION, FAKIR. BUT A LITTLE... RANDOM, DON'T YOU THINK?
WHAT'S THE THEME?

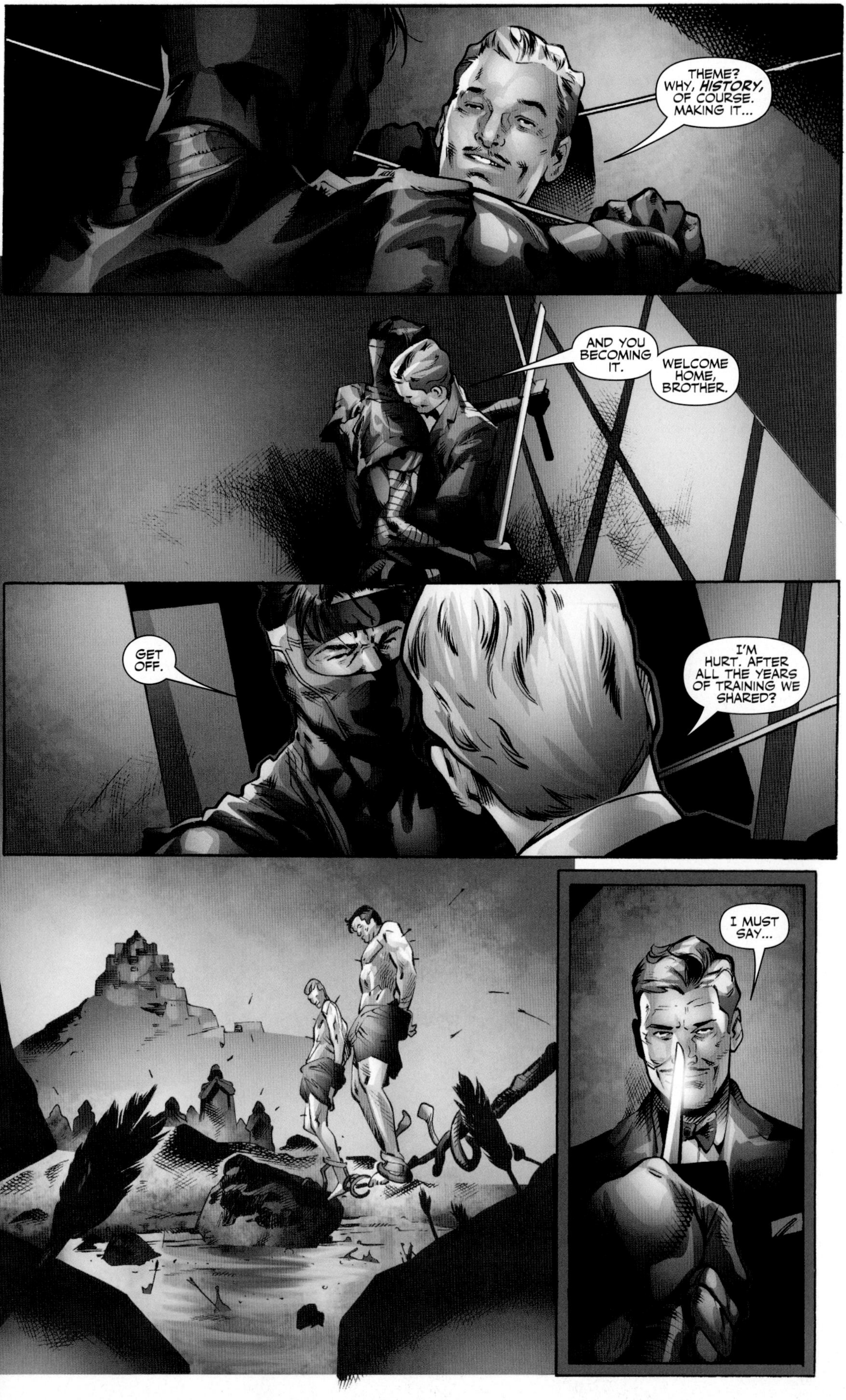
THEME? WHY, *HISTORY,* OF COURSE. MAKING IT...
AND YOU BECOMING IT.
WELCOME HOME, BROTHER.
GET OFF.
I'M HURT. AFTER ALL THE YEARS OF TRAINING WE SHARED?
I MUST SAY...

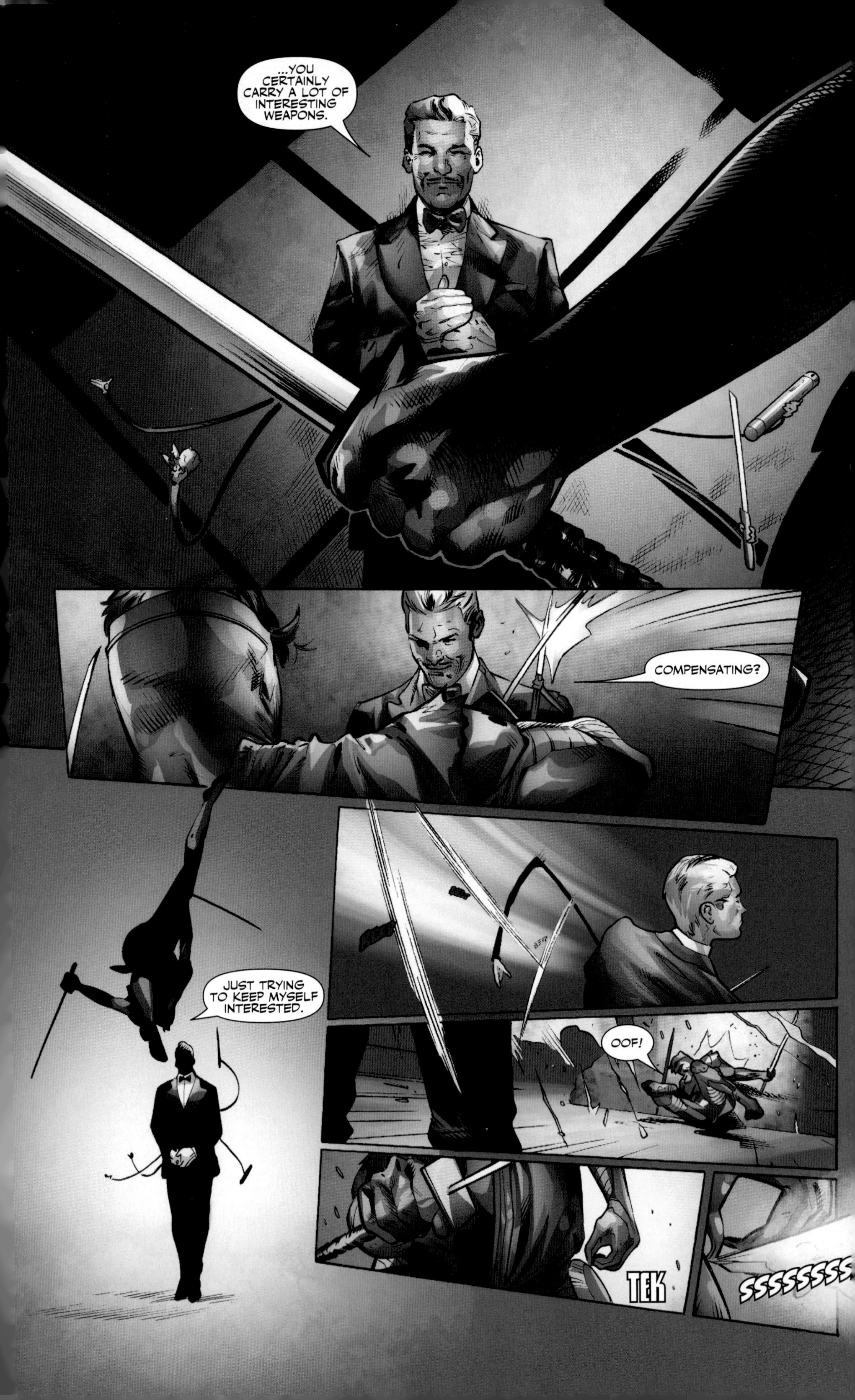
...YOU CERTAINLY CARRY A LOT OF INTERESTING WEAPONS.
COMPENSATING?
JUST TRYING TO KEEP MYSELF INTERESTED.
OOF!
TEK
SSSSSSSS

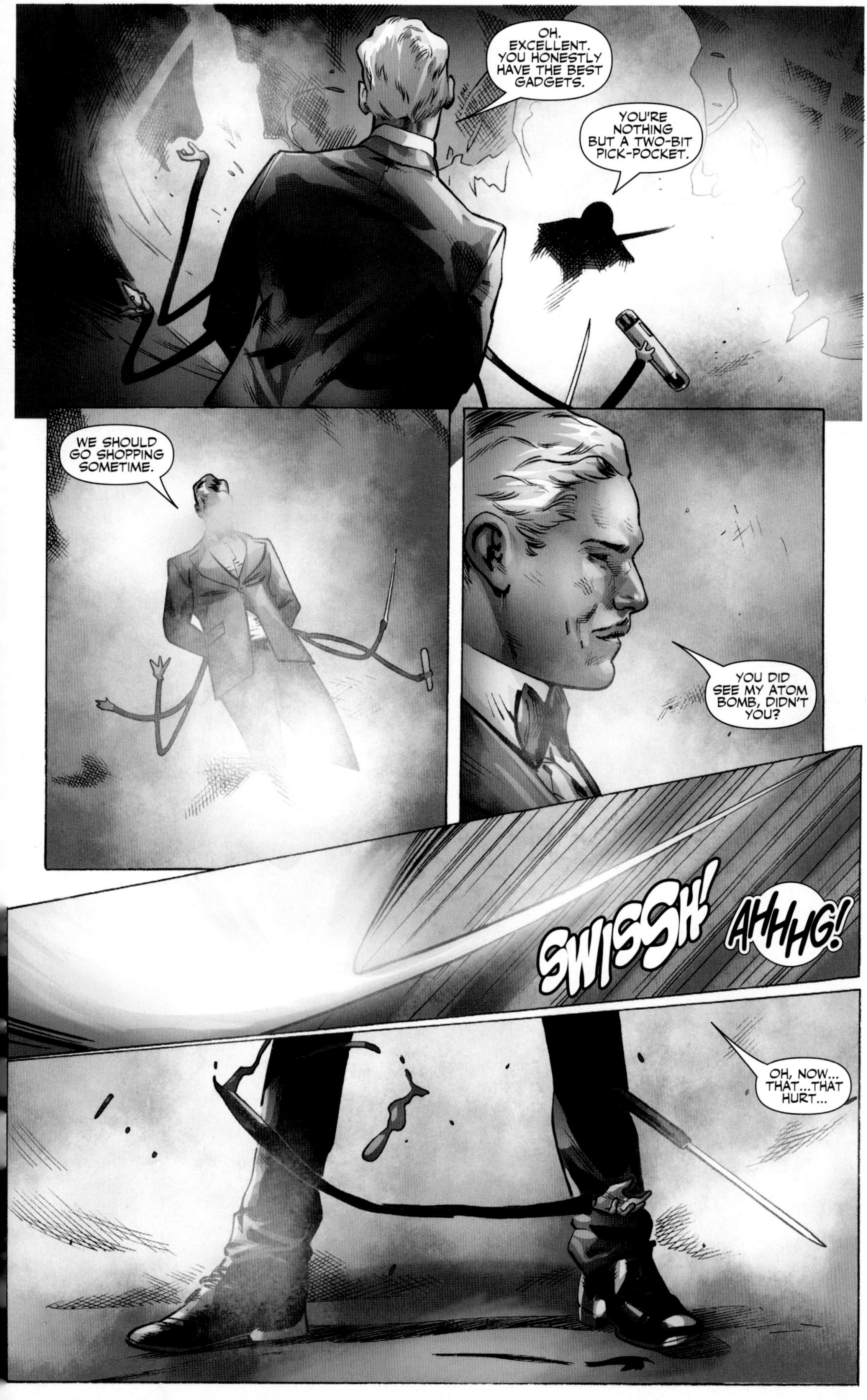
OH. EXCELLENT. YOU HONESTLY HAVE THE BEST GADGETS.
YOU'RE NOTHING BUT A TWO-BIT PICK-POCKET.
WE SHOULD GO SHOPPING SOMETIME.
YOU DID SEE MY ATOM BOMB, DIDN'T YOU?
SWISSH!
AHHHG!
OH, NOW... THAT...THAT HURT...

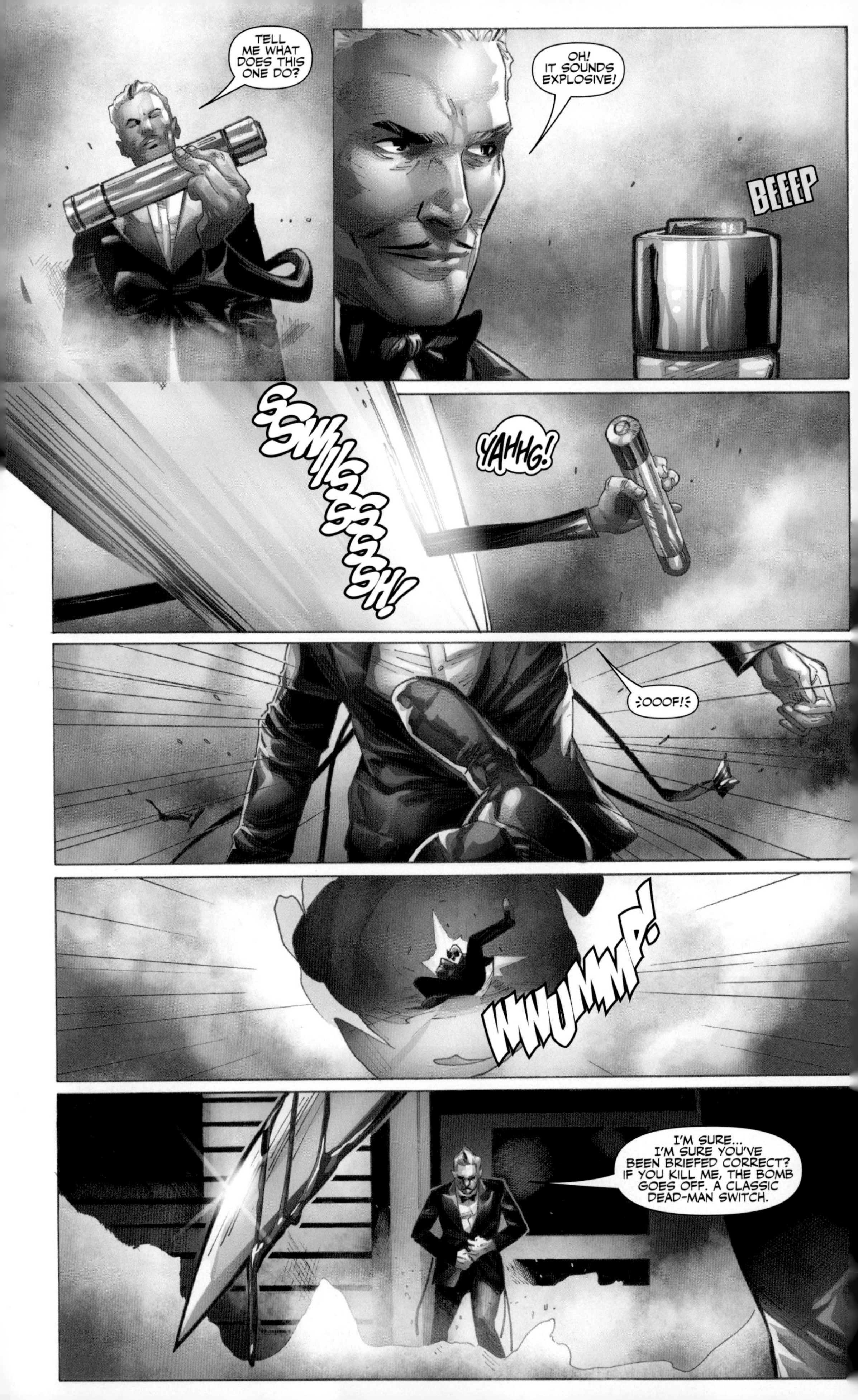
TELL ME WHAT DOES THIS ONE DO?
OH! IT SOUNDS EXPLOSIVE!
BEEEP
SSWIISSSSSH!
YAHHG!
OOOF!
WWUMMP!
I'M SURE... I'M SURE YOU'VE BEEN BRIEFED CORRECT? IF YOU KILL ME, THE BOMB GOES OFF. A CLASSIC DEAD-MAN SWITCH.

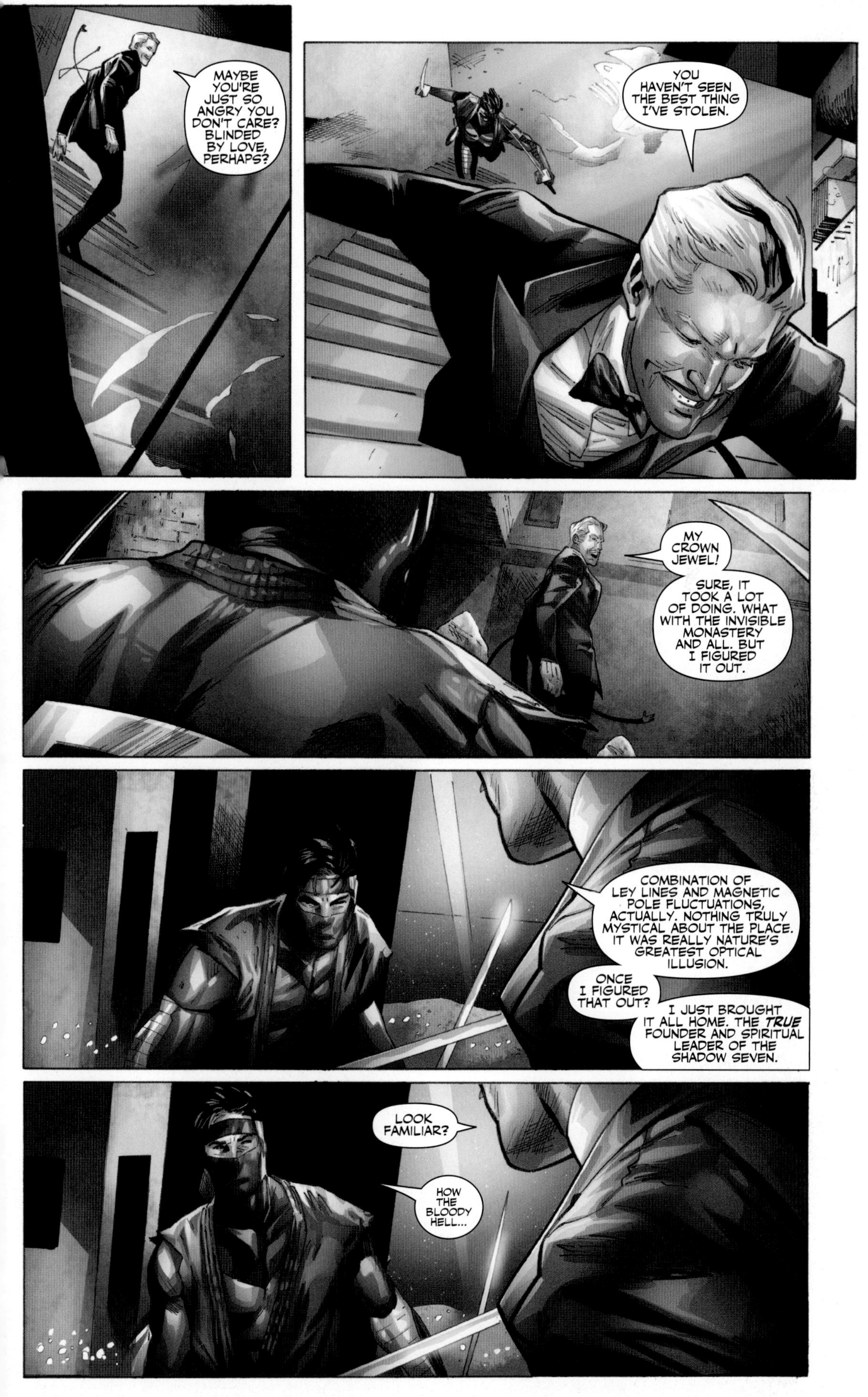
MAYBE YOU'RE JUST SO ANGRY YOU DON'T CARE? BLINDED BY LOVE, PERHAPS?
YOU HAVEN'T SEEN THE BEST THING I'VE STOLEN.
MY CROWN JEWEL!
SURE, IT TOOK A LOT OF DOING. WHAT WITH THE INVISIBLE MONASTERY AND ALL. BUT I FIGURED IT OUT.
COMBINATION OF LEY LINES AND MAGNETIC POLE FLUCTUATIONS, ACTUALLY. NOTHING TRULY MYSTICAL ABOUT THE PLACE. IT WAS REALLY NATURE'S GREATEST OPTICAL ILLUSION.
ONCE I FIGURED THAT OUT?
I JUST BROUGHT IT ALL HOME. THE *TRUE* FOUNDER AND SPIRITUAL LEADER OF THE SHADOW SEVEN.
LOOK FAMILIAR?
HOW THE BLOODY HELL...

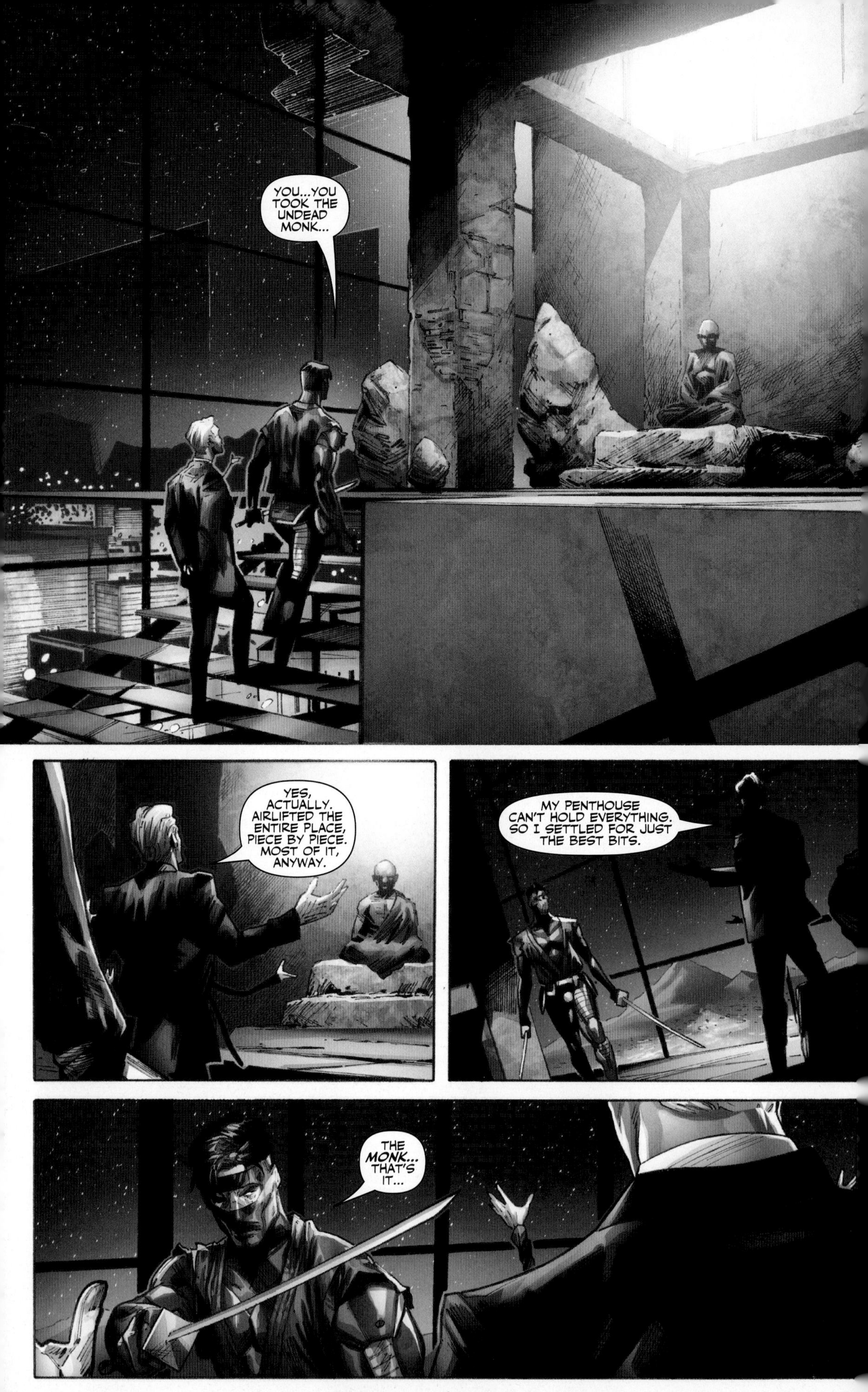
YOU...YOU TOOK THE UNDEAD MONK...
YES, ACTUALLY. AIRLIFTED THE ENTIRE PLACE, PIECE BY PIECE. MOST OF IT, ANYWAY.
MY PENTHOUSE CAN'T HOLD EVERYTHING. SO I SETTLED FOR JUST THE BEST BITS.
THE *MONK*... THAT'S IT...

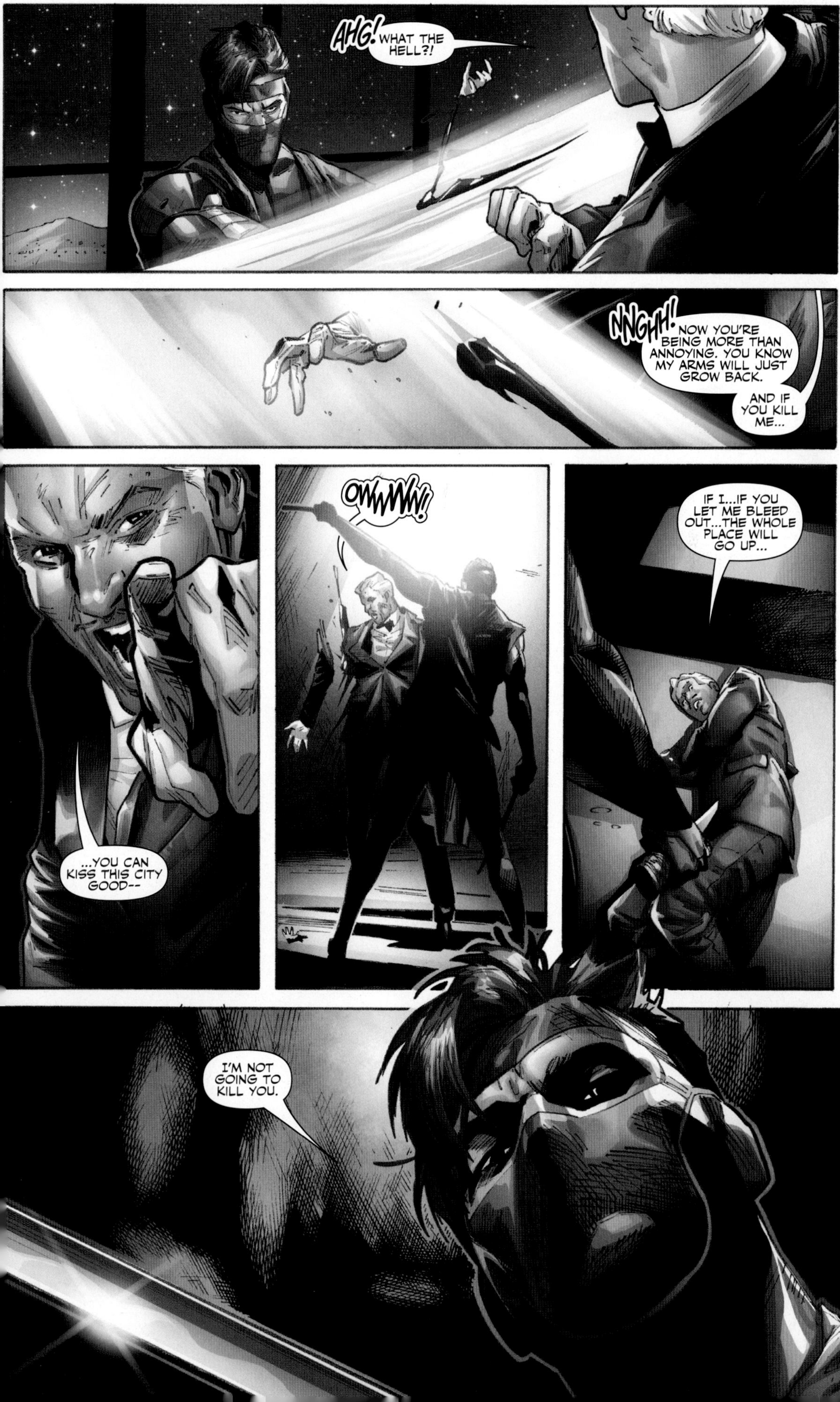
AHG! WHAT THE HELL?!
NNGHH! NOW YOU'RE BEING MORE THAN ANNOYING. YOU KNOW MY ARMS WILL JUST GROW BACK.
AND IF YOU KILL ME...
...YOU CAN KISS THIS CITY GOOD--
OWWWW!
IF I...IF YOU LET ME BLEED OUT...THE WHOLE PLACE WILL GO UP...
I'M NOT GOING TO KILL YOU.

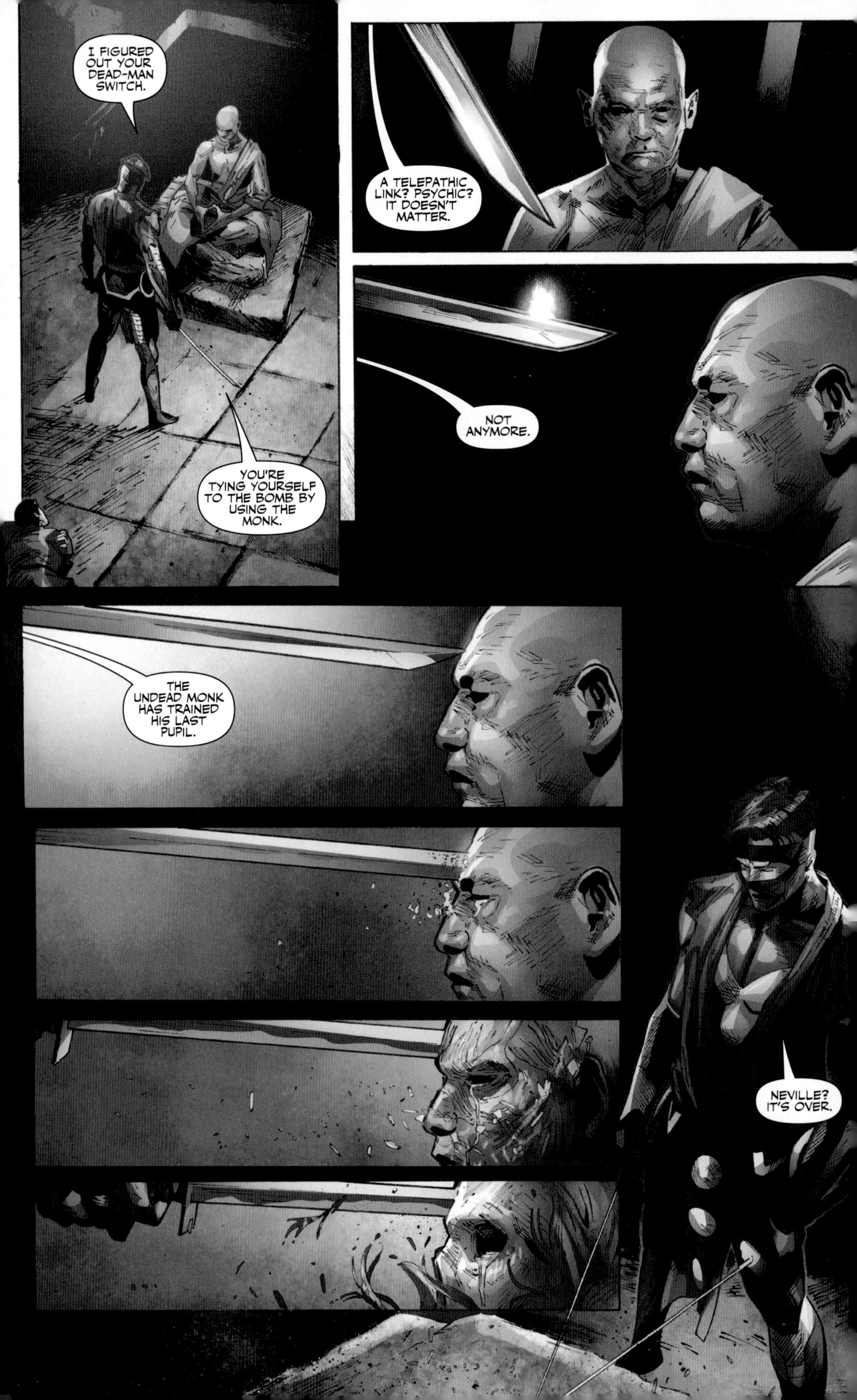
I FIGURED OUT YOUR DEAD-MAN SWITCH.
YOU'RE TYING YOURSELF TO THE BOMB BY USING THE MONK.
A TELEPATHIC LINK? PSYCHIC? IT DOESN'T MATTER.
NOT ANYMORE.
THE UNDEAD MONK HAS TRAINED HIS LAST PUPIL.
NEVILLE? IT'S OVER.

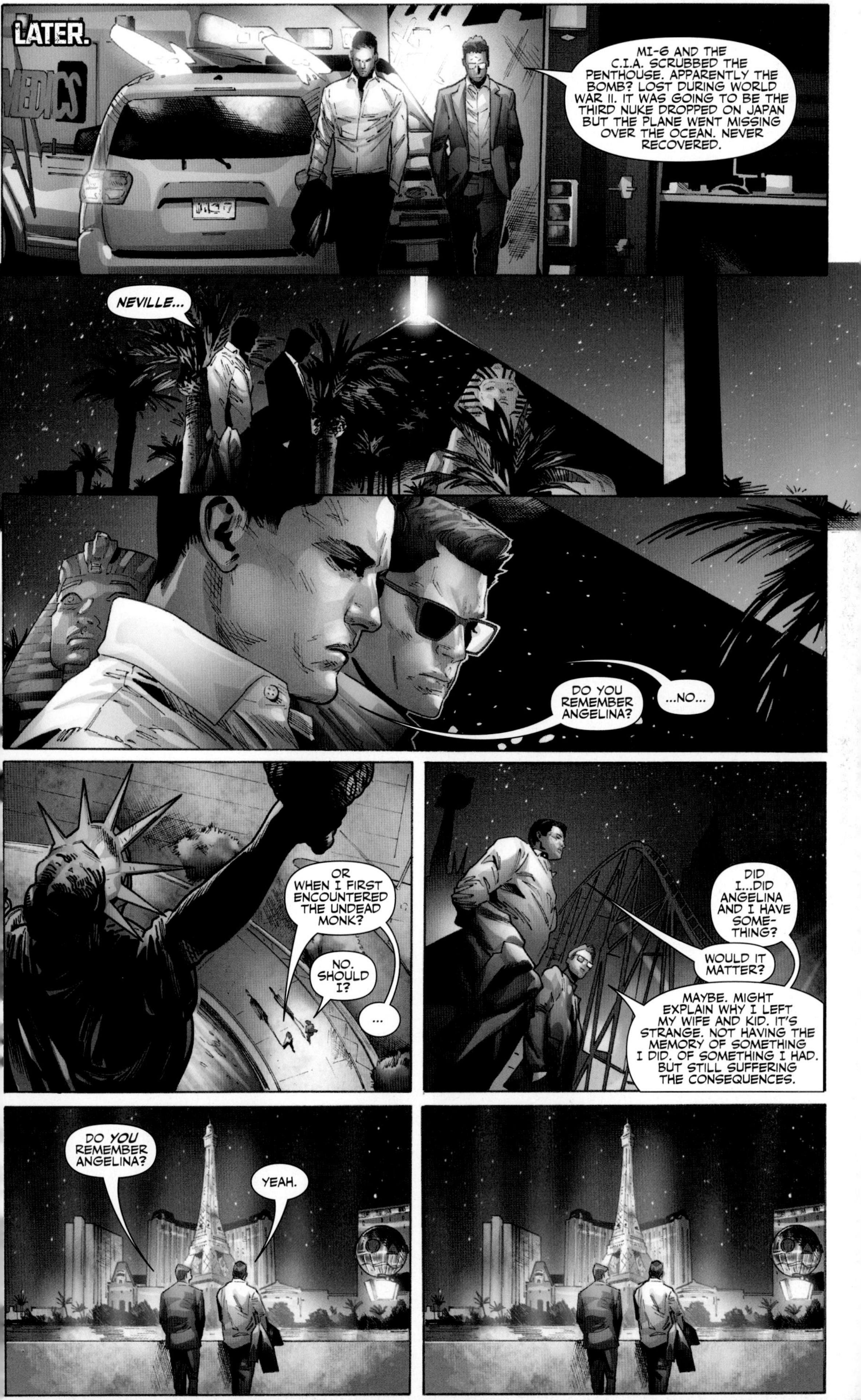
LATER.
MI-6 AND THE C.I.A. SCRUBBED THE PENTHOUSE. APPARENTLY THE BOMB? LOST DURING WORLD WAR II. IT WAS GOING TO BE THE THIRD NUKE DROPPED ON JAPAN BUT THE PLANE WENT MISSING OVER THE OCEAN. NEVER RECOVERED.
NEVILLE...
DO YOU REMEMBER ANGELINA?
...NO...
OR WHEN I FIRST ENCOUNTERED THE UNDEAD MONK?
NO. SHOULD I?
...
DID I...DID ANGELINA AND I HAVE SOME-THING?
WOULD IT MATTER?
MAYBE. MIGHT EXPLAIN WHY I LEFT MY WIFE AND KID. IT'S STRANGE. NOT HAVING THE MEMORY OF SOMETHING I DID. OF SOMETHING I HAD. BUT STILL SUFFERING THE CONSEQUENCES.
DO *YOU* REMEMBER ANGELINA?
YEAH.

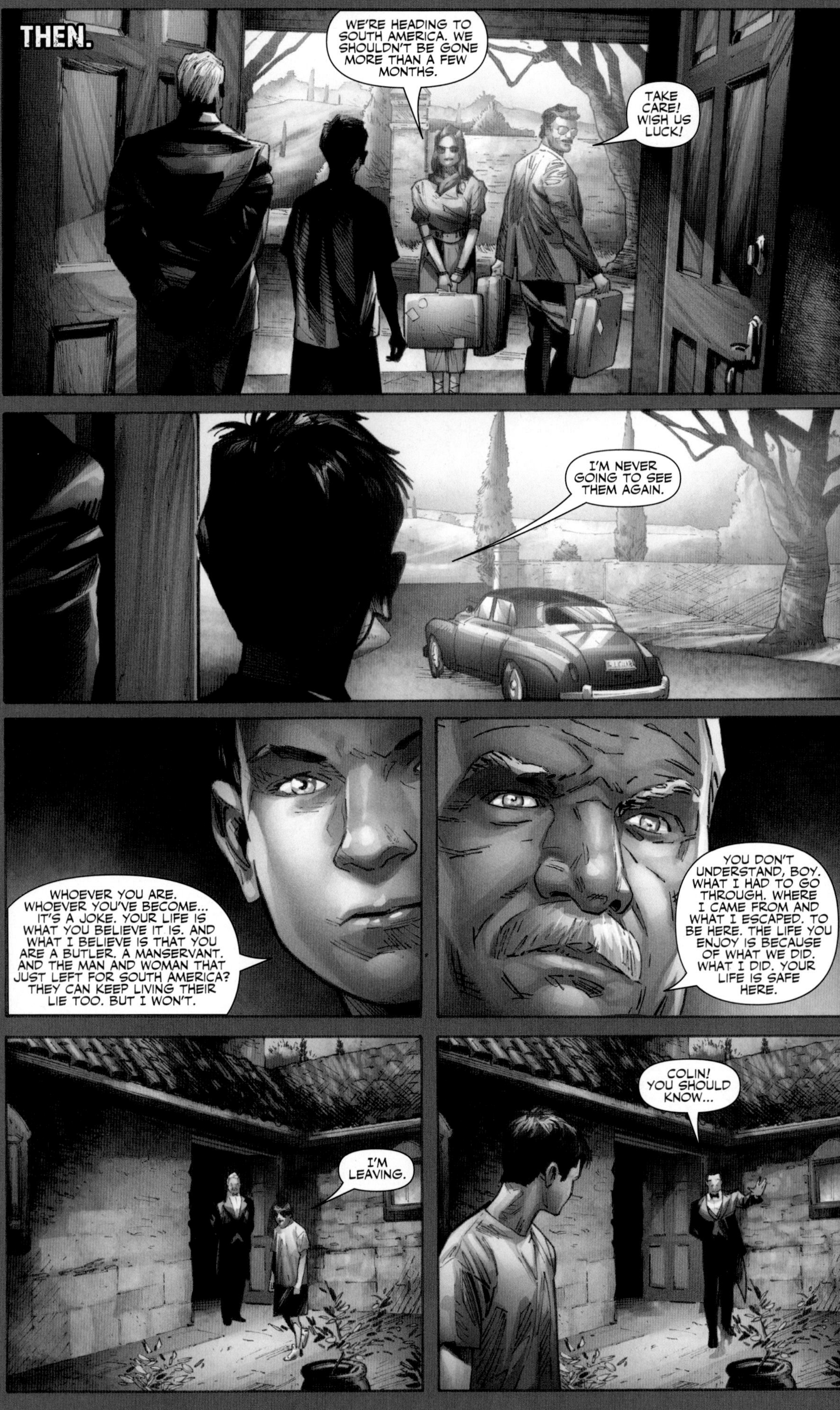
THEN.
WE'RE HEADING TO SOUTH AMERICA. WE SHOULDN'T BE GONE MORE THAN A FEW MONTHS.
TAKE CARE! WISH US LUCK!
I'M NEVER GOING TO SEE THEM AGAIN.
WHOEVER YOU ARE. WHOEVER YOU'VE BECOME... IT'S A JOKE. YOUR LIFE IS WHAT YOU BELIEVE IT IS. AND WHAT I BELIEVE IS THAT YOU ARE A BUTLER. A MANSERVANT. AND THE MAN AND WOMAN THAT JUST LEFT FOR SOUTH AMERICA? THEY CAN KEEP LIVING THEIR LIE TOO. BUT I WON'T.
YOU DON'T UNDERSTAND, BOY. WHAT I HAD TO GO THROUGH. WHERE I CAME FROM AND WHAT I ESCAPED. TO BE HERE. THE LIFE YOU ENJOY IS BECAUSE OF WHAT WE DID. WHAT I DID. YOUR LIFE IS SAFE HERE.
I'M LEAVING.
COLIN! YOU SHOULD KNOW...

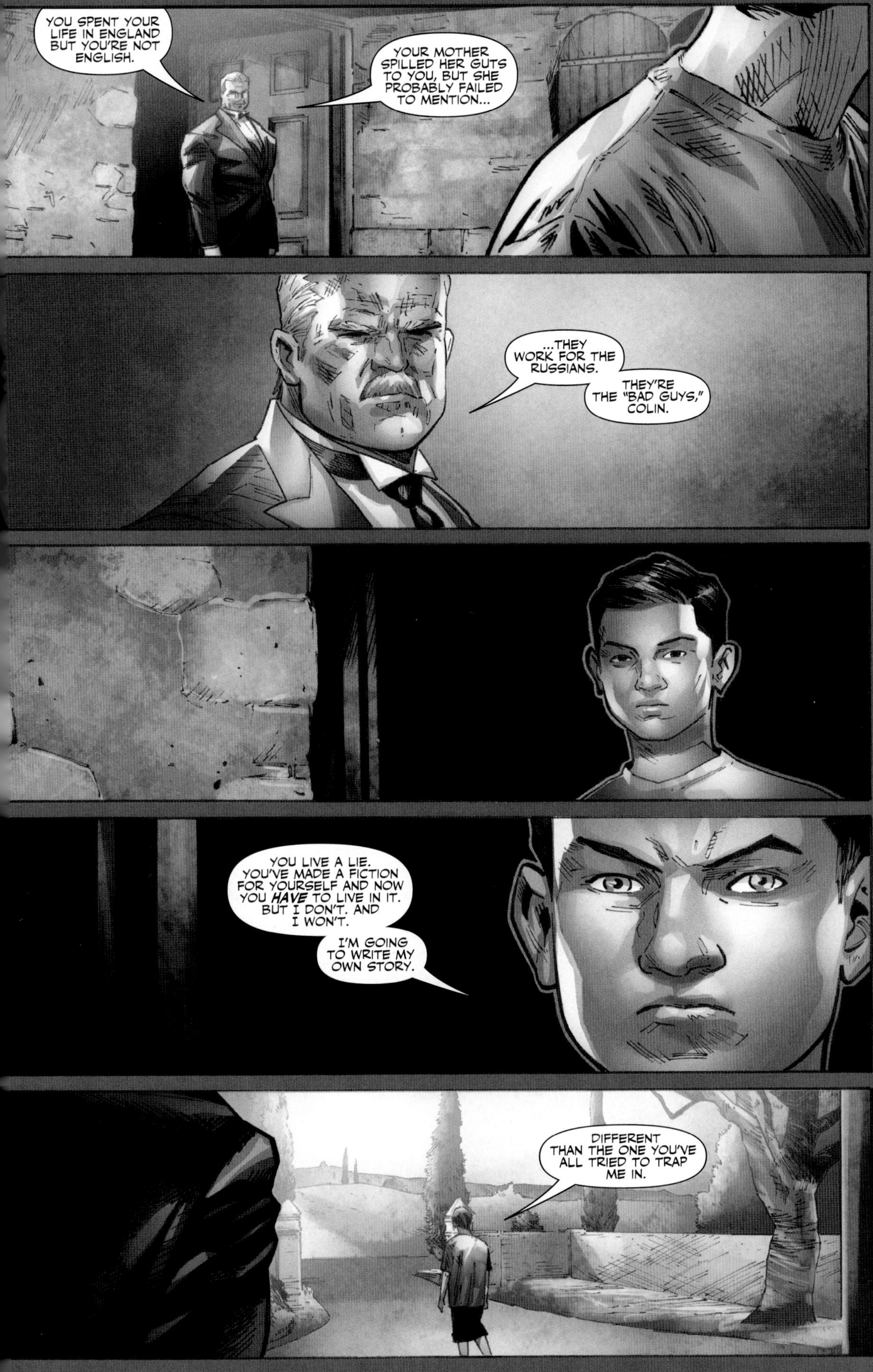
YOU SPENT YOUR LIFE IN ENGLAND BUT YOU'RE NOT ENGLISH.
YOUR MOTHER SPILLED HER GUTS TO YOU, BUT SHE PROBABLY FAILED TO MENTION...
...THEY WORK FOR THE RUSSIANS.
THEY'RE THE "BAD GUYS," COLIN.
YOU LIVE A LIE. YOU'VE MADE A FICTION FOR YOURSELF AND NOW YOU *HAVE* TO LIVE IN IT. BUT I DON'T. AND I WON'T.
I'M GOING TO WRITE MY OWN STORY.
DIFFERENT THAN THE ONE YOU'VE ALL TRIED TO TRAP ME IN.

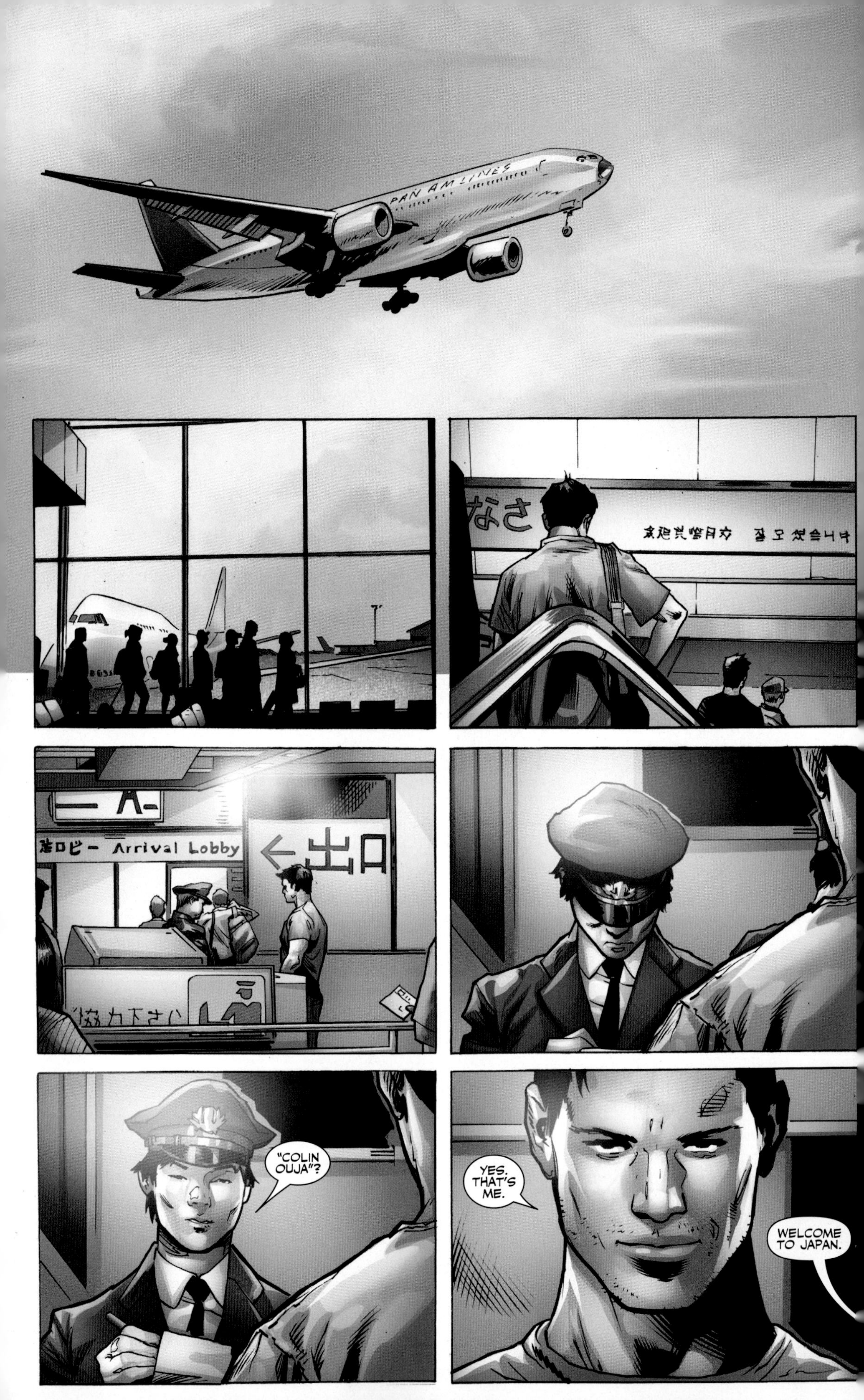
PAN AM LINES
Arrival Lobby
← 出口
"COLIN OUJA"?
YES. THAT'S ME.
WELCOME TO JAPAN.

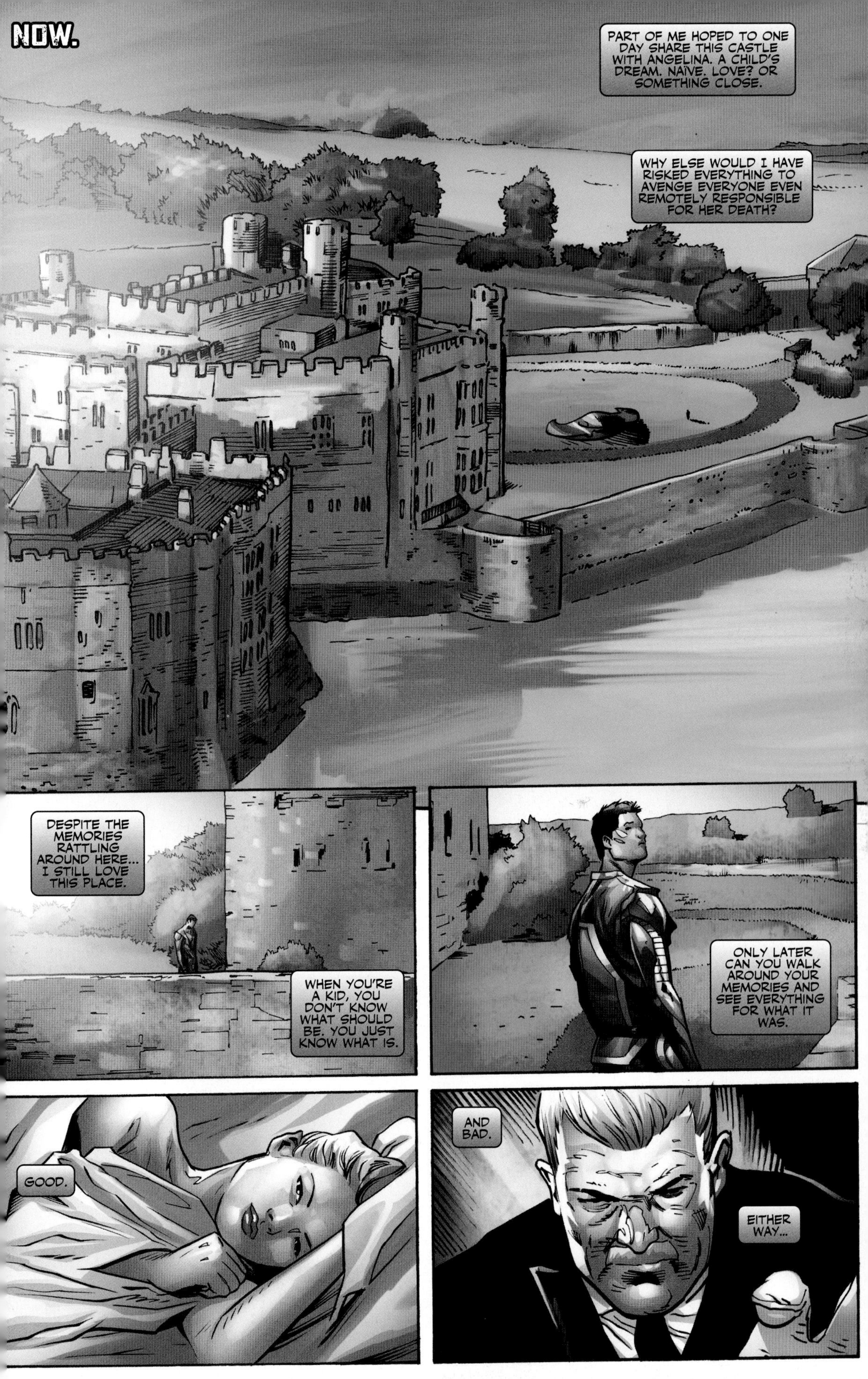
NOW.
PART OF ME HOPED TO ONE DAY SHARE THIS CASTLE WITH ANGELINA. A CHILD'S DREAM. NAÏVE. LOVE? OR SOMETHING CLOSE.
WHY ELSE WOULD I HAVE RISKED EVERYTHING TO AVENGE EVERYONE EVEN REMOTELY RESPONSIBLE FOR HER DEATH?
DESPITE THE MEMORIES RATTLING AROUND HERE... I STILL LOVE THIS PLACE.
WHEN YOU'RE A KID, YOU DON'T KNOW WHAT SHOULD BE. YOU JUST KNOW WHAT IS.
ONLY LATER CAN YOU WALK AROUND YOUR MEMORIES AND SEE EVERYTHING FOR WHAT IT WAS.
GOOD.
AND BAD.
EITHER WAY...

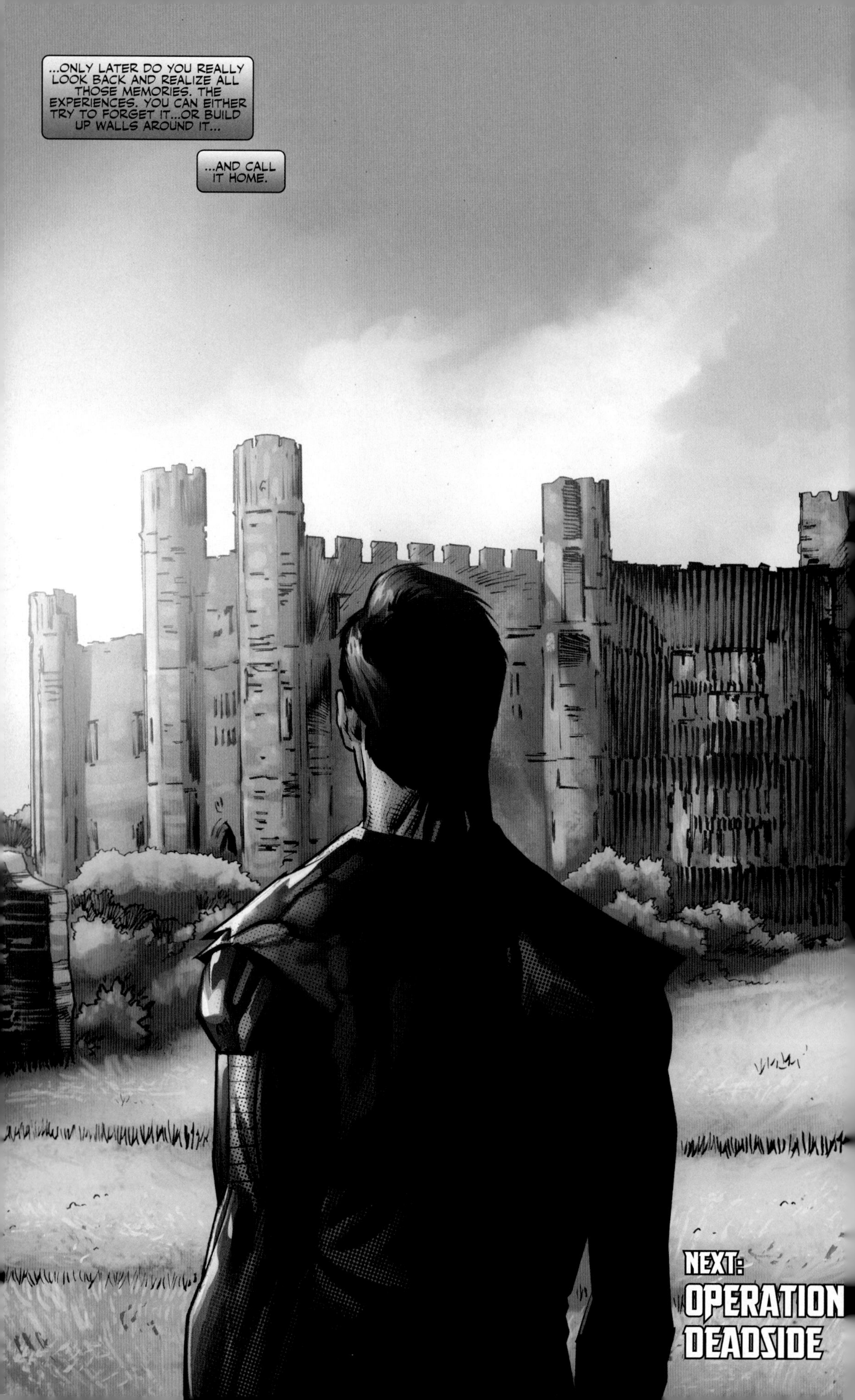
...ONLY LATER DO YOU REALLY LOOK BACK AND REALIZE ALL THOSE MEMORIES. THE EXPERIENCES. YOU CAN EITHER TRY TO FORGET IT...OR BUILD UP WALLS AROUND IT...
...AND CALL IT HOME.
NEXT: OPERATION DEADSIDE

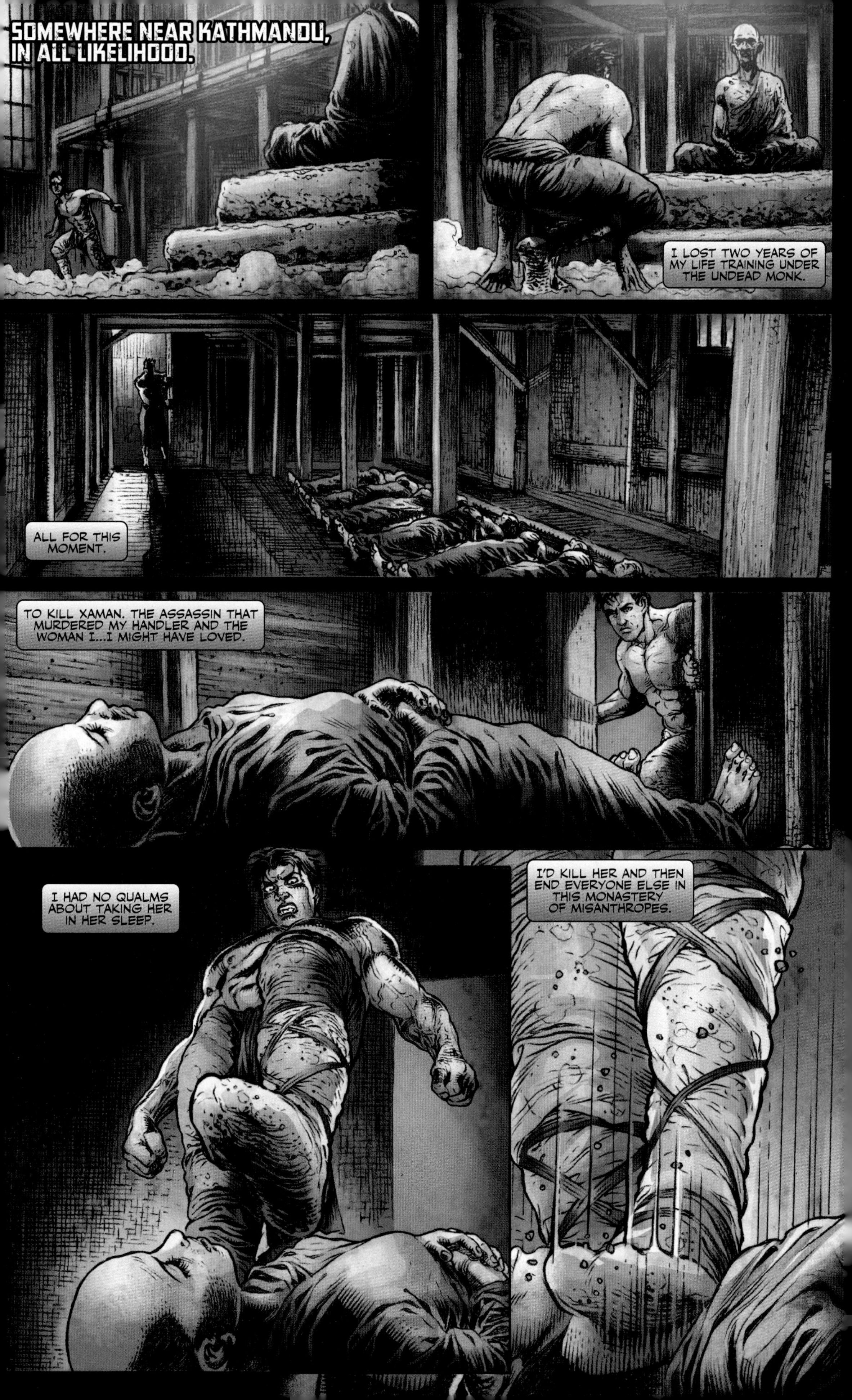
SOMEWHERE NEAR KATHMANDU, IN ALL LIKELIHOOD.
I LOST TWO YEARS OF MY LIFE TRAINING UNDER THE UNDEAD MONK.
ALL FOR THIS MOMENT.
TO KILL XAMAN. THE ASSASSIN THAT MURDERED MY HANDLER AND THE WOMAN I...I MIGHT HAVE LOVED.
I HAD NO QUALMS ABOUT TAKING HER IN HER SLEEP.
I'D KILL HER AND THEN END EVERYONE ELSE IN THIS MONASTERY OF MISANTHROPES.

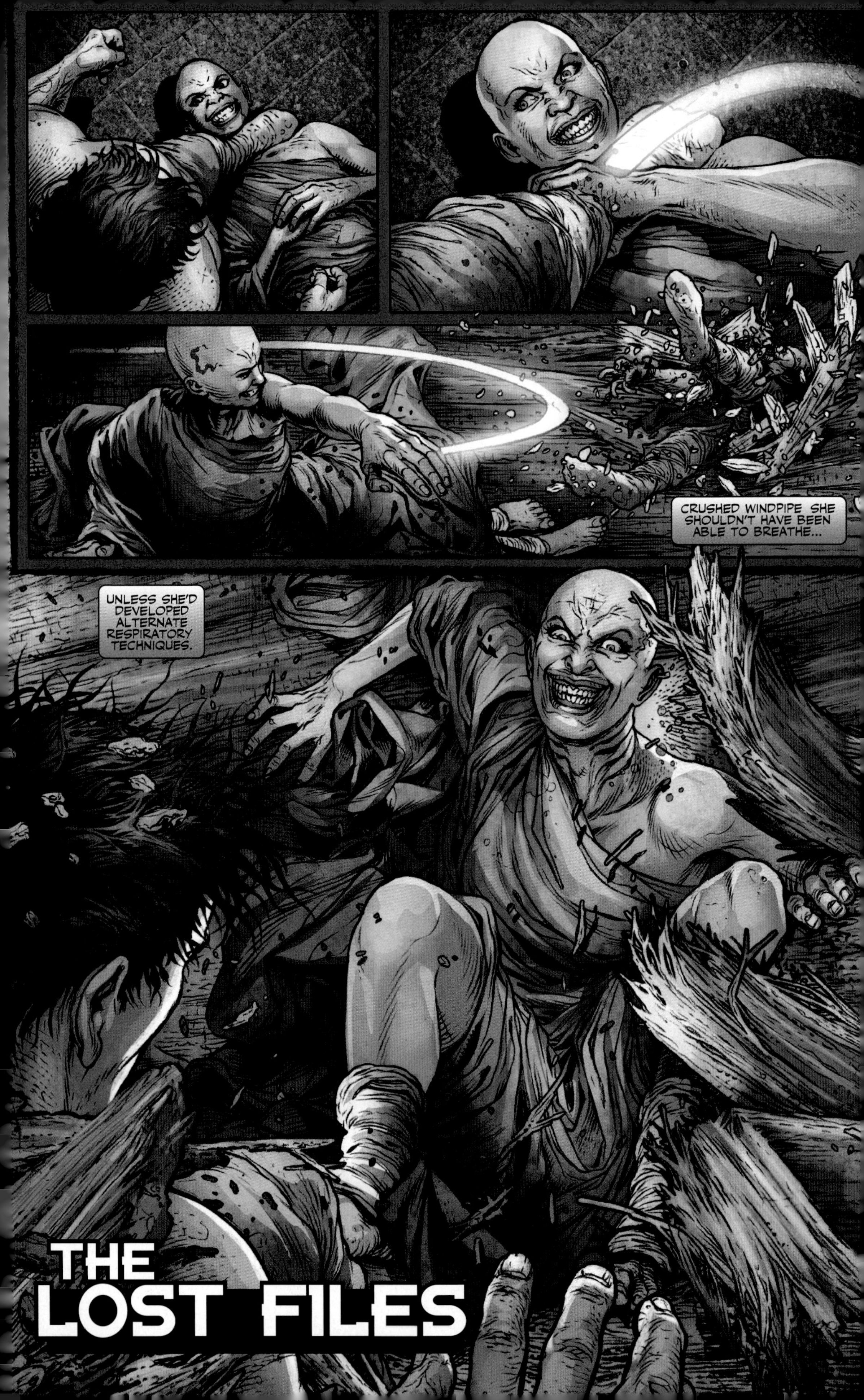
CRUSHED WINDPIPE SHE SHOULDN'T HAVE BEEN ABLE TO BREATHE...
UNLESS SHE'D DEVELOPED ALTERNATE RESPIRATORY TECHNIQUES.
THE LOST FILES

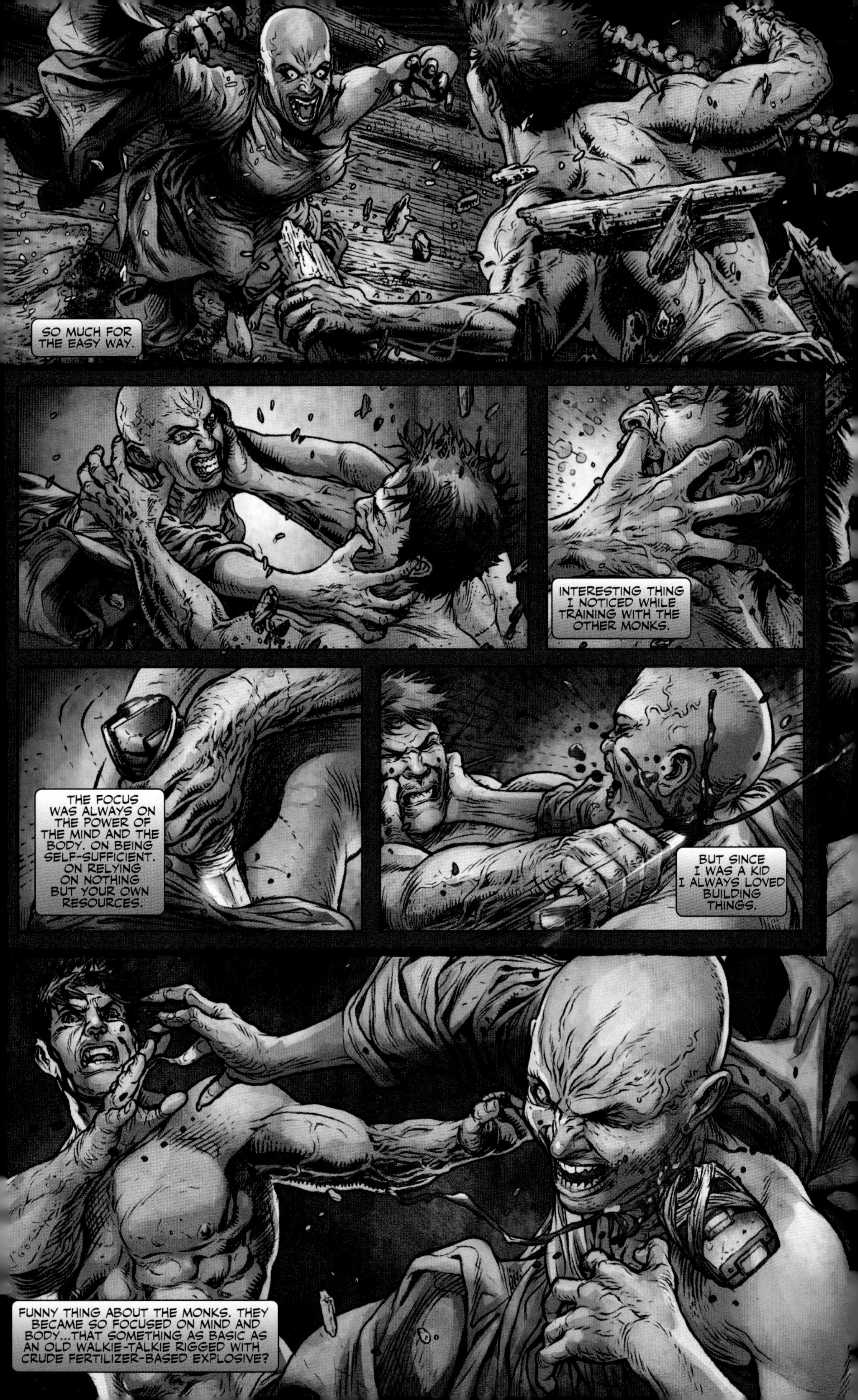
SO MUCH FOR THE EASY WAY.
INTERESTING THING I NOTICED WHILE TRAINING WITH THE OTHER MONKS.
THE FOCUS WAS ALWAYS ON THE POWER OF THE MIND AND THE BODY. ON BEING SELF-SUFFICIENT. ON RELYING ON NOTHING BUT YOUR OWN RESOURCES.
BUT SINCE I WAS A KID I ALWAYS LOVED BUILDING THINGS.
FUNNY THING ABOUT THE MONKS. THEY BECAME SO FOCUSED ON MIND AND BODY...THAT SOMETHING AS BASIC AS AN OLD WALKIE-TALKIE RIGGED WITH CRUDE FERTILIZER-BASED EXPLOSIVE?

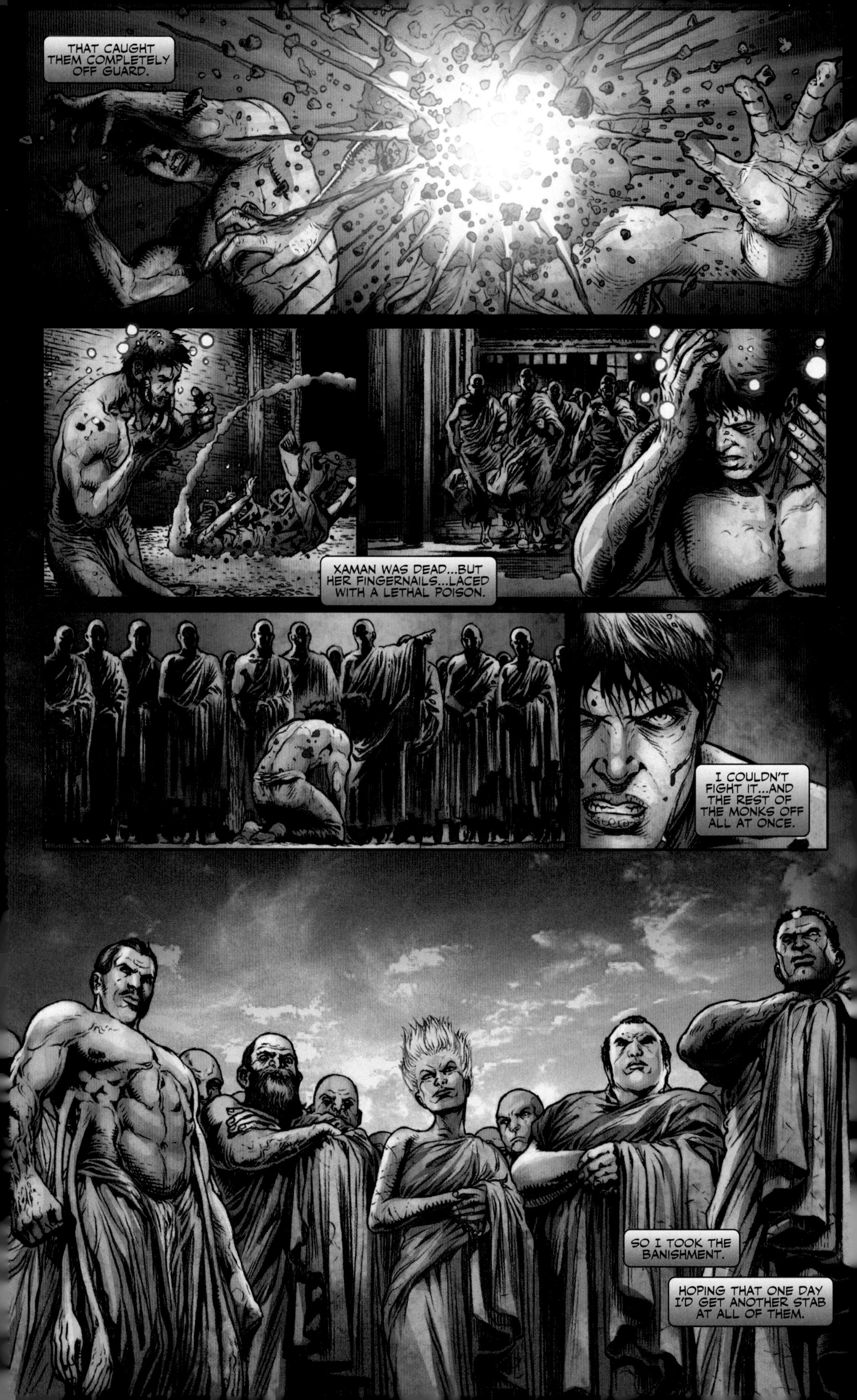
THAT CAUGHT THEM COMPLETELY OFF GUARD.
XAMAN WAS DEAD...BUT HER FINGERNAILS...LACED WITH A LETHAL POISON.
I COULDN'T FIGHT IT...AND THE REST OF THE MONKS OFF ALL AT ONCE.
SO I TOOK THE BANISHMENT.
HOPING THAT ONE DAY I'D GET ANOTHER STAB AT ALL OF THEM.

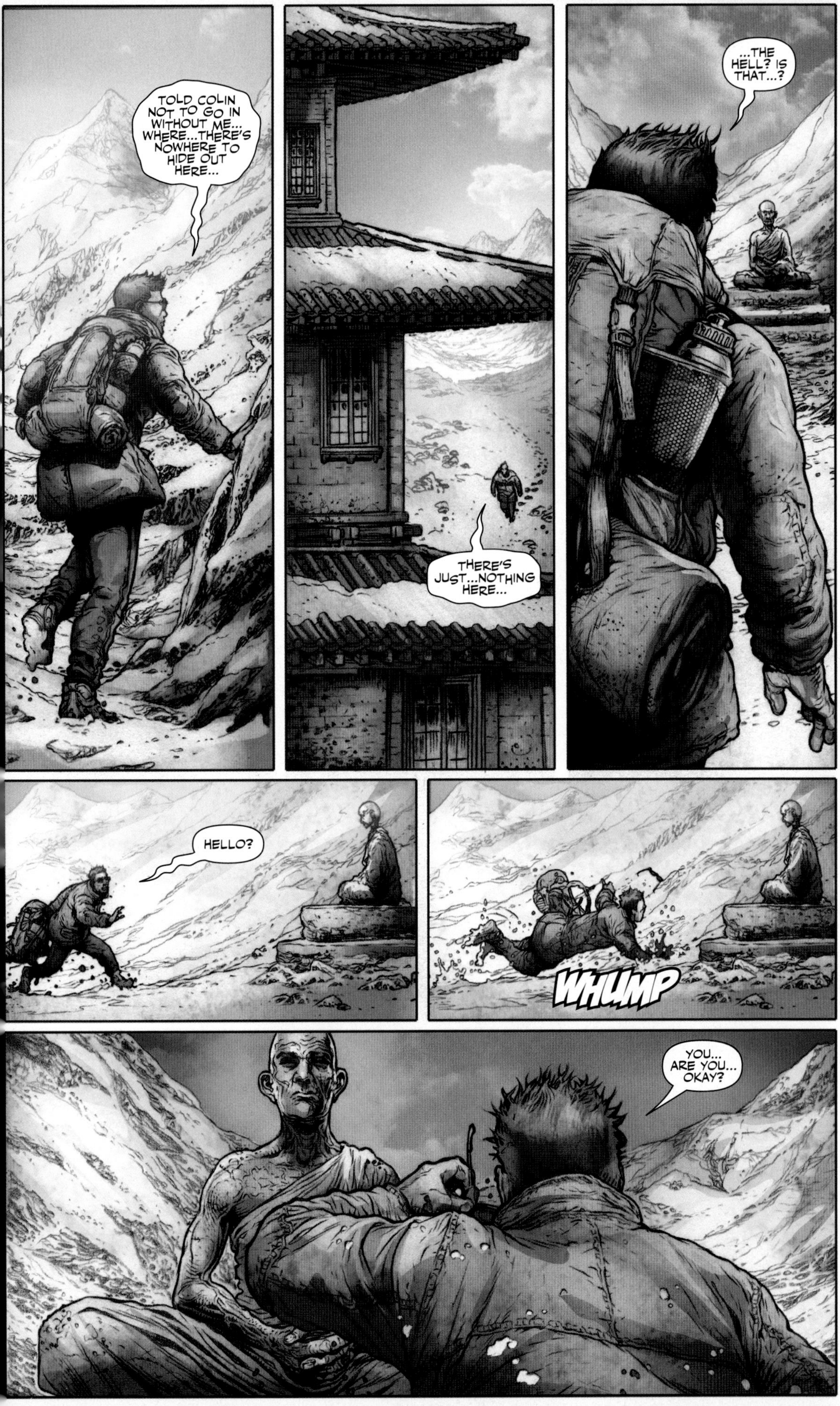
TOLD COLIN NOT TO GO IN WITHOUT ME... WHERE...THERE'S NOWHERE TO HIDE OUT HERE...
THERE'S JUST...NOTHING HERE...
...THE HELL? IS THAT...?
HELLO?
WHUMP
YOU... ARE YOU... OKAY?

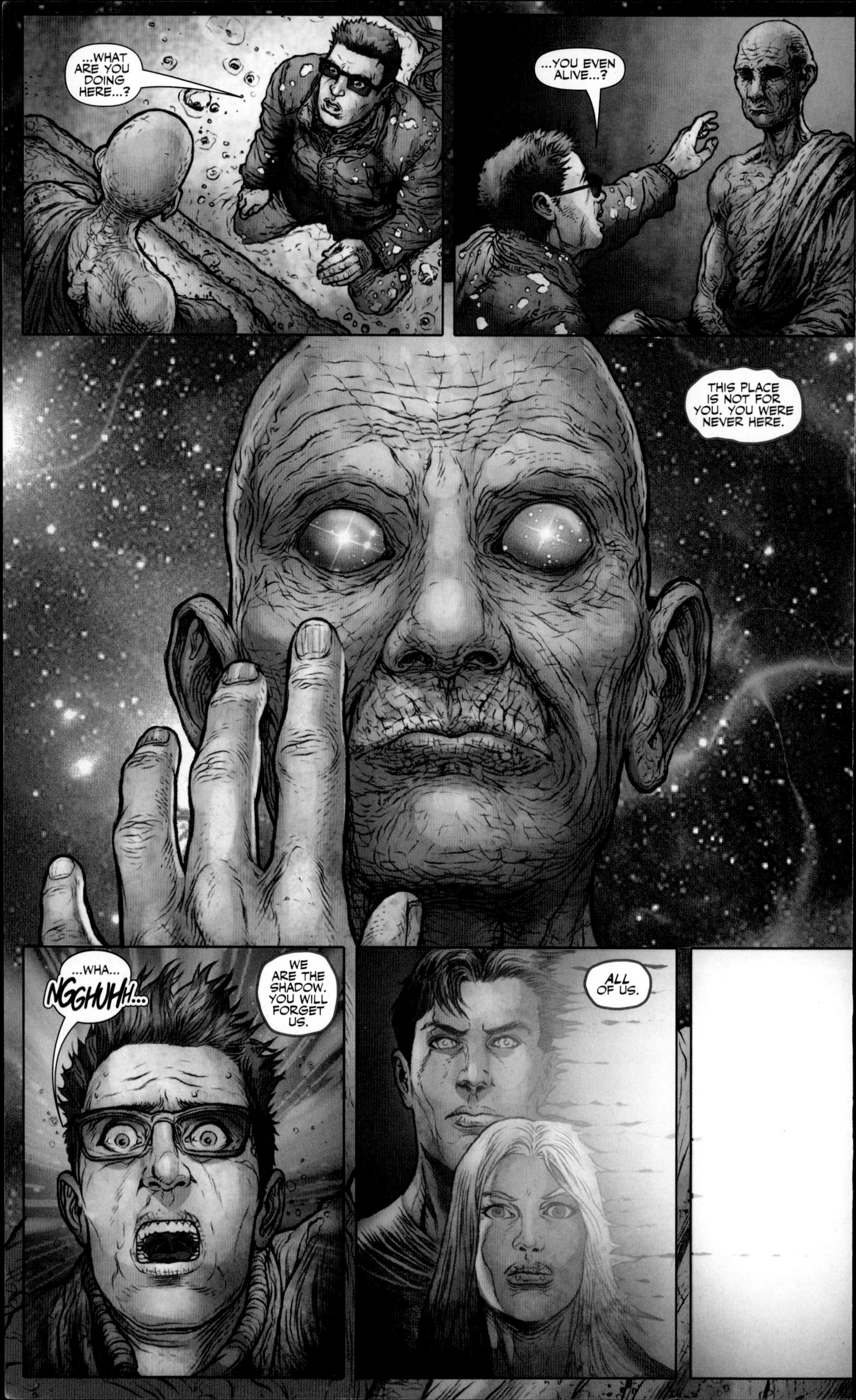
...WHAT ARE YOU DOING HERE...?
...YOU EVEN ALIVE...?
THIS PLACE IS NOT FOR YOU. YOU WERE NEVER HERE.
...WHA...
NGGHUHH...
WE ARE THE SHADOW. YOU WILL FORGET US.
ALL OF US.

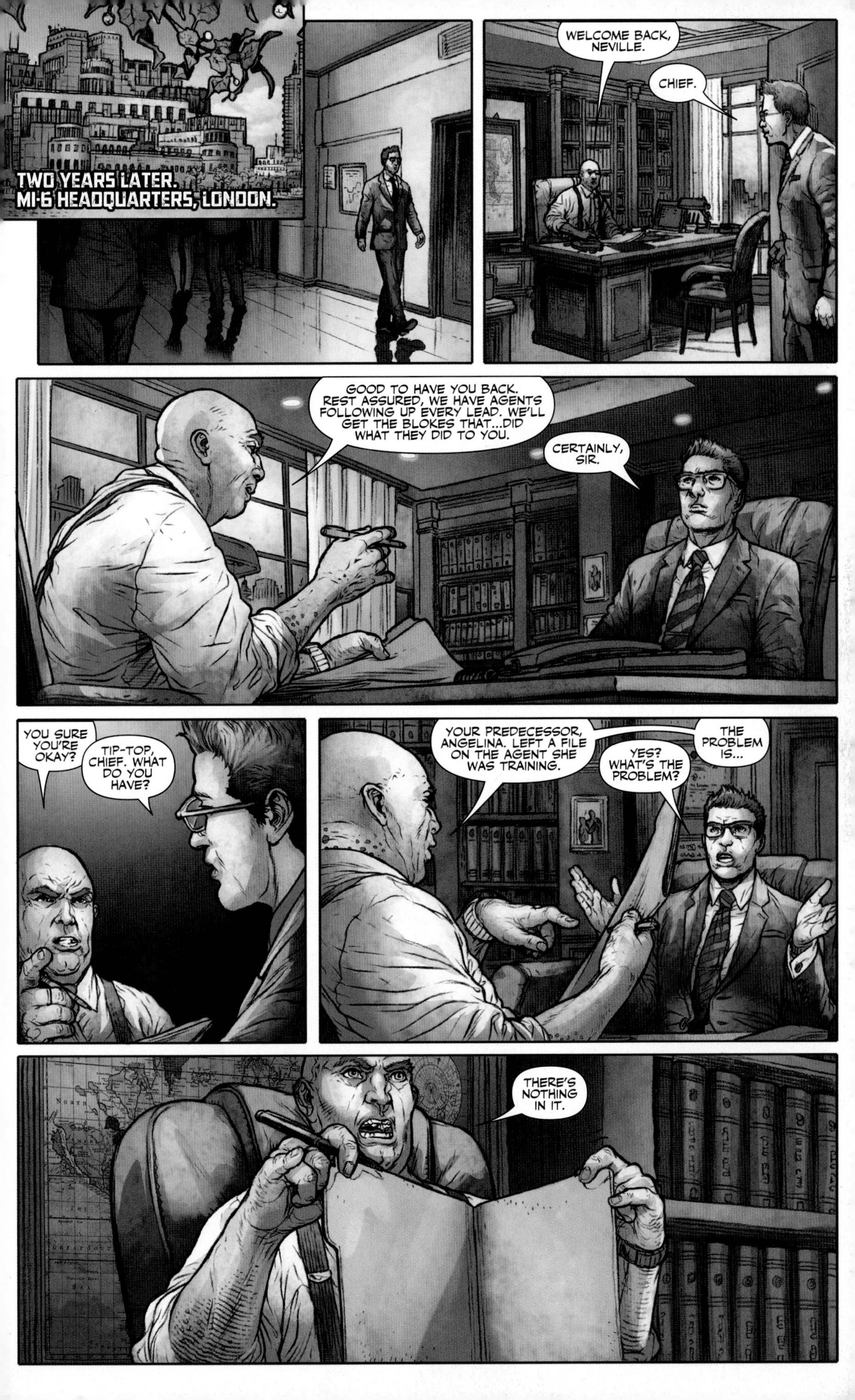
TWO YEARS LATER.
MI-6 HEADQUARTERS, LONDON.
WELCOME BACK, NEVILLE.
CHIEF.
GOOD TO HAVE YOU BACK. REST ASSURED, WE HAVE AGENTS FOLLOWING UP EVERY LEAD. WE'LL GET THE BLOKES THAT...DID WHAT THEY DID TO YOU.
CERTAINLY, SIR.
YOU SURE YOU'RE OKAY?
TIP-TOP, CHIEF. WHAT DO YOU HAVE?
YOUR PREDECESSOR, ANGELINA. LEFT A FILE ON THE AGENT SHE WAS TRAINING.
YES? WHAT'S THE PROBLEM?
THE PROBLEM IS...
THERE'S NOTHING IN IT.

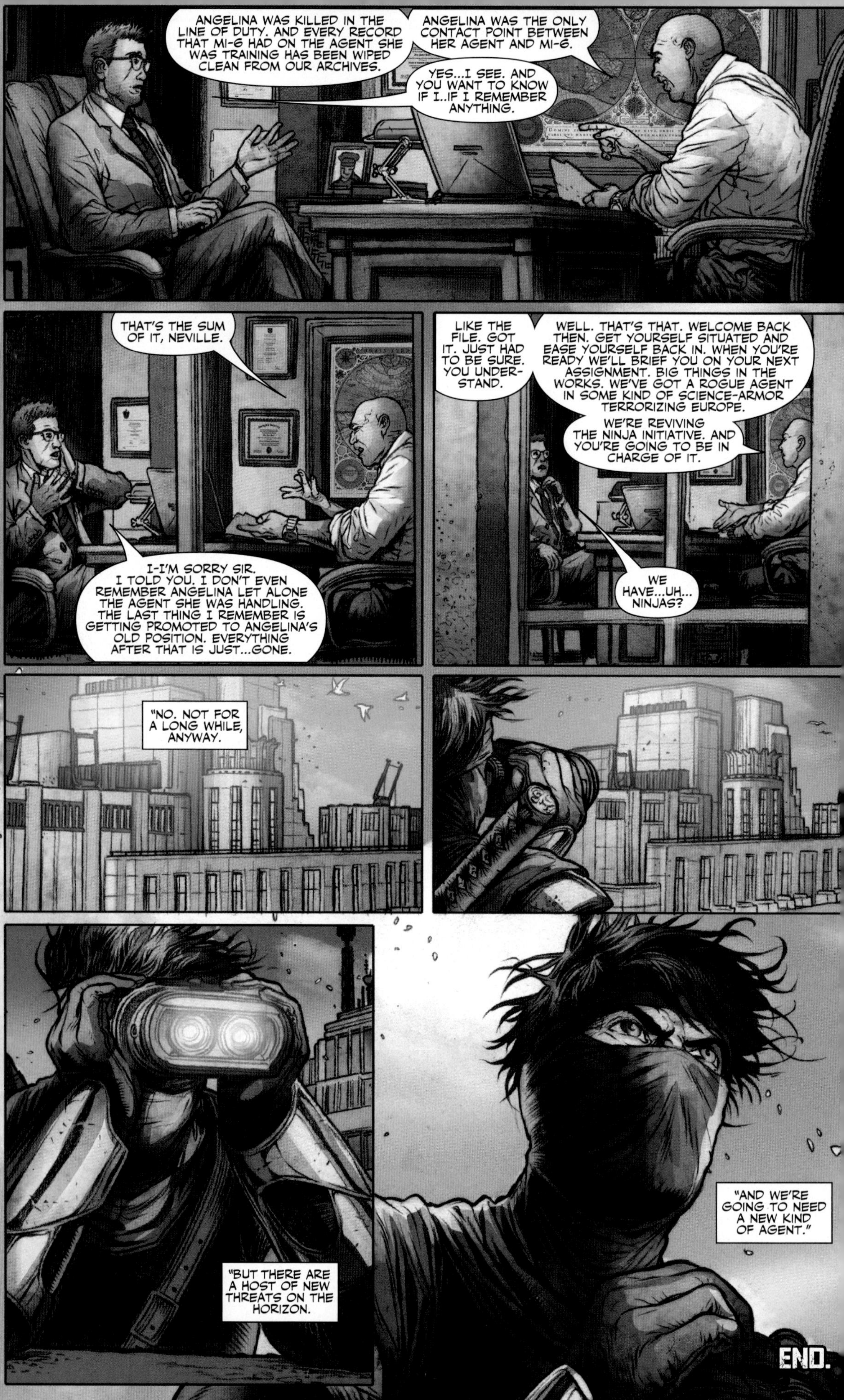
ANGELINA WAS KILLED IN THE LINE OF DUTY. AND EVERY RECORD THAT MI-6 HAD ON THE AGENT SHE WAS TRAINING HAS BEEN WIPED CLEAN FROM OUR ARCHIVES.
ANGELINA WAS THE ONLY CONTACT POINT BETWEEN HER AGENT AND MI-6.
YES...I SEE. AND YOU WANT TO KNOW IF I..IF I REMEMBER ANYTHING.
THAT'S THE SUM OF IT, NEVILLE.
I-I'M SORRY SIR. I TOLD YOU. I DON'T EVEN REMEMBER ANGELINA LET ALONE THE AGENT SHE WAS HANDLING. THE LAST THING I REMEMBER IS GETTING PROMOTED TO ANGELINA'S OLD POSITION. EVERYTHING AFTER THAT IS JUST...GONE.
LIKE THE FILE. GOT IT. JUST HAD TO BE SURE. YOU UNDER-STAND.
WELL. THAT'S THAT. WELCOME BACK THEN. GET YOURSELF SITUATED AND EASE YOURSELF BACK IN. WHEN YOU'RE READY WE'LL BRIEF YOU ON YOUR NEXT ASSIGNMENT. BIG THINGS IN THE WORKS. WE'VE GOT A ROGUE AGENT IN SOME KIND OF SCIENCE-ARMOR TERRORIZING EUROPE.
WE'RE REVIVING THE NINJA INITIATIVE. AND YOU'RE GOING TO BE IN CHARGE OF IT.
WE HAVE...UH... NINJAS?
"NO. NOT FOR A LONG WHILE, ANYWAY.
"BUT THERE ARE A HOST OF NEW THREATS ON THE HORIZON.
"AND WE'RE GOING TO NEED A NEW KIND OF AGENT."
END.

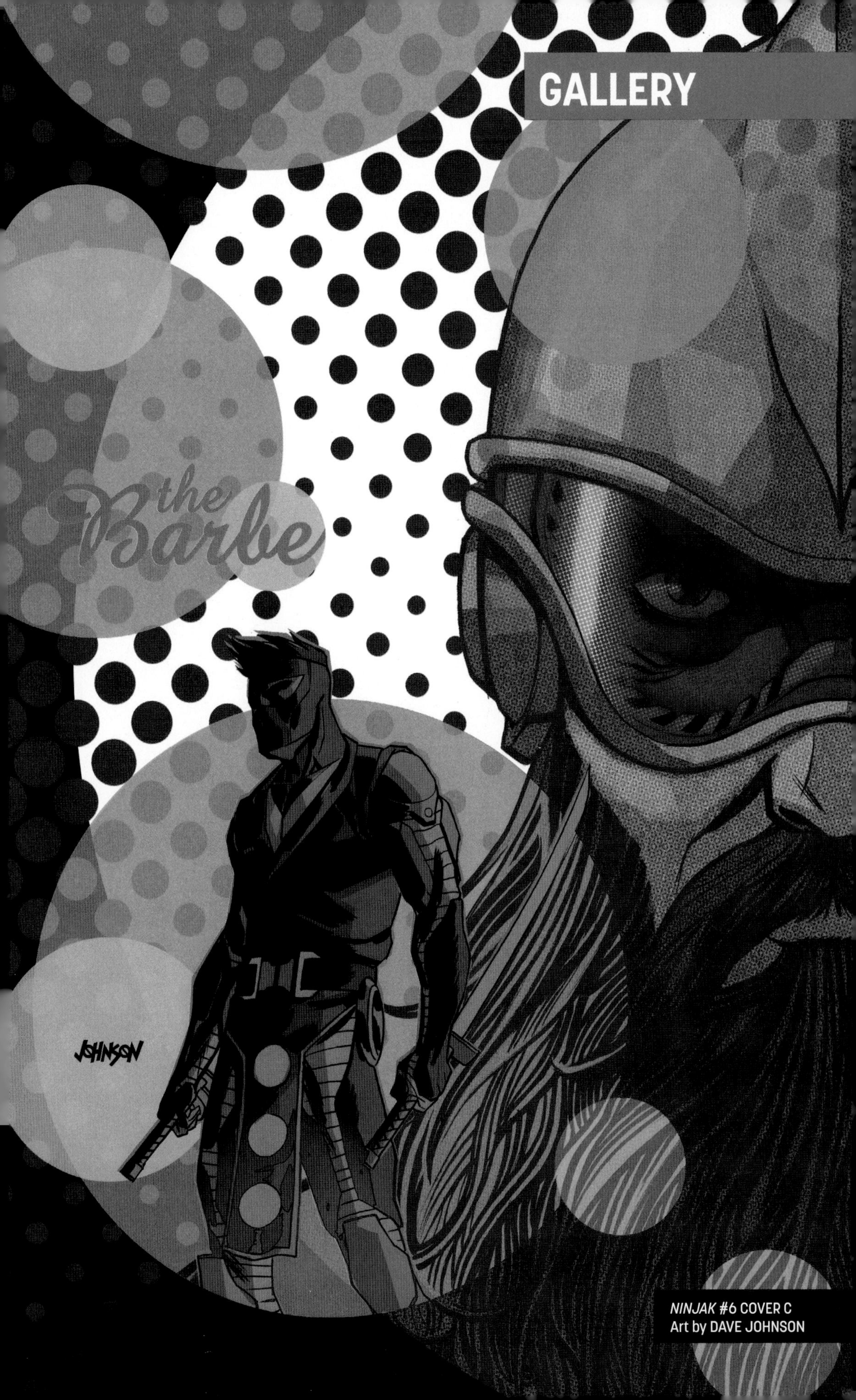
the Barbe
JOHNSON

NINJAK #6 COVER C
Art by DAVE JOHNSON

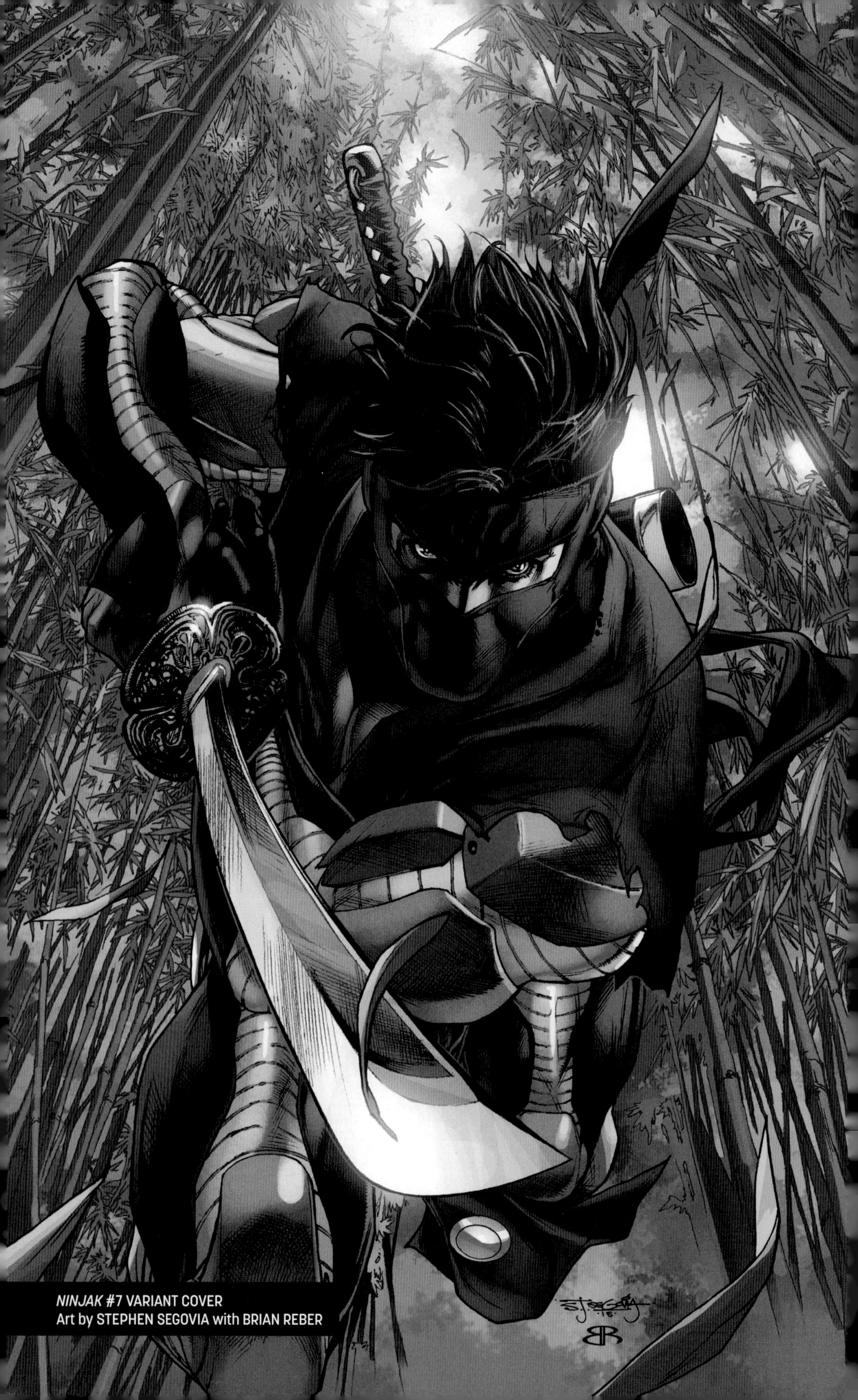

NINJAK #7 VARIANT COVER
Art by STEPHEN SEGOVIA with BRIAN REBER

NINJAK #7 COVER B
Art by JELENA KEVIC-DJURDJEVIC

NINJAK #9 VARIANT COVER
Art by MITCH GERADS

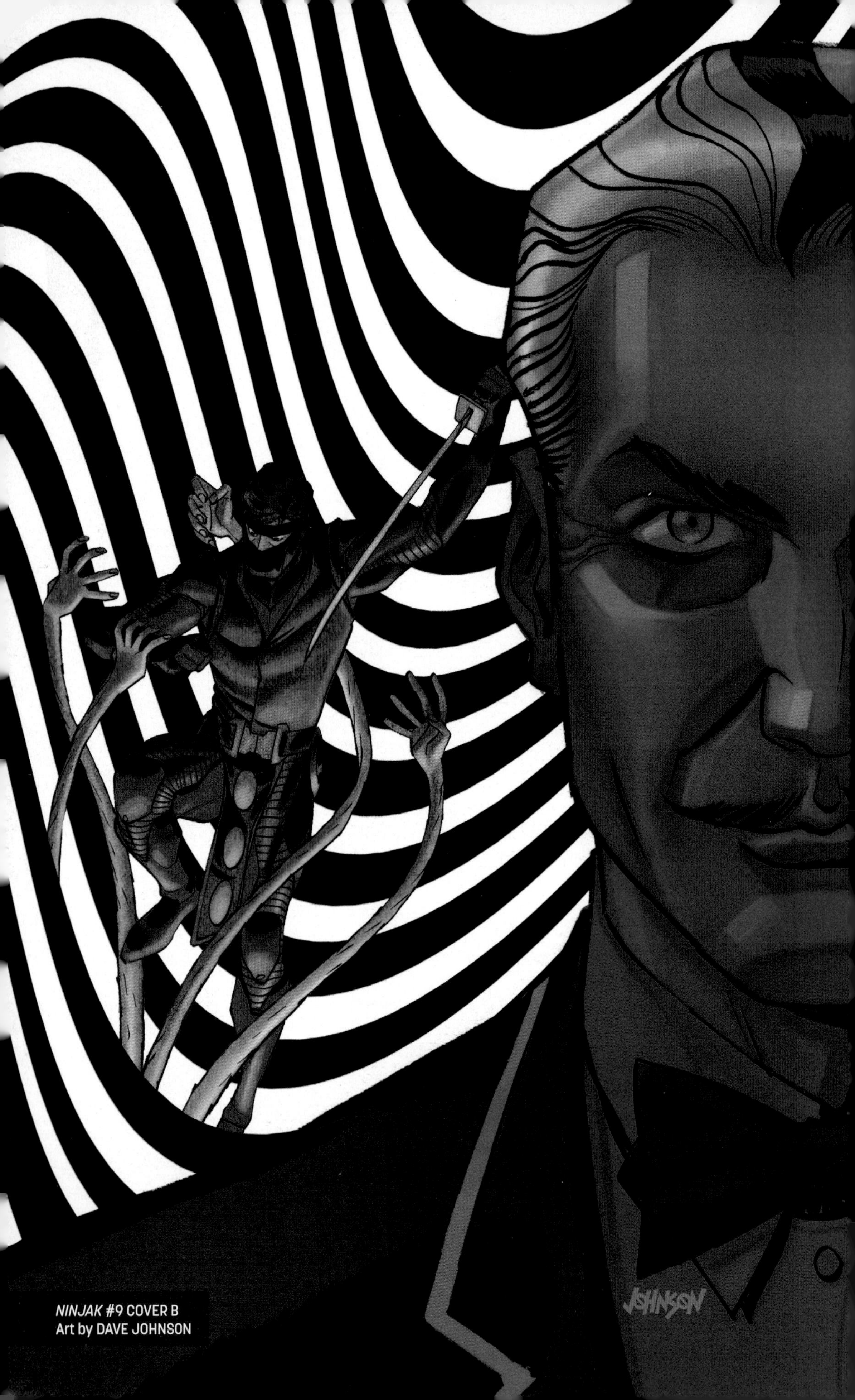
JOHNSON

NINJAK #9 COVER B
Art by DAVE JOHNSON

NINJAK #7, p. 12
Pencils by JUAN JOSÉ RYP

NINJAK #7, p. 16
Pencils by JUAN JOSÉ RYP

NINJAK #8, p. 15
Art by STEPHEN SEGOVIA and RYAN WINN

NINJAK #8, p. 19
Art by STEPHEN SEGOVIA and RYAN WINN

NINJAK #9, "THE LOST FILES" p. 2
Pencils by JUAN JOSÉ RYP

NINJAK #9, "THE LOST FILES" p. 6
Pencils by JUAN JOSÉ RYP

EXPLORE THE VALIANT UNIVERSE

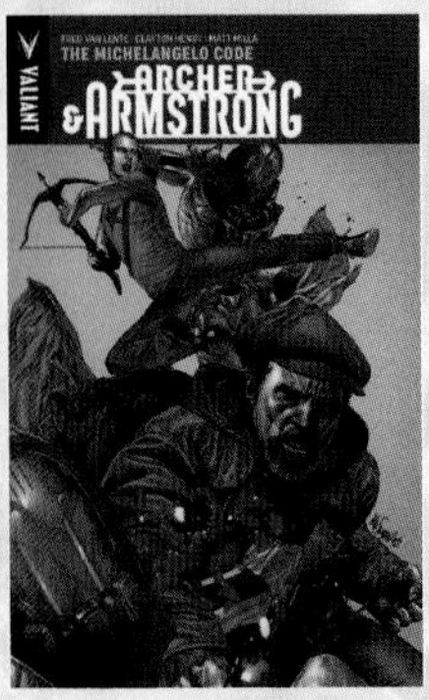
VALIANT
THE MICHELANGELO CODE
ARCHER & ARMSTRONG

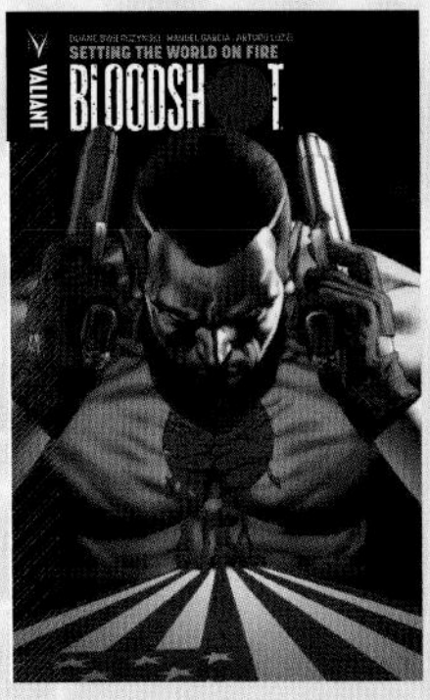
VALIANT
SETTING THE WORLD ON FIRE
BLOODSHOT

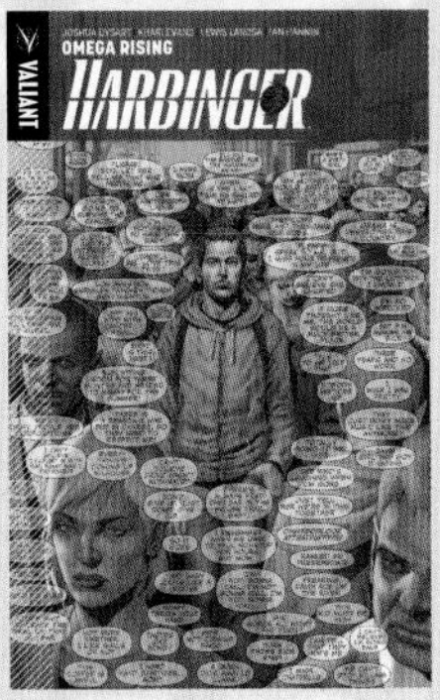
VALIANT
OMEGA RISING
HARBINGER

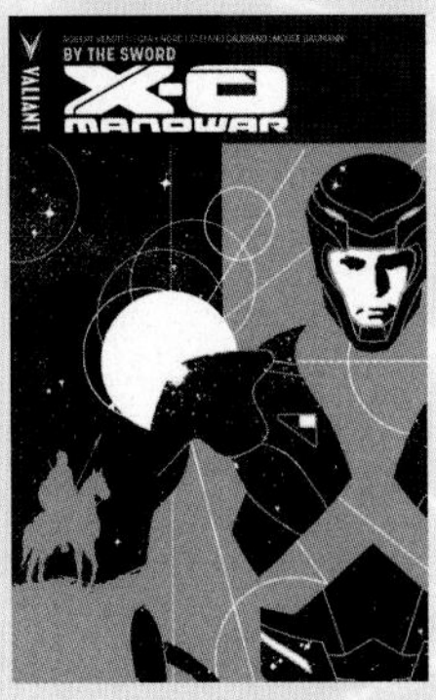
VALIANT
BY THE SWORD
X-O MANOWAR

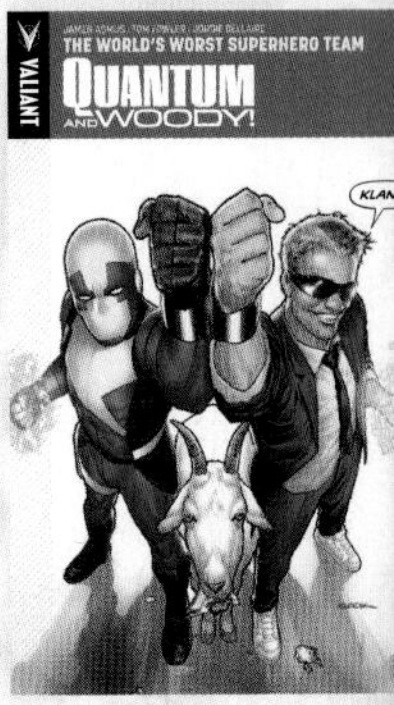
VALIANT
THE WORLD'S WORST SUPERHERO TEAM
QUANTUM AND WOODY!

ARCHER & ARMSTRONG

Volume 1: The Michelangelo Code
ISBN: 9780979640988

Volume 2: Wrath of the Eternal Warrior
ISBN: 9781939346049

Volume 3: Far Faraway
ISBN: 9781939346148

Volume 4: Sect Civil War
ISBN: 9781939346254

Volume 5: Mission: Improbable
ISBN: 9781939346353

Volume 6: American Wasteland
ISBN: 9781939346421

Volume 7: The One Percent and Other Tales
ISBN: 9781939346537

ARMOR HUNTERS

Armor Hunters
ISBN: 9781939346452

Armor Hunters: Bloodshot
ISBN: 9781939346469

Armor Hunters: Harbinger
ISBN: 9781939346506

Unity Vol. 3: Armor Hunters
ISBN: 9781939346445

X-O Manowar Vol. 7: Armor Hunters
ISBN: 9781939346476

BLOODSHOT

Volume 1: Setting the World on Fire
ISBN: 9780979640964

Volume 2: The Rise and the Fall
ISBN: 9781939346032

Volume 3: Harbinger Wars
ISBN: 9781939346124

Volume 4: H.A.R.D. Corps
ISBN: 9781939346193

Volume 5: Get Some!
ISBN: 9781939346315

Volume 6: The Glitch and Other Tales
ISBN: 9781939346711

BLOODSHOT REBORN

Volume 1: Colorado
ISBN: 9781939346674

Volume 2: The Hunt
ISBN: 9781939346827

DEAD DROP

ISBN: 9781939346858

THE DEATH-DEFYING DOCTOR MIRAGE

ISBN: 9781939346490

THE DELINQUENTS

ISBN: 9781939346513

DIVINITY

ISBN: 9781939346766

ETERNAL WARRIOR

Volume 1: Sword of the Wild
ISBN: 9781939346209

Volume 2: Eternal Emperor
ISBN: 9781939346292

Volume 3: Days of Steel
ISBN: 9781939346742

HARBINGER

Volume 1: Omega Rising
ISBN: 9780979640957

Volume 2: Renegades
ISBN: 9781939346025

Volume 3: Harbinger Wars
ISBN: 9781939346117

Volume 4: Perfect Day
ISBN: 9781939346155

Volume 5: Death of a Renegade
ISBN: 9781939346339

Volume 6: Omegas
ISBN: 9781939346384

HARBINGER WARS

Harbinger Wars
ISBN: 9781939346094

Bloodshot Vol. 3: Harbinger Wars
ISBN: 9781939346124

Harbinger Vol. 3: Harbinger Wars
ISBN: 9781939346117

EXPLORE THE VALIANT UNIVERSE

VALIANT
KICK ME
QUANTUM AND WOODY
BY PRIEST & BRIGHT
VOL 1: KLANG

VALIANT
BATTLE FOR NEW JAPAN
RAI

VALIANT
THE VALIANT

VALIANT
THE DEATH-DEFYING
DOCTOR MIRAGE

VALIANT
DIVINITY

インピリアム
IMPERIUM

olume 1: Collecting Monsters
SBN: 9781939346759

olume 2: Broken Angels
SBN: 9781939346896

NINJAK

olume 1: Weaponeer
BN: 9781939346667

olume 2: The Shadow Wars
BN: 9781939346940

QUANTUM AND WOODY!

olume 1: The World's Worst Superhero Team
BN: 9781939346186

olume 2: In Security
BN: 9781939346230

olume 3: Crooked Pasts, Present Tense
BN: 9781939346391

olume 4: Quantum and Woody Must Die!
BN: 9781939346629

QUANTUM AND WOODY BY PRIEST & BRIGHT

lume 1: Klang
N: 9781939346780

lume 2: Switch
N: 9781939346803

lume 3: And So...
N: 9781939346865

lume 4: The Return
N: 9781682151099

RAI

Volume 1: Welcome to New Japan
ISBN: 9781939346414

Volume 2: Battle for New Japan
ISBN: 9781939346612

Volume 3: The Orphan
ISBN: 9781939346841

SHADOWMAN

Volume 1: Birth Rites
ISBN: 9781939346001

Volume 2: Darque Reckoning
ISBN: 9781939346056

Volume 3: Deadside Blues
ISBN: 9781939346162

Volume 4: Fear, Blood, And Shadows
ISBN: 9781939346278

Volume 5: End Times
ISBN: 9781939346377

Ivar, Timewalker

Volume 1: Making History
ISBN: 9781939346636

Volume 2: Breaking History
ISBN: 9781939346834

UNITY

Volume 1: To Kill a King
ISBN: 9781939346261

Volume 2: Trapped by Webnet
ISBN: 9781939346346

Volume 3: Armor Hunters
ISBN: 9781939346445

Volume 4: The United
ISBN: 9781939346544

UNITY (Continued)

Volume 5: Homefront
ISBN: 9781939346797

Volume 6: The War-Monger
ISBN: 9781939346902

THE VALIANT

ISBN: 9781939346605

VALIANT ZEROES AND ORIGINS

ISBN: 9781939346582

X-O MANOWAR

Volume 1: By the Sword
ISBN: 9780979640940

Volume 2: Enter Ninjak
ISBN: 9780979640995

Volume 3: Planet Death
ISBN: 9781939346087

Volume 4: Homecoming
ISBN: 9781939346179

Volume 5: At War With Unity
ISBN: 9781939346247

Volume 6: Prelude to Armor Hunters
ISBN: 9781939346407

Volume 7: Armor Hunters
ISBN: 9781939346476

Volume 8: Enter: Armorines
ISBN: 9781939346551

Volume 9: Dead Hand
ISBN: 9781939346650

Volume 10: Exodus
ISBN: 9781939346933

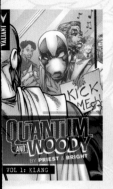

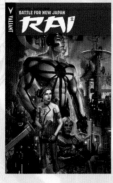

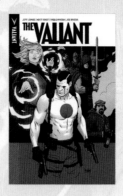

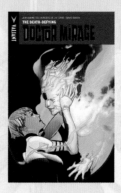

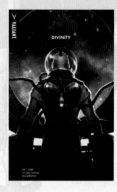

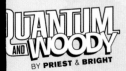

EXPLORE THE VALIANT UNIVERSE

VALIANT
HARBINGER DELUXE EDITION 2

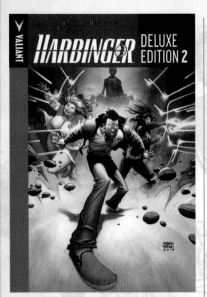

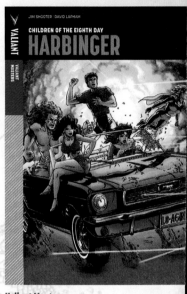

Omnibuses

Archer & Armstrong:
The Complete Classic Omnibus
ISBN: 9781939346872
Collecting ARCHER & ARMSTRONG (1992) #0-26, ETERNAL WARRIOR (1992) #25 along with ARCHER & ARMSTRONG: THE FORMATION OF THE SECT.

Quantum and Woody:
The Complete Classic Omnibus
ISBN: 9781939346360
Collecting QUANTUM AND WOODY (1997) #0, 1-21 and #32, THE GOAT: H.A.E.D.U.S. #1, and X-O MANOWAR (1996) #16

X-O Manowar Classic Omnibus Vol. 1
ISBN: 9781939346308
Collecting X-O MANOWAR (1992) #0-30, ARMORINES #0, X-O DATABASE #1, as well as material from SECRETS OF THE VALIANT UNIVERSE #1

VALIANT
ROBERT VENDITTI MATT KINDT JOSHUA DYSART JOE HARRIS ROBERT GILL
DOUG BRAITHWAITE DIEGO BERNARD TREVOR HAIRSINE STEPHEN SEGOVIA
ARMOR HUNTERS DELUXE EDITION

Deluxe Editions

Archer & Armstrong Deluxe Edition Book 1
ISBN: 9781939346223
Collecting ARCHER & ARMSTRONG #0-13

Archer & Armstrong Deluxe Edition Book 2
ISBN: 9781939346957
Collecting ARCHER & ARMSTRONG #14-25, ARCHER & ARMSTRONG: ARCHER #0 and BLOODSHOT AND H.A.R.D. CORPS #20-21.

Armor Hunters Deluxe Edition
ISBN: 9781939346728
Collecting Armor Hunters #1-4, Armor Hunters: Aftermath #1, Armor Hunters: Bloodshot #1-3, Armor Hunters: Harbinger #1-3, Unity #8-11, and X-O MANOWAR #23-29

Bloodshot Deluxe Edition Book 1
ISBN: 9781939346216
Collecting BLOODSHOT #1-13

Bloodshot Deluxe Edition Book 2
ISBN: 9781939346810
Collecting BLOODSHOT AND H.A.R.D. CORPS #14-23, BLOODSHOT #24-25, BLOODSHOT #0, BLOODSHOT AND H.A.R.D. CORPS: H.A.R.D. CORPS #0, along with ARCHER & ARMSTRONG #18-19

Divinity Deluxe Edition
ISBN: 97819393460993
Collecting DIVNITY #1-4

Harbinger Deluxe Edition Book 1
ISBN: 9781939346131
Collecting HARBINGER #0-14

Harbinger Deluxe Edition Book 2
SBN: 9781939346773
Collecting HARBINGER #15-25, HARBINGER: OMEGAS #1-3, and HARBINGER: BLEEDING MONK #0

Harbinger Wars Deluxe Edition
ISBN: 9781939346322
Collecting HARBINGER WARS #1-4, HARBINGER #11-14, and BLOODSHOT #10-13

Quantum and Woody Deluxe Edition Book 1
ISBN: 9781939346681
Collecting QUANTUM AND WOODY #1-12 and QUANTUM AND WOODY: THE GOAT #0

Q2: The Return of Quantum and Woody Deluxe Edition
ISBN: 9781939346568
Collecting Q2: THE RETURN OF QUANTUM AND WOODY #1-5

Shadowman Deluxe Edition Book 1
ISBN: 9781939346438
Collecting SHADOWMAN #0-10

Shadowman Deluxe Edition Book 2
ISBN: 9781682151075
Collecting SHADOWMAN #11-16, SHADOWMAN #13X, SHADOWMAN: END TIMES #1-3 and PUNK MAMBO #0

Unity Deluxe Edition Book 1
ISBN: 9781939346575
Collecting UNITY #0-14

The Valiant Deluxe Edition
ISBN: 97819393460986
Collecting THE VALIANT #1-4

X-O Manowar Deluxe Edition Book 1
ISBN: 9781939346100
Collecting X-O MANOWAR #1-14

X-O Manowar Deluxe Edition Book 2
ISBN: 9781939346520
Collecting X-O MANOWAR #15-22, and UNITY #1-4

JIM SHOOTER | DAVID LAPHAM
VALIANT
CHILDREN OF THE EIGHTH DAY
HARBINGER
VALIANT MASTERS

Valiant Masters

Bloodshot Vol. 1 - Blood of the Machine
ISBN: 9780979640933

H.A.R.D. Corps Vol. 1 - Search and Destroy
ISBN: 9781939346285

Harbinger Vol. 1 - Children of the Eighth Day
ISBN: 9781939346483

Ninjak Vol. 1 - Black Water
ISBN: 9780979640971

Rai Vol. 1 - From Honor to Strength
ISBN: 9781939346070

Shadowman Vol. 1 - Spirits Within
ISBN: 9781939346018

KEVIN VANHOOK | DON PERLIN
VALIANT
BLOOD OF THE MACHINE
BLOODSHOT
VALIANT MASTERS

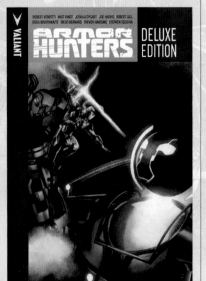

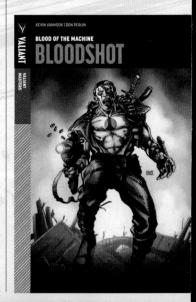

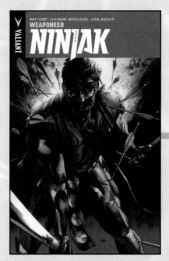

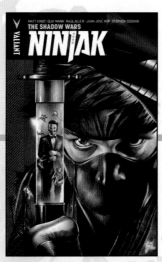

NINJAK READING ORDER

VALIANT
WEAPONEER
NINJAK
Ninjak Vol. 1: Weaponeer

VALIANT
THE SHADOW WARS
NINJAK
Ninjak Vol. 2: The Shadow Wars

VALIANT
OPERATION: DEADSIDE
NINJAK
Ninjak Vol. 3: Operation: Deadside

Read the smash-hit debut and earliest adventures of the Valiant Universe's deadliest master spy!

VALIANT
ENTER: NINJAK
X-O MANOWAR
X-O Manowar Vol. 2:
Enter Ninjak

VALIANT
TO KILL A KING
UNITY
NOMINATED FOR THREE 2014 HARVEY AWARDS
Unity Vol. 1:
To Kill a King

VALIANT
TRAPPED BY WEBNET
UNITY
Unity Vol. 2:
Trapped by Webnet

VALIANT
ARMOR HUNTERS
UNITY
MULTIPLE HARVEY AWARD NOMINEE
Unity Vol. 3:
Armor Hunters

VALIANT
THE UNITED
UNITY
MULTIPLE HARVEY AWARD NOMINEE
Unity Vol. 4:
The United

VALIANT
HOMEFRONT
UNITY
MULTIPLE HARVEY AWARD NOMINEE
Unity Vol. 5:
Homefront

VALIANT
THE VALIANT
The Valiant

VALIANT
DIVINITY
THE BEST NEW SUPERHERO OF 2015
Divinity

VALIANT®

NINJAK®

VOLUME THREE: OPERATION DEADSIDE

SHADOWMAN STRIKES AGAIN IN *OPERATION: DEADSIDE*!

In December of 2015, a covert military intelligence unit sent a team of twenty agents and one special operative into a parallel dimension. Only one came back.

The purpose of their mission was classified. Now, out of options, MI-6 has recruited their most elite operative - codename: NINJAK - to follow the doomed mission's sole witness back into the dimension called Deadside...and bring her missing teammates home.

What will they find there? And who will be waiting for them? Jump on board here as New York Times best-selling writer Matt Kindt (DIVINITY) and superstar artists Doug Braithwaite (ARMOR HUNTERS) and Juan José Ryp (*Clone*) reunite for a terrifying journey into an unknown plane of existence...and bring NINJAK head-to-head with Shadowman.

Collecting NINJAK #10-13.

VALIANT
MATT KINDT | DOUG BRAITHWAITE | JUAN JOSÉ RYP
OPERATION: DEADSIDE
NINJAK

TRADE PAPERBACK
ISBN: 978-1-68215-125-9

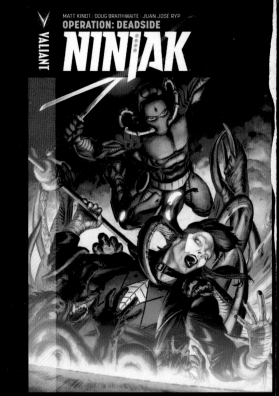